Lucy ... Hampshire ... Leeds, ... her hus...

An Almost Perfect Holiday is her fifteenth novel, and the idea for this particular book came to her when she was lying by a swimming pool in France, shamelessly eavesdropping on the family who were holidaying next door. She apologizes if that was you, but is very grateful for all the juicy material she overheard. In fact, she couldn't have written this one without you.

LUCY DIAMOND

An *Almost* Perfect Holiday

PAN BOOKS

First published 2020 by Macmillan

First published in paperback 2020 by Macmillan

This paperback edition first published 2020 by Pan Books
an imprint of Pan Macmillan
The Smithson, 6 Briset Street, London EC1M 5NR
Associated companies throughout the world
www.panmacmillan.com

ISBN 978-1-5290-2698-6

3 5 7 9 8 6 4

A CIP catalogue record for this book is available from the British Library.

Typeset in Dante by Jouve (UK), Milton Keynes
Printed and bound by CPI Group (UK) Ltd, Croydon, CR0 4YY

Visit **www.panmacmillan.com** to read more about all our books
and to buy them. You will also find features, author interviews and
news of any author events, and you can sign up for e-newsletters
so that you're always first to hear about our new releases.

For everyone longing to get away from it all . . . This book's for you.

Please note – I have taken some geographical liberties with the setting of this book, inventing roads and other locations to suit the purposes of the story. Humour me!

Prologue

The women were still sitting by the swimming pool, even though it was almost midnight. Up above, the stars were a handful of silver glitter against the inky black while the moon cast glimmering ripples of light into the water. The air smelled of wine and chlorine, with just a faint hint of ozone from the distant sea carried on the breeze.

A collection of empty glasses and plates around them signalled that this had been a long night. At an earlier point, as the sun vanished and the temperature began to plummet, one of the women had suggested bringing their duvets out to keep themselves warm, and now they were comfortably rugged-up and cosy on the sun loungers, laughing and exchanging confidences like girls on a sleepover.

'This has been such a strange holiday,' said the first woman just then. Strange but also surprisingly good in a lot of ways, she was thinking. Everything had changed. Even *she* had changed. For the first time in years, the future felt . . . interesting.

'You're telling me,' said the second woman. Her mood wasn't quite so optimistic. In fact she'd go as far as to say that the holiday had been a complete disaster. Would she ever get over what had happened this week?

Silence fell, except for the faint glugging of the water in the swimming-pool filter and the soft bumps of an inflatable flamingo against the metal steps as it cruised in slow, blind circles.

The third woman had been gazing up at the night sky, turning things over in her mind. Now she spoke. 'I might regret this tomorrow,' she said after a moment, 'but I was wondering . . . can I tell you guys a secret? Like – something really big?'

Chapter One

FIVE DAYS EARLIER

There was a lot riding on this holiday, thought Em, folding T-shirts and packing them into a suitcase. Back when she'd made the booking – miserable and alone on Christmas Day – she'd had no idea that it would turn out to be anything other than another summer break for her, Izzie and Jack: two weeks of trying to force her teenagers out of bed before midday to enjoy the beautiful Cornish countryside and beaches, plus at least one waistband-punishing cream tea for good measure. But now . . . Well, everything was different now. Their fortnight away was shaping up to be a whole new kind of trip.

If only someone could have told her, back on that desolate afternoon, that life was about to take an exciting upward turn! She still hadn't quite forgiven Dom for making it the worst Christmas ever. Off she'd gone on Christmas Eve, driving the kids over to the posh new Cirencester house he shared with his bimbo girlfriend Michelle, with him assuring her – *promising* her – that of course he would drive them back home after lunch the following day. And what had he done? Forgotten his so-called promise and tucked into the gin, champagne and port over his roast turkey and trimmings so that he was over the limit, the selfish jerk. 'Michelle's plastered too,' he'd told her sheepishly over the phone when he rang to confess. 'Christmas spirit and all that. We'll drop them back tomorrow, okay?'

No, it was not remotely okay. Em had gone from shocked to devastated to downright fuming in the space of about ten seconds. And of course, by then, she had already put away two massive glasses of wine herself – well, you had to, didn't you, when you were without your kids and finding the whole solo Christmas thing horribly unfestive – and didn't feel it was her destiny to get arrested for drunk-driving on Christmas Day, either. The upsetting news that she was now unable to see her own children for the whole day had sent her nose-diving straight into the Baileys, as well as polishing off an entire family pack of pigs-in-blankets and most of the cheeseboard, hacking into the Stilton as if she was committing a murder. If only. Afterwards she'd resorted to quite a lot of spontaneous spirit-boosting online purchases in order to endure the festive marathon – including a holiday, she had discovered, waking up on Boxing Day and blinking at the emailed receipts with a thumping head. A holiday in a gorgeous four-bedroom barn conversion down in Cornwall, which had cost practically a month's wages, no less.

She had clicked on the details with a degree of trepidation – her impulsive nature had seen her paying for some particularly duff decisions over the years (those neon-yellow ski boots for one, when she'd never been skiing in her life) – but Briar Cottage still looked lovely in the cold light of day, thankfully, despite being far roomier (and far more luxurious) than they actually needed. There were three holiday homes altogether, arranged around the sides of a pool, as well as a separate games-room building that Izzie and Jack might make use of. Plus the cottages were situated in the middle of gorgeous countryside, with the shops and beaches of Falmouth a short drive away. Good work, drunken me, she had congratulated herself in relief, before going on to examine her subsequent purchases with rather more eye-rolling and despair: a home rowing machine (why? she hated exercise!), several wildly extravagant cocktail dresses that she'd never actually wear and a fabulous black bouclé coat that she absolutely could not afford. And then, of course, January had begun with the usual hangover and list of impossibly strict resolutions, at which point she'd put the holiday entirely out of her head.

By the time summer eventually rocked up, with its delights of chilled rosé and dreamily golden evenings, everything had changed anyway. Changed for the better! In a nutshell, George Macleod had appeared in her life and cast a new and wonderful haze across it. George was her perfect fit – easy-going and comfortable in his own skin, so much more her kind of person than moody, controlling Dom had been. He had the best laugh she'd ever heard: loud and unrestrained, the sort you couldn't help joining in with. How could anyone *not* fall in love with a man who laughed with such generous abandon? Added to which, he was successful in his career, confident at all times and there was just this steadiness about him, this unflappable nature that Em really appreciated now, as a forty-four-year-old woman, in a way that her feckless twenty-something self hadn't particularly cared about. Plus – had she mentioned it? – he was sexy as hell. Sexy. As. Hell.

My God! It had been such a shock for her, all of that. Five years of smarting from the divorce and its fallout, five years of assuming no way would she ever so much as play footsie with another man under the table, let alone find herself romping and flirting with hedonistic glee. Not least because the post-divorce years had been relentlessly tough; a juggling act of single motherhood, career ambitions and domestic grind. As she tried to keep herself sane and her children happy, as she paid each bill, heaved the bins out every week, swore at the lawnmower and hung out a thousand loads of laundry single-handedly, she had felt herself ageing, as if the fun, free-spirited Em of her youth was shrivelling grimly away into this tight-lipped middle-aged drudge, with no way back.

It had therefore hit her like a landslide the first time she and George had kissed. They'd gone for dinner in Martino's and somewhere between the risotto verdure and the peppermint tea, he had leaned forward across the table without warning, his mouth grazing hers, and it was as if her body had woken right up following its years-long state of coma, shocked into life by his touch, like someone on an operating table receiving the 500-volt defibrillator pads. *Stand clear!* WHAM!

Just a kiss, and yet she'd experienced this physical force of lust that had swept through her entire body like a randy tornado. His mouth felt urgent yet confident against hers, as if he knew exactly what to do (and oh, he *did* know what to do, he really did). There had been stars in her eyes afterwards, like a dazed cartoon character. Hello, brave new world. I like the look of *you.*

'Sorry,' he'd murmured, seeing her stunned expression as he leaned back, although he was smiling as if he wasn't actually all *that* sorry. 'I couldn't help myself. You just looked so pretty and lovely. Was that outrageously presumptuous of me?'

'No,' she'd said, blinking. *Pretty and lovely!* she repeated to herself rapturously, storing up the phrase to bask in later on. She collected compliments with the avidity of a miser hoarding pennies; her own private Greatest Hits moments that she could replay in times of low morale. 'Not in the slightest. In fact why don't we do it again?'

Her friends, of course, couldn't believe what they were hearing. They were so used to her being *Poor Em* that they struggled to get their heads around this glittering new version. After all, they'd known where they stood with sad old divorced loser Em, who was doing her best but had such a tension about her jaw, bless her, it must be hard. (And didn't we always say that Dom was a bastard? Cheating on her all that time with that fake bitch Michelle. We never liked him in the first place.)

Yet look at Em now: getting her nails done and buying skimpy knickers in her lunch-break, blushing like a teenager at the drop of a hat. Her body, which had resembled an abandoned field in recent years, with numerous unpleasant weeds sprouting here and there, was now waxed and plucked, smooth and scrubbed. Alive and kicking. She walked down the street and felt her bottom swing with a new jauntiness. She looked in the mirror and arched an eyebrow at her own sassy reflection instead of ducking her head away to avoid eye contact. Poor Em had been banished, replaced by Delighted Em, this fabulous new edition who couldn't believe her luck.

'Have you lost weight?'

'Have you had your hair done?'

'You look different!' her colleagues commented in surprise.

Her friends were rather more blunt. 'Are you having loads of sex?' they asked, some with more horror than envy, admittedly. Perhaps even a certain measure of mistrust. 'I mean, how do you have the *energy*?' a few of them wondered aloud. 'Or the inclination? Don't you feel too *old* to be doing that sort of thing?'

As for her sister Jenny, she had cut straight to the chase, as she invariably did. 'It's all sounding a bit too good to be true,' she had remarked. 'What's the catch?'

Em deflected these questions with her radiant shield of happiness, but in truth, there *was* a tiny catch. Wasn't that simply a part of being a human, though? Surely no person on earth reached their forties without some kind of baggage trailing along behind them, unless there was something a bit odd going on. Right?

In George's case, the baggage was fairly minimal at least; practically hand-luggage levels, really, consisting of one ex-wife, Charlotte, and one small daughter, Seren. Em hadn't yet met Charlotte, but had done enough furtive Internet searches to have discovered that she was both glamorous and beautiful in a way that freckle-faced, soft-bodied Em was never going to be. Charlotte was also an intimidatingly successful high-flier in the field of genetic engineering and often jetted around the world to present scientific findings to other brainy types.

So far so disconcerting, admittedly, although Em was

trying not to let any of this get to her. According to George, he and Charlotte had split up because they had grown apart, but further prying had revealed that Charlotte was now living with another man, one of George's mates, just to put the boot in. From what Em could gather, they had got together *very* quickly after the split – suspiciously quickly, you could say – and were now engaged, so at least that was her off the scene. Technically, anyway. The sticking point was that, due to the fact that Charlotte and George had a child together, their lives would be linked pretty much forever, like it or not.

Em herself knew the score, of course. Despite the anger and loathing she'd felt towards Dom since their marriage broke down, there were still school parents' evenings and concerts to attend together, still weekends and holidays and Christmases to negotiate, in terms of the children and who had them, and you just had to be grown-up and civil about it all, even if that meant rictus grins and swearing under your breath each time. Even if, deep down, you would rather never see that cheating, lying, Christmas-wrecking pig again. George and Charlotte appeared to have avoided quite such bad blood, though. In fact they seemed positively amicable with one another. What decent, caring people they both were, Em tried to convince herself admiringly, although it did seem at times as if Charlotte was on the phone to George every ten minutes with some new query or update regarding their daughter. This had happened! That had happened! Had George remembered this? Would he be able to do that?

Em was making a supreme effort not to comment or get involved, but Christ, it was really starting to get on her wick.

As for George's daughter Seren, she was seven years old and Em wasn't quite sure what to make of her. Prior to their meeting, she had felt – not super-confident exactly, but on safe ground at least. She knew kids. She was good with kids, everyone said so. 'Hello. Lovely to meet you! Those are very cool trainers,' she had said warmly the first time they'd been introduced.

Seren's expression had been downright withering in response. 'I'm not a baby, you know, you don't have to talk to me like that,' the scornful retort had come. 'Anyway, Mummy says that it's patronizing and sexist when people talk about my clothes. Would you say that if I was a boy?'

Em had blinked, thrown off-guard by this irate young feminist. 'I might have done,' she'd replied weakly, to which Seren had merely snorted.

That was just the start of it. Seren had a very direct stare – the type that seemed to measure a person and find you wanting every time. Her favourite topic of conversation was how wonderful, clever and talented Charlotte was, and she made it abundantly clear that she found Em lacking, in comparison. Em was not used to dealing with such disdain. She worked in marketing and was surrounded by enthusiastic, smiling people who could put a positive spin on anything. Was it melodramatic of her to say that she found Seren quite unnerving?

Just the other evening, Em had gone round to George's flat, where Seren was already present. She'd been taking her shoes off in the hall when she overheard the little girl say, 'I don't like this girlfriend, Daddy. She has mean eyes', and Em's hand had flown straight to her throat, her mouth a shocked O. For starters, it sounded as if George had had loads of girlfriends (which he'd assured her he hadn't); and for another thing, she so *didn't* have mean eyes! She'd always flattered herself that her eyes were one – two, rather – of her best features!

'Do *you* like my eyes?' she had found herself fretting on the phone to her friend Kathy the next day. 'They don't seem mean to you, do they?' It was as if she was fourteen again, and crying because one of the boys at school had made fun of her pimples. When she was forty-four, for heaven's sake! For the record, Kathy had told her she had sexpot, bushbaby eyes and not to worry for a second, and it was all Em could do not to get a fridge magnet made up with the words, like some kind of proof.

Anyway. So that was Seren: basically, like no child Em had ever come across before. Her own two, Izzie and Jack, were both easy-going, sporty types and there were always hordes of their friends trooping in to sprawl all over Em's sofa and ransack her fridge. Some of Izzie's friends – Lily, for instance – called her 'Ems' as if they were mates themselves; she couldn't in a million years imagine Seren ever being so pally and affable. She'd be more likely to kick Em in the shins and flick her the Vs when George wasn't looking.

Not that Em was moaning. Of course she wasn't. Well, maybe just a tiny bit. But it wasn't as if they were joined at the hip and Em had to deal with Seren twenty-four/seven or anything, was it? Until now, that was. Until this very summer holiday in fact.

It had happened like this: as June had ripened into July, it had dawned on Em that she wasn't actually looking forward to getting away quite so much now, luxury cottage or not. All she could think about was George, and how desperately she was going to miss him while they were apart. She would *pine* for him like a doomed heroine, a swooning girl. Was that completely tragic of her or wildly romantic? ('Wildly romantic,' Kathy assured her. 'Completely tragic,' Jenny had decreed. 'Pull yourself together!')

Whichever, a few weeks ago Em had rashly taken the plunge and asked George if he'd like to join them for the break. As soon as she said the words, she knew it was too much, too keen of her: ridiculously short notice, for starters; he surely wouldn't be able to get time off work and must already have his own plans for the summer. So she'd been both thrilled and astonished when instead he'd said yes.

'He said *yes!*' she had whooped down the phone to Jenny, unable to believe her good fortune.

'Wow, that's brave,' her sister replied, in a voice that meant 'Wow, that's insane'. 'And you've been seeing each other for, what? Three whole months? How well do you actually *know* this man?'

'Five months,' Em corrected her, stung by this palpable lack of excitement. 'And I wouldn't say it's *brave*,' she felt compelled to go on. 'More like, when you know, you know. And I just know.' Did that sound smug and annoying, when Jenny and her husband were constantly sniping at one another and lived in a permanent state of acrimony? Em didn't care, she discovered. In fact she hoped it *did* sound smug and annoying, seeing as Jenny was being so damn unenthusiastic about the whole holiday business, when if she'd been any kind of supportive sister, she'd have been cheering her on with pom-poms. 'Besides – it's a fortnight in a very nice barn conversion in Cornwall, with a pool,' she'd added scathingly. 'It's not as if we're trekking across the Sahara together. What could go wrong?'

'Er . . . you decide you hate him? The kids hate him? He hates you?' Jenny suggested with naked unhelpfulness.

'Thanks for your support. Ever thought about volunteering for the Samaritans?' Em had replied, before hanging up and making a loud growling noise, as she often seemed to do following their sisterly conversations.

She rolled her eyes now, remembering Jenny's pessimism, and stuffed her hiking boots into a plastic bag. Damn it, but it had almost been the perfect getaway, as well! Two weeks with her wonderful new man, two weeks of waking up together every morning, blissful days in each other's company, not to mention the even more blissful nights she'd been imagining. George was the reason she had ceremoniously ditched her sensible, years-old one-piece swimming costume with the baggy elastic for some flattering new bikinis (she could *just* about get away with them if she didn't breathe out). And you bet she was packing all her frothy new undies, with their lace, ribbons and hand-washing instructions too. Into the case also went some sensual massage oil and bubble bath, followed by a rather slinky satin dressing gown she'd bought recently, which, when it wasn't screaming 'Fire hazard', was most definitely pouting, 'Come and get me.'

Granted, this was still a holiday in the UK and she wasn't a complete fantasist, so there was a hoody and a jumper amidst the pile of clothes too, as well as five pairs of hiking socks and some comfortable bras, but hey. This already felt like a huge departure from her usual frigid single-mum holidays, where she avoided all the perfect nuclear two-parent families on the beaches, where she felt under torturous, stifling pressure to give her children a great time. Or, at the very least, a better time than they'd have with Dom and sodding Michelle.

Until the phone call two days ago. *There's been a slight hitch*, George had said. Yeah, you're telling me, mate. The slight hitch being that Charlotte had been asked to go abroad at the last minute, to speak at a conference in Berlin, and, because she was currently 'between nannies', George had been lumped with Seren instead.

Not 'lumped with', Em corrected herself in the next moment. Because George had actually sounded quite excited about the prospect of getting their children together like this, as if they were one of those modern blended families who moved in and out of each other's spheres with ease. 'I know it might seem a bit sudden, but I'm sure the kids would get on okay,' he had said.

'Mmm,' Em had replied, unable to sound very convincing.

'And didn't you say it was a big place you'd rented? So there'd be room for another little one, right?'

'Ye-e-e-es,' she'd said, reconfiguring bedroom allocations in her head.

'Otherwise I guess I would have to miss the first week and just catch up with you guys for the second half of the holiday,' George suggested regretfully, when Em didn't offer any further encouragement. 'What do you think?'

What did she think? Her instinct was that George plus Seren would almost certainly be better than no George at all. Even if it did mean the slight risk that she would wake up in the night to find Seren leaning over her with a bread knife, of course. Or that she would receive a hard, unexpected shove down the stairs by the girl and end up paralysed for life, even dead. Perhaps Seren would spy on Em and send video evidence of her dreadfulness to perfect Charlotte. Oh God, the possibilities were endless and alarming. The holiday could easily turn into a nightmare!

'Em?' George prompted, before unwittingly going on to crank her doubts right up to What-the-Hell? level. 'Charlotte's really sorry,' he'd said. 'And don't worry, I asked her to come and pick up Seren when she's back, so that I don't have to go shuttling back and forth again, and she said that was fine. Which is something.'

Em had gasped for breath like a goldfish plucked from its bowl. 'Right,' she somehow managed to say weakly. Yeah, George, that *was* something. The ex-wife turning up on holiday, passing judgement on Em, her kids, her choice of accommodation, her step-parenting skills? George cheerfully telling her, 'Don't worry' as if it wasn't a big deal, like she wasn't going to be tying herself in knots over the encounter from now until then? That really was something. Could a holiday *get* any more stressful?

Em was not the sort of person who went hating on other women – she'd never done that competitive-girlfriend thing, not even with Michelle, Dom's new wife. (Well, okay, she'd done it a *bit* with Michelle, she supposed, but then she *had* been severely provoked, in fairness. Many times.) But she really tried not to be judgey and sneering about other women for the sake of it; she'd always seen herself as better than that.

Turned out she wasn't all that much better. Turned out, in fact, that as soon as she heard that Charlotte was going to be joining them, however briefly, on holiday, Em had dissolved into a puddle of self-loathing, instantly putting herself on a crash diet, booking in an emergency haircut and doing brutal sets of sit-ups whenever she remembered. What was she going to *wear*? How long would Charlotte want to spend with them? Should she organize food? A sit-down meal? Should she bring some recipe books or nice accessories from home? Perhaps some summer lanterns, which she could string up along the front of the cottage so that it looked like a holiday straight from the pages of a catalogue; or . . .

Standing now in her bedroom, supposedly packing for their imminent departure, Em found herself clutching the flattering fitted evening dress she'd just taken from the wardrobe as if it was another person. She had to remind herself to breathe before her head exploded. *Come on, Em, get a grip.* It was one measly encounter with one other human being that would probably last less than an hour. She could do it. Of course she could do it! Charlotte would probably be just as terrified as she was. Okay, perhaps not terrified, but at least slightly trepidatious. At the very least curious, anyway. Interested. Wouldn't she?

She stared glumly at herself in the mirror, worried that her new haircut – meant to be breezy, choppy and young – actually looked a bit wonky and amateurish. Did her neck look strange now? Would Charlotte think she was odd-looking? 'God, George has lowered his standards big-time since me,' Charlotte might laugh unkindly to her new part-ner. 'Such a weird haircut. And—'

Stop it, Em. Seriously. STOP. IT!

Folding the dress, she rolled her eyes and tried to channel Kathy, the most chilled person she knew. A devoted fan of self-help books, Kathy had once told Em that you should stand in front of a mirror every day, look yourself in the eye and say affirming things. It was worth a go, she supposed.

'It's going to be a great holiday and everyone will get on brilliantly, and Charlotte won't judge me,' she mumbled to her reflection.

Whoa, whoa, whoa, is that seriously the best you can do? Rub-bish! Try again, this time with a bit of oomph, Kathy chided her. She was quite bossy at times, for someone so laidback.

'It's going to be a great holiday and everyone will get on brilliantly, and Charlotte better not bloody well judge me,' Em repeated to herself. Not so much with oomph as sav-agery, but never mind. It would have to do.

'First sign of madness, you know, Mum,' Jack said, passing the open bedroom door just then and making her jump.

She pulled a face at her reflection, hoping he hadn't heard the details of her cringey mirror affirmation. 'Only the first?' she called back. 'I'm doing better than I thought.'

Deep breath, she told herself, chucking the last few things into her case and heaving the zip along. Seren coming with them was not a disaster, just a slight change of plan. Charlotte turning up as well was not an experience to be dreaded, but a chance for Em to show her best self. Yeah! She would not let either of them ruin her perfect, romantic holiday, that was for sure. Em was a born optimist, after all. These two weeks away were going to be absolutely wonderful. The best.

'Kids? Are you ready?' she yelled as she lugged the suitcase downstairs. 'Going in ten minutes. Repeat: ten minutes. Let's do this!'

It was going to be a great holiday and everyone was going to get on brilliantly, she said once more under her breath as she put her shoes on. Just see if they didn't!

Chapter Two

A skylark soared high above the old stone cottages that nestled in the dip of a wooded hillside, its sweet cheerful melody ringing through the air. The swimming pool was a perfect azure rectangle at the centre of the buildings, glinting and still as the sun rose steadily in the sky. A lone pink inflatable flamingo bobbed on the surface of the water, sent on a leisurely meandering circuit by the breeze. Nearby, amidst the clumps of fragrant lavender, a bee was bumping between the flower heads, humming busily to itself.

The cottages stood still and empty, their old brick walls enjoying the silence after all the frantic activity that had taken place there earlier that morning: cases packed, damp swimming things rolled up in plastic bags, fridges emptied, beds checked underneath for small essential toys and misplaced socks. Even, in one particular bedroom, for the underwear that had been thrown off the night before in a heady moment of passion.

Then the cars had been loaded up, and away the families

had driven, each with their new holiday memories and souvenirs, with sand still speckling the inside of the cars, with freckles and tanned skin; the nagging feeling of having forgotten something gradually replaced by thoughts of arriving home again, with every mile that accumulated between here and there.

It was Friday, changeover day, when holidays began and ended, when the cycle reset itself all over again. In a matter of hours there would come a whole new set of arrivals, hoping for fun, adventures and relaxation; looking forward to a slice of time that was removed from all the demands of their real worlds. Shrieks of laughter would ring out around the pool, along with noisy splashes. The barbecue would be lit once more, the table football would click and clack with competitive games, the beds would sigh beneath the weight of their new sleepers' dreams and desires. Wine would be popped, kisses would linger, arguments might flare.

But all of that was yet to come. For now, the cottages stood quietly, waiting for their next temporary residents and all of the dramas that would unfold within their walls. In the meantime, the skylark flew on through the blue, its song spiralling down to earth.

Lorna was hauling sheets off the bed when her phone rang downstairs in the kitchen. 'Just coming,' she called down to it, knowing that, had her husband Roy been there, he would have made an affectionate comment about her talking to technology again. She couldn't help herself. Those annoying self-service checkout tills at the supermarket were the worst. *Unexpected item in bagging area. Please check and try again. Have you swiped your loyalty card?* 'Yes, all *right!*' she would end up saying crossly every time.

She dumped the pile of bedding into the basket, then hurried down the narrow stairs. Mawnan Cottage was the smallest of their three holiday lets, with one good-sized bedroom and a smaller single room, but it had the nicest sea views of all the cottages: perfectly framed rectangles of the countryside sweeping down to the sea. On a summer's day like today you could see the boats on the water; could practically hear the halyards slapping against the masts as the wind blew. But on a Friday – changeover day – she was always far too busy to stand and gawp out of a window, however wonderful the view. Besides, that phone was ringing and if she didn't get a shift-on, she'd miss the call altogether.

'Hello? Lorna Brearley speaking?' she said, snatching it up. Sometimes, even now, she still half-expected to hear Aidan's voice whenever she answered a phone. *Is that you? It's me,* he'd always said; that easy shorthand you only got between people who loved one another. Back in the real world, however, the kitchen smelled of bleach and cleaning spray from when she'd done the rounds earlier, but there was a crumb on the table, she noticed in annoyance, dabbing it up with her finger and flicking it into the sink. She was only sixty-three and not planning to retire for at least a decade, but sometimes she worried that her eyesight was going. That she was losing her attention to detail.

'Hi, my name's Jonathan Woodward, I'm booked in to stay at Mawnan Cottage from today,' a deep male voice said into her ear. There was something agitated about his tone, and Lorna braced herself for trouble. Here we go. He and his wife were going to be late, she guessed. They had deleted the email with her set of directions and didn't know how to get there. They had changed their minds, wanted to rearrange or – worst of all – cancel.

'Yes?' she said guardedly. Well, it was too late for any cancelling or rearranging, she reminded herself. Not if they expected to receive any money back, anyway. Roy had made it very clear on the website that a month's notice was required in order to cancel a booking, and that rearrangements would only be made at the discretion of the owners. 'And no going soft on them either, mind,' he'd warned her, raising his silvery eyebrows. 'We're meant to be a business here, not a charity, remember.'

'There's been a change of plan, I'm afraid,' said the deep-voiced Jonathan Woodward now, as these thoughts spun in Lorna's head like clean laundry in the tumble-drier. 'Clara – my wife – went into labour six weeks early last night. And so—'

'Oh my goodness,' gulped Lorna. 'Is she all right?'

'She's fine. Actually . . .' His voice cracked on the words. 'She's more than fine. We've had a little boy.'

'Oh!' She clapped a hand to her chest, the soppy old fool that she was. You could hear the emotion in his voice, how choked up he was to be saying the words out loud. Their first baby, it must be, seeing as the cottage had only been booked for two. That precious first child. 'Congratulations! Are they both all right?'

'They're doing really well. Obviously he's very small still, being so premature, and it's all a bit of a shock, becoming parents when we weren't quite ready for it.' He seemed to check himself, as if remembering that he was speaking to a stranger. He had probably been telling all his relatives the same thing the whole morning.

'I can imagine,' she said kindly. 'So what time will we be expecting you then?'

There was a horrified silence for a moment, then an awkward-sounding 'Ahh . . .'

'I'm kidding,' she laughed, before remembering that he was probably stunned from the unexpected arrival and perhaps not up to recognizing a joke. 'I understand. You're ringing to cancel your holiday.'

'Yes, I'm afraid so, because obviously Clara will be in hospital for a while and—'

'Of course she will,' Lorna soothed. 'Absolutely. Well,

my very best wishes to you both. To the three of you, I should say.' *Please don't ask for a refund,* she thought, her fingers tightening on the phone. *Please don't do that. You sound so nice, you and your wife and child, and it's not as if you planned this to happen, but I really can't let you off all that money, when we need it. Roy will kill me if I do.*

'Thank you very much,' he said. 'And we're sorry to mess you around. We were both really looking forward to the holiday. In terms of the payments we've made . . .'

She knew it. Didn't she know it? She felt her face twist in a grimace, anticipating the unpleasant moment when he asked and she had to say no, even though every instinct in her body wanted to acquiesce. How could she refuse him when he was so happy and emotional, when he had just become a father?

'Obviously I know it's too late to get any kind of a refund, and that's fine,' he went on, to her surprise. 'But hopefully we can come down some other time as a family; maybe in the spring.' He laughed, sounding tired. 'Although I get the impression that holidays aren't really the same when you've got a small person in tow.'

Her shoulders sagged in relief at how decent he was being, and how grateful *she* was in return, that he wasn't going to argue or start trying to haggle her down. You'd be astonished at how many people did, and it never ended well. Left a nasty taste in your mouth every time. 'Thank you,' she replied. 'Tell you what,' she heard herself adding, because she was soft, too soft, just like Roy always said, 'if you do decide to come back in the spring, remind me of this phone call and you can have the cottage for half-price. Our little gift to you all.'

'Oh!' That had surprised him. 'That's so kind. Thank you very much, Lorna.'

'You're welcome. Thanks for letting me know your news. And all the best. Welcome to parenthood.'

She had tears in her eyes as she hung up. Don't you dare, Lorna Brearley, she told herself fiercely. Don't you dare start feeling sorry for yourself. Not now, when you've still got two cottages to clean and all that laundry to do. Stop right there, this minute!

It was particularly hard this summer, that was all. Particularly thorny. If she could just get past Monday without losing her head, if she could keep it together for another few days and somehow make it through the weekend, then she knew her grief would subside once more. The tide would drop. She might even stop feeling as if she was full right to the brim with emotion the whole time.

Squeezing her eyes shut, she clenched both fists and counted her breathing. In and out. In and out. In. Out. She focused on the smell of bleach from the sink. The soft ticking of the clock on the wall. The warmth on her skin from the sun as it shone through the small square windowpane.

She was all right. She was here, she was breathing, she was absolutely fine. It was still going to be a good day.

Now then – she had the beds to finish stripping, and afterwards she would head over to Briar and Parr, and hope that nobody else cancelled on her. As long as she kept busy she would survive the next few days. 'Come on, Lorna,' she said to herself, striding back upstairs. 'You've got work to do.'

Two hundred and fifty or so miles east, Maggie Laine was in her living room, ticking items off a neatly written list. Geological hand-lenses and maps, her wildflower guide, the books that Paul had lent her, one about Cornish tin mines, another about Arthurian legends: all packed. Binoculars. Waterproofs. Notepad. Backgammon set. Marmite. Underwear. Jumpers . . .

Amelia walked in just then and threw herself on the sofa with a loud groan, joggling Maggie's hand and sending the pen shooting over the list. 'Careful,' Maggie scolded, but her daughter was busily scooping her long dark hair over the arm of the sofa so that it fell like a shiny waterfall towards the carpet and took no notice. Amelia was fourteen and had recently started communicating with all kinds of new melodramatic noises: exasperated sighs, moans of complaint, deep huffs of frustration. As a secondary-school teacher, Maggie recognized these sounds from the classroom, from other people's teenagers, but it was still kind of unsettling to have your own child making them at you. Your own child who, until a few months ago, had always seemed pleased to see you and wanted nothing more than to spend time with you and share all your hobbies. 'Thick as thieves, the pair of you,' her own mum had often commented, seeing them both with their heads bent over a map, or poring over some rock samples Maggie had brought home from school.

But that had all changed when Tara appeared on the scene.

'All ready to go?' Maggie asked now, trying to block Tara from her head. They were heading off on holiday after all, away from the wretched girl, and she wasn't willing to give her any mental space whatsoever for the next fortnight.

Amelia lifted a shoulder, which might have signalled yes or no, Maggie wasn't sure.

'You've shut your window, haven't you?' she added, going over to the television and switching off the power at the wall. 'Packed your toothbrush? Knickers?'

'Mum!' groaned Amelia. 'I'm not five years old. I do know how to put a few things in a suitcase. Christ on a bike!'

Maggie stiffened. 'Can you not say that, please.'

'Why? You're not religious. What do you care?' Amelia retorted.

'Other people are religious, though. Like Grandma. Think how—'

'She's not here, though, is she? Hey, Grandma, are you there?' Amelia pretended to listen, one hand curved around her ear. 'Nope. We're okay. Hallelujah! Praise the Lord!'

Maggie ignored the sarcasm. 'Have you packed plenty of warm tops?' she asked, trying to keep her tone even. 'Pyjamas? I'm not sure how cold it's going to get there at night.' She'd packed some thermal socks herself, just in case the nights proved nippy. It was wise, in her experience, not to gamble on other people's ideas of comfort, especially when it came to insulation and a proper tog duvet. Maggie always felt the cold, particularly in her feet. Her ex, Will, had often complained that it was like sleeping with a couple of ice-blocks in the bed. ('Better cold feet than a cold heart,' Maggie should have said to him. If only she'd thought of it before he'd gone and walked out.)

'I'm sure they'll have blankets there. Not to mention brick walls,' Amelia replied. 'If we're really lucky, a roof too.'

Maggie pressed her lips together, trying not to show how much she disliked her daughter's smart-alec remarks. This is just normal teenage behaviour, she told herself. This is just boundary-testing and button-pushing. All the same, she was surprised how much it hurt each time. How their tight little partnership of two seemed to be encountering unprecedented stress-points. 'Here's hoping,' she said, refusing to rise to the bait. 'Although there's something to be said for sleeping under the stars. Remember that time we stayed on the dig in France, and it was so hot that everyone slept in hammocks outside?'

'Yeah, and there were loads of gross bugs and weird noises – it was horrible,' Amelia said, seeming to disregard the fact that, going home from this particular trip, she had told Maggie, shiny-eyed, that it had been her best holiday ever.

Maggie decided not to remind her of that now. Amelia was apparently so set on forging this cool new image for herself that she would rather rewrite any parts of her history that might be viewed by others as dorky or strange. And so archaeology was now 'really boring'. Historical ruins were 'totally lame'. Geological investigations were for wcirdos. Instead, thanks to the influence of wretched Tara Webster and the rest of her gang, Amelia was now mostly interested in applying flicky eyeliner and clumpy mascara, the latest banal YouTuber and obsessed with social media.

But Maggie was not thinking about Tara Webster, she reminded herself. 'Let's get going anyway, before the Friday traffic becomes too heinous,' she said instead. 'Ready?'

'Suppose so,' grunted Amelia with all the reluctance of someone facing several hours of root-canal work at the dentist. She forced herself off the sofa and upright, a weary *If I have to* expression on her face.

'Great,' said Maggie, feeling her voice becoming tighter

with each word, in her desperation to remain cheerful. 'In that case, the holiday starts here!'

Amelia had been a sickly little thing as a baby: sallow and small, suffering terribly from eczema until she was five, when Maggie had finally discovered the precise combination of washing-powder brand, medication and non-dairy products that seemed to help. Those early years now felt like a blur of despair and exhaustion: all the dreadful nights they'd shared weeping together, Amelia's sheets covered in specks of blood where she'd been unable to stop scratching, however much emollient cream Maggie slathered on her, however many scratch-mitts and soothing baths they tried. It had bonded them, though, such horror, forging a deep primal alliance between the two of them, partners in combat. When Will had walked out seven months after Amelia's birth, claiming he couldn't cope, the bond between mother and daughter only strengthened.

Maggie had never forgiven Will for leaving them in their darkest hour. She despised him for caring so little about their child that he could leave like that, with barely any contact over the ensuing years. He was a photographer, footloose and fancy-free, and she would occasionally see his work pop up in glossy magazines, immediately feeling a rush of anger at the sight of his name. For years she had been unable to help comparing whatever exciting thing Will might be doing at any given moment with her own humdrum life.

He is crouching in a warzone right now, she would think dully, *with heavy gunfire shattering the air around him, seeing men die through a camera lens. I, meanwhile, am raking the nit comb through our daughter's hair and examining the white teeth for telltale dark specks.*

He is having lunch in an expensive hushed hotel with a magazine editor who wants to commission a reportage special. Over in suburbia, however, I am cajoling our toddler to eat peas and sweetcorn.

His world was big, bristling with danger around each corner, boundless in its scope and urgency. Hers was as small as a held hand, a pinecone on the ground, a storybook pored over on a lap.

Not that Maggie begrudged her daughter their shared domestic world at all. Not for a moment. She had tried to shower Amelia with so much love and attention that there simply wasn't space for her to feel as if she'd missed out by having an absent dad. Maggie had retrained from geologist to geography teacher, so that she could be around for every school holiday. She'd turned down countless invitations to book clubs, parties, dinner, drinks – most evening things, in fact, because she would rather spend time with her wonderful, sparky girl.

And for fourteen years Amelia had gazed lovingly back at

her with those faithful dark eyes and been glad of her mother's company. They'd moulded a comfortable life together, full of rituals and favourite things and in-jokes. Series they binge-watched together. Recipes they both enjoyed making. It had been delightful for Maggie – enriching and plentiful. Yet all of a sudden their relationship was no longer enough for Amelia, it seemed. Worse, it had apparently become an embarrassment.

The trouble with you, Maggie, Will had said to her once – and truly, was there any way in which this sentence *didn't* end badly? – *is that you're too bloody intense. You're needy. You consume people with your need. And I can't live like this.*

Maggie had never been able to forget those damning words. They had buzzed and circled around in her head like wasps in a jar. She knew she shouldn't take anything to heart from Will, of all people, Mr Terrified of Commitment, but all the same, the sentiment smarted. He made her sound as if she was some monstrous parasite, leeching off her loved ones. When she'd only ever tried to do her best!

She glanced across at Amelia, her adored girl, slumped in the passenger seat beside her, earphones unsociably attached. It was her worst fear that one day her daughter would reject her in the same way that Will had. *The trouble with you, Mum –* oh God, she couldn't even bear to imagine the rest of the sentence. It would kill her. It would break her heart clean through.

She must have let out an involuntary moan at the thought because Amelia turned, yanking out an earbud, and gave her mother a suspicious sideways look. 'You all right?' she asked grudgingly.

Maggie blinked away her doom-laden thoughts and smiled brightly. 'Absolutely fine,' she said, starting the engine and carefully pulling out of her parking space. Tara might have taken Amelia by the hand lately and led her down a terrible new path of alcopops, short skirts and sarcasm, but Maggie was determined to win her back over the next two weeks, or at least die trying. The bond between them would be repaired, made good as new. 'Cornwall here we come!' she cried, with all the valour of King Arthur himself.

Chapter Three

There was something about going on holiday, Em thought, unpacking provisions in Briar Cottage's kitchen, that allowed you to reinvent yourself, just for two weeks at a time. You could snip yourself out of your usual real-life frieze like a paper doll and position yourself in new, exotic surroundings. With a bit of luck you might even become a new, exotic person in the process. It was a beguiling thought.

Not that all of her holidays in the past had been exotic occasions, obviously. Her childhood holidays had been a succession of damp and drizzly campsites, all welly boots, tinned meatballs and petty squabbles. She could picture her mum now, wearing two jumpers and an anorak on the beach, pouring coffee from a Thermos flask with a rigid jaw as the clouds huddled threateningly in the sky. The gritty texture of sand at the bottom of a sleeping bag. Vanilla ice-cream dribbling stickily down a cone onto her fingers.

The holidays she'd spent as a teenager were best forgotten, frankly, especially the summer they'd camped at the

Gower when she was fifteen. The tent had leaked and she'd had back-to-back arguments with her parents, including one particularly explosive row over the wearing (or the non-wearing, rather) of her hated orange cagoule in a freezing downpour. 'I'd sooner catch pneumonia and *die*' had been her passionate, if grandiose declaration. 'At least that would give us all a break from having to listen to you shouting,' her dad had replied mildly. As for the trouble she and Jenny got into the next morning, having sneaked off to the campsite bar with some boys they'd met and ending up violently sick, her ears rang even now to recall the thunderous recriminations. She'd never been able to stomach cider and black since.

Holidays with mates had been more fun at least: easygoing, sun-drenched weeks in cheap European resorts where flirting with the sloe-eyed waiters became an art form. Pounding nightclubs, tiny dresses, shots of ouzo thrown back with abandon, and the worst sunburn of her life, thanks to falling asleep on the beach hungover at midday, once and once only. Ah, to be young and stupid. Those were the days.

Sexy, romantic holidays with Dom had followed in her late twenties, back when he was still Dom the Bomb rather than Dom the shitty ex-husband. Holidays where she'd packed seven bikinis, a few strappy dresses and scented body lotion. Very little else. Dreamy nights beneath a rotating ceiling fan, rubbing after-sun into each other's tanned bodies. Not that she'd want to do such things with Dom now, mind, especially with the paunch he'd developed in recent years, but at the time it had felt like paradise.

Hard on the heels of the romantic holidays and then the honeymoon had come the summer breaks with their young children, when there was no longer anything remotely holi-dayish or relaxing about the experience. In fact those weeks away turned out to mean exactly the same old exhaustion and drudgery in a different place, where the babies wouldn't sleep and developed prickly heat and they were all packed into a one-bedroom apartment, and it was hell. Then, once Izzie and Jack had grown up into small, toddling wrecking-machines, she would spend the entire time away worrying that they were going to topple off a balcony or plunge head-first into the nearest pool, if she took her eyes off them for a second. Over the years she had assembled an impressive line of foreign phrases, namely 'My child is drowning!', 'I need a doctor!' and 'Help!' in various languages, ready to scream the appropriate words at any given moment.

It was always such a relief to come home after these 'holidays', even if she did then find herself yearning, quite ferociously, for a week on her own in a hotel somewhere to recover, with room service, silence and a well-stocked minibar.

Still, if she'd thought those years were tough, then the first summer as a single mum had been the worst yet. Izzie was eleven and Jack ten, and Em had been so determined to give them a brilliant time and show the world she could manage just fine without Dom that the three of them had gone to Florida for the so-called holiday of a lifetime. Yes, so the photos might show the kids beaming with Bart Simpson and Goofy, and dive-bombing each other in a turquoise pool, but they sure as hell didn't show Em accidentally rear-ending the hire car and bursting into tears, or Izzie picking up a vomiting bug on the second day, or Jack getting stung by a wasp and having an allergic reaction that had seen them racing for the nearest hospital in a heart-pounding adrenalin dash. She had returned to the UK a complete wreck beneath her mahogany tan; jet-lagged, skint and vowing 'never a-bloody-gain'.

Forget all that, though. This year's holiday was going to be *great*. Without the day-to-day hassles of work, school and domestic chores grinding her down, she would be a new Em, albeit one in several different variations. She'd be the easy-going, non-nagging mum for Izzie and Jack. She'd be the fun-loving girlfriend without a care in the world for George. For Seren, she'd be kind and considerate and infinitely patient. For Charlotte, she'd be the gracious hostess, relaxed and at home in her beautiful surroundings. Ha! See, maybe this would be okay after all. In fact, in many ways it was probably better for Charlotte to see her here in the gorgeous cottage, rather than in her scruffy, messy Cheltenham home, which almost always had somebody's sports socks or work tights drying on a radiator, and rude messages chalked up on the kitchen blackboard.

'They're here,' Jack called just then, from where he was perched on the windowsill of the living room.

Em had had to contend with various scathing complaints from the teens about Briar Cottage's dodgy Wi-Fi and the even worse phone signal since they had arrived twenty minutes ago, but apparently her son had now discovered the best place in the house in which to keep up with his social life, which was a relief to everyone. What was more, the spot seemed to double as a lookout post.

'Hooray,' she replied, unloading her last carrier bag in the kitchen. You never knew, with these holiday cottages, if they were going to welcome you with a bottle of wine in the fridge and assorted tasty goodies, or if they would be the stingy type of place that didn't so much as leave you a single toilet roll. She well remembered the horror of having slogged all the way up to the Lake District one summer to a house in the middle of nowhere, to be greeted in the latter way, and had almost burst into tears at the realization she'd have to get back into the hot sweatbox of a car once more, before being able to make herself a much-needed cup of tea with milk.

Since then she'd always travelled as if preparing for siege conditions, squeezing bags of bread, fruit and tinned beans into the boot of the car, packing toilet rolls and pasta packets around the children as if rearranging Tetris pieces. Wouldn't you know it, this was the more generous kind of holiday cottage, and she had been gratified to discover paper bags containing a loaf of fresh bread and some sultana scones awaiting them on the table, along with milk, butter, eggs, jam and a decent-looking Sauvignon Blanc in the fridge. *There, see!* she'd thought, with a slightly pathetic stab of triumph. She might have been drunk when she'd booked this holiday, but her instincts had guided her to a good place at least.

And it did, on first appearances, seem very nice there. The three stone-built barn conversions must once have formed the edges of a stable yard, she guessed, but were now set up as a trio of holiday homes around a swimming pool, which also boasted a small lawned area with deckchairs and sun loungers arranged in clusters. There was a fourth, smaller building set further back from the pool, which housed the games room, according to Izzie's investigations, alongside a communal barbecue area. To the left of their cottage stretched rounded green hills, and if you peered out of the bedrooms at the front, you could just about see a sliver of petrol-blue sea down below.

Inside, the cottage was clean and tasteful: big stone hearths and beamed ceilings, neutral paint shades with bright pops of colour here and there. Huge beds and monsoon showers awaited them upstairs, with deep soft sofas and shelves of paperbacks down in the living area. 'The girl done good,' she had thought to herself with a smile, heaving her suitcase up to the master bedroom, where she stood for a few moments to admire the cherrywood fitted wardrobes, the spotless white bed-linen and the vintage washstand in the en-suite. Just the place, she'd thought, flopping backwards on the bed, for a romantic getaway for two. Plus their three assorted children, of course. She found herself casting a wary eye over the bed, hoping that Seren wouldn't end up squeezed in between her and George too many times.

Now in the kitchen, she rushed about, trying to get everything put away before the others walked in. Originally she'd assumed they'd all be travelling down to Cornwall together, but since George had been roped into bringing Seren along, he'd decided to drive his own car there too, claiming it would make life easier. Was it also his means of escape, she wondered, in case he wanted to make a quick getaway? A rush of nerves assaulted her in the next moment. What if her sister and friends were right, and this was all too much too soon? Would she and George still be quite so besotted with each other by the end of the fortnight?

'I never expected to feel like this again,' he had told her on Wednesday night. They'd been out to the cinema together and were back at her place, slotted around each other like spoons in the cutlery drawer as they lay in bed.

'Me neither,' she'd replied happily. Oh, so happily! 'I honestly thought I was done with all that love and romance business. That it was a young person's thing, and that I was far too cynical and jaded ever to go there again.'

He'd laughed, and it was warm and ticklish against the back of her neck. 'Same. Who knew that we jaded old cynics would find each other? The perfect match!'

'The perfect catch,' she echoed. They had a tendency to be very cheesy with each other, she and George; the exact shade of mush she'd always turned her nose up about previously. How come she had never realized just how enjoyable it was to act like a complete sap? She couldn't get enough of such behaviour these days.

It seemed hard to believe that it was only five months since they'd met, at Laura and Sam's house-warming party. She hadn't even been intending to go – she'd had one of those crazy weeks at work and had been thinking longingly of a pyjama-clad Friday night in, getting up close and personal with a bottle of gin and a box-set on the sofa – except that she'd bumped into Laura on her way back from the station and been nobbled. 'See you about eight then?' Laura had asked, after recounting details of the hours she'd spent preparing party food and play-lists. Only the most churlish of people could have said no.

Okay, so she would just stay for a bit, she'd vowed: long enough to be polite, before she went scuttling home to her pyjamas and sofa. Laura and Sam's new house was a scant two streets away from her own, so at least it wasn't as if she had to drag herself across town. 'I'll see you later,' she promised the TV, before locking the back door and issuing the kids with strict instructions about remembering not to let in any paedophiles or murderers.

'Burglars?' Jack had asked. 'Psychopaths?'

'Them too,' she said. 'Especially if it's Amanda from next door. Joking! Do *not* tell her I said that.'

Once at the party, she'd got chatting to George in the kitchen and found him so interesting and funny and handsome that she completely changed her mind about leaving early. A TV binge in pyjamas had never seemed less appealing. He kept making her laugh and his eyes were gorgeously dark and crinkled at the edges when he smiled. He smelled nice too, and she found herself pretending she couldn't quite hear what he was saying a few times so that she could lean in closer and get a good whiff. Mmm. Delicious.

Before she knew it, the kitchen clock was showing midnight – how had that happened? It was the latest that Em had ever stayed out, without there being a responsible adult in the house with her kids. Despite text reassurances from Izzie (*I'm still up watching Netflix anyway, it's fine*) and Jack (*I punched a couple of paedos and shot the burglars, don't worry, I got this, Mum*), she decided, reluctantly, that she should head back. 'Alas, Cinderella has to return home to her teenagers, who may or may not have been at my pathetic drinks cupboard,' she confessed to George, weighing up whether she was drunk or brazen enough to ask for his phone number.

Sod it – nothing ventured, nothing gained and all that. 'I was wondering . . .' she began recklessly in the next moment, just as he said, 'I don't suppose I could have your number?'

They'd smiled at each other dreamily. *Kapow!* she thought, her heart thudding. Get in there, Cinders.

'Wait,' Jack was saying now. 'Does George drive a shitty beige Volvo?'

Em shut the fridge door, sensing an imminent anticlimax. 'No,' she said. 'He's got a black BMW.'

'False alarm,' said Izzie with a snort of laughter. 'Unless George has turned himself into a spoddy-looking woman, that is.'

'I certainly hope not,' Em said, coming to peer through the window with them at the small shared car park that was in view. Out of the car (Jack's description of a 'shitty beige Volvo' turned out to be pretty accurate) emerged a tall, rather hunched-over woman in a dark-green anorak and corduroy trousers, with a faintly harassed air. She looked as if she was Em's age, slightly older perhaps, with shaggy brown hair. 'Nope,' Em said, 'that's definitely not George.'

As the woman turned in their direction, Em dodged abruptly away from the window, embarrassed that she and her children were being so nosy. 'Stop staring,' she hissed, but then Jack murmured an approving 'Excellent!' and curiosity got the better of her. Peering over again, Em was just in time to see a teenage girl clamber out of the passenger seat with an air of resignation. The girl had long black hair that fell into her eyes and was wearing a ripped black vest-top, a bottle-green miniskirt and high-heeled DM boots. She folded her arms across her chest and took up the stance that Em recognized from her own two as Combative Teen, then said something they couldn't hear.

'Someone's not happy,' Izzie commented, glued to the scene.

Just then, as the three Hugheses gawped on, the girl noticed them and glared. Em ducked back again, mortified to have been caught snooping, but not before she saw the girl stretch out an arm and flip them the finger.

'Whoa,' cried Izzie. 'Harsh.'

'She is *fit*,' said Jack, grinning back at her.

Oh God, thought Em, startled, was that actually a *wink* as well? Since when had her son shown the slightest bit of interest in girls? Until today she would have said that precisely nothing went on in his head other than football, YouTube, snacks and sleeping, but apparently he had turned into Casanova during the journey down from Cheltenham. Marvellous. She stared at him as if seeing him for the first time in months, noting the faint fuzz of hair that had recently sprouted along his jaw, as well as how broad his shoulders were these days. Blink and your children changed before your eyes. All of a sudden, he was half-boy, half-man. All hormones, apparently.

'Gross,' Izzie was telling him in disapproval. 'Didn't your mother ever teach you not to objectify girls?'

'Clearly not explicitly enough,' Em said. Oof, Jack getting the horn. Now she was imagining torturous holiday romances, a Romeo and Juliet between the barn conversions (were there any balconies? She hadn't spotted any) and fumbly first kisses. She'd have to have a serious chat with him about responsibilities and respect. About not being a git to the opposite sex, like his dad, moreover.

Casanova, still smirking, slid down from his perch and headed for the kitchen, with what looked like a new swagger in his step. 'Well, this place suddenly got a *lot* more interesting anyway,' they heard him drawl, before adding in his normal voice, 'Hey, Mum, can I open these crisps?'

'I wish it was just going to be us,' Izzie said in a quiet voice, before Em could reply to Jack. 'Here, I mean. I wish the others weren't coming.'

'What? Oh!' Now Em felt a pang of guilt. And surprise too, not least because on their last summer holiday, to Snowdonia, Izzie had barely wanted anything to do with her or Jack. Every time Em had tried to drag her out on a day-trip or off on a walk, she'd resisted, saying she just wanted to stay in the house that day; please, did she *have* to go? 'Really? But I thought . . .'

'I mean, we don't even *know* this George bloke. I don't want to sleep in a strange house with a random man hanging around.'

'I'm opening the crisps then, I'm taking that as a yes,' Jack bellowed from the kitchen, but Em was too startled by Izzie's words to pay him any proper attention.

'I *do* know him and he's not a *random man*,' she replied, stung, 'and he won't be *hanging around*, either, he'll be in with me, so—'

'Yeah, and I'm not wildly happy about *that*, either, Mum.' Izzie pursed her lips, her small pert nose in the air. She wound a thick lock of honey-coloured hair around her hand, then tossed it back over one shoulder. 'Our rooms are right next to each other and I don't want to *hear* anything, all right? It's disgusting, at your age. It's kind of desperate, too.'

At *her* age! Izzie made it sound as if Em was geriatric rather than in the prime of her middle years. That jibe about being desperate hurt too. *Hardly!* she wanted to cry in nettled self-defence. She had all but given up on men until George had come along and surprised her so delightfully; she had been fully prepared to see out her old age alone, nursing the remaining shreds of her dignity in spinsterly solitude. That was not what a desperate woman looked like, in Em's opinion.

Nonetheless, Izzie's words gave her pause for thought. *I wish the others weren't coming.* Had Em made a colossal error in inviting George along? she wondered with renewed unease. Izzie and Jack spent so little time with her usually – they were out with friends, or playing for their hockey and football teams – that the three of them didn't often socialize as a unit. She had anticipated – perhaps wrongly, admittedly – that they might want to do their own thing down in Cornwall too, *sans* Mum. Or had she been kidding herself on this front, so that she could throw herself into the arms of George, guilt-free?

'I'm sure we'll still do some things together, just the three of us,' she promised, trying hastily to think of one. 'George will have his daughter too, remember, who's a bit younger and won't be able to cope with long bike rides, for instance, so you, me and Jack could—'

'Can I open this beer as well?' yelled Jack from the kitchen. 'Mum?'

'No, you cannot – don't you dare,' she called back. 'I've counted the bottles, before you get any ideas,' she added for good measure. She gave Izzie a beseeching look, taking in the jut of her chin, the squaring of her shoulders. Izzie was sixteen now, and Em felt as if a countdown clock was permanently ticking in her head as her children grew up at seemingly astonishing speed. This might be the final holiday that her daughter would want to spend with them before opting for the wilder temptations of festivals and interrailing with her mates in future summers. Em had been hoping for at least a few joyful, idyllic days together this time, to add to the photo albums and memory banks, but perhaps she'd been too ambitious. 'Come on, love. It'll be fine.'

'Yeah, but . . .' Izzie dug the toe of her trainer into the soft carpet, despite Em having told her several times to take her shoes off while they were inside the house. 'It's not the same, is it?'

'Well . . .' Em felt stumped. She wished they'd had this conversation earlier, back at home, rather than here, when George might appear at any moment. 'I mean, Dad takes you on holiday with him and Michelle, doesn't he, so . . .'

'Yeah, but we like Michelle. She's really cool.'

Ouch. Double-punch from Izzie. 'What, and you don't like George?' she asked, feeling hurt on his behalf. How could anyone not like George? And – hello! – since when had *Michelle*, the Queen of Flammable Hair and inch-thick make-up, been 'really cool' anyway? It wasn't all that long ago that Izzie was bitching and moaning about her, and Em, although aiming for detached neutrality, was secretly drinking in every delicious insult.

Izzie shrugged in a way Em couldn't interpret. 'He's a bit . . . fake,' she replied.

What, and Michelle *wasn't*, with those new knockers and all that collagen in her face? Put her too close to a naked flame and she'd combust (with a bit of luck). 'He is not!' Em protested.

'Yeah, he is. He's like – too nice. I don't trust him.' Izzie's face had sealed up like a tomb suddenly, her eyes down on the floor.

Em opened her mouth then shut it again, taken aback. Izzie had never even hinted at such feelings before. When did her children become such mysteries to her? Had she taken her eye off the ball with the distraction of being swept up in her own romance, and turned into one of those negligent, selfish parents she was always tutting about with her friends? 'Well . . . look . . . You just don't know him very well, that's all. But I promise you—'

'Exactly! We don't *know* him. So why have you invited him on holiday with us? How do you think that makes me and Jack feel, shunted aside for your bloody love-life?'

Just then – of course it had to be just then, with their voices raised and a horrible un-holidayish tension in the air – there was a knock at the open door and George came in. 'Hello! We made it,' he said jovially, and Em's heart almost stopped, both with panic at the conversation he'd just walked into, and at how extremely handsome he was, even after a five-hour drive with a seven-year-old. Look at him, so tall and tanned, in his pale-blue T-shirt and jeans, dropping an overnight bag to the floor with a grin. She couldn't tell from his expression if he'd heard what Izzie had just said or not, though. *Not*, she hoped, her stomach tying itself in knots.

'Whoop-dee-doo,' muttered Izzie, stalking out of the room, while Em tried to gather herself with heroic effort.

'You made it! Hello. Welcome to Cornwall,' she said, rather stupidly, as if she owned the county. 'I mean . . . Did you have a good journey? We've only been here half an hour or so ourselves. Hello, Seren,' she added, as the little girl sidled in beside her dad, wheeling a small pink suitcase. Awkwardness forced Em's face into a rictus smile and she crouched down, hoping that she sounded friendly and maternal. *Don't gush*, she reminded herself. 'Lovely to see you! We're all set for a great holiday, aren't we? Do you like the seaside?'

'Not really,' said Seren, lifting a shoulder as if she couldn't care less about some old seaside.

George roared with laughter. 'Of course she does,' he said, ruffling her hair.

'Yeah, I liked it when we went to the Bahamas with Mum, obviously,' Seren said. 'But . . .' Her scathing look around the cottage was enough to get Em bristling. *Er, excuse me, darling, but this cost me an arm and leg, so button it*, she felt like saying. She didn't, because she was rising above such things. Being the better person. Also because she was forty-four, and not seven herself, she remembered, plastering on a smile.

'The Bahamas! Lucky you,' she said. 'Right then, drinks: can I get anyone a drink? Is it too early for wine?' (She was desperate for wine.) 'Not you, Seren, ha-ha,' she went babbling on, 'although I do have some squash, if you're an orange-squash kind of girl.'

'I'll have wine,' Jack said, appearing from the kitchen with a hopeful look on his face.

'Not you, either,' Em told him, and George laughed.

'Nice try,' he said, then came over and put his arms around her. All of a sudden Em found that she could breathe again. 'Hello, holiday fun,' he said.

'Hello, good times,' she replied, not caring how hokey they sounded. She hadn't realized how much knotty tension she was holding in her shoulders until he was there, crushed against her. He smelled reassuringly scrumptious. It felt really good to have his arms around her, and her whole body went limp with relief in response. The drive, the worry, the argument with Izzie . . . it all melted away. Or most of it, anyway. She'd have to dissect Izzie's words properly later, when she had some time to think. Ask her exactly what she meant and why she'd said it. But in the meantime she was too happy about George's arrival to go there. 'Is it me, or did the sun just get a touch brighter?' she added cheesily. Five minutes he'd been here and she was already approaching peak *fromage*. Oh, who cared? Bring it on!

Out of the corner of her eye, she could see Jack slap a hand to his face. 'Jesus Christ,' he groaned. 'Please, Mum. There are children present. Children with sensitive dispositions.'

She felt George's laugh rumble against her and felt better than she had done all day. Lighter. 'Come on through, both of you,' she said. 'I'll show you around. Seren, do you need a wee? The loo's just here . . .'

It was all going to be okay, she insisted to herself as she picked up the little pink suitcase and began leading them upstairs. The kids would adjust and settle down. They'd all muddle into the holiday together and have a great time. Of course they would!

Chapter Four

'I'm going to the pool,' Amelia called through from the hallway.

'Oh. What, now? I thought we could—' Maggie broke off as the door clicked shut and she sighed. 'I thought we could look at the map together,' she finished quietly to herself, spreading it out on the table. Maybe not. Less than an hour after arriving at their holiday cottage, her daughter couldn't wait to get away from her, it seemed

She smoothed a hand across the paper, trying not to feel rejected. She'd taught Amelia how to read maps from an early age, explaining to her about contour lines and grid references, how to interpret all the tiny symbols. Maggie prided herself on being a patient, encouraging teacher, letting a child's interest guide the exploration, and had loved seeing her daughter work out routes across an Ordnance Survey charted landscape, her finger tracing lines between destinations. One of Amelia's favourite games as a little girl had been to go on imaginary adventures around their house, using Maggie's maps; it had delighted them both. The kitchen would become a lake or forest. The downstairs loo a cave or train station. The dining table an island off a rugged coastline that they'd have to swim to for lunch.

Even now, for Maggie, the unfolding of a map promised so much interest and discovery. She'd been looking forward to having Amelia to herself this fortnight, the two of them poring over the marks on the paper together and plotting their days out, as a return to old times, a nod back to all the other maps they'd enjoyed studying in summers gone by. But that could wait, she supposed. They could check out the area later on, make some plans then. And anyway, look on the bright side, Maggie, she ordered herself. This was a good thing, really – Amelia being positive about the holiday and heading out for a swim of her own volition. When Maggie had rather pessimistically been expecting her to plug straight into the Wi-Fi, then go up to her bedroom and catch up on all her social media in sulking solitude until it was time to eat. She'd been steeling herself for battles about going out anywhere interesting, now that Amelia was claiming to find everything boring and lame. And yet here was her daughter, choosing exercise and fresh air for herself after all and, in so doing, completely defying her mother's low expectations. How could she possibly complain about *that*?

Swimming was a great idea. They'd had a long and rather fractious journey, the roads clogged with traffic and the air-con in the car seemingly suffering an existential crisis. The prospect of sliding underwater into cool, tranquil blue was immensely appealing.

Hurrying up the narrow staircase to her bedroom with its pleasing, pared-down simplicity – every time Maggie went on holiday, she found herself vowing to live with fewer possessions, to adopt a more spartan lifestyle, although it never lasted – she began unpacking her clothes. Jumpers, hoodies, T-shirts, hiking leggings . . . ah, her swimming costume, there it was. She shut the curtains and stripped off, briefly noticing that her legs could do with a shave, before squeezing herself into the black one-piece.

There were two towels folded in a neat pile on the end of the bed and she picked them both up, in case Amelia hadn't remembered one, in her haste – and hoped with a small shiver of trepidation that the water wouldn't be *too* cold. The pool was heated, apparently, but this was England, after all, and although it had been a warm sunny day, it was now almost six o'clock and the air temperature was starting to fall. A quick dip before dinner would be lovely, though, she reminded herself bracingly, imagining the two of them laughing together as they attempted wonky underwater handstands and tried to remember how to do tumble-turns. It would be a really holidayish thing to do. Perhaps even start the mother–daughter bonding!

Voices floated up to her from outside, interrupting her

daydream, and she opened the curtains again and peered out, just in time to see a boy leaping into the water beside Amelia with a massive splash. Amelia shrieked and Maggie gasped in alarm, her hand fumbling immediately with the window catch, meaning to tell the idiot off in no uncertain terms. How dare he? What a foolhardy thing to do! Was Amelia all right?

In the next second, though, she realized her daughter's shriek was one of laughter, not distress. In fact the two of them, Amelia and the boy, were now splashing each other deliberately, with great armfuls of water fountaining up between them, and the air vibrated with their loud squeals of merriment.

Maggie took a step back from the window and caught sight of her reflection in the long pine-framed mirror that hung nearby. She saw a tall, spindly woman staring back at her, with broken veins and cellulite marbling her pale stubbled legs. An unflattering swimming costume. Bushy armpits and bingo wings, her unkempt mud-brown hair in sore need of a trim, or even a style. Maggie might be at odds with her daughter these days, but she still had just about enough self-awareness to realize that Amelia would not thank her for joining her in the pool right now. In fact, if she went out there like this, Amelia would be shrieking for all the wrong reasons.

Maggie put the towels down again, then sat heavily on

the bed beside them. After a moment, she unpeeled her shoulder straps and put her bra back on, then dressed once more and tucked the swimming costume in a drawer. Okay, she said to herself. Change of plan. This was fine, though. This was good! Amelia had made a friend. Amelia would think twice about the holiday being boring. Meanwhile, Maggie would make dinner and listen to Radio 4, and then they would have a lovely evening together.

Forty-five minutes passed. It was now seven o'clock, and Maggie's risotto had reached the point where it needed to be eaten, or risked cooling to an unpalatable stodge. Amelia, meanwhile, had still not returned.

Maggie had resisted going outside to the pool for this long, knowing that her appearance there could well result in a frosty look from her daughter or, worse, accusations of spying or interfering. Ever since Amelia had become best friends with the awful Tara, she had recast her mother as Embarrassment Number One, to be avoided at all costs. But it was perfectly reasonable to go out and announce that dinner was ready, surely?

She began to open the front door then found herself hesitating there on the mat as their voices drifted over to her. 'You should come with us, it's only a couple of miles away, I think,' the boy was saying, and Maggie stiffened as she tried and failed to make out Amelia's indistinct reply. Come with him? Miles away? What, now, when she had dinner ready to serve?

Through the gap in the door, she could make out their two heads at one edge of the pool, sleek as seals, companionably close. Their wet folded arms propped on the side reminded Maggie of angular mathematical brackets, the late sun splashing gold across their damp skin.

She hadn't caught Amelia's reply, but the boy was now speaking again. 'That's all right, you can borrow my mum's,' she heard him say. 'She'll be cool about it.'

Then came one of Amelia's sarcastic snorts, a muttered reply at which the boy laughed. Maggie felt herself flush hot all over, wondering if that had been a rude comment about her *not* being cool about anything much. She had only herself to blame for eavesdropping, a voice reproached in her head, but all the same: suspecting your child was betraying you to a complete stranger was hurtful, whatever the circumstances.

The boy briefly turned his head towards the biggest cottage, presumably where he was staying, as if checking nobody was listening, then said, 'Mine's madly in love and *very* negligent right now. Plus she's brought tons of booze. I'll easily be able to sneak some out, so if—'

Maggie prickled all over. No, thank you very much, she thought, as a protective maternal instinct – her inner lioness! – propelled her from the house immediately. She strode out with such vigour, in fact, that the door flew right open and banged against the stone wall behind her. 'Dinner's ready,' she said, her voice clipped and hard-sounding. She had changed her mind completely about any kind of friendship between Amelia and this boy; she would not be encouraging it in the slightest. Quite the opposite.

The boy regarded her with interest, then gave her a dazzling smile. 'Hello,' he said. 'I'm Jack. We're staying in—'

'Yes,' Maggie interrupted, paying him no attention. She knew boys like him from her years of teaching: the confident, cocky ones, all good looks and charm. They turned into the worst kind of men. 'Dinner, Amelia,' she said.

Amelia had turned red, no doubt from Maggie's brusque dismissal of her new friend. Well, so be it. 'I'm not hungry,' she said, before turning back to Jack. 'Want to do a few more lengths?'

'Er . . .' His gaze tick-tocked between them. He was polite, Maggie gave him that, because he clearly felt uncomfortable about siding with Amelia against her mother. 'I should probably go in for dinner soon myself,' he said after a moment. 'Let me know about tomorrow, yeah?'

Amelia smiled at him and Maggie's heart twisted a little because she looked so beautiful when she smiled like that, with her whole face relaxed and her eyes sparkly. 'Yeah, nice one,' she said. Her expression froze over as she turned back to Maggie, though. 'You don't have to loom over me like that,' she hissed. 'I *am* coming.'

Jack eased himself out of the pool and slouched off to where he'd left a towel on a lounger, water dripping from his limbs. He had golden hair, sort of lion-coloured, and was athletic in build. Probably captain of the school football team, Maggie guessed darkly. Breaking a different heart with every new term. Well, not today, sunshine.

'Bye, Amelia,' he called as he loped away.

As soon as he'd gone, Amelia's anger flared. 'God, Mum! You don't need to embarrass me,' she snarled. 'For Christ's sake! Why do you always have to *do* that?'

'Do what? Make dinner for you and tell you it's ready?' Maggie replied caustically. You couldn't win with teenagers, once they'd convinced themselves that you were the enemy. You simply couldn't win. 'Should I communicate by flags and semaphore next time? Sign language through the window?'

Amelia rolled her eyes, as if even speaking to her mother had become an ordeal. 'Please don't,' she huffed, hauling herself out of the water and stalking over to the lawn to retrieve her towel.

Maggie bit her lip, feeling as if she'd made a hash of everything, but unsure how she could have handled the situation any differently. Why didn't human beings come with a manual, a clear set of instructions that one could follow? 'I'll go and dish up,' she said, walking back towards the front door.

*

Dinner was something of a damp squib, not least because of the unappetizingly clumpy risotto that refused to redeem itself, even with the additions of roasted butternut squash and cubes of feta, but also because Amelia was in a towering mood with Maggie, barely saying a civil word. After ten minutes or so of strained silence, she pushed her plate away. 'I'm not really hungry,' she muttered. 'Think I'll head off to the games room for a bit.'

'Oh,' said Maggie, brightening. It might be fun to have a few rounds of table tennis, she supposed. Laugh over a game of table football or whatever was there. 'Okay. I'll come and join you, when I've washed up, shall I?'

'Er . . .' Amelia's face went red. 'Well, the others might be there, that's all, so I thought I'd hang out with them.'

'Oh,' said Maggie again, disappointment sinking through her like coloured dye in water. Was this how it was going to be for the entire fortnight this fruitless pursuit? 'It's the first night of our holiday, though, I thought we could play cards or . . . ?'

Amelia sighed. You would think she'd just been asked if she wanted her fingernails ripped out one by one. 'Do I *have* to?'

'Or I've brought Yahtzee?' Maggie persisted, trying not to hear how pleading her own voice sounded. 'If you fancy it?'

Amelia shook her head. 'Not really,' she said. 'Look, I kind of already said I'd meet them, so . . .'

So that was that. 'Okay,' Maggie said, defeated. 'But don't—'

The front door shut before she could finish her sentence. She wasn't even sure what she'd been about to say. *Don't do anything silly. Don't get into trouble. Don't . . . forget about me.*

Too late, anyway. Maggie was left with all the washing up and then an evening in morose solitude. Not exactly the holiday unity and camaraderie she'd hoped for.

The following day was a new start, though, and Maggie was determined to put her disappointment from the previous evening behind her. Amelia had come in at ten the night before, and seemed more cheerful at least, although she hadn't been remotely forthcoming on what she, Jack and his sister had been doing the whole time. 'Stuff,' she'd said airily with a shrug. 'Just hanging out, you know.'

No, Maggie didn't know. That was the problem. But Amelia hadn't smelled of either cigarettes or alcohol, at least, so perhaps the others were innocent and well behaved, like Amelia. Small mercies.

'Morning!' she said, as Amelia came down for breakfast now, trying not to appear too startled by the fact that her daughter was wearing a full face of make-up, a clingy white vest top and a tiny black denim skirt. Maggie poured her a cup of tea and slotted two pieces of bread into the toaster, Amelia being very much a creature of habit when it came to the first meal of the day. 'So today I thought we could pack up some lunch things and head over to Cligga Head,' she began brightly, wishing Amelia would sit down at the small round table with her, rather than leaning slouchily against the door-jamb like that. 'Remember, we researched it a few months ago and it's got that granite exposure, which looked really interesting and—'

But Amelia was already shaking her head. 'I'm going out with Jack. We've arranged to cycle into Falmouth. I'm borrowing a bike from them.'

Maggie felt her heart sink. 'Oh, but . . .' she bleated in disappointment. 'No,' she heard herself saying in the next moment. 'No, I don't think so.'

Amelia folded her arms across her chest. 'Yeah. I am,' she said. 'Look, it's my holiday too, Mum. And I don't want to go and look at boring old granite, or whatever it is, this time. I'm not into that, okay? Anyway, I already said I'd go, so—'

'Well, I'm saying no,' Maggie said again, hardening; she'd be every bit as tough as granite herself in a minute. 'You don't know anything about this boy, or his family. Plus you haven't been on a bike for ages, let alone going off cycling along major roads. Especially in that skirt! You don't even have your helmet.'

'I can borrow one. And they'll hardly be *major roads*, out here in the sticks,' Amelia said scathingly. She glanced down at her outfit and shrugged. 'And I can put on some shorts – big deal.'

There was a pain in Maggie's chest as if she'd swallowed something too hot. This was not Amelia speaking to her, she reminded herself, this was Tara Webster's voice. Cool, streetwise Tara of the thick mascara and side-eye glances. The girl who thought nothing of bringing cherry brandy to Amelia's birthday sleepover, and whose sole hobby appeared to be pouting suggestively into a camera. 'But we've already got plans,' she said, trying to claw back some control. 'Come on, Amelia. The holidays are about us, me and you, spending a bit of time together.'

As soon as the words were out, she knew they were a mistake. 'What if I don't *want* to spend time with you?' Amelia retaliated. 'What if I don't *want* to look at a load of old rocks? I mean, who *does*?'

It was like being under attack: every exchange a new blow, a new wound. *Who does?* Well, Maggie did for one, as they both knew. And Amelia too had loved investigating geological sites not so long ago, before she had decided they were too uncool for the likes of her and Tara. 'But—'

'Mum, you don't get it. I'm telling, not asking. I'm going out with Jack, so—'

She was already making her way towards the door and Maggie leapt up and followed her into the small hallway. 'No, you are *not*, young lady,' she said, grabbing Amelia by the wrist. There came a time when you had to put your foot down as a parent, and this was it. High noon. 'You haven't even had any *breakfast*.'

'Get off me,' shrieked Amelia, pushing her off. 'God, Mum! If I've got bruises because of you, I'm going to . . .'

They were interrupted by a knock at the door, mere inches away, and they both froze on the spot in a tableau of horrified surprise. For a hysterical moment, Maggie thought it might be the landlady of the cottage, Lorna, coming to have a stern word with them about making so much noise, but then Amelia, who was nearest, dodged away and yanked the door open to reveal someone else altogether. There on the doorstep was a forty-something woman with strawberry-blonde hair in a wavy shoulder-length bob and a smiling face that was covered with freckles. Maggie felt extremely hot and embarrassed that this woman had presumably just heard her and Amelia screaming at each other.

'Hi, I'm Em,' said the woman. 'Emma Hughes, your neighbour. From Briar Cottage, or whatever it's called over there.'

Maggie blinked, trying to assimilate all of this information as the woman pointed behind her. Emma Hughes had a cheery sort of confidence, standing there in a pink-and-white striped T-shirt and pale-blue cropped trousers, and Maggie guessed that this must be Jack's mum. Great, she thought, trying not to let her dismay show. 'Hi,' she managed to croak in reply, mortified to still be in her cotton shortie pyjamas in front of a stranger.

'Just thought I should pop round and introduce myself, as I gather our offspring have cooked up a plan between them,' the woman – Emma – went on to Maggie. She was wearing make-up, and had sparkly blue stud earrings and clinking rose-gold bangles on her wrist. What kind of person went to so much effort at nine o'clock in the morning? On holiday?

Emma twinkled her eyes at Amelia in a knowing sort of way. 'You're Amelia, I take it. My son is *very* keen to go off on a jaunt with you.'

Amelia blushed, but Maggie noticed a small, pleased smile play around on her lips as well. Even though if *Maggie* had been the one to use a word like 'jaunt' in front of someone else's adolescent, Amelia would be pulling sick faces and hissing at her to stop being weird, rather than smiling in quite such a winning way.

'Yes,' said Maggie, seeing as her daughter had been struck uncharacteristically dumb. 'We were just having a discussion about that.' *You probably heard us screeching like banshees from the other side of the door, in fact.*

'Well, I thought I'd swing by to say hello and that it's fine by me, as long as you're in agreement,' Emma said, turning to Maggie. 'Izzie, my eldest, is sixteen and she's going with them too – she's very sensible,' she assured her. 'And, Amelia, you're welcome to borrow my bike, if you don't have one of your own here; it's not *too* old-ladyish, I promise you. Jack was thinking ten o'clock or so? Give you a bit of time to have breakfast and whatever. He's not actually showered yet, the stinking pig, but don't worry, I'll make sure he's decent before I release him from the house.'

'Cool,' Amelia said, risking a bold side-eye at Maggie, who felt completely backed into a corner by now. 'I'll be over at ten.'

'Wait,' said Maggie, feeling as if this was all happening too fast. 'You don't have a bike helmet, Amelia, so—'

'It's fine, we've got a spare she can use,' Em said. Then she peered a little closer at Maggie. 'Is that okay? I did tell Jack you might have plans or . . .'

Maggie swallowed, thinking about her dad and wanting to put a stop to this whole expedition but too embarrassed to trot out her worries in front of this breezy, smiling stranger. *You can't wrap Amelia in cotton wool!*, her mum had warned in the past. Yes, but why not?

'It's okay,' she managed to say after a moment. She put her arms around herself, wishing she had on a dressing gown at least. The material of her pyjamas was horribly thin and a little bit coffee-stained, come to think of it. 'We hadn't made any plans.'

The woman grinned. 'Same! Oh, good. I can never understand people who go on holiday with this full agenda.

An itinerary! What's that all about?' She gave a hoot. 'Nice to meet you, anyway. Oh – I didn't catch your name.'

'Maggie,' she said miserably. Maggie of the pyjamas and unbrushed hair, that's me. Not to mention the daughter who can't wait to be shot of me.

'Maggie, got it. I'm Em, as I said, and I'm here with George and . . .' Spots of colour rose in her cheeks suddenly, for some reason. 'Well, you don't need to know all of that, obviously. Right! I'll leave you to your breakfast anyway. Just come on over when you're ready, Amelia, okay? Have a lovely day, Maggie.'

Maggie shut the door again, her heart thudding, feeling as if she'd lost face terribly. Lost a battle too. 'So there we are,' she said after a moment. 'Looks like you're going, after all.' She was unable to look at Amelia in case there was a gloating light of victory in her eyes; she didn't think she could bear it. 'You'd better go and butter that toast before it gets cold,' she added, as Amelia skipped away from her, a new bounce in her step.

Leaning against the wall, Maggie had the tight, miserable feeling of having been outplayed. Cycling on unknown roads, on an unfamiliar bike, with teenagers she barely knew, one of whom had been boasting about being able to sneak out some alcohol . . . This was not at all what she wanted for her girl. This was not remotely the lovely start to the holiday she had hoped for.

More to the point, she realized, with a startled jolt, if Amelia was departing for these new horizons this morning, what on earth was Maggie going to do with herself in the meantime?

Chapter Five

'So I'll see you tomorrow,' Mack said, bending down to kiss her. Olivia was still in her dressing gown at the kitchen table, hair lank and unwashed on her shoulders, while the detritus of family breakfast lay all around: the smeary Weetabix bowls, the explosion-splatter of toast crumbs and the blobs of raspberry jam quivering like bright scarlet jewels beside the butter dish.

'Yep,' she said, not leaning into him like she might once have done. *You could at least have helped me clear this lot up first*, she thought with weary reproach.

'Probably around five, depending on the traffic, but I'll text if I'm going to be much later than that, okay?' he went on, not seeming to notice how still she held herself, how tightly her hands were clenched around her mug. 'Right, where are those rascals? Stanley? Harry? Come and say bye to Daddy. I'm going now. Boys?'

In they roared like a double blond whirlwind, her three-year-old twin tearaways, whose hobbies were wrestling, resisting naps and smashing things. 'Where are they? Where are those boys of mine?' Mack repeated, pretending to peer into cupboards and the fridge. 'Don't say I've lost them. Don't say they've gone missing again.'

He crouched down to look under the table and this was their cue to launch themselves with whoops and war cries onto his back. 'Whoa,' he yelled, as their small plump arms fastened around his neck. 'I'm being attacked! They've got me! They've got me!'

'CHOP! CHOP!' yelled Stanley, bashing the side of his hand against his father's neck. 'Chop off your HEAD!'

'No chopping,' Olivia said weakly, but her voice was unheard, unnoticed by the scrum of her husband and sons. They reminded her of a comic-strip fight, one depicting arms and legs emerging from a cloud of dust. Through the back window she could see next door's cat saunter along the fence, a vision of leisurliness compared to the melee this side of the glass.

'Who's chopping me? Who's daring to chop the mighty Daddy?' bellowed Mack, straightening from his crouched position so that the boys, thrilled, were forced to cling onto him tighter in order to avoid falling to the floor. 'And where are my boys?'

'Here we are,' squeaked Harry breathlessly, wriggling and squirming, drumming his small bare feet against his father's hip. 'Here we are!'

'Aha,' cried Mack, grabbing a foot as Harry giggled and yelped. 'And another one!' he cheered, clutching Stanley's ankle with his other hand. 'I've got me two boys now. What shall I do with them?'

'Mack . . .' Olivia said, because neither he nor they ever knew when to stop with these rough-and-tumble games, whipping each other into such a state of frenzy that they almost always ended in injury and tears. It drove her mad that he would work them up like this just before he left the house, so that she'd have to deal with the fallout once he'd gone. It was still only eight-thirty in the morning and they were already wild. Meanwhile the cat outside had dropped in one liquid movement to the flowerbed, like a commando trained in stealth, and she felt a pang of envy for its freedom to go where it pleased. 'MACK,' she said again, louder this time, because the three of them were still grappling and yelling. 'Don't you need to go?'

He stopped and the game was over, but the boys weren't ready for it to end and charged at his legs, pummelling his thighs and trying to haul him over, with protesting shouts. 'No, no,' he said, holding up his hands. 'Mummy's right, that's enough. I need to go.'

Mummy's fault, more like, Olivia thought dismally as the boys howled and stamped. Mummy the killjoy ruins every-thing again. She could smell her own unwashed body as she bent to try and console Harry, and wished she'd had time to shower before Mack left. With the boys now wound up like battling clockwork toys, it would be ages before she could manage five minutes to herself for such a luxury.

'See you tomorrow,' he said over the ruckus, extricating himself first from one red-faced twin, then another, and walking quickly away. 'Bye, boys. Be good for Mummy!'

Olivia sat there like a piece of stone while the boys roiled and boiled around her. She put her head in her hands and tried to calculate how many minutes and hours it would be before he walked back through the door again, but her brain was too fogged with the bad night she'd had to compute that far. A lot of minutes, anyway. Too many hours. They stretched out before her like empty boxes on a conveyor belt and she wondered how she would fill them. If she would ever reach the end.

Pinned up on the fridge with a Peppa Pig magnet was one of their wedding photos, and her gaze rested numbly on it for a moment. It was like looking at a pair of strangers. There they were, she and Mack, so happy on their special day. Olivia in her lace-sleeved dress, her hair pinned up in an elaborate style, her face so bright and joyful as she leaned against her handsome husband, the two of them with their arms around each other beneath a rose-covered arching trellis in the hotel grounds. She loved the way that Mack's shock of unruly brown hair was just starting to loosen from its previously controlled neatness, that his tie was already askew. It was as if the real Mack, who was happiest in a pair of knackered shorts and a beat-up old T-shirt – the Mack who resisted suits and hair products as if he had some kind of allergy – was on the verge of bursting through Wedding Mack in all his finery.

Just look at them both, though, innocents that they were. They had no idea that eleven months later they would be parents of hell-raising twins and would never sleep again.

Meanwhile the boys were still fighting, she could hear their muffled thuds and yells and knew she should go and separate them before one of them was hurt or something got broken. And yet inertia had already settled upon her. A deadening sort of paralysis. Annoyance – no, actually, *anger* – at the fact that Mack, having worked long hours out at work all week, could then just go off on a bender with his mates for the whole weekend like this without a second thought. As if she didn't matter. As if she had nothing better to do than the endless laundry and cleaning and childcare. Her next job would presumably be to disentangle her blood-thirsty boys without any of them losing a finger or eye in the process. Great.

His life hadn't come to a screeching halt three years ago, had it? Oh no. Quite the opposite in fact. Mack's star was very much in the ascendant, with great demand for his company, which specialized in turning around struggling businesses. He was proud of his longer days in the office, proud that he could support the family with his run of big contracts.

For Mack, fatherhood was having a picture of the boys in his wallet; it was wrestling matches and water fights, for as long as he felt like it. He was the Mighty Daddy, the fun parent, who still got to go to football matches and stag weekends and drinks with his mates, assuming all the while that Olivia would be there to hold the fort in his absence. And to be fair, she had gone along with this division of labour initially: they both knew she was so determined to be a good mother to the boys that she wanted to be there for them for every night-waking, every feed, every cry. Call it atonement, call it proving a point, she was dogged in her belief that this was her work, the least she could do.

Until she realized just how hard it was anyway, how utterly exhausting. How broken she was starting to feel. Was it pride or embarrassment that kept her from telling Mack she was struggling? Or sheer maternal guilt? Which-ever, he didn't seem to have noticed her feelings of failure.

His parents didn't help matters, either. They were up in Aberdeenshire and had traditional ideas about child-rearing, namely that it was solely the preserve of a mother and cer-tainly not to be farmed out to any third parties, even the child's own father. 'Don't tell me she's got you changing nappies,' Olivia had overheard her mother-in-law exclaiming with horror the first time they'd come down after the boys had been born. 'For heaven's sake! When you're out work-ing hard and earning all the money for the family, as well. Whatever next?'

Like Olivia was lounging around eating peeled grapes all day, like she *wasn't* working hard. There were times when she looked back on her old job in the university library and it seemed an oasis of calm concentration, practically a holi-day, compared to her current job as a mum. Sometimes she could weep for that civilized life of politeness and order, of lunch-breaks and set hours, where nobody was fighting or throwing things or bellowing urgently that they needed the toilet. To think that before the boys she had taken such lux-uries for granted!

This was her world now, though. 'No need to worry about rushing back to work,' Mack assured her whenever she broached the subject, to the point where his success and wealth had begun to feel like a prison door slamming shut on her. He thought he was being kind, doing her a favour, but in truth she was gripped by the queasy conviction that she was just not cut out for full-time motherhood. Oh, of course she loved the small rampaging tyrants who had to-tally annexed her life, she adored every inch of their grubby, wriggling bodies, right up to their flaxen-haired heads, but if she was honest with herself, she loved them most when they were asleep. At the end of the day, when they were lost to dream worlds, side by side in their junior beds, long eyelashes fluttering on perfect peachy cheeks, she felt her love for them unfurling, albeit in a creaky, reluctant sort of way sometimes, if they'd had a particularly punishing day. It returned every night, a well that never quite ran dry.

Yet, anyway. That was what worried her.

'Ow! That hurt! Mummy!'

'Get OFF! *Mummy!*'

She was jerked back to the present by indignant yells from the next room. She should probably go and do something about it, she supposed dully. Mack, meanwhile, would be halfway across town by now, the radio burbling cricket scores from his car speakers; he would have switched off thoughts of Olivia and the boys, and would be looking forward to his session with the lads. Left here to fend for herself, his wife was drowning, her head sinking beneath the surface, uncertain if she could make it back to shore again.

'Mummy! He hit me!'

'He hit me first! MUMMY!'

The boys deserved better than her, she thought. They deserved a proper, capable, fun mother, who wanted to build forts with them and bake biscuits and play football for hours on end in the garden. A laughing, energetic woman who didn't keep dissolving into hopeless tears. Who didn't feel half-dead with exhaustion.

'*MUMMY!* Come and tell him!'

And yet here she was, lumbering to her feet like a weary

old mule, knowing that her work for the day had only just begun. Knowing, too, that if this was her penance, then it was the very least she could do. 'Coming,' she said miserably. 'Just coming.'

Izzie's long caramel-coloured hair streamed out behind her as she freewheeled down a hill with Jack and Amelia on the way towards Falmouth. This was her Summer of Yes, the summer that was supposed to be changing everything – and yet here she was, forced into chaperoning her annoying brother and the girl he fancied. It was not going to earn her any points on the group chat leaderboard, that was for sure.

'This summer,' Lily had said, shortly after their last exam, when a group of them had been lying in the park passing around cans of raspberry cider, 'we should all pledge to be wild. To say yes to everything!'

Perhaps it was the sweet intensity of freedom from school and GCSEs, perhaps it was the lukewarm fruity cider they were sharing, but everyone, Izzie included, had seized upon the suggestion. Yeah! This would be the summer when they lived life to the full and grabbed every opportunity with both hands. They were sixteen and ripe for adventures of whatever kind.

Since then, a leaderboard had started running on their group chat, with points being allocated for various daring acts of behaviour:

Ruby had scored ten points for dirty dancing with the boy she fancied at a house party, then another fifteen for kissing him, tongues and everything.

Tej had scored ten points for nicking a bottle of vodka from the corner shop and then another ten for gatecrashing a sixth former's party in her street.

Miko had chatted up a hot boy at the Sandford Park Lido the other day (ten points) and apparently flashed him her boobs behind the changing-room door (fifteen).

Lily had bagged herself twenty points for some naked snogging – 'heavy petting', she called it coyly – with her boyfriend Jordan and looked set to earn quite a lot more, having wangled the two of them tickets for a music festival in August. *How many points do I get for sharing a tent with Jordan?* she'd asked the others.

Depends what else you're sharing . . . Ruby had replied, with a load of winking emojis

Izzie, meanwhile, was yet to register a single point. Clearly she was hopeless at being as cool as her friends. She felt squeamish whenever they talked about sex or boys and never knew what to say. The smell of cigarettes grossed her out, and she privately thought alcohol was disgusting. Being on holiday in the middle of nowhere wasn't exactly going to help her score either, not least because Seren kept barging into her room all the time and was a total snitch; it would be impossible to get away with *anything*, let alone go as wild as her friends. *Izzie didn't wash her hands,* Seren had reported last night at dinner. *Izzie was on her phone really late last night,* she had said at breakfast, presumably having been creeping about spying, like the annoying weirdo she was. *Izzie won't let me join in,* she had moaned earlier, when Izzie was having a conversation with George and ignoring all Seren's attention-seeking interruptions. *Yeah, no shit,* Izzie had thought, rolling her eyes.

It didn't help that her mum was being so sickeningly happy and loved-up all the time. Was there anything more pukesome than your mum with a new boyfriend? Hello? If anyone should be blushing and feeling fluttery in their family, it was her, the actual sixteen-year-old, not her cringey old mum. Even Jack was having more luck than Izzie, now that he'd clapped eyes on Amelia and seemed revoltingly pleased with himself. It made Izzie feel more of a freak than ever.

As for George, well, he was a whole other problem.

Izzie still burned with embarrassment whenever she thought about the first time she'd seen him back in the spring. She'd been out at Wagamama in town for Tej's birthday treat, and a group of them were sitting at a table by the window, cracking open their chopsticks and tucking into steaming mounds of yaki soba, as the conversation turned to boys at school. Miko was swooning on about Ryan Michaels, in the sixth form, and Ruby was sighing shiny-eyed about

Conor Perry; and even Tej, who had recently come out, was joining in, confessing her crush on Lia Mendelson in a breathless, excited sort of way. Izzie had kept quiet, not really having anything to contribute, until Lily had elbowed her and said, 'Go on then, who do you fancy at school, Iz?'

'God, no one at *school*,' Izzie had said, possibly too quickly and defensively. 'They're all so lame and immature. Give me an older guy any day.'

She wasn't even sure where this had come from – a bluster, a bluff, to try and throw the limelight away from herself. There was no older guy on her mind whatsoever. The whole idea of falling in love with *anyone* seemed remote and impossible to her; it was something for other people to get all weird about. Unfortunately, her friends took her comment at face value.

'What, an older guy like him?' Tej sniggered, pointing across the restaurant to where an elderly gentleman with a magnificent curly white moustache sat alone with a bowl of noodle soup.

The others fell about tittering and Izzie felt her face grow hot. She had very pale skin that went from milk to lobster in the space of seconds, and she hated wearing her embarrassment so publicly. 'Not like him! Like . . .' Izzie scoured the restaurant for inspiration – absolutely none – then turned her attention to the world outside. 'Like *him*,' she said triumphantly, pointing a chopstick.

They'd all stared at the good-looking guy striding confidently along Clarence Street in dark jeans with a cool purple shirt. Okay, so he was middle-aged, she realized in the next moment, nearer her dad's age in fact, but he was undeniably handsome, tall and with this sexy sort of walk. Yeah, he'd do.

'Mmmm,' said Miko approvingly, and Izzie's tension eased a fraction. 'That's definitely a man, not a boy.'

'You dirty girl,' Ruby said, one eyebrow raised, but she was smiling and it was obvious she was mucking about.

That might have been the end of it – the moment slipping into the tidal pull of conversation and forgotten, as a new topic surfaced – if it hadn't been for the fact that, just then, as they were all looking at the man, a woman approached him. Izzie gulped in a stunned breath and watched with disbelief as the smiling woman touched a hand to the man's arm. In the next moment the two of them were locked in a passionate kiss. Izzie's mind pounded. Her mouth dried to chalk. What the *hell* . . . ?

'No way,' Tej had whooped. 'Is that your *mum*?'

'Are you kidding me?' Lily squawked. 'Wait – so is that your *dad*?'

'*No!*' Izzie cried, her face scorching again. 'I don't fancy my *dad*. Jesus!' She had blinked and stared, unable to believe what she was seeing, as her mum and this man – this handsome purple-shirted man! – eventually disentangled from their kiss and went into a nearby café together. Her heart was going nuts. Mum was *dating*? Since when?

'Oh my God,' Miko was laughing. 'You fancy your mum's new boyfriend. Awkward!'

'No wonder she didn't want to talk about him,' Ruby spluttered.

'This is like *EastEnders*,' Tej added gleefully. 'So are you two, like, *rivals*? So juicy!'

However hard Izzie protested, the teasing went on mercilessly, the subject apparently of the greatest hilarity to her friends. And of course ever since then, there had been sly digs and questions, raised eyebrows and smirks. Especially when Lily found out they were all going on holiday together. *How's the dad-bod looking in trunks??? Get in there!!* she had put on the group chat just that morning, to Izzie's mortification.

Yeah, we want pictures of the budgie smugglers!! Ruby added

Go on, we'll give you five points if you can get a flirty selfie with him, Tej wrote, with crying-laughing emojis.

Ten points if you're both wearing swimming gear and actually touching each other's bodies, Miko added. *Dare you!!!!*

Obviously they were only mucking about, but it was starting to get a bit annoying. Because Izzie totally didn't fancy George, all right? She *didn't*! He was old and kind of wrinkly around the eyes, and he told really bad dad-jokes all the time, and liked Formula One, which was surely the most boring thing on earth. This was what she kept telling her friends anyway. What she wasn't telling them, and what she could hardly even bear to admit to herself, was that yes, okay, there was something about George's laugh that made her feel peculiarly liquid inside. And how when he teased you, or really paid attention to you, it was like basking in the warmth of the sun; a sun that was almost too bright, too dazzling to remain comfortable under, after a while.

She liked how he whistled around their house whenever he stayed over, really loudly and cheerfully, and made scrambled egg for breakfast – tons of it, with piles of toast, as if he was used to feeding an army. He was generous too, thinking nothing of leaving a large tip for the waiting staff if they went out, or slipping her and Jack a tenner each if they wanted to see something at the cinema. If he was a colour, he'd be something classy and cool, she thought. A charcoal grey, maybe, or a dark red, like wine. You could trust someone who was that colour. You could feel enchanted by them too.

Oh, it was torture, trying to keep a lid on her feelings! He had picked her up from babysitting the other week because Mum hated driving in the dark, and she'd even found herself appreciating the way he *drove*, confident and decisive; noting favourably to herself how nice his car smelled compared to Mum's. She had leaned back in the seat as the dark world outside rushed past them, the street lights blurring into streaky lines, and she'd imagined for a crazy, heady moment that George was her lover. Wondered what he would do if she pulled her shirt off over her head and offered her bare breasts to him. *Here I am. How do you like me now?* Was this how it felt to be in love?

Of course she hadn't done any of those things – as if! She cringed every time she thought about it now, but at the time her heart had galloped so loud at the images she'd conjured up that she'd half-expected him to notice. How she would *die* if he noticed!

The sobering fact, however, was that he was *Mum's* boyfriend. Also he made Mum super-happy, like singing-in-the-shower happy, which she hadn't been for years. So for Izzie to be having these tumultuous, crazed thoughts left her feeling confused and disloyal, as if the ground was tilting beneath her feet. Her friends might think it was all a big joke, but she was starting to feel weird about being in the same room with George. And yet it was so hard to stay away from him.

That morning over breakfast he had started asking her about her plans for sixth form and when Izzie said she wanted to do Art as an A-level, he'd said 'Oh!' in a really pleased-sounding way, before telling her he'd done that as an A-level too and always wished he'd gone on to art college, rather than heading into business. They had bonded, you know? George had got out his iPad and shown her some Caravaggio paintings that he'd seen in Rome, and she'd been able to say some reasonably intelligent-sounding things in response – in between Seren's attempts to sabotage the conversation, that was – and they'd ended up having a really good chat. She had felt noticed, properly listened to, especially when Mum, overhearing, had said, 'Oi, you, I've been trying to persuade her to do something vaguely useful like Economics instead of Art' and George had pulled a face at Izzie and replied, 'Sorry, Em, but I'm on your daughter's side for this one.' A thrill had gone starbursting through her at his conspiratorial grin. Did that mean she fancied him or was it something else?

Jack shouted just then and Izzie snapped out of her reverie to find herself back on her bike and passing a small cove, with a row of painted beach huts on their right. The sea was spread out before them, its dark-blue ripples winking and twinkling under the morning sun, with a couple of people out on the water in kayaks.

Down on the shingly sand there were kids building sandcastles and dads using big rocks to hammer in the poles of windbreaks, and one family starting a game of beach cricket. For a moment Izzie had a lump in her throat, remembering holidays when her parents had still been together; how they'd all been obsessed with beach cricket themselves one summer, ridiculously competitive, playing for the prize of chicken and chips from their favourite takeaway. And then she was tumbling all the way back down memory lane, thinking about how her dad would always insist on walking miles down the sand on any given beach until he found the perfect spot, and how Mum would roll her eyes affectionately in his wake. How she and Jack would spend ages building forts near the shoreline and carving out a moat and channels, so that when the tide started coming in, they would fill with frothing sea water . . .

Sometimes she wished you didn't have to grow up. She'd have liked to be a small girl on holiday forever, collecting shells in a plastic bucket and sprinkling a paper packet of salt on her chips before being tucked into bed at night, safe and sound, all responsibilities taken away from her. It would be a lot easier than trying to compete with her daring friends in their Summer of Yes, that was for sure.

'Is this it?' Jack had stopped in a small car-park area and now gestured at the beach, looking confused.

Izzie braked beside him 'No! Of course not,' she scoffed, getting her phone out to check the map. 'There's the whole town further ahead.' She showed Jack the screen with the route marked out. 'See? We have to keep going, past this lagoon thing.' She said the last bit hurriedly because she wasn't sure if 'lagoon' was the right word for the large pool over on their left. Geography had never been her strong point, as would no doubt be proven when her exam results came in later that summer.

'What are we going to do when we get there anyway?'

This was Amelia, the girl from the neighbouring cottage, who had the most badly pencilled eyebrows Izzie had ever seen, along with some seriously terrible orange foundation. She was from Reading, apparently, although Izzie had heard her saying to Jack that it was 'near London'. Even Izzie, geography failure of the year, knew that this description was stretching the truth way past the point of elasticity.

Jack hesitated, then looked at Izzie.

'Don't ask me!' she retorted snottily. 'I didn't even want to go in the first place.'

Jack glanced back to the beach. 'Skinny-dipping?' he suggested, raising an eyebrow at Amelia.

Izzie guffawed, not wanting the other girl to feel under pressure. Her brother was all mouth and no trousers. 'Go on then, you first,' she told him. 'Me and Amelia will watch and give you marks out of ten for execution.'

Amelia snorted. 'Bonus marks if you make any small children cry,' she said.

Unperturbed, Jack slouched over his handlebars with a shrug. 'You suggest something then,' he said.

Amelia looked pleased to be asked. 'Well,' she said, delving a hand into her bag and pulling out a bottle with golden liquid inside. It glittered under the sun like something magical as she turned the bottle so that they could read the label. 'José Cuervo Especial,' it said, followed by the words 'Tequila Reposado'. 'I did bring *this*.'

'Whoa!' Jack was easily impressed. 'Good one!'

Izzie did her best to look nonchalant, like it was no big deal. Amelia was fourteen, two years younger than Izzie, and she couldn't allow herself to be bested. 'Okaaaaay,' she said, in her coolest drawl. 'That's going to make the day more interesting. Let me just get out my amyls and we'll have a party.'

'You don't have any—' Jack began saying, but she glared at him.

'I'm *joking*, dickhead. Obviously,' she said. She eyed Amelia, trying to channel Lily, her most worldly-wise friend. Head tilted. *You don't impress me.* 'So are you opening that, or what? Or is it just for show?'

Amelia gave a lazy smile. 'Let's go into town first. It's boring here,' she said, stuffing the bottle back in her bag. Then she tossed her long dark hair over one shoulder and pedalled away.

Jack and Izzie looked at each other, then followed.

A short while later they'd found their way into Falmouth and wheeled their bikes through the busy shopping area and out towards the docks. 'This'll do,' said Amelia, gesturing at a bench and flopping down without waiting for any kind of consensus.

Jack, who appeared to be her new devotee, sat down beside her at once and Izzie stifled a prickle of annoyance.

All of a sudden Amelia was the one calling the shots, as if the tequila bottle had gifted her the power of authority. When Izzie, as the eldest, should rightfully be the one in charge. With an audible sniff, she tried to convey her pique by sitting down at the far end of the bench, facing slightly away from the others.

'So who wants to play Truth or Dare?' Amelia asked, waggling an eyebrow at Jack.

Izzie, already feeling like a gooseberry, stood up again. 'I think I'll leave you two to it,' she said, as Amelia uncapped the tequila. 'I'm going for a wander.'

'She's scared,' said Jack, the traitor, and made a chicken noise.

'I am not!' Izzie retaliated.

Amelia tilted back her head and took a swallow of the tequila, and Izzie found herself staring at the girl's soft exposed throat as she gulped it down. Then Amelia held out the bottle towards Izzie: a challenge.

Izzie hesitated, knowing that if she refused, the other two would cackle and call her a coward. Yet if she went ahead and drank, she'd have to stay and get drawn into whatever game Amelia was playing. Who knew where that could lead? Then she imagined herself reporting back to the group chat later: *Got smashed on tequila down by the docks. Party time!* – and the prospect of finally scoring a few points was enough to make her snatch the bottle from Amelia's hand.

She put it to her lips before she could change her mind. The tequila smelled absolutely disgusting, like nail-varnish remover, but the others were both goggling at her, so she raised the bottle and drank. 'Oh my God,' she blurted out afterwards, passing it on to Jack. Her eyes watered as the alcohol slammed into her bloodstream and her head swam. The taste, meanwhile . . . How did anyone drink that stuff for pleasure? 'Not bad,' she managed to say, wiping her mouth.

'Jesus,' croaked Jack as he too took a glug – a big one, no doubt trying to impress Amelia. 'My head's on fire.'

Amelia laughed. 'You two are a right pair of light-weights,' she said, swigging out of the bottle again. Then she gave Izzie a long, cool stare. 'So. Izzie – Truth or Dare?'

Chapter Six

Several miles inland, Em was sitting on an uncomfortable plastic chair, drinking black coffee from a cardboard cup and waving intermittently at Seren and George as they became visible in one of the corners of the vast soft-play area before vanishing again. The air was thick with the sound of shrieks and the smell of wet nappies, her coffee had come from a vending machine and was atrociously bad, and the couple at the next table to hers were having a massive hissy row. Everything was brightly coloured and seemed unpleasantly dazzling to the eye, not least because of the scant amount of sleep she'd had the night before. Her head throbbed. Maybe *this* was the catch to the relationship, after all. *Terms and conditions apply.*

Admittedly the lack of sleep had been mostly due to the combination of unfamiliar bed and very handsome boyfriend, and she certainly wasn't complaining about *that*, but then Seren had come in at three o'clock in the morning, saying plaintively that she'd had a bad dream, and Em had spent the rest of the night in a half-awake hinterland, alert to every last creak and groan of the cottage's timbers, unable to drift into slumber once more. (George, meanwhile, had fallen instantly back asleep, thereby proving that it wasn't only Dom, Em's ex, who possessed this enviable skill.)

The bad night had had its coffin nails hammered fully in when Seren returned shortly after seven, to say that she was hungry and wanted breakfast. Any normal person might have grunted and let the child's actual parent take over this duty, but idiotic Em had insisted on getting up and playing the part of hostess, hurriedly dabbing on some tinted moisturizer and a lick of mascara and then getting stuck in. Hot drinks for her and George, warm milk for Seren, and then she'd whipped up a batch of fluffy American pancakes, which she served with streaky bacon and maple syrup. 'Wow,' laughed George as she presented him with a plate heaped high. 'I'm coming to this restaurant again.' Even Seren stopped looking quite so surly for a few minutes as she drowned the pancakes with syrup and dug in.

'This looks like a fun place to go!' Em had cried later that morning, holding up the leaflet for the petting zoo she'd found amidst the cottage's information pack. Jack had already informed her that he was going out with a girl he'd met from the next cottage; and Izzie, facing the prospect of being the sole teen stuck with the adults and Seren, had grudgingly opted for her brother's company instead. No problem, Em had thought, trying to maintain her holiday sparkle. In that case, Seren could be the centre of attention.

'There are loads of animals, a little train ride, a playground . . . all sorts of stuff,' she went on. 'What do you think, Seren?'

Seren, arranging some Sylvanian Families dogs into a circle on the kitchen floor, completely ignored her – rude little madam – and so George had stepped in, repeating the same offer to her, pretty much in the exact same words, to which Seren had given him a willing smile and lisped, 'Yes please.'

'Great,' said Em through gritted teeth. 'That's a plan then.'

Her own two had always loved such places when they were of a similar age, clamouring to go on tractor rides and enjoying being able to stroke and feed assorted animals. This one was a mere five miles from where they were staying, the forecast was good, and she was sure they would all have a lovely time. Day one of the holiday and she was already winning.

Unfortunately, the reality was not working out quite as idyllically as she'd envisaged so far.

First stop: the petting zoo, where Seren had been scared of the pygmy goats. No, she didn't want to hold a baby rabbit. She definitely didn't want to feed the ponies. She didn't even want to go down the big astro-slides.

'Come on! It'll be really fun,' Em said encouragingly. 'Look, I'll go first to show you it's not scary, okay?'

How to feel like a complete weirdo, shoving your feet into a sack, gaily crying 'Wheeee!' and praying that your bottom wouldn't become wedged in the rather too-narrow sides as you slid down, she found herself thinking moments later. Other kids were staring at her – possibly in alarm, rather than awe – but Seren didn't even give her that courtesy, which made her feel even more of a chump. (George at least had been gallant enough to put a thumb up and wink. 'Incredibly athletic performance there, Em,' he'd said, as Seren tugged at his hand to go elsewhere.)

'How about soft-play, then?' Em suggested weakly in the end when they entered its deafening arena. 'Me and your dad will sit here and have a coffee while we watch you, Seren. Doesn't it look cool?'

Izzie and Jack had never needed the slightest bit of encouragement when it came to these primary-coloured monstrosities, flinging off their shoes and racing in without a backward glance, leaping joyfully into the ball-pit and crawling through tunnels with abandon. Seren, though, was less keen. 'Daddy, you come with me,' she'd said, clutching at his hand and towing him towards the entrance.

'Oh, but I think it's really for children,' he had said, eyeing up the café counter. 'I'm not sure daddies are allowed to—'

'They *are*. That man is,' said Seren, pointing. 'Please?'

'Go on then,' he'd said with an apologetic glance back at Em. 'Just for a few minutes.'

Em managed a gracious smile. 'Have fun!' she'd cried to them both as they took their shoes off and plunged in. Of course Izzie and Jack had always had each other as company, she reasoned, and Seren just wanted someone to play with too. Fair enough. No problem! This was all part and parcel of holidaying with kids, she supposed. And if Seren was happy, then so was she.

Her phone started ringing just then, with Izzie's name on the screen.

'Hello, love,' Em said. 'How's it going? Are you in Falmouth now?'

'Yeah. But, um . . .'

Izzie sounded very far away. Was that trepidation in her daughter's voice? Em hunched over her phone, trying to block out the cacophony around her. 'What is it? Everything okay?'

'Mum? Something's happened.'

'What?' Instantly her blood ran cold. Her heart accelerated straight into fifth. Shit. 'What's up? Are you all right?'

'It's Jack. He . . .' There was a pause and Em's imagination rushed helplessly to fill it with all manner of dreadful endings. 'He's in a bit of trouble,' Izzie went on, with a maddening lack of detail. 'Can you come?'

So there it was: proof, if anyone needed it, that she was a dreadful mother. An optimistic fool who should have known better. She had sent off her children – and someone else's daughter too! – to Falmouth by themselves, with a few quid and a bottle of water, and assumed they'd have a lovely time and manage perfectly well. Hadn't she and her cousins all gone off similarly at that age? Her parents had barely turned a hair at the thought of them cycling around the country-side, and that was before there was any such thing as a mobile phone. And yet if she'd bothered to think about it longer than five seconds that morning, she'd have remem-bered all the scrapes she'd got into herself as a teenager: dodgy blokes leering at her and Jenny in their shorts and bare legs; straying onto farmland and being threatened by shotgun-wielding farmers; and how her cousin Neil's habit of setting fire to things, aged fourteen, had almost resulted in a hay-barn inferno. Hardly the stuff of ginger beer and innocence, really, when she foraged a little further past her hazy gilded memories.

It turned out that not much changed, from teenager to teenager over the decades, either. Because on arrival in Fal-mouth, having caught a hair-raisingly pricy cab there alone ('You two stay here! Have fun! I'm sure I won't be long,' she had trilled to George, on the verge of hysteria), she dis-covered exactly what the 'bit of trouble' Izzie had referred to, so cagily, actually entailed. For a start, when she tracked them down in a small gift shop, the three teenagers were all chewing minty gum with suspiciously glassy eyes (booze?

cannabis? Em speculated, narrowing her own eyes to slits). The second item of note was that there was a large balding, rather angry-looking man standing alongside them, with a meaty hand clamped on Jack's shoulder.

'This your lad, is it?' the man said when Em burst breathlessly onto the scene, still shoving her purse back in her bag from paying the cab driver.

'Yes,' Em said, blinking rapidly as she tried to take in her surroundings. Watercolour seascapes on the walls. Jewellery in glass boxes. Small clay birds on a white shelf. Postcards and prints and cards. And the three kids huddled together, heads down, guilt written all over their faces. 'It is. What's happened? What's he done?'

'It was just a stupid dare, I wasn't going to *nick* it,' Jack protested without preamble, and Em's heart sank into her sandals.

'Yeah, but you did, mate,' the man pointed out. 'You stuffed it in your pocket and left my shop. Without paying. Which, I think you'll find, definitely counts as "nicking it".'

A blonde woman browsing at the rack of postcards turned her head in interest just then, although she turned it straight back again, upon encountering Em's eyeball-blistering scowl.

'What a stupid thing to do, Jack,' Em said. 'Especially in a shop like this, where everything has been hand-made by artists, rather than mass-produced in a factory for some faceless corporation or—' She broke off, aware this might be the wrong thing to say. 'Not that it's okay to steal *any-where*, obviously,' she added in her most severe voice, for the benefit of the shopkeeper, plus the eavesdropping woman, who didn't seem in any great hurry to move on. 'Honestly, Jack, I thought I'd brought you up better than this. I'm ashamed. What have you got to say for yourself?'

'She said the thirteenth shop, and this was the thirteenth shop, so I had to—'

'JACK!' Em said loudly. 'I didn't mean in terms of making more excuses. I meant, what do you have to say to the shopkeeper? To this man whose family depends on his shop, whose mortgage probably does as well. How about apologizing and seeing if there's any way you can make it up? For all we know,' she added, getting into her stride, 'he might want to call the police.' She eyed the shopkeeper anx-iously. *Please don't call the police,* she begged him, with her best stab at telepathy. *You wouldn't, would you?*

'Sorry,' Jack mumbled.

He'd tanned during the last month, from all the tennis and cricket he'd been playing, but he seemed to have paled under the shop's bright lights. He was actually kind of nauseous-looking, now that Em scrutinized him closer. Oh, Christ. He wasn't about to throw up, was he? What on earth had they been drinking? Thank goodness George wasn't here to see what reprobates her children were.

'Anything else?' she prompted sternly, when this turned out to be the extent of his apology. 'Jack?'

'I'm really sorry,' he said, a little louder this time and with more sincerity. His green eyes were troubled as he raised them to the angry shopkeeper. 'It was a stupid game – a dare. I shouldn't have done it.'

He glanced sideways just a fraction towards Amelia, and something flashed across his face – reproach perhaps or irritation, Em couldn't tell. Then realization dawned: this whole little drama had been about impressing the girl, she was sure of it. Showing off. Oh, Jack. Trust him to go too far and get caught. Typical!

'Well . . .' the shopkeeper said, his eyebrows furrowing as he considered his next move, and Em, spotting his hesitation, leapt in.

'Can I buy something lovely from your shop to make up for it?' she blurted out, on impulse. 'And have my son promise never to set foot in here again? He really is sorry. We've all done daft things as teenagers, right?'

The item that Jack had pocketed and attempted to steal turned out to be one of the carved stone birds, and for a moment she thought about buying it to leave on their mantelpiece at home, as a reminder to him: crime doesn't pay. But then the shopkeeper said, 'Or, of course, if you wanted something a bit special . . .' before gesturing to a rather beautiful oil painting of the harbour, with a definite hint of threat about his body language.

Em was not an idiot and sensed very clearly how she was being directed, and so she ended up buying the beautiful oil painting. There was two hundred quid she'd never see again, she thought waspishly, giving Jack a cross look, as the shop-keeper taped bubble-wrap around it for her. Talk about blood money. With a final gritted-teeth apology, she marched the three out into the street, where she dumped the bubble-wrapped picture down by her feet so that she could put her hands on her hips.

'Right,' she said, eyes like lasers as she gave them all her hardest stare, one after another. So much for happy blended families on holiday, she thought. So much for George getting to know and love her fantastic special children! Thank God she'd had the foresight to leave him safely in the soft-play hellhole while she dealt with this. 'Let's hear it then. Exactly what have you three been up to?'

Chapter Seven

This was the life, Maggie told herself, albeit with a certain grim determination. Here she was, draped on a sun lounger by a pool, enjoying the gentle plash of water as a light breeze drove ripples across it. There were birds singing in the trees behind the cottage, the air was warm and soft, and there was a nearby shrub festooned with pink flowers that smelled deliciously of honey. This is what other people longed for on holiday, wasn't it?: complete rest and relaxation in beautiful surroundings. Nothing whatsoever to do except admire the scenery, pick up a tan and get lost in the pages of a good book. Bliss!

Except . . . well, she was struggling to feel very blissful, unfortunately. She had sent Amelia off with strict instructions to be careful on the road but still felt compelled to keep checking her watch and phone, wondering where Amelia was now and if she was all right. Instead of settling into her novel, her mind insisted on raking relentlessly over the events of the morning, all those sharp words they'd hurled at one another. Also, she felt horribly public, sitting there on her own, as if showing to the world that no, she didn't have anyone to spend time with right now. No, even her own daughter didn't want to be with her! Who would? It was the fortune-cookie moment all over again.

Her thoughts turned with dismal predictability to a scene from several weeks earlier, a scene that kept coming back to jab her whenever she was feeling inadequate. It had been her brother Ross's birthday and Helena, his wife, had organized a celebratory family dinner at their Berkshire home: a catered Chinese buffet served in the wood-panelled dining room.

'Fortune cookies!' Helena cried at the end of the meal, holding up a plate as if it was some kind of oracle. Maggie didn't have any truck with that sort of nonsense – a load of superstitious rubbish, she thought privately – but gamely took a cookie when the plate came her way. When they broke them open, it seemed as if everyone else had rather oblique fortunes: *You will find light amidst darkness* was Amelia's, for instance, which could have meant anything ('Turn your bedroom lamp on tonight,' Maggie joked at the time); and Helena's said *Life moves like a serpent*, which she seemed to be interpreting in a smutty way ('Hear that, Ross? Snake-hips are go!')

Then someone said, 'Go on then, Maggie, what's yours?'

Maggie opened the piece of paper and read aloud, 'True

passion awaits', only to be greeted by a gale of laughter. Honestly – a gale. 'Yeah, right!' Helena had shrieked. 'Well, they got that wrong, didn't they? Ha-ha!'

'True passion – brilliant,' Ross had chuckled, as if it was the most hilariously unlikely thing he'd ever heard.

Maggie had turned hot all over and she'd crumpled the paper in her fist. Was that how everyone saw her – as a passionless old spinster? A dried-up old stick? Was that how Amelia saw her too? she wondered miserably now, gazing out at her perfect surroundings and feeling nothing but dismay. Poor old Maggie, the laughing stock of the family. No wonder Amelia had been so keen to escape with some new mates.

A bird was flying high overhead, gliding on a thermal; she watched it soar away into the blue. The night of the fortune-cookie debacle she had felt so alone in the world. Her mum, at least, seemed to have noticed her humiliation and spoke to her about it later on, as the two of them stacked the dishwasher (Maggie and her mum always seemed to end up doing this in Ross's house, as if they were the natural skivvies of the pecking order). 'Come on, they were only having a bit of a fun, don't take it so personally,' she soothed.

Maggie had felt like a small child again, needing comfort from a sympathetic parent after having been teased. She was an adult, she should be able to let these things glide off her, but they always snagged on her prickles. Besides, it hurt to have been laughed at like that. 'Is it so outlandish, though, that I might fall in love?' she asked quietly. 'Am I such a figure of ridicule that it's an impossible thought?'

'No! Of course not. They were only joking,' her mum said, scraping slithery chow-mein noodles into the compost bin. 'Everyone's been teasing Ross all night about his so-called advanced age, haven't they, but he laughs along with it. Water off a duck's back!'

Maggie said nothing. She didn't seem to have been born with that duck's-back gene. But nobody liked a sulker, so she said, 'I know' and tried to think of a way to change the subject. Her mum beat her to it, though.

'Although if it's passion you're after, you should head out to Zennor while you're in Cornwall,' she went on. 'You know it's where your dad proposed to me, don't you?'

'No.' Maggie slotted cutlery into the plastic holder, grimacing as a stray piece of beansprout landed on her hand. It *wasn't* passion she was after, and her mum knew that full well. 'Tell me the story,' she added. 'What happened?'

'Oh! Well, we were down there as a group – there must have been fifteen or sixteen of us. We had our bikes and tents, we were there for a fortnight.' There was a faraway smile on her mum's face and Maggie felt a pang inside. Her dad had died ten years ago and they both still missed him hugely. 'Your father and I, we had been dating for a few months by then and we were very much in love.' She clapped a hand to her heart and sighed. 'I can see him now, all young and handsome, freewheeling down the hills on his bike as if he were king of the land.'

Maggie tried to smile, but she felt a twist of pain at the same time. Her dad had loved being out on a bike, but had been a reckless, over-confident cyclist who thought cycling helmets and reflective clothing were for sissies. Who knew if such things would have saved him when he was clipped by the van driver at fifty miles per hour, but his head injuries had been so catastrophic that he had died before the ambulance even reached the hospital. 'At least he went doing something he loved,' people had said, imagining these words to be comforting, as if it was all right for a fit and healthy man to die suddenly because he was too macho to slow down and act responsibly, too vain to put a protective helmet on his head.

'Go on,' she said to her mum after a moment, stacking tumblers upside down on the top shelf of the dishwasher.

'We went to Zennor for the day, just the two of us, and heard the legend about the mermaid – such a romantic story – you know, how a local man was entranced by the unearthly singing of a mysterious young woman who appeared every week in the church, and how they fell in love and disappeared, presumably to live in the sea together . . .'

'Hmm,' said Maggie, whose idea of happy-ever-after did not involve a watery grave.

'Anyway, there's a chair carved with a mermaid design in the church there – hundreds of years old, it is, and we went to see it. Perhaps your dad was caught up in the romance of the story, because that was where he asked me to marry him. Down on one knee and everything, once we were outside – he made a right spectacle of himself.' Her mum straightened up, her face soft. She'd always enjoyed scolding her husband for one misdemeanour or another. No doubt at the moment of proposal she'd said, 'Get off your knee, you daft chump, you'll get grass stains!' as if that was the most important consideration.

'Maybe you could visit while you're down there, anyway,' she went on, folding a tea-towel. 'Take some photographs of the place for me, so that I can see it again.'

'I'm sure there are pictures online,' Maggie said, posting a dishwasher tablet into its compartment and setting the machine running. 'Do you want me to look on my phone for you?'

'You could pay your respects while you were there,' her mum went on, as if she hadn't heard Maggie. 'I'd go myself, but with my hip, I'm not so mobile these days. Go on, I would really appreciate it. And you never know, you might be overcome by romance and passion yourself.' She'd nudged Maggie, who promptly scowled. 'Just like that fortune cookie said, eh?'

'What, prompted by an old *chair*?' Maggie scoffed.

Romance and passion had not been on her agenda since Will had walked out on her fourteen years earlier, but she allowed her mother's remark to pass without further comment nevertheless. That said, she rather liked the thought of her young, handsome father dropping impulsively to one knee and proposing, to hell with any grass stains, so she elbowed her natural scepticism aside for once. 'I'll see what I can do,' she promised.

Lorna was leafing through her scrapbook. *Is that you? It's me,* Aidan said in her head as she turned the pages. There he was, in a newspaper clipping, aged eleven as he collected his chess trophy from the south-west finals, looking up through those long dark lashes of his with a shy smile.

There he was, suited and booted with Roy, in a photo from his baby cousin's christening. Sixteen he must have been there, but already taller than Roy by a good inch. How he'd loved that! How he'd milked it too, resting an elbow on Roy's shoulder with a big grin, as if he wasn't the young whippersnapper!

There he was as a baby, with such round chubby cheeks you couldn't help but chuck them between your thumb and forefinger. Those bonny black curls too. Had there *been* a more beautiful baby?

And there was the last Mother's Day card he'd sent her, with 'Love you, Mum' written inside; a splodgy painting brought home from his infant class; the school report he'd had aged fifteen, where one of the teachers had written, *If Aidan Brearley doesn't become a very successful engineer or physicist in years to come, I will eat my hat!*

It always gave her a lump in her throat, that line. She turned the page quickly.

When Lorna reached the first page with an empty space, she glued in the piece of paper where she'd written down the memory that had occurred to her that morning. Every little detail concerning Aidan that floated into her head, however trivial or inconsequential, she tried to jot down and stick in the book, along with all the other pictures and memorabilia. Just so that she had as much of him as it was possible to have. Just to try and keep him from drifting away from her altogether.

I remembered the party he and his friends had after their GCSEs, at Jason Fisher's house. How they'd started playing football with a melon in Jason's garden, and after a few kicks it had ended up splattered all over the roses. Mr and Mrs F were so cross they banned Jason from having friends round – and melons in the house! – for the whole summer.

She smoothed a hand over the newly added paper, as if stroking his beautiful face. She could almost picture the melon as it broke into juicy pieces, outlined against the blue sky. Smell its sweet sticky flesh as it showered everywhere, hear the boys guffawing.

'Teenagers, eh?' she murmured to herself with a little smile.

'Teenagers!' said Em that night, once she and George were cosily snuggled in bed together. What a day it had been, she thought. One of those when you were glad to see the back of it, frankly.

'So they got pissed and went on a robbing spree – is that about the size of it?' George asked, his arm heavy and warm where it was slung across her.

'No!' Em spluttered. 'It wasn't like that.' She sighed, nestling a little closer into him. 'Well, all right, I suppose it *was* like that, a bit,' she conceded glumly.

The trip to Falmouth hadn't been the most successful, all in all. From what Em could gather, Amelia had produced a bottle of tequila and they'd all tucked in ('It was rank, I only had a sip, I swear,' Izzie said meekly) and then Amelia – her again! – had suggested that old teenage classic: a game of Truth or Dare. Having glossed hurriedly over what the 'Truths' might have been – don't think she hadn't noticed, Em thought – Jack then revealed that his dare had been to steal something from the thirteenth shop they had come across. That, of course, had been the little gallery, and he had been stupid enough to pocket a seventy-pound ornament. Even the world's most bored, lackadaisical shop assistant wouldn't have allowed him to get away with that, let alone the irate sculptor and gallery co-owner himself.

Perhaps sensing her slight despondency as she replayed the scene in her head, George took her hand and folded it in his. 'So. It seems I am dating the mother of a shoplifter,' he teased. 'And let me tell you, I'm horrified. What other torrid tales are you going to spring on me?'

'Stop it! He's not a shoplifter. He's a fifteen-year-old boy trying to impress a girl and getting it badly wrong.' She traced a finger along his knuckles. 'I, meanwhile, am the fool who shelled out two hundred quid on a painting that will always remind me of my mothering nadir. I'm not sure who needs to learn more of a lesson here.'

'If it makes you feel any better,' he began, then stopped. 'No, forget it, I'm not sure I can bear the shame.'

'What?'

'My own terrible youthful misdemeanours. My most shocking secret.' Em could hear the laugh in his voice behind the sombre words and she smiled to herself, feeling a tiny bit better already.

'You can't leave it there,' she scolded 'Come on. What did you do? What's this dreadful confession?'

'I'm worried it will put you off me,' he said. 'Are you sure you want to know?'

'Yes! Of course I do. Spill!' She always wanted to know

people's dark, terrible secrets. Didn't everyone? It made her feel special, as if she was being admitted to a private, exclusive club, welcomed into an inner circle.

'Well, I was a bit older than Jack's age. Seventeen, I think. Bunked off college and had a few lunchtime beers with my mates,' George began. 'These were the Dark Ages, obviously, when a pub would serve any skinny, acne-ridden little turd.'

'You're painting a very attractive picture of yourself here,' she said, feeling a giggle rise in her throat. 'Is that the bit that's going to put me off you?'

'Oh, Christ no, there's far worse to come,' he went on. 'Far worse. Now brace yourself and picture the scene: four or five lanky lads, can't handle even the weakest lager, blinking in the daylight as they emerge from the den of vice – that's the pub, obviously.'

'Good, I was wondering.' Her glumness had evaporated and she was enjoying this peek into George's youth. 'Carry on.'

'So the lads emerge, wobbling and a bit giddy. There's the Friday fruit-and-veg market on in town – this is in Shropshire, where I grew up. And wait, who's this in front of the lads? It's only Nicola Hulme, the fittest girl in the sixth form.'

'Oh dear,' said Em. 'Let me guess. The boys feel obliged to show off in front of young, innocent Nicola Hulme.'

'She wasn't all that innocent, allegedly, but let's gloss over that. One particularly stupid boy who shall remain nameless—'

'You?'

'Me. Picks up some oranges from a nearby stall and starts juggling.'

Em smirked. 'Ah, yes. Scientifically proven to be the fastest way to a girl's heart.'

'Indeed. His mates are jealous of his skills and start trying to snatch the oranges. Some fruit-throwing ensues. They're going everywhere. Meanwhile, the owner of the fruit stall is rightfully pissed off and grabs hold of the ringleader.'

'Not you again?'

'Me again. Who is hauled off down the nick, for a bollocking from the bored copper on the desk – thus ruining my chances with Nicola Hulme forever and earning me a criminal record.'

Em snorted. 'You've got a criminal record for lobbing a few oranges about? That is the most . . .' She burst out laughing. 'That is the most tragic criminal record I've ever heard of in my life.' She poked his leg with her toe. 'Still, I've always loved a rebel. Even one without a cause.'

'Without a cause? You're forgetting foxy Nicola Hulme, mate. Not easy to do, believe you me.'

She smiled, feeling a whole lot better. '*Orange Is the New Black: The George Macleod Diaries*,' she said in a dramatic voice, giggling at her own wit.

'TV rights *are* available for the dramatization of my memoir,' he said. 'For a very reasonable price.'

'You surprise me.'

'But at least now you know that I think your son is a perfectly normal fifteen-year-old boy and I'm not judging him in the slightest.' His arm tightened around her. 'Come on, he didn't even get a criminal record out of the whole experience. He's a total lightweight, to be honest. Not trying hard enough.'

'Good point,' she said. 'Thank you.' She wiggled around so that she was facing him and slid her leg over his. 'I'm not sure how I feel about dating a delinquent with a criminal record, though,' she added in a breathy voice. 'Slightly miffed that you haven't tried to impress *me* with your juggling skills, mainly.'

'All in good time,' he murmured, laughing.

'However, I would like to remind you,' she said huskily into his ear, 'that oranges are *not* the only fruit, George.'

She was tipsy enough that she might have begun making lewd remarks about bananas, but thankfully they started kissing at that moment. Slowly at first, both still smiling at one another, but quickly becoming more passionate and intense. Now *this* was what she needed . . .

'Daddy!' came a howl just then, and their door was flung open to reveal Seren rushing towards them. 'Daddy, I had a bad dream!'

You had to laugh, Em thought, rolling discreetly away. Didn't you?

Summer of Yes group chat

Izzie – tequila and shoplifting session in Falmouth today . . .
  banned from art gallery and called a delinquent. How
  many points??!

Lily – you rebel, Iz. Ten points!

Miko – don't think we haven't forgotten about your selfie
  with the older man, though. Get on with it!!

Tej – she's chicken. Bwark! Bwark!

Ruby – give her a chance, she's been on the tequila all day.
  (But yeah, crack on, Iz. We're waiting!)

Izzie – GUYS. Doing my best here.

Lily – don't let us down.

Chapter Eight

The wind was picking up strands of Maggie's overgrown bob and throwing them into her eyes and mouth as she strode around the headland. It was Sunday, the following day, and she and Amelia had come out to explore Pendennis Castle, Henry VIII's squat stone fortress up on the cliff. The sky was overcast and sullen, and thin spitty needles of rain fell periodically, as if a storm was swelling above them, ready to let go at a given signal. Maggie's spirits remained resolutely sunny, however. She had abandoned geological trips for the day and tried history instead, luring Amelia out with promises of the gift shop *and* a café lunch. To her great surprise, her daughter had agreed to the excursion without too much of a fuss.

'According to the leaflet, there was a five-month siege here in 1646, during the English Civil War,' she said to Amelia, gazing back at the circular fort and mentally conjuring up the shouts and fervour, the smell of gunpowder, the boom and thud of a battering ram. Maybe this could be their new shared hobby, she thought, with a sudden flash of optimism. Cornwall was steeped in history – they could immerse themselves this summer. She might even go the whole hog and join English Heritage on the way out today. 'Five *months*! Can you imagine?'

'Mmm,' said Amelia, her face blank.

Was she even listening? Maggie thought, deflating again.

Amelia had been rather subdued since going out to Falmouth with the other children the day before. ('How was it? What did you get up to? Did you have a lovely time?' Maggie had pressed, only to be met with a shrug and a set of abbreviated replies. *It was okay. Not much. They were all right.*) She'd probably found them a bit intimidating, Maggie imagined, seeing as they were a year or two older than her. Peer pressure could lead vulnerable younger ones into all kinds of trouble, as she'd seen at first hand, working as a secondary-school teacher. She just hoped Amelia had enough resilience to say no to any older teenagers trying to encourage her into bad behaviour.

'We could wander inside to have a look at the underground magazine next,' she went on brightly, striding across the tussocky grass. Out at sea, she noticed a cruise liner moving slowly through the water, plus a few sailing boats, and she found herself imagining cargo ships returning from faraway shores, full of gold and pearls and spices. 'Did you know the word "magazine" has two meanings, by the way?'

she went on, just in case Amelia was confused by her suggestion. 'In this instance it means . . .'

Amelia didn't seem very interested in the issue of etymology, though. 'Um, so, Mum, anyway, I've got something to tell you,' she blurted out just then, interrupting Maggie's explanation.

'Oh,' said Maggie, disconcerted. She pulled her jacket around her a little tighter – that sea breeze was quite something. 'What is it?'

'Just that I've been in touch with Dad lately,' Amelia said, the words dropping like – well, like a whole magazine of weapons, frankly, Maggie thought to herself in horror. *What?* 'And – yeah. Basically, I want to meet him.'

It suddenly felt like the most enormous effort to breathe. Maggie stared at Amelia's perfect cupid's-bow mouth as she said these impossible words, the wind whipping long strands of dark hair around her face, like Medusa's snakes.

'Mum,' prompted Amelia. 'Now you need to say something.'

'I . . .' Maggie cast about wildly, but the words simply weren't forthcoming. Amelia had been *in touch* with *Will* and wanted to *meet* him, she told herself, incredulous. She glanced over her shoulder as if half-expecting him to come striding over towards them from the gift shop. *The trouble with you, Maggie . . .*

How could this be happening? She couldn't take it in.

'Right,' she said, her mind reeling. It wasn't as if she had shut Will out of her *or* Amelia's lives – far from it! She had done her best to keep in touch with him, doggedly emailing news and sending Christmas cards to his mum's address in Newton Abbot at first – PLEASE FORWARD written neatly and hopefully on the envelopes. He had been a poor correspondent in return: the occasional halting phone call, the even more occasional visit where Maggie felt tense the whole time, praying that this time he would fall in love with Amelia; would properly see how wonderful she was and have an about-turn in attitude. His mum, Philippa, did her best to maintain relations, but on the whole Maggie felt cut adrift.

Then, when Amelia was about five, Philippa had died, suddenly and horribly, following a massive stroke and, almost in tandem, Will's career had gone stratospheric. Suddenly he was off undertaking reportage work in dangerous cities or wildlife series in remote places far from civilization, and contact became even more sporadic. Maggie had sent updates via his photographic agency instead: pictures on birthdays and Amelia's first day at school, news about piano exams and netball captaincy and great exam results. The edited highlights that said: *This is our child. Look how fantastic she is. How can you not want to be part of her life, for heaven's sake?*

It was as if Will had died too, because he hardly ever replied. A birthday present, three months late. An email that seemed to be all about him and how busy he was. A

Christmas card with an airmail sticker and exotic-looking stamp, the envelope so battered and creased it was as if the postman had walked it personally to Maggie's house all the way from Colombia, or wherever Will was these days. ('Where *is* my daddy?' Amelia had said a few times when she was at primary school and discovered that lots of the other children in her class had dads, and brothers and sisters, and pet rabbits and dogs and – oh, all of the things that Maggie hadn't been able to give her, basically. *Good bloody question*, she had fumed, trying to cobble together an upbeat response.)

She swallowed hard because Amelia was still looking at her, now with a slight frown as if worried that Maggie was on the verge of collapse. Well, and quite right too, because she *was* on the verge of collapse all of a sudden, and had to lean against the 600-year-old wall and hope it would stay standing a while longer, at least until she got her breath back. 'I . . . Gosh,' she stammered. 'When did this happen? I mean, how did you even . . . ?'

'I looked up his website,' Amelia said, as if this was a given. 'He's not exactly hiding away, Mum; his work's all over the Internet. Then I followed him on Twitter and we just started to chat.'

Blood was roaring around Maggie's brain, shock beating through her that this had all been going on without her having the slightest idea. Why hadn't Amelia said anything earlier? Why hadn't she confided in Maggie that she might approach him, asked her opinion? She could have warned Amelia off, braced her to expect disappointment – and gone to Will herself, to threaten him, *Don't you dare break her heart.* Because he would. You bet he would.

She found herself thinking about the chunky silver bracelet he had bought her one birthday. It was heavy and made her wrist ache, and privately it reminded her of a manacle, but she'd told him she loved it and wore it nonetheless. She even went on wearing it for years after he'd left, just in case he came back unexpectedly and noticed it there on her arm, recognized the symbolism of her having waited loyally all this time. But he hadn't come back and eventually she had taken it off and shoved it in her jewellery box, where it had lain ever since. It was going a bit green now, as she hadn't taken care of it, and smelled musty, of old metal. Something had stopped her from getting rid of it, but right now she felt like driving home and throwing it straight into the nearest river. There! What do you think of *that* for symbolism?

'I see,' she said in a strangled voice. Stay neutral, she reminded herself. Don't antagonize her. The quickest way to ensure Amelia's shutters came rattling down was to argue. 'And . . . how's that going?'

'He's really cool,' Amelia said, and it was as if a sixteenth-century battering ram had punched Maggie's heart right out of her body. It was all she could do not to whimper in pain.

'Great,' she said weakly. 'Good.'

The man who had used her up and tossed her away, the man who had washed his hands of them both and walked out, with barely a backward glance at his ex-wife and infant child. *This* man was cool? No, he was not. He really was not. But now he was back in her head, looking at her with that curled lip. *The trouble with you, Maggie, is that you're too bloody intense. You're needy. And I can't live like this.*

Her mouth trembled, remembering. *I'm not the problem here, mate,* she wished she'd shouted. *Better intense than not caring!*

'So I was thinking, maybe I could go and meet him,' Amelia was saying, not seeming to have noticed that her mother was visibly crumbling, just like the ancient fortress wall currently propping her up.

'Right,' Maggie managed to say, thinking fast. Obviously she couldn't deny Amelia this meeting, but she could smooth the way for her, make it as easy as possible, she supposed, because Amelia was sure to be shy when it came to the crunch. And who wouldn't be? She could invite Will over for Sunday lunch or something, back when they were in Reading, she thought grudgingly. Lay on some cordial conversation along with the food, take tentative steps towards a new relationship. If that wasn't too 'intense' for Will of course, she thought, bristling. If that wasn't too 'needy' of Amelia too, for wanting to see her own dad for the first time in years. 'Okay,' she said, trying to sound supportive. 'Perhaps we could—'

'I was thinking, maybe tomorrow?'

Maggie gulped. *'Tomorrow?'* Her voice was almost a shriek. 'Well, I don't think—'

'Yeah, if you don't mind dropping me at Falmouth train station and sorting out the ticket,' Amelia went on doggedly. 'He said I could stay over anyway, meet his family . . .'

This was all happening way too fast, the conversation streaking from her grasp as if it were greased. Maggie couldn't keep up. Meet his *family*? Amelia *was* his family – or was there some other wife and kids she didn't even know about? Did Amelia have a half-brother or sister? Oh God. She wasn't ready for this. All these years she'd waited for Will to reach out to his daughter and yet she wasn't remotely prepared for the actuality.

'Hold on a minute,' she said, her hands flying up into stop signs. Or the symbol of surrender, whichever way you chose to look at it. 'What do you mean, "stay over"? I thought he was living in London.'

'He's in Devon now, though. He inherited his mum's house or something. My gran, I guess.'

Maggie's throat was tightening with every new insult. Amelia's gran was Maggie's own mum, thank you very much – the woman who had shown her granddaughter boundless love over the years, in the form of knitted garments, a massive collection of charity-shop and eBay Lego sets, bedtime stories, extra sneaked pocket money, babysitting and, more recently, a shared love of *Strictly*, book recommendations and baking sessions. *That* was Amelia's gran.

The rest of her daughter's words percolated through belatedly. So Will was in *Devon*, the neighbouring county. In Newton Abbot, presumably. And suddenly Maggie had flashed right back in time to the weekends they'd spent there at Philippa's house in years gone by, when she was young and life was still carefree: tramping through verdant countryside with Philippa's dog Bonnie, stopping now and then at a riverside pub along the way; the comfortably scruffy kitchen with its battered black range-cooker and the bunches of herbs drying along the wall. She could vividly remember being curled up on the baggy old sofa with Will in the evening, the smells of red wine and wood smoke in the air, feeling blissfully happy. She had never allowed herself to feel so happy with a man again. For a second, the memories pained her. She felt as if her heart might rupture, even thinking about that time.

'So . . . can I, then?' Amelia asked, impatient to have her question answered. 'Go and stay with him?'

There were so many reasons why Maggie wanted to say no. No, this is our holiday and we're meant to be having fun here in Cornwall together. No, because Will's a bad person and you'll get hurt, and then I'll be livid and quite possibly murderous. No, because this has been sprung on me and I can't make a decision like that on the spur of the moment, here at Pendennis bloody Castle, with a coach load of tourists milling around us.

But Amelia was looking at her with such hope and determination that all such words stopped in Maggie's throat. 'Okay,' she heard herself saying, 'on one condition. That I take you there. It's my final offer, take it or leave it.'

Amelia looked as if she was about to protest, but Maggie's expression was so steely, so stern, that she must have changed her mind. 'Cool,' she said. She even added a meek 'Thanks, Mum', before beaming and giving a little skip. 'I'll give him a ring,' she said and, before Maggie could say anything else, she'd whipped out her phone and punched in a number. 'I ll, it's me, Amelia. So tomorrow's looking good.' She grinned. 'Yeah, I know. I can't wait!'

Chapter Nine

Olivia had been having a trying weekend ever since Mack had left for his stag-do. On Saturday morning she'd taken the boys to the playground, hoping they would wear themselves out with all the fresh air and charging about, but a mere ten minutes after arriving, an older boy had pushed Harry down the slide too hard, making him bump his head and cry; and then Stanley, fired up by injustice and fraternal solidarity, had punched the other boy and they'd ended up grappling in the sandpit. Olivia had raced over to separate them, but had clearly been so ineffective that the older boy's mum felt the need to intervene too, with a few choice remarks about Olivia's children for good measure. 'Come on, Arthur, let's stay away from these nasty boys' had been her parting shot, arm around her smirking son.

On Saturday afternoon Olivia took them swimming, something they usually did as a family, and always a big treat for the boys. Both Stanley and Harry loved the way Mack would throw them up in the air and catch them in the pool, and would shriek in delight whenever he let them ride on his back, clinging around his neck, their small froglet legs pumping with glee. As soon as the three of them got into the water this time, though, it was apparent to them all that swimming was going to be a lot less fun without Mack there. Olivia was more fearful than her husband, more worried about drowning or choking possibilities, despite the boys' neoprene swim-vests keeping them safe, and she couldn't relax into rough-and-tumble games in the way he could. She did her best to entertain them, but it felt forced, artificial, and she kept eyeing other mothers, laughing and playing with their children, and wondered what was wrong with her that she couldn't behave similarly. Was she boring her own sons? Why had she thought she could manage this alone?

The excited squeals and shouts of the happy families around Olivia seemed to rebound from the walls, loud and distorted, mocking her own shortcomings. She thought longingly about how, as a teenager, she'd loved to swim in the sea with her friends, how confident and free she'd felt when buoyant and weightless in the water. This was hell in comparison. 'Shall we go?' she asked the boys when they started splashing each other peevishly, and felt guilty at just how relieved she was when they said yes. Unfortunately she'd somehow managed to lose her locker key and the three of them had to stand around, shivering and goosepimpled, in the chlorine- and pee-scented changing area while a member of staff did his best to track down and open the locker with all their towels and clothes. People were staring at her nosily as they went past, and Olivia felt her cheeks burn particularly hotly when Harry started to cry. Yes, I *am* the most terrible mother. No, I don't deserve to be responsible for any children. Yes, you're right to judge me – I am totally doing the same thing myself.

By the time they were finally dressed and leaving the leisure centre, still a bit damp and cold, Olivia felt as if she was having to hold herself together very, very tightly to avoid some public crying of her own. Then, on the way out of the car park, she managed to clip a bollard with the car and it was the final straw. The breaking of the dam. Tears spurted from her eyes, a strangled howl burst from her throat and then she was sobbing with such abandon that she had to indicate and pull over for a moment in order to gather herself and blow her nose.

'Mummy's CRYING,' said Stanley in interest, while Harry, rather more callously, drummed his feet against his seat and wailed, 'I'm HUNGRY.' Then a car beeped impatiently behind her and Olivia had to gulp back her sobs, put her hand up – *Sorry* – and move on.

Sorry. So sorry. It seemed as if she had been saying that word for years. Would a time ever come when she *didn't* feel sorry?

Saturday night, she had got them into bed as fast as possible, then lay on the sofa staring dumbly at bright, flickering television programmes. It was the first stretch of time she'd had to herself all day, but she barely had the energy to lift her head. She tried Mack's number but he didn't answer, and she couldn't think of another person she felt like talking to. Sometimes motherhood seemed like the loneliest place in the world, Olivia thought. She'd lost touch with her work friends — they didn't seem to have much in common any more – while lots of the women she'd met when the boys were tiny babies were now back at work and busy trying to juggle everything. Whenever she did see them, they would all keep telling her how lucky she was, having Mack earning so much money that she wasn't forced back into an office. Then, after a glass of wine, they'd start confessing their guilt at not being a full-time mum like her, how terrible they sometimes felt when dropping their little ones off at nursery. It was as if nobody could win the game. (Olivia had once admitted that actually she sometimes *longed* to drop her boys off at a nursery for a whole day, and the others had looked at her with such raised-eyebrow condemnation that she had felt herself turn bright red.)

Now it was a grey, drizzly Sunday and she and the boys had so far weathered the baking of biscuits (flour everywhere), some arts and crafts (glitter everywhere), the bad-tempered building of a looping train track (resulting in a fight), followed by a picnic under the kitchen table for some reason (Olivia no longer had the stamina to say no). They had watched some telly. Played some games. Been out for a quick walk to the swings when the drizzle held off for half an hour. A mere ninety minutes remained before Mack was due to return, and Olivia was hanging by a single fraying thread by this point, desperate for him to come home and take over.

Washing up in the kitchen with one eye on the clock while the radio burbled companionably, she found herself relishing this brief respite, pretty much the only time she'd had to herself that entire day so far. But then, from overhead, there had come the inevitable sound of an almighty crash and a yell, followed by breathless sobs.

'MUMMY!' shouted Harry and she raced upstairs and into her bedroom to find Stanley flat on his back there with a crumpled photo in his hand, and one of her drawers pulled out beside him.

'What on earth is going on?' she cried. 'Stanley, are you all right? Boys, you're not even supposed to be in here – you know that!'

Stanley sat up, apparently only winded, but tearful and shocked. 'We was looking for some treasure,' he said, wiping his nose on his arm. 'And Harry said "Mummy's bedroom"—'

'No, I did not!' yelled his brother in outrage.

'And we looked in the drawer and found a picture, but Harry said—'

'No, I did NOT!' yelled Harry, before he even knew the accusation.

'Open another one and – yes, you did! He did, Mummy! And it fell out and I bumped and – GET OFF ME! OW! He hurt me AGAIN!'

And now they were grappling and rolling around the floor like bear-cubs, the crumpled picture Stanley had been holding discarded, so that he could land a punch on his brother's head. Olivia barely registered their shouts of protest and war, because on seeing the dropped picture, she'd let out a cry of dismay herself.

'Oh, *boys*,' she said wretchedly, her hand swooping for the photo, which was now completely ruined. She must have sounded particularly anguished because they actually stopped brawling for a moment to stare at her. 'Boys, this is . . .' She couldn't speak for a moment because she was staring down at the picture of her first love, the teenage boy who had captured her heart so completely back in Cornwall, and she found herself overcome with desolation at how far away those carefree days now seemed. How had she turned into this frazzled, miserable housewife since then? 'This was Mummy's special photo,' she said, trying and failing to swallow back the sob that was building in her throat.

If only you could reverse through time, she would go now and stay there, she thought. Do everything differently.

The boys, unperturbed, merely resumed their scrap, rolling and bowling around on the floor, and she stepped over them and retreated to the living room, where she sank into the sofa and cried. Not just a tear or two, not just a whimper, but a proper shoulder-shaking weep where her feelings completely overtook her. Where she felt as if she might never stop crying.

It was no good, she thought desperately. She couldn't do this. She simply couldn't do this any more. Other women had their own mums popping round, helping out and dispensing loving advice. They had sisterly wisdom passed on to them, kind mothers-in-law even, who would descend and provide practical assistance (albeit with judgemental looks at the laundry pile and dusty skirting boards, if the women she'd overheard complaining at toddler group were to be believed). Olivia had no such support network, though – no mum, no sisters and few friends she felt able to confide in. On days like these, she always felt so alone. Even her own mother-in-law descending from Scotland for her annual visit, raising a disapproving eyebrow at the state of her fridge drawer – *Are the boys getting enough nutrition, do you think, dear?* – would have been welcomed as company right now.

The boys' fight rumbled on into the same room as her and then two things happened, one after the other. The first was that a small wooden block, hurled by Stanley, presumably at his brother, missed its target and hit her smack on the head. 'Ow!' she yelped as pain buzzed through her temple. 'Be careful!' And then her phone chirped with a text from Mack – *Back in an hour* – and as she looked at it, she noticed what date it was that day. It was the shove she needed. The sign.

I'm going, she thought. *Right now. I'm out of here. He'll be back soon. He can have them.*

Everything happened very quickly after that. She couldn't even remember some of the details; it was like coming up on a nightclub drug, fast and vivid, the rest of the world blurring about her. There was the writing of a note to Mack, although she had no idea now what gibberish she might have written. She had calmly taken the boys round to her neighbour, Brenda, asking if she could just keep an eye on them for half an hour or so, until Mack got home, while she popped out.

(Popped out, indeed. *You look after them, because I can't any more* was more like it. *I've given up, Brenda. I've thrown in the towel!*)

And then she'd stuffed some clothes in a bag and she was in her car, heading for the motorway, like a dream where she was running away, where she was escaping, only it was real. She was doing it – it was happening this minute. She felt drunk on adrenalin, wild but strangely still at the same time, as if there was a silent scream in her head that nobody else could hear. Something had taken hold of her.

As she drove on, she expected sirens to pursue her at any moment, she expected other drivers to see her and sound their horns in alarm – *She's getting away! That woman there, that mother just walked out on her children, and now she's getting away!* – but nobody stopped her. Nobody took any notice of her. She was so used to being the very visible mother of twins, with people smiling and commenting on them wherever she went – 'Double-trouble!' – but all of a sudden it was just her. A pale, plump woman hurtling along the motorway while her life collapsed behind her.

'Oh my God,' she said aloud and then she was shouting and crying like a maniac, and had to pull over at the next services because she was shaking so much. What was happening to her? Was this what a nervous breakdown felt like? What was she *doing*?

She should go home, she knew that. She should go home and just knuckle down to the job of being Mum, like every other woman managed to do so well. Do the sensible thing. There was still time, if she turned around now and headed back, to rip up the presumably garbled note she'd left and collect the boys from Brenda's; Mack never needed to know about this alarming interlude.

She hesitated, her hands on the steering wheel, tears wet

on her face. Home or away? she thought, stricken by doubt. Onwards or back?

Her dad's face flashed into her mind, and then her brother Danny's, but she ruled them both out in the next moment, because Cornwall was calling to her loudest of all, like the seductive song of a mermaid. The past engulfed her and there was no turning back. The boys would be fine without her; they would probably be better off in fact. And so she started the engine again, released the handbrake and carried on westward-bound, trying not to think about anything much at all.

It was only when she'd got as far as Exeter that a new thought struck her. *It's happened. I tried so hard to be the perfect mother this time, to do everything right, but instead I'm as bad as my own mum. In fact I'm worse.*

Say what you like about Sylvia Asbury – and plenty of people had done, on the small housing estate where the family lived – but she had managed a while longer than Olivia at least. She'd notched up ten whole years of motherhood in fact, before washing her hands of the job. There had been no warning, no build-up to her departure – she had simply disappeared into thin air.

On the day it happened, Olivia had been annoyed at first, having to wait and wait outside school with her younger brother, as all the other mums arrived and took their children home. It wasn't as if Sylvia had ever been particularly reliable – she was often late, for one reason or another, but on this particular day she simply didn't come at all. They had stood there together, she and Danny, where they always waited near the netball hoop, and the playground emptied out until it was just the two of them left, the November chill sliding insidiously through their thin coats. It was a horrible feeling, being forgotten; to this day, Olivia still felt anxious having to wait for anyone, never quite able to shake off that worry of having been overlooked, left behind.

Eventually a kind teacher noticed them still there and asked if they were all right; did they want her to phone Mum to see what was going on? Olivia had felt embarrassed – she'd been a shy child and hated being singled out for any kind of attention, and so she mumbled an excuse, before grabbing Danny's hand and making a brisk exit. She was ten, she knew the way home and was sensible about crossing roads, although Danny had whined all the way back about wanting a lolly, until Olivia had felt like slapping him.

It was only when they arrived home to find the house empty, and nobody answering the door, that Olivia felt the first pricklings of fear. She could remember even now the hollow feeling in her stomach as she'd knocked and knocked, then pressed her finger to the bell in a long loud DRRRRRRRRING. Something had dropped away inside her stomach, a hot, loose sensation of uncertainty. *Mum wasn't there. Nobody was there.*

After a short while they'd gone round to the back and peered hopelessly into the kitchen window, but still there was no sign of Mum. Alarm started to punch holes in her and a bad feeling poured in – the conviction that she must have done something wrong, that this was her fault. She and Danny had sat there, shivering like two little orphans on the back step, for nearly two hours as the freezing darkness gathered like clouds of ink around them, until Olivia's dad had finally come home from work and found them.

Nothing had ever been the same, after that. The family had broken, never to be fully repaired. There had been no reconciliation, no attempts to explain or reunite. Nothing at Christmas or birthdays – not a word. Rumour had it that Sylvia had moved to Redruth, there were sightings now and then, according to the neighbours' gossip, but it might as well have been the moon. The police added her name to the register of missing persons, but said there was nothing else they could do. Was she alive? Was she dead? She had simply gone and not come back.

It was the waiting that was the worst. The gradual crumbling away of hope, year after year. Olivia's dad was angry and drunk for a while, and his Devonshire parents came to look after the children and the house, as their son fell apart before their eyes. Within two years he had pulled himself together and married again, though: to Gail, a quiet owlish sort of woman, who didn't like to have Sylvia's name mentioned in the house. Olivia couldn't give up so easily and, with the advent of the Internet, continued to search for her mother, a sighting, a reference. Nothing. It was like an ache inside. A hole that could never be filled.

She and her brother would talk about it now and then, with the conversational shorthand that came from mutual trauma. 'Do you ever think about her?' one of them would say. 'All the time,' the other would reply. It was almost better to believe that she had died, they decided. That she had died all those years ago and her body must never have been found. Surely she would have come back, otherwise? Surely she would have made contact with her own children?

Finally, five and a half years ago, word had come through via their aunt, Sylvia's sister, that apparently she had died in the US. She had been there for the last twenty-one years, it turned out, although details were thin on the ground. A lawyer had passed on the news; it was a surprise to everyone. A horrible surprise, as it turned out, the worst kind. So she'd been alive all that time, but didn't want her family to know. Didn't want to see them or hear them. She had wiped the slate clean, left the country and started over. It had hurt so badly, Olivia could hardly bear the pain. Was it any surprise that when she had met Mack a few weeks later – Mack, who seemed so sturdy and together and solid – she had clung to him like a drowning woman reaching a life-raft? He had made her feel safer. He seemed reliable, the kind of person who wouldn't abandon another without warning.

And yet here was Olivia now, being the one to abandon *him*. Leaving their children with Brenda Hollins next door because she couldn't cut it any more. It was the moment she had always feared would come; that she'd turn out to be just like Sylvia. Hadn't she known it all along?

What a rubbish person she was, she thought, gulping back a sob. Weak and spineless and shit. It would be better for everyone if she kept on driving until she reached the coast and went sailing right on over it.

Chapter Ten

Here they were again: the day had arrived, as it always did, every single year. It was Monday and therefore the anniversary of the most terrible episode in Lorna's life. And this year marked two whole decades since it had happened.

He'd be thirty-eight now, her Aidan, if he'd survived. Thirty-eight years old, a middle-aged man! He'd have married his teenage sweetheart, no doubt – he was the most loyal boy you could imagine – and they'd have had children too by now, she guessed. A girl and a boy, she liked to daydream, both with his blue eyes and wide smile. And wouldn't Lorna and Roy enjoy spoiling their grandchildren rotten? Her friends were all nannies and grandmas and grannies these days, but nobody would be calling Lorna one of those names, unfortunately.

At the time of Aidan's death, he'd been hoping to go to university to study Mechanical Engineering. He'd always been such a clever lad, such a hard worker. Neither Lorna nor Roy had ever had anyone in their families go to university, so they'd practically burst with pride when he'd been offered a place by both Leeds and Liverpool to study there. As a child, he'd been fascinated by taking things apart to see how they worked – clocks, dynamo engines, Lorna's hairdryer once, you name it – and always managed to put them back together again, still working. (Well, pretty much. The hairdryer had developed an alarming singeing sort of smell, but Lorna wasn't one to dampen a boy's ambition.)

Six weeks after his death, two envelopes had come through the door for him, and it had been such a bittersweet experience, opening the first one to see that he'd done so well in his A-levels: two Bs in Maths and Chemistry and an A in Physics. She'd opened the second envelope to see that it was a letter from Leeds, his first choice, congratulating him on earning a place on the degree course, with a list of accommodation options. Seeing that parallel future for him on typed pieces of paper had been like a punch in the stomach. *This is what you could have won.*

But instead he was gone, nothing more than their memories and a headstone in the local cemetery: *Aidan Brearley, Rest in Peace.*

One of the worst episodes in the whole nightmare – and there were plenty to choose from – had been the day Roy had to ring up the university and tell them, his voice catching on the words, that there had been a change of plan and that Aidan Brearley wouldn't be attending after all. No, he wasn't deferring a year, he would never actually be making the trip up the M1 to sit in their lecture halls and laboratories, because he'd driven his car off the road and was dead.

Roy had sobbed for a full forty minutes after that phone call, God love him. They both had. It seemed so final, that door closing in Leeds, a name crossed off the list; Aidan's place on the course filled by some other student who'd never know the circumstances of their belated acceptance. At the time, Lorna had been unable to imagine any kind of future without her son, when each day brought such emptiness, and yet somehow twenty years had passed. Today was the anniversary of his death all over again, and they had a full fifteen hours of it to get through yet, before the calendar slipped on to another day, another morning. Lorna wondered if she'd survive that long.

Was there anything worse than losing a child? Could any pain be more sharply felt? The suddenness of his death had felt like an act of violence in itself. Aidan and his girlfriend had been out for the evening together, seeing some band or other in Truro, and he'd been driving them home. It was dark, and the road was wet following an earlier cloudburst and his tyre treads had been on the elderly side, according to the police report, so when he took a bend too fast, the car had left the road, tumbling down the steep embankment until it came up hard against a sturdy oak tree. Aidan had died on impact, a stunned look on his face, as if he'd seen death coming for him and couldn't believe his bad luck. The girlfriend, meanwhile, had been trapped in the car with his body until the paramedics got her out, and suffered whiplash and concussion, but at least she had survived.

Oh, Lorna had raged and raged at the injustice of Aidan's loss, at the cruelty of the world. She had screamed and wept into her sofa cushions like a madwoman, she had smashed things against the kitchen wall, she had dropped to her knees and sobbed in his bedroom, before collapsing to the floor and lying there on the carpet that still smelled faintly of him, for what might have been minutes or hours. And then, after all that raging, she had taken to her bed, wrung out, and had stayed there for a whole week.

Depressed, the doctor called her, as if it was possible to sum up the maelstrom of her emotions with one single labelling word. As if anyone else had ever felt so tormented, so robbed of the brightest light in their lives! How could anyone possibly understand how she felt?

Time was a great healer, people kept telling her, and in the twenty years that had passed, admittedly the pain had lessened. She and Roy had clung tightly to one another through the darkest days and nights, seeing the heartbreak out together. They'd had a succession of dogs – Patch and Murphy and Meg – who, to Lorna's surprise, had helped tremendously in getting her through each day, forcing her back out into the world again, rain or shine, and, most unexpectedly, making her laugh at their daft antics and naughtiness. Not to mention easing a bad day with their innate doggy kindness. How was it that dogs always sensed when you were having a wobble, and knew exactly when to offer a sympathetic nose-push, a head on the knee, a warm bodily lean against the legs in canine solidarity? It didn't compare to hearing her son's rich, happy laugh bouncing off the walls, mind. There were some things that even the most loyal of dogs couldn't make better.

Work had helped her too, though, keeping her busy. She and Roy had bought up the derelict farmhouse and its old barns fifteen years ago, and it had been a labour of love to gradually transform first the house for themselves, and then the barns into holiday cottages. They were a good team, the two of them, both adept at practical tasks and neither of them afraid of getting their hands dirty. She'd planted up a kitchen garden as well as beds full of flowers, and found that being outside as the seasons slowly turned around her was soothing and helped her sleep better.

She was doing pretty well, all in all. Holding strong. There was just today to see through and then she could get back to normal again.

'Here we are,' said Roy, parking the car, and Lorna felt her mouth dry up as she realized they'd arrived. It was a warm, muggy sort of day with heavy showers forecast, exactly the sort of weather they'd had twenty years ago.

Getting out of the car, her fingers tightened around the cellophane-wrapped flowers she'd brought. Sunflowers, his favourite. They'd planted some together in their old garden one summer when he was a little boy, eight or nine, and he'd loved how they'd grown taller than him by the time it was July. She sniffled, feeling the tears gather in her eyes. They were never far away at the best of times, but when it came to the anniversary, anything would set her off. She was like a leaking tap.

Come on, girl, she said to herself. *Chin up.*

As usual, they walked arm-in-arm through the creaking cemetery gates. She popped in there most weeks to say hello to Aidan and pass on the news, but Roy tended only to visit on the anniversary these days. He said he preferred to think of his son as a young man, not a headstone. Fair enough. They all had their ways of dealing with bereavement. Hers was to believe that she could still communicate with him; that somewhere, on some spiritual plane or other, her boy was able to hear every single thing she said to him and know how much he meant to her. *I will never forget you,* she told him now in her head. *Never!*

The Victorian cemetery was deserted, as it so often was, just the faint rustling of the branches of the gnarled old yew trees as the breeze sighed its condolences. You'd see a dog-walker passing through occasionally, but there were seldom other mourners. 'You were lucky to get a spot here,' the funeral director had said at the time. 'This place is pretty much full up nowadays.'

Lucky, she'd repeated back at him with an angrily raised eyebrow and he'd turned red all the way down to his throat.

They walked along the winding path in silence. The grass needed cutting, but there was sorrel and vetch blooming, and the air smelled sweet. Rituals were comforting when you had lost someone, she had learned. Today, for instance, like every year, the anniversary would be stitched together with one tradition after another, journeys they repeated because it made them feel closer to their son, places to revisit and mark the passing of time. They always began with this annual visit to the headstone, and the laying of flowers. Lorna liked to tidy up the plot, if necessary, and then they'd say a few words each, usually about how much they missed him. After that, they would—

'Who's that?' Roy asked suddenly, as they rounded a corner and came to a halt. Because there, beside Aidan's grave, was the unexpected sight of a kneeling woman.

Lorna stared, dumbfounded. The woman was leaning against the stone with one arm around it, as if confiding secrets to a lover.

Lorna tightened her own arm on Roy's. It felt as if someone was trespassing on her heart. 'What on earth . . . ?' she said, breaking free from his grasp and marching hurriedly on. Emotion whirled up through her like a tornado: anger and hurt and pain. Of all the days, of all the moments, she did not want to encounter some weirdo here, on the twentieth anniversary of Aidan's death. Who was this woman touching his gravestone as if she had some kind of right to it? Was she on drugs? Was she mentally unwell? *Go away*, she thought. *Get your hands off my son and get out of here!*

'Hello?' she called out, her voice strident and accusing, but with just a hint of a crack in it. A crack that Lorna knew could either turn into a sob or a roar. 'Can I help you?'

Then the woman turned, her eyes bloodshot, her cheeks puffy where she'd been crying, and Lorna stopped dead again, staring as her brain tried to assimilate this face with the one she'd known many years before. 'Olivia?' she whispered, unable to tear her gaze away. 'Olivia, is that you?'

The woman rose. She had put on weight in the last twenty years – haven't we all? thought Lorna – and her blonde hair, which had once been a pixie cut with a swooping fringe when she was eighteen, was tugged messily back into a ponytail. But Lorna recognized those storm-grey eyes and the woman's beautiful alabaster skin, even if there was now a fretwork of lines etched on her forehead.

'Lorna,' she replied, her voice almost a whisper, as if she had seen a ghost. 'Roy.' Her mouth trembled as they approached and she took a step back. 'I . . . I hope you don't mind me being here.'

'*Mind?* Oh goodness, no, of course we don't. It's lovely to see you.' Just like that, her mood had changed to one of wonder and Lorna couldn't help herself, she threw her arms around the woman just as soon as she reached her, the cellophane around the flowers crinkling in surprise. Olivia Asbury, the girl Aidan had mooned over in the sixth form! The girl who had prompted a new, never-before-seen interest in hair gel and ironed shirts and enthusiastic applications of aftershave. The girl who had been sitting next to him in the car when he died.

Lorna swallowed hard as the memories spiralled around her. 'You're in Bristol these days, is that right?' she managed to say, releasing Olivia after a moment. 'I saw your dad – gosh, it must be four or five years ago now – and he said you'd been living there a while.'

'Bristol, yes,' Olivia said faintly. Her eyes had a haunted look about them, her nails were gnawed down to the quick, Lorna noticed, taking in the details. She had been such a little livewire once upon a time. 'I just . . .' She bit her lip, her hands flying out as if they were trying to pluck the right words from the air. 'I just wanted to come today. I hope that's okay. Twenty years, isn't it? I still think about him.'

There was such a lump in Lorna's throat that she could hardly speak. She wanted to hug Olivia again, even though she knew she probably shouldn't. But Olivia had *remembered*. She had cared enough to come here, all the way from Bristol. It was like receiving a gift, when you least expected it.

Nodding hard, she gripped Olivia's hands in hers, unable to express how moved this left her feeling.

'Hello there, love,' said Roy, noticing that his wife was speechless. 'It's good to see you again. You've never driven all the way here from Bristol this morning, have you? You must have got up with the lark!'

Trust Roy, Lorna thought, wanting to laugh and sob at the same time. Typical man! He hadn't set eyes on this girl – woman, rather – in years and years, and the first thing he wanted to ask about was her journey? 'Roy,' she managed to splutter. 'What are you like? Next you'll be asking her did she take the motorway or the back roads, when that's not remotely the point. The most important thing is that she's here. It's Olivia and – oh, I'm sorry, I just have to hug you again. Come here, pet.'

Now Roy was giving *her* an exasperated look, as if to say, *Get off her, you daft old woman*, and then Lorna began thinking the same, that Olivia almost certainly didn't want a second hug from Aidan's old mum, the first was probably more than enough – except that, in the next moment, Olivia let out a sob and leaned hard against Lorna, winding her arms around the older woman's back so tightly that Lorna feared for the stems of her sunflowers. 'Oh, darling,' she crooned, taken aback by the passion of Olivia's tears. 'I know. We're sad too. We're so, so sad.'

'Sorry,' Olivia said, disentangling herself after a moment

and blowing her nose. She seemed to make an enormous effort to regain her composure, after which she repeated, 'Sorry' and cleared her throat. 'This isn't about me. I'll leave you to it.'

'You don't have to,' Roy told her, but she was insistent.

'No, no, I've had my little chat with him. Poured out my problems.' She gave a shaky laugh, but looked so miserable Lorna felt worried for her. 'He's all yours.' Then her hand was up in a self-conscious sort of wave and she took another step backwards. 'It's good to see you both again. Even under these circumstances.'

'Wait,' said Lorna as Olivia turned to depart. 'Please. I'd like a minute with him, yes, we both would, but after that . . . Well, all we usually do from here is go and have a fried breakfast in Aidan's favourite café. If you're not busy, then . . . you could join us?' She caught Roy's eye, worried suddenly that he wouldn't want an extra person there with them for their ritual anniversary eggs on toast, but he was nodding in agreement.

'You'd be very welcome,' he said.

Olivia's mouth folded into itself, in a weak approximation of a smile, although the anxiety was still visible around her eyes. 'I'm not busy,' she replied. 'Thank you, that would be nice, if you're sure. I'll wait for you on the bench near the entrance, shall I? Obviously take as long as you want.'

Tears were rolling down Lorna's face, but they were not

the usual tears of devastation. She felt . . . was it odd to say that she felt *happy* for Aidan in that moment, that his girlfriend had come back? Happy that she still thought about him and cared? What a wonderful person he had been, to have inspired such devotion!

Blinking, she knelt at the grave and fussed about, putting the sunflowers into the holder there. 'So many visitors today, my love,' she said. 'What a nice surprise! We're all thinking of you, you'll always be in our hearts.' Okay, and now the devastated tears were kicking in. Now she had shifted into the gear of full-blown grief and was losing him all over again. She was remembering how they'd been watching television together, she and Roy, when the knock on the front door came. A normal evening, Roy with his bottle of stout, her with a white-wine spritzer, watching her favourite soap, *Ebberston Terrace*, and then some programme about the restoration of a stately home, both of them yawning a bit and thinking they'd have to turn in for the night soon. The cat purring on her knee.

Oh, but she'd give anything to go back to that moment, to freeze-frame it right there, staying in that safe little bubble of time forever! When the world was still good, when everything was steady and ordinary!

But then there had been a police car pulling up outside, and two officers walking up her front path, caps in hand. 'Mrs Brearley? There's been an accident,' one of them had said, hardly able to look her in the eye. It was Richard Abrahams, her friend Valerie's son, who was usually the most amiable of young men, always ready with a smile and a hello if she saw him in town. Not that night, though.

Out poured her sorrow now as she spoke to her son, lovingly, tenderly. All the things she'd ever wanted to tell him: hopes, memories, words of love. It was not enough, this one-sided conversation, it would never be enough, but it was all she had left.

Once she was spent, it was Roy's turn. Lorna stepped back to give him some privacy, wiping her eyes and trying not to listen to his gruff words of sadness. Already she could feel the enormity of her pain receding a little for another year, as if a tide was washing away the top layer of heartache and taking it out to sea. Numbness was setting in, a welcome balm, and she shut her eyes, grateful for the weak sunshine and the birdsong. She felt exhausted by the ordeal, as she always did, but she was comforted – just a crumb – by the fact that Olivia would be there waiting for them at the cemetery gate.

Marco's Café was full of its usual incongruous mix of clientele: teenagers, young mums and truck drivers. Aidan, Olivia and the rest of the gang had been frequent customers back as sixth formers, thinking themselves sophisticated for drinking milky coffees there after college lectures, and often congregating for a proper fry-up and builders' tea on week-end mornings. The decor might have changed over the years – a revamp here, a paint job there – but it had retained its cosy, rather scruffy-round-the-edges feel. More import-antly, Lorna could still imagine the eighteen-year-old Aidan here at a table, laughing as he and his mates shared a joke, and that was all that mattered.

Hello, my love, she thought, as she always did when walk-ing in, as if she might catch one last spectral glimpse of him there.

It was the only time of year that she and Roy ever came to the café, but there always seemed to be just one table free, as if somehow Aidan had reserved a place for them. This time it was the nicest table of all, the one in the window, and she sent a grateful smile up to the ceiling as they settled themselves into the wooden chairs and con-sidered the laminated menus.

'Gosh,' said Olivia, gazing around. 'I had forgotten about this place. I haven't been in for years.'

Now that they were under the bright café lights, there was a peaky look about her, Lorna noticed with a small frown of concern. Terrible bags under her eyes too, the poor thing. Was she well? 'So how are things with you?' she asked, resisting the urge to reach over and take Olivia's hand in hers. There was something about having Aidan's former girlfriend here with them, in person, that made Lorna want to keep touching her. As if she couldn't quite believe she was real. 'Your dad's okay, is he? I'm guessing you're staying with him and Gail while you're down here, are you?'

'Um,' said Olivia, fiddling with the salt cellar. There was no wedding ring on her finger, Lorna noticed. Had she never been able to find anyone to match Aidan? Her heart ached for the poor girl, who had clearly been so affected by his death. 'Actually, no, he and Gail moved to Torquay a couple of years ago. I . . .' She shrugged sheepishly. 'It was a bit of a whim, me coming down here. I slept in the car last night, because I didn't know where else—'

'Oh!' said Lorna in surprise. 'In your *car*?' she repeated dumbly, as if she might have misheard. Was Olivia in financial troubles? Homeless? No wonder she looked so pale.

'Yeah, it was kind of a last-minute decision,' Olivia said, her cheeks colouring. 'I knew everywhere would be booked up, so I . . . It was fine. I didn't mind. Anyway.' The subject was clearly embarrassing her. 'I think I'm going for the poached eggs on toast with mushrooms. How about you two?'

They ordered their food and talked about Aidan for a while. This was the only part of the anniversary day that Lorna could bear. When they sat at a table in his café and reminisced, it briefly brought him back to life, as if he was there, sharing the moment with them. What was particularly nice today was hearing Olivia's stories of him – ones that

Lorna hadn't heard before, or had quite forgotten about. In fact she found herself leaning forward greedily, drinking in every word, as Olivia recounted a tale about a sixth-form Halloween party where Aidan had taken it upon himself to wear a huge real pumpkin on his head, carving it so that it fitted like a crash helmet. 'Oh yes! The state of his hair later on when he took it off!' Lorna exclaimed, the memory of it coming back to her as clear as day. She would write this up in the scrapbook later, she thought, mentally storing away every word that Olivia had said. 'Seeds and orange pumpkin smears, and that sticky juice everywhere . . .'

Olivia laughed. 'He had it all over his face too, the juice kept leaking down as we were dancing. His eyebrows were full of it by the end of the evening.' Her eyes were bright. 'He was the funniest person, wasn't he? You never knew what he was going to do next.'

'Oh, he was,' Lorna agreed in delight at once. The image of Aidan in a pumpkin helmet kept coming back to her with a feeling of wonder. How had she forgotten that? Having the memory restored was the nicest thing that had happened to her in weeks. It actually felt like a gift, wrapped up with shiny paper and a ribbon.

'He was such a daft one at times.' She gazed at Olivia fondly, so grateful for her arrival today. There had been a fragility about Olivia when she was seventeen; she remembered a traumatic tale involving her mum abandoning the family, but look at her now, appearing out of the blue like a good fairy and offering around her stories as if they were sweeties to share. 'And you're a love for being here today too. An angel!'

She must have spoken out of turn, though, because Olivia's eyes filled with tears all of a sudden and she was shaking her head. 'No, I'm not,' she replied. Then her mouth was wobbling and creasing, and her fingers were trembling on her coffee cup. She looked dreadfully upset. 'I'm a terrible person, Lorna. And I've done such a terrible thing!'

Chapter Eleven

The most stupidly dangerous thing Maggie had ever done had been to explore an old quarry at Wye Downs in Kent without telling anyone where she was going. It was overgrown with brambles, and she hadn't spotted a chalk scree until it gave way beneath her foot, at which point she had skidded and tumbled right down to its base, twisting her ankle so badly she couldn't walk. She might have been stranded there for hours, overnight even, if it hadn't been for a fleece clad couple from Folkestone who came to her rescue. Still, that all seemed like a stroll in the park, compared to the stupidly dangerous thing she was doing now: driving to Devon so that Amelia could stay with Will in his mother's Newton Abbot house. There were some trips when even a hard hat and all the latest kit couldn't protect you.

'How are you feeling?' she asked her daughter, who wasn't saying very much in the passenger seat.

'Excited. A bit nervous,' Amelia replied, fiddling with her earbuds and shrugging. She'd taken care with her appearance that morning, Maggie noticed: a lot of make-up had been applied, hair had been straightened, her favourite mustard-yellow striped Breton top selected. Would Will notice, or appreciate, just how much effort had been put into this ensemble? Probably not. The tosser.

Maggie meanwhile felt absolutely no excitement about the day ahead. Instead she was a vat of curdling dread. Will had been easier to deal with when he had remained merely a silent reproach in her mind, an enigma kept safely at a distance. Now that the details of his life were being inked in once more, she found herself wanting to look away from them, to put her hands over her ears and remain in ignorance, just as he had done to her. For starters, it turned out that Will was living in Philippa's old house with his new partner Celeste (!) and their two young children (!!). So Amelia had half-siblings on top of everything else. Why had nobody thought to tell them *that*, either? And, more pertinently, how come Will had deigned to stay and look after these other offspring, when he had run a mile from his first child? She felt deeply, bruisingly hurt on hearing this piece of news; way more disconcerted than being told that he had settled down with another woman.

As for Amelia . . . 'How do you feel, knowing you've got – wait, are they boys or girls? Sisters or brothers?' she had asked cautiously the night before, as the details began emerging. They were in the cosy living room together, one sofa each, warm rain beating a tattoo against the window, and it had been like having a live grenade chucked through the front door, hearing about these mystery children. BOOM! There goes your quiet evening.

Amelia hesitated and Maggie couldn't help remembering with a pang how she had asked for a sibling repeatedly as a small child, as if she thought Maggie might be able to whip one out of a cupboard for her. Ta-dah! And now she had not one, but two. Gifts from Will that Maggie hadn't been able to provide.

'Thistle's a boy, Rain's a girl,' Amelia said. 'Cool names, aren't they?'

Maggie had almost sprayed a mouthful of wine across the floor. 'Thistle and *Rain*? Aren't those Farrow and Ball paint colours?' she scoffed. 'Heavens, how did they come up with those – stare out the window and pick the first dreary thing they saw? Ah, Pondweed, that'll do. Or how about Drizzle? Perfect!'

Amelia had shot her a disapproving look and Maggie felt bad for sneering. It was hardly the poor children's fault they'd been given such daft names – and these were Amelia's half-brother and half-sister, more to the point. Any more criticism and she knew which side Amelia would pick.

Come on, though, she thought now, remembering the conversation. Thistle was bad enough, but Rain was just mean. Who liked rain? She certainly didn't.

The journey to Newton Abbot took about two hours, but even when they had parked and were walking up towards the house, the situation still didn't feel quite real. Maggie found herself assaulted by a punch of memories that she hadn't even known were there, as she approached the familiar front door; all of a sudden she was twenty-eight again, with a swingy ponytail and jeans. She was hand-in-hand with Will, holding a bunch of flowers for Philippa, their overnight bags at their feet as they rang the bell.

Then she blinked and was all grown-up again, with a sprinkling of grey hairs on her head and crow's feet around her eyes, and it was her teenage daughter who held the overnight bag now. The jeans Maggie had once lived in had become fawn-coloured chinos, teamed with a cap-sleeve white blouse with pretty embroidering; the unofficial uniform of every Middle-Aged Fart this summer, she realized too late. An army of invisible, nothing-to-see-here women doing all the grunt work of their families. Maybe she should have put more effort into her outfit today, like Amelia had, she thought, glancing down at her mum-clothes. Well, everyone had to grow up eventually, she told herself. Maybe even Will.

Talk of the devil, here he was answering the door and – oh goodness, yes, how her traitorous heart twisted at the sight of him, still as handsome as ever, with those exquisite cheek-bones and the sweep of glossy dark hair that Amelia had inherited. Wearing scruffy jeans and a blue T-shirt with some band logo emblazoned across it, he apparently hadn't received the memo about the uniform of middle age. Which only left her feeling frumpier than ever.

'Hey!' he said, drinking in the sight of Amelia there before him. 'Look at you. My God. All grown-up!'

Yes, funny how that happens over fourteen years, Maggie somehow managed not to say out loud.

'Hi, Dad,' said Amelia, then blushed violently. 'That sounds weird. Can I call you that?'

'If you want,' he said and shrugged in such a casual, care-less way that Maggie felt like throwing her hands up into the air and screaming at his lack of sensitivity. 'Or you could call me Will?'

'What do your other children call you?' Maggie asked through gritted teeth.

'Well . . . Daddy,' he replied, shrugging again as if the answer was obvious.

'Right, so Amelia can call you that as well,' Maggie said, flint-eyed. They hadn't even crossed the threshold yet and she was already braced for a fist-fight. He didn't get it, did he? He still didn't get it!

'Mum! Don't be weird,' Amelia hissed, elbowing her as Will remembered his manners at last and invited them in.

Philippa's house had been cosy and comfortable, back in the days when Maggie had come visiting. Although there had always been a hint of wet-Labrador detectable in the air, the place had been spotless and uncluttered, with fresh flowers and hoovered carpets, and a clean-swept hearth. Following Will into the hall now and through to the kitchen, Maggie blinked, as her memories of how things used to be clashed up against the reality of the present day.

The hall carpet, for example, was now dirty and stained, strewn with assorted parts of a wooden train, while someone had idly peeled away strips of the wallpaper below the dado rail, leaving it dangling in sad papery curls. In the kitchen there were small painty hand-prints ascending one wall, a laundry basket full of dirty clothes abandoned in the middle of the floor, and an unidentifiable pan of some yellow-brown slop – curry? casserole? nappy contents? – that bubbled and plopped on the hob. A scraggy black cat with a torn ear walked daintily along the worktops, past smeary jars of rice and lentils and an overloaded spice rack, before pausing to sniff at a crumb-littered bread board.

Maggie thought of how welcoming this kitchen had always been when Philippa was alive, how fragrant the air was with roast dinners and apple crumbles, how it had been the very heart of the home. Now the room felt like a student squat and left her anxious about food hygiene. Glancing sideways at Amelia, she saw that listeria concerns were far from her daughter's mind, though.

Wide-eyed, Amelia was staring around, beaming. 'This is so cool,' she said.

Well, of course she found it cool, Maggie thought, trying not to roll her eyes. She was fourteen and had always lived in a house with clean tea-towels and bleach squirted regularly down the sink. This sort of lifestyle must look glamorous and bohemian to her, just as it would have done to Maggie at the same age. Nowadays her instinct was to put on a pair of rubber gloves and possibly a biohazard suit, and start thoroughly disinfecting the surfaces.

'Very nice,' she said tightly, trying not to look as if she was sneering. It would play right into Amelia's views of Maggie being the boring parent and Will being the exciting one, if she started acting disparaging or patronizing now. 'Love what you've done with the place,' she added for good measure, although she couldn't help a sarcastic edge creeping in. But then her gaze turned to the window, through which she noticed a woman and two small children outside in the garden, and all comments about decor and food-poisoning risks vanished from her mind altogether.

So there they were. The ones who had tamed Will Evans and persuaded him to stay, where Maggie had failed. Her breath tightened in her lungs. She wished now that she had bothered to put some make-up on, just to act as armour, a buffer between the situation and the real, vulnerable Maggie underneath. Had she even brushed her hair properly that morning? Why had she not thought this through?

Will went and banged on the window. 'Guys! They're here,' he called.

The woman – Celeste, presumably – had aubergine-coloured, rather stringy hair that fell down to the centre of her back. (It didn't look as if she had brushed it, either, at least. Or even washed it for a while.) She was small and slight, dressed in a billowing Indian-print dress with grubby bare feet, and Maggie immediately felt every inch of her five-foot-ten height. ('Don't *hunch*, Maggie,' her mother's catchphrase had been, when Maggie was a self-conscious teenager. She could feel herself hunching again; she was a huge, lumbering carthorse compared to this slender foal of a woman.)

'Hello,' she managed to croak as Celeste entered the room. So this was Will's type now, was it? About as different as you could get from enormous, solid Maggie. Good to know.

The children were introduced, but in such earnest terms – 'This is Thistle, he's five and loves wind turbines. This is Rain, she's three and wants to protect the Amur leopard' – that Maggie started to wonder if the whole set-up here was one colossal parody. Come on, *seriously*? Was she actually meant to be impressed by a three-year-old's contribution to feline conservation efforts?

'Lovely,' she managed to say, when the silence that followed let her know that yes, clearly she was.

'Green tea, anyone?' said Celeste, who had a dreamy air about her, as if she existed on a high spiritual plane at all times. Before anyone could answer, Thistle started running a pencil back and forth along the metal radiator, leaving bumpy, scribbly lines as the lead banged up and down the uneven edges.

The noise set Maggie's teeth on edge. 'Oh,' she said politely. 'Do you want him doing that? He's—'

'He's *so* creative,' Celeste sighed, interrupting her. What was she, late twenties? Thirty, maybe? She had a bindi between her eyes and thick black eyeliner in a Cleopatra style, and appeared to be smiling with pride. 'He just loves music. Doesn't he, Wilf?'

Maggie goggled. That was music, was it? And wait – had Celeste just said *Wilf*? Will had always strongly resisted nicknames back when she'd known him, perhaps a hang-up from having been called 'Willy' by a group of girls all the way through secondary school. Feeling vaguely hysterical, she eyed him with interest, watching for a flicker of irritation. But Will – Wilf, rather – didn't appear irritated in the slightest. In fact he was smiling lovingly back at his waifish partner and saying, 'Yeah, he's a proper little muso. Loves expressing himself' to Maggie and Amelia, as if having someone scrawl noisily all over your radiator was a well-respected form of culture. Then he turned to Amelia. 'Hey, so tell me about you. What are you into?'

'Well,' said Amelia, deliberately not looking at Maggie, 'I'm quite political. And I, you know, care about the world. Like, I stopped using plastic bags and that, because it's just so wrong, filling up the planet with bits of plastic that will hang around for millions of years? And . . .' She had run out of steam. 'Yeah. So I'm into that sort of thing,' she said.

Oh God, it was painful, it really was, seeing how desperate Amelia was for Will's approval. How she blossomed at his smile of agreement, his murmured 'Absolutely.'

Come *on*, Will, thought Maggie. Give her more than that. Tell her how great she is. She's waited all these years to hear those words from you. But Amelia was already speaking again.

'I hope this isn't, like, super fangirl-ish or whatever, but I really love your work,' she went on, emboldened. Enthusiasm shone from her eyes. 'I've actually picked Photography as one of my GCSE options, I can't wait to start the course. So I'd love some tips from you or—'

'Sure, sure,' Will said distractedly, as Rain flung herself against his leg and demanded to be picked up. 'Hey, watch it, tiger!' he laughed, not noticing that Amelia had stopped talking.

As he leaned down to scoop the toddler into his arms, Maggie noticed two things: one, that she felt a pain like a knitting needle stabbing into her side to see her ex cuddling a small daughter with such tenderness, when his eldest child was trying her hopeful, bravest best to form a relationship with him. The second thing she noticed was that his black hair appeared to have a tiny grey line at its roots. Will dyed his hair? For some reason that cheered her up immensely. Even the knitting-needle stab seemed to ease just a smidge.

'Amelia's got a real talent,' she felt compelled to add, nonetheless. 'She certainly doesn't get it from me!' So just look at Amelia for a moment, you prick. Look at her properly and take her seriously. Would it kill you to put that other child down for five minutes, when we've come all this way?

He turned his gaze on her and, for a terrible moment, Maggie thought she might just have said all of that out loud and blushed furiously.

'So you'll pick her up . . . what, Friday?' he asked, joggling Rain on his hip. She had gorgeously springy russet curls that bounced with every joggle, and giggled at the bouncing, poking him lovingly in the cheek.

'Kiss Daddy,' she announced, leaning in for a rather slobbery face-plant.

Friday? Wait . . . what? Maggie was on holiday mode, where time had already lost its importance as a concept, the days of the week melding into a pleasingly indistinguishable blur, but even so, she was pretty sure Friday was fairly distant from now. 'Isn't it only Monday today, though?' she asked. Will must have got it wrong. Too busy being organic and mindful to check the calendar, she expected. 'I was just assuming she'd be here for one night and then—'

'Please, Mum,' Amelia said immediately. 'Can't I stay till Friday? We do have a whole week of the holiday left after that, so . . .'

Maggie opened her mouth to argue, but the pleading light in her daughter's eyes was impossible to ignore. 'Well . . .' she began. Ever since they had left home, she seemed to have been making one weedy protest after another and losing every time, she realized, her heart sinking. By the time it was Friday, though, half their holiday would be over.

Celeste was scooping dusty-looking tea leaves into a health hazard disguised as a teapot and Maggie's eye was caught by the chunky silver bracelet on her wrist. One that resembled a manacle. Clearly Will wasn't all that original with his gifts.

'They haven't seen in each other for almost ten years,' Celeste said mildly. 'Can't you spare her for four nights?'

Maggie's hackles rose in disbelief. Er . . . Yeah! Correct, Celeste. It *had* been almost ten years. And whose bloody fault was that?

'Believe me, sweetheart, I am *delighted* that Will has finally seen the light and decided to get to know Amelia after so long,' she said through gritted teeth. She could feel Amelia frowning at her – Maggie never usually called people 'sweetheart' or pet names, and this one had come out with a properly sibilant hiss of contempt. 'And about time too! He's missed out on so much over the years, believe me! However, seeing as we are currently on *holiday*, I—'

'Mum, it's fine, don't make a fuss,' Amelia said, and Maggie's words faltered, then died in her throat. Where was the justice in the world, she thought, when her only child was siding with him, with *them*, when for so long Will had been completely absent from the picture? She actually felt as if she might be sick with the sheer wrongness of it all.

Will put his hands up. Like it or not (*not*, thought Maggie), he still had the charisma she had fallen for in the first place. He still had that crooked smile, that insouciant manner; the magnetism that drew people in. Everyone had always wanted to be Will's best friend. 'Listen, I don't want to come between the two of you,' he said. 'We don't argue in this house. Bad for the vibes.' He gave Amelia his special twinkly grin to show he was joking, that he didn't really believe in 'vibes', and Maggie saw her melting a little in adoration. Oh, sod off, Will. 'So if your mum says you have to leave tomorrow, then . . .'

Right. You shit. In other words, he was assigning himself the role of easy-going Good Cop, and leaving Maggie to be the uptight bad guy. Thanks a bunch, mate. Rule number one of parenting: solidarity with other parents. Especially when it came to the woman who had spent the last fourteen years raising your first-born. What a creep he was. It was on the tip of her tongue to tell him to shove his good vibes somewhere extremely painful.

They all knew she had lost, but she gave him a hard, appraising look nonetheless, one that left him in no uncertainty about what she thought. 'Friday it is,' she said, her heart cracking a little as Amelia gave a cheer and clapped her hands together. 'If you've got enough clean clothes to last that long, that is . . . ?'

Amelia rolled her eyes. 'You're so funny, Mum. Bye, then!'

Celeste smiled sweetly, mashing tea leaves in the pot. 'Bye, Maggie. Good to meet you.'

So Maggie was to be dismissed then, just like that, before the tea had even been poured? Well, *fine*. She wanted to go anyway – or rather she needed to, before she did anything embarrassing, like angry crying. 'Bye, love,' she said to Amelia, ignoring Celeste. Her eyes smarted and she gave a quick watery smile before turning for the door.

'Safe journey,' said Will, following her out down the hall. 'Hey,' he added as she reached the front door, then hesitated. For the first time since she'd arrived Maggie sensed a new uncertainty about him; a glimpse of the real Will behind the confident persona. 'Thanks for this. It's really good of you,' he said.

She hoped her resulting snort was suitably contemptuous. 'Yes,' she said. 'It is, isn't it?'

'I know I don't deserve this,' he said. Was that actually a humble note in his voice? He was looking . . . well, kind of shell-shocked actually. As if he was struggling to conflate the beautiful young woman now in his kitchen with the teeny daughter he'd left behind. 'I'm ashamed of myself, Mag. I totally let you down. And Amelia too, obviously.'

She was *not* going to forgive him in a single moment, just because he had discovered his own guilty conscience. However hangdog those glossy brown eyes of his might be. 'Yes,' she said again. 'You did. And you need to tell her that. Make it up to her.'

'I will. I want to,' he said. He sighed, shuffling his feet together in the doorway. 'She seems amazing, by the way. You've done a great job. We really appreciate you letting her stay with us, getting to know the family.'

She wished he hadn't said 'the family' like that. Up until then, she had almost been starting to warm back up to Will, just a tiny bit, remembering all the things she had liked about him – liked very much for a long time. With those two short words, though, it was as if a door had been slammed in her face. The family that neither Maggie nor Amelia belonged to, was what he meant. The family that he had bothered to make a go of.

'Right,' she said, swinging her face away. 'I'll be in touch with Amelia about when to pick her up on Friday, et cetera.'

With that, she walked stiffly back down the drive, feeling him watching her all the way.

God, she's not aged well, she imagined him thinking. *When did Maggie Laine get so old and boring?*

She got into the car, trembling all over. Why, when it was her leaving Amelia now, did she feel as if she was the one who'd been abandoned?

Chapter Twelve

With Lorna's kind maternal gaze fixed on her in concern, Olivia tried to pull herself together. 'I'm finding . . . I'm finding life a bit tough at the moment,' she confessed. She had been on the verge of saying that she was finding motherhood tough, but at the very last second remembered who she was talking to. How crass it would have been of her, how insensitive, to have sat there complaining about being a parent, when Lorna and Roy were sitting opposite her on the twentieth anniversary of their only child's death. Lorna and Roy, who would have given anything to have their son back.

Guilt wormed inside Olivia that she could have driven away from her own boys with such comparative ease yesterday. It had been such a strange moment, though, sitting there on her sofa, clutching her spoiled photograph of Aidan and remembering that summer when everything had changed. And then, noticing the date on her phone, her mouth had dropped open as she worked out that the very next day would be twenty years exactly since the accident, that fateful car journey.

'Oh, Aidan,' she'd gulped, pressing the photo to her heart. Twenty whole years. She couldn't believe it. 'I'm so sorry.'

She had been a different person back then. A girl, still finding her place in the world, with her head full of dreams. Now look at her: a hopeless, hapless, fat housewife. Good for nothing. She wished she could run away to that old life of hers, turn the clock back and do things differently. If only she could start all over again!

Glancing back down at the photo, she had remembered the afternoon it had been taken: how she and Aidan had been mucking about on a boat in the estuary. A perfect summer's day, just after they'd finished their A-levels when the world seemed wide and welcoming, opportunities stretching before them far out to the horizon. Happier times. And now look at his picture – ruined forever.

Then she'd found herself thinking about the moments in the car before he'd died; what she'd said to him. How he'd looked at her. The instant when the wheels went skidding off the tarmac, the sound of her own screams echoing around them, the meaty smack of his head against the steering wheel . . .

She'd whimpered in distress, tearing her gaze away from the photograph, but it was as if his eyes followed her, cold and accusing. *You did that to me,* they said. *It's your fault I'm dead.* She remembered the moment of silence after the impact, as if the night was holding its breath in shock. His terrible staring eyes, fixing her with reproach as she sat beside him screaming. Thank goodness for the paramedic who had eventually pulled the lids gently down, like blinds on dark windows.

Twenty years ago, almost to the day. The past had called out to her, too loud to be ignored.

An hour or so after she'd left, her phone had begun buzzing with texts from Mack, but she couldn't bring herself to open them; she had turned the phone off again after sending a brief *I'm okay* holding message in reply. It wasn't until she'd arrived in Falmouth that evening that she realized she'd left her wedding ring by the kitchen sink, where she'd taken it off to wash up. He was probably imagining the worst – but even so, she just felt numb about the situation: she didn't even miss them. There was white noise in her brain where any normal mother would have been thinking incessantly about her precious children; static where any normal wife would feel concerned about her husband. Olivia just felt too used-up to care any more; too broken and tired.

So no, it was probably best that she didn't mention any of this to Lorna, on reflection. And no, she wouldn't confess in blank emotionless tones that she actually had no desire to go hurrying back to Bristol today; no inclination whatsoever to walk back through her own front door, knowing that she'd be immediately swallowed up in toddler chaos and her own feelings of inadequacy. Right now she couldn't imagine herself ever being able to deal with it again.

'Oh, darling,' said Lorna. You could see the confusion on her face, 'I'm sorry to hear things are difficult. You're not a terrible person, though, whatever's happened. I know you, Olivia, and you're not.'

'Is there anything we can do to help?' asked Roy.

'Not really,' she said. They *didn't* know her, she thought. For one thing, they wouldn't be so sympathetic if they knew what she'd done twenty years ago. But Lorna and Roy were the last people she wanted to hurt. Back when she and Aidan had been an item, Olivia had loved going round to his house for tea or Sunday lunch, because they would both make such a fuss of her, especially Lorna. It was the first time in years that she'd felt properly mothered, and she had drunk it up like someone dying of thirst.

Innate politeness forced her to pull herself together now, remembering that Lorna and Roy did not need to be burdened with her misery, today of all days. 'But thanks anyway.'

'Maybe you just need a break,' Lorna said, her brow furrowed with concern. 'Is there any chance you could take a few days off, recharge your batteries? Because . . .' Then she stopped and looked at Roy. 'I was just thinking: Mawnan's empty, isn't it?'

He nodded. 'I was thinking the same. We've become property tycoons, the pair of us, believe it or not,' he explained to Olivia, then gave a self-deprecatory chuckle. 'Well – I say that, but we're just running a few holiday cottages, that's all. Three altogether, barn conversions that—'

'And we've had a cancellation,' Lorna interjected, before Roy could go off on a tangent. He was rightfully proud of their little lettings business, but give him five minutes and he'd be talking you through the entire process, complete with drawing out the floor plans on a napkin. 'A dear little cottage, minutes away from us, if you want it. All newly decorated. Sea views. Your own kitchen and living room.'

'It's empty until Friday,' Roy put in. 'You'd be doing us a favour, really.'

'You'd be very welcome,' Lorna agreed.

They were both beaming at her, delighted with their own idea. Olivia blinked, unable to respond for a moment as she took in what they were offering. It was peak holiday season and every last guesthouse and B&B in Falmouth would be stuffed to the gills. Where else could she go? A hideaway, a sanctuary, a cottage of her own for a few days would be a million times nicer than sleeping in the car again, facing the music at home or answering tough questions at her dad's place. At Lorna and Roy's holiday cottage she could prolong any big decisions, at least for a short while. She would have privacy. A bed to herself.

'There's even a pool,' Lorna added proudly, as if Olivia needed any more persuading.

Olivia could hardly take it all in. She felt stunned with gratitude that they were willing to scoop her up like this, that they could provide the exact thing she needed. With quiet, empty rooms and the luxury of time to herself, it would be a holiday from real life. God knows she needed one. 'Yes, please,' she said.

Mawnan Cottage turned out to be the loveliest place imaginable. Originally a stable, it was built of stone and still retained its chunky original door, but inside was a haven of cool greys and crisp white, spotlessly clean, with a huge comfortable sofa and a huge comfortable bed. All for her. She became quite overwhelmed as Lorna showed her round. 'I can't – this is too much. At least let me give you some money,' she protested, as they reached the bathroom with its power shower and gleaming bath (with not a squirty toy or Hulk flannel to be seen. She had forgotten such bathrooms even existed).

'Nonsense,' Lorna told her. 'Aidan would want us to help his girlfriend, wouldn't he? Seems daft to leave the place empty anyway. Now then: there's a new supermarket ten minutes out of the village on the other side, so you can stock up with bits and pieces, and you're welcome to use all the facilities . . . Make yourself at home, okay? Relax.'

It was an enormous kindness, of course, but being called 'Aidan's girlfriend' did slightly give Olivia the heebie-jeebies. For the first time since crossing the threshold of the cottage she hesitated, feeling that it was wrong to take advantage of the other woman's generosity. Wondering if Aidan might not rather have had her shooed off the premises, had he been capable of expressing an opinion on the matter.

She tried not to think about that as she went out to buy a few provisions and then, once back in the cottage, ran herself a hot, deep bath full of bubbles. Closing her eyes, she listened to the cry of a seagull through the open window, and the faint comings and goings of other holidaymakers, but it was no good. She couldn't stop thinking about Aidan. 'I'm sorry,' she said into the quiet steamy air after a while. 'I'm so sorry.'

Shutting her eyes, she slid beneath the surface of the trembling water for a moment, feeling tired, so desperately tired. It had been a strange few days. Already Bristol and her home there seemed to have retreated far into the back of her head, while memories of her life here had crowded in, taking up the space. Aidan's face, bloodied and battered, floated into her mind, his eyes the blue of an autumn sky even in death, his expression one of disbelief.

She surged up through the bath-water, cringing and trying to shake the image from her head. Oh God, she thought. What was she doing? What was she doing here?

Chapter Thirteen

'So, what's the dirt then?' said the face on Izzie's phone screen, waggling a suggestive eyebrow.

It was the following morning and Izzie was up in her room, FaceTiming her friend Lily. Having listened to lurid details of Lily's antics with her boyfriend Jordan for some time, the conversation had recently turned to Izzie, and her low rating on the Summer of Yes leaderboard. 'Anything happening with the Sexy Older Man?' Lily asked before Izzie could reply.

Ugh, not this again. 'Don't call him that!' Izzie spluttered. 'You make him sound like a pensioner. And nothing's happening with him, funnily enough. Seeing as he's my *mum's boyfriend* and all. Jesus!'

Lily rolled on some dark-brown lipstick and pouted glossily at the screen. 'Go on. What happened to that bikini selfie anyway? Or even a kiss?' She peered at herself critically. 'What do you think of this colour, by the way?'

'Nice,' said Izzie. 'But I'm so not going to kiss him. That is just not happening, all right?'

And then she heard it. A giggle from outside her bedroom door. The room seemed to lurch around her as she glanced back in horror to see that the door was open a crack and there was a small Seren-sized person lurking, in order to eavesdrop on the conversation. Izzie's stomach plummeted. Shit. How much had she heard?

'Got to go,' she said quickly, ending the call, before leaping off the bed and striding over to the door. 'Hey! Don't spy on me,' she snapped.

Seren didn't seem bothered to have been discovered. She looked excited in fact, hopping from foot to foot, her long hair swinging around her pale face. 'You were talking about kissing,' she said gleefully. She was holding a Sylvanian Families cat in each hand and pushed them together in a grinding clinch. 'Have you got a *boyfriend*? Have you done *sex* with him?'

Izzie felt like throttling her. 'None of your business, you little shit,' she growled before she could stop herself, at which point Seren's eyes became big and round and her expression went from gleeful to positively thrilled.

'That's a *very* bad word,' she said severely. 'You said a bad word to me.' And then she turned and was hurrying off downstairs as if she couldn't wait to broadcast the news.

'Izzie said a bad word to me,' she announced at the top of her voice. 'And she was talking about *kissing*. I heard her!'

'No, I wasn't,' Izzie blustered, thudding after her. 'Stop being an annoying brat.'

'And she called me an annoying brat,' Seren added immediately. 'Daddy?' She had reached the ground floor by now and went racing into the kitchen. 'Daddy! Izzie said I was an annoying brat and said a bad word *and* was talking about kissing. *And* she said—'

'And *you* were eavesdropping on a private phone conversation between me and my friend,' Izzie yelled hotly. The last thing she needed was for Seren to work out exactly who they had been talking about and dob her in for that, too. Had the little girl actually heard Izzie say the words 'He's my mum's boyfriend'? If so, it was surely only a matter of time before she put two and two together and rumbled Izzie to the adults. And how utterly excruciating would *that* be?

Storming into the kitchen, Izzie saw that George was washing up while Em was tracing a route on a map at the kitchen table. Jack, meanwhile, was finishing a mid-morning bowl of cornflakes with enough milk to have turned it into soup. They all looked round at the noisy entrance of the two girls.

'Whoa,' cried George, hands in the sink. 'Seren, calm down and stop shouting.'

'Izzie, what's going on?' Em asked, her finger still on the map.

'I want to know about the kissing aspect,' Jack teased. 'Has someone got a mystery boyfriend? Or girlfriend, come to that?'

'Oh, shut up, Jack,' said Izzie, her hands curling into impotent fists as the blood rushed to her face.

'I think she said it was *somebody else's boyfriend*,' Seren said, head cocked slightly, eyes glittering, but her face unreadable.

Oh, crap. Did that mean she *had* heard?

'No way! Izzie, you bad girl,' said Jack, smirking. 'What happened to sisterhood?'

'Yes, I hope that's not true,' Em said with a frown.

Izzie thought she might throw up. Christ, if only Mum knew the half of it. But what did *Seren* know? Had she heard Izzie's actual words or just the boyfriend bit? 'It's nobody's business!' she shrieked, whirling out of the room, trembling with embarrassment.

'*And* she said "shit",' she heard Seren add with a note of triumph as she pounded back upstairs again. 'That's a bad word, isn't it, Daddy?'

'I hope you *didn't* say that in front of a child, Isabel,' her mum's voice followed her up, disapproval loud and clear with every syllable.

Izzie said several even worse words under her breath as she threw herself back on her bed, punching the pillow a few times. 'AAAAARRGGHHH!' she screamed into the mattress.

Aaarrgh, thought Em, rolling her eyes and mouthing 'Sorry' to George. Why were their kids so intent on sabotaging this holiday? First it had been her two, swigging alcohol down at the harbour in Falmouth, lucky not to have ended up in the nearest police station following the gallery debacle. Then, first thing that morning, Seren had made a comment over breakfast about hearing some funny noises in the night. 'It sounded like *you*, Emma, saying, *Ooh ooh ooh!*' she had said, wide-eyed, within everyone's earshot. Izzie had groaned. Jack had looked distinctly revolted. George, meanwhile, had laughed unhelpfully as Em had to think fast and explain: Ah yes, that was probably when she'd stubbed her toe, nothing to worry about. And now the two girls had had a bust-up, and Izzie had gone off, slamming doors in her wake, just in case anyone was in doubt as to her feelings. Fabulous!

It's going to be a great holiday and everyone will get on brilliantly, she remembered herself saying to the mirror back home, channelling her wise friend Kathy. Well, she'd got that one wrong.

'Aren't you going to tell her *off*?' Seren was demanding now, hand on hip. She had luscious pink lips, Seren, and the bottom one was currently sticking far out in extreme indignation.

'Well, if you were eavesdropping on a private conversation, then I can see why Izzie got annoyed with you,' Em replied. In other words, no, she wasn't about to tell her off. Not that she would spell *that* out quite so specifically. 'So don't do it again, okay?'

'I'm sure Izzie will say sorry to you later, poppet,' George said, glancing over at Em as he put the frying pan in the draining rack.

Jack snorted. 'I'm sure she won't,' he muttered, ambling over towards the door.

'Er – bowl in the dishwasher, please,' Em reminded him, feeling her fuse becoming shorter by the second. 'Anyway. Who wants to go to the beach today? I've found one that sounds lovely. Come and see, Seren,' she added, holding up her iPad, where she'd found the description online.

Seren didn't move, though. 'I want her to say sorry now,' she whined, leaning against George at the sink. 'Daddy,' she prompted when he didn't react. 'I want her to say sorry *now*. She upset me.'

'Here we are,' Em persisted, reading aloud from the iPad. 'Gyllyngvase Beach is one of only five beaches in Cornwall to be awarded the Blue Flag. There's great swimming and rockpooling, beach volleyball nets, a café . . . Ooh, and sometimes you can see dolphins, apparently.' She read a little further. 'Ah. If you have binoculars, it says. Anyone brought any binoculars? No, me neither. Well, anyway, we can sit on the sand

and imagine the dolphins out there, which will be nearly as good, won't it?'

'Not really,' said Jack, kicking the dishwasher door shut, which sent everything rattling inside. He'd been in a proper grump since yesterday, when bad-influence Amelia had gone off to Devon on an impromptu visit to see her dad, or something. (Unlike her son, Em wasn't terribly sorry about *that* little departure.)

'*And*,' she went on, ignoring this unhelpful interruption, 'it's only a few miles away, so there's no boring long car journey. We can make up a picnic, grab our swimming things and towels – and Bob's your uncle. One fantastic day coming up! Who's with me?'

Jack had sloped out of the room and Seren was staring petulantly at the lino, but at least George was twinkling his eyes and smiling. 'Right behind you, Captain,' he said, with a soapsud-speckled mock-salute.

'Ooh, good, I hope so,' she replied flirtatiously, feeling marginally better. She got to her feet and then bawled, 'Going in fifteen minutes' up the stairs to her bad-tempered teens. 'Brush your teeth, find your swimming things, shout me any sandwich requests. Let's get this show on the road!'

Em put every single fun thing she could think of in the car – cricket set, Frisbee, buckets, spades, flippers, snorkels, you name it – and tried to gee herself up as they set off soon afterwards. Who didn't love a day at the beach? Everyone would get over their differences and enjoy themselves, she told herself bracingly.

It felt as if the universe was on their side for once, at least: there was an easy parking space on arrival at Gyllyngvase, the clouds obligingly melted away from the sky as they stepped onto the sand, and there was a busy, happy atmosphere with people enjoying themselves, but not so many crowds that they couldn't find a good spot to lay down their towels and beach mats. Perfect choice, Em, she congratulated herself. Maybe, just maybe, this could end up being one of those rare days when everything just clicked smoothly into place, as if all part of some very carefully and expertly engineered design.

George suggested a game of Frisbee and Izzie and Jack were both enthusiastic, while Em seized the chance for some bonding with Seren by helping her make sandcastles. Kneeling beside the little girl on the warm sand, the sun casting freckles on her shoulder-blades, Em felt a new optimism wash through her. This was going well, she told herself proudly, scooping sand into a red bucket. Everyone was having a nice time. She and George were bonding with each other's children. They would look back on this day as the turning point of the holiday, after which—

'My mummy is prettier than you.'

Ouch. Was Em's deep-seated paranoia making her hear

voices now? 'Sorry, what, darling?' she asked, taken aback. She turned the full bucket upside down and plopped it onto the sand. 'Do you want to bang the top with your spade to make sure the sand doesn't stick?' she asked pleasantly. Surely she'd misheard. Of course she had!

'My mummy is really pretty. And kind. She makes *very* good sandcastles,' Seren said, her face unnervingly blank as ever. '*And*,' she went on, with a glance at Em's pale dimpled thighs, 'she's not fat.'

'Oh,' said Em. Double-ouch. 'Well, that's nice,' she managed to say evenly. *Do not rise to it.* 'Good for Mummy. But we're going to make some great sandcastles ourselves now, aren't we? We're going to make an absolute palace!' She gave her best and kindest smile as she patted the bottom of the bucket and then slowly lifted it, to reveal the moulded sand shape beneath. 'Ooh, that's come out well,' she said, feeling rather pleased with herself. Let it not be said that Em Hughes was an amateur sandcastle-maker, she thought with a flash of triumph. She'd certainly had a few more years practice than . . . 'What are you doing?' she yelped in alarm as Seren, without warning, picked up a yellow plastic spade and smashed in Em's sandcastle, with all the ruthless abandon of a psychopath.

'*I* want to do the castles,' Seren said, chopping the blade of her spade through the sandy wreckage.

'Right,' Em said weakly, unsure what else to say. She

actually felt quite taken aback at the ferocity Seren had just displayed. *Don't take it personally,* she told herself. *Cut her some slack. She's testing boundaries, that's all. Seeing what she can get away with.* 'I'm going to build a moat,' she announced after a moment, deciding to act as if the sandcastle-pulverizing hadn't just occurred. 'What are you going to build next?'

From where they were sitting on the sand, they could see the Frisbee game in full swing and both turned their heads as Izzie's whoops of triumph drifted over on the sea breeze. Em smiled to see her daughter doing this strange little victory dance with the orange Frisbee held aloft, before she sent it skimming across to her brother. 'They're having fun,' she commented, when Seren didn't answer her question.

Seren had a rather tight look about her face as she began arranging a group of Sylvanian Families foxes on the coolbox, then dumped spadefuls of sand into a purple bucket. 'My mummy is in another country now, because she has a very important job,' she said grandly.

Great, back to everyone's favourite subject: George's wonderful ex-wife. 'Wow, that's exciting,' Em replied, marking out the edges of her moat. 'What job do you think *you* might want to do when you're older? Let me guess . . . A lion tamer!'

'No,' said Seren, and just for a moment, Em thought she was on the verge of provoking a giggle for once. A scowl was forthcoming instead, though. 'That's not a proper job.'

'An astronaut, then. A robot designer. Um . . . An ice-cream tester.' Her own children had loved this game back when they were little, coming up with their own wild fantastical ideas amidst gales of laughter. Not Seren, apparently.

'No! Those are silly jobs.' She sat back on her haunches and eyed Em with a patronizing air, as if she was far too old for such childish nonsense. 'I need some shells,' she announced.

'Right,' said Em, whose ideas of cutting children a bit of slack did not extend to allowing them to boss her about like a minion. 'You'd better get some then, hadn't you?'

'You get them,' Seren countered.

Over my dead body, love. 'I'm busy digging my moat,' Em said sweetly. 'Why don't you look for some in the rock pools over there? I bet you can find some really cool ones.'

Seren's nostrils flared. 'My mum would find the best shells,' she said.

Charlotte was obviously a woman of many talents. 'I'm sure she would,' Em replied, deadpan. She glanced longingly at the folding chairs they'd brought, wishing she could retreat into her novel now, thus escaping this interminable conversation about Seren's amazing, highly skilled mother who was better than Em in every way. She turned back just in time to see Jack leaping athletically to get the Frisbee further down the beach. 'Good catch!' she yelled as he snatched it out of the air. George went over and clapped him on the back and

Em smiled at the scene, but Seren meanwhile had a face like thunder. '*My* daddy,' she growled under her breath.

Okay, so not everyone was having a perfect day on the beach, Em thought wearily. But she wouldn't let one small mardy person spoil everything. Absolutely not. 'Ah, here's Izzie,' she said, as her daughter appeared, apparently in need of a hair bobble. 'Izzie, do me a favour, love, and take Seren for a shell hunt, will you? Just for two minutes? Thank you. See who can find the best one.'

Izzie glanced back longingly at the Frisbee game. 'Do I have to? Can't she go on her own?'

'It appears not,' Em replied before she could stop herself. 'Go on,' she cajoled. 'Make an effort, please. Be nice.'

Izzie shot Seren a murderous glare, but acquiesced. 'Come on then,' she muttered to the younger girl.

'Daddy Fox is coming with us,' said Seren, plucking him from her little woodland line-up, while the other figures stared blankly on.

'Whoopee-doo,' growled Izzie, stalking away.

Em sank gladly into her chair and retrieved her sand-speckled book. The sun was dancing on the sea in front of her. Jack and George were shouting with laughter as they attempted diving Frisbee-catches nearby. The girls would hopefully forge a friendship over some rock-pool discoveries. Meanwhile she could indulge in what the glossy mags called 'me-time', which in Em's eyes meant doing bugger all for anyone else. For a change.

Barely five minutes later, though, a high-pitched shriek ripped through the air. A high-pitched shriek, moreover, that came from the direction of the rock pools. Em whipped her head round just in time to see Seren clambering out of a pool, dripping wet and in floods of tears. Oh Lord.

Snatching up a towel, she went running straight over. George too charged across at once. They just needed the red swimming togs to go the full *Baywatch*. 'Are you okay?' he called to his daughter.

Seren stumbled towards him. 'She pushed me,' the little girl accused through gasping sobs. 'She pushed me in!'

Izzie looked stricken. 'What? No, I didn't,' she cried hotly, meeting Em's eye. 'I did *not*!'

'*And* she said she didn't want to collect stupid sh-sh-shells with me,' Seren sobbed. 'She said it was babyish and she wanted to play Fr-Fr-Frisbee!'

This did, admittedly, have the ring of truth about it and Em felt her face suffuse with heat. Izzie had been peevishly reluctant about looking after Seren, but all the same, she wasn't the sort of girl who pushed little children around. Was she? 'Did you say those things?' Em demanded of Izzie, while draping the towel around the younger girl's shoulders.

Izzie's face reddened. 'Well – yeah, but I didn't *push* her. She's lying!'

'Hey,' George gave her a stern look. 'That's a very serious thing to say, young lady.'

'I'd say it was pretty serious for someone to make a false accusation too,' Izzie retorted, glaring.

George's face stiffened as he bent over his daughter. 'All right, Noodle,' he soothed, wrapping the towel more tightly around her. 'You're all right. Did you bump anywhere? Tell me what hurts.'

'I bumped my head,' Seren said plaintively. 'And my leg hurts a *lot*. There's blood!' She broke into fresh sobs. 'Daddy Fox got wet too,' she sobbed.

'He's probably drowned,' Izzie muttered meanly.

'Iz—' warned Em, frowning.

'I want Mummy!' howled Seren.

Em and Izzie looked at each other. 'I didn't push her,' Izzie said again, folding her arms across her chest. 'You do believe me, don't you, Mum?'

Em hesitated, feeling George's eyes on her too. *Did* she believe Izzie? The two girls had already had one spat that morning, after all. 'I didn't see what happened,' she said after a moment. This is what it must be like being a politician, she thought, her mind scrabbling for the right words. The most delicate of balancing acts required, to keep everyone sweet. 'If there was a push, then I'm sure it was an accident and nothing deliberate, so—'

'There *wasn't* a push at all. She's making it up!' Izzie said.

'That's enough,' said George in a voice Em didn't recognize, as he scooped Seren into his arms and began carrying her towards their towels and bags. 'Come on, poppet,' they heard him say as he walked away. 'We can dry Daddy Fox back at the house, don't worry.'

Em opened her mouth, then shut it again, feeling miserable. And just like that, a wall had sprung up between her and George. This was the problem with mixing up different families, she thought to herself, sliding a hand into Izzie's in a show of solidarity as the two of them set off in silent pursuit. When it came to contradicting accounts, like now, there was always going to be a taking of sides; you would be in your own child's corner every single time. As had just been demonstrated. At least when she and Dom had been together, there'd been no automatic tribalism; they could judge each situation fairly without the tug of loyalties clouding their vision.

'Don't worry, it'll blow over,' she said to Izzie in a low voice. 'There's no harm done, I'm sure.'

Famous last words. With Seren still sobbing and blood dripping onto the sand, George decreed that they should go back and clean her up. 'She might need a stitch, but let's see how her leg's looking, once we're back and able to assess it properly,' he said.

Em felt her spirits plummet. A stitch? If Seren ended up

in A&E – or, worse, came back from this holiday with a scar – Charlotte would never forgive George *or* her, especially if it was Em's child to blame.

The mood in the car was sour, with Seren still sniffling tearfully, and Izzie scowling. George had gone all serious and a little bit cold, and Em felt worse and more responsible by the second. If she hadn't been so quick to fob Seren off on Izzie, this would never have happened. Why had she been so petty and stubborn about not collecting shells with the little girl? She had behaved abominably!

Back at the cottage, they had barely got through the front door before Seren was saying, 'Phone Mummy. Phone Mummy!' again and again. 'You promised, Daddy! I want to talk to her!'

'Oh, great, so you can lie to *her*, too?' Izzie muttered, scowling, but unfortunately her voice carried to George, who gave her a frosty look.

'Izzie, that's enough. She's only seven and she's upset,' he snapped, as they trooped inside. 'Have a bit more sympathy.' He turned back to Seren, his features softening. 'Let's get that leg cleaned up first, lovely.'

'She's so mean to me!' wept Seren, tears pouring copiously now. 'Just because I heard what she said. About kissing a man's boyfriend.'

'WHAT?' yelped Jack, honking with laughter. 'Kissing a man's boyfriend?'

'Oh, shut up, Seren, you little—'

'IZZIE!' roared Em as Izzie lunged towards the girl. 'That's quite enough.'

Izzie's face clenched and for a moment Em feared she was about to turn on *her* – she'd always had a hot temper, right from when she was tiny and her favourite word had been 'NO!' – but Izzie merely swung away, eyes glittering, and pounded upstairs.

Em tracked down the first-aid kit and George began dabbing some of the sand away from the scrape on Seren's leg. And it *was* only a scrape, thank goodness. It had already stopped bleeding, leaving a graze where the top layer of skin had come off. 'There, all done,' George said, sticking a plaster on top. 'I think you'll live.'

'I'll set the picnic lunch up on the table,' Em said in relief, remembering that Izzie's moods were particularly volatile when she was hungry. Maybe they could all calm down now, put the drama behind them and eat some sandwiches, which, hopefully, hadn't become too cardboard-like since she'd made them earlier that morning.

'I still want Mummy,' Seren pouted, apparently not in any hurry to relinquish her spot in the limelight. Had this been her own daughter, there would have been an end to the saga now, Em thought privately: she would have been brisk and firm; enough was enough, they would just move along. George was obviously a lot nicer and more patient a parent than she was, though, because he wearily acquiesced to Seren's demands and began setting up Skype.

Oh dear! Is my baby safe there with such hoodlums? Em imagined Charlotte asking George in concern. She hoped George wouldn't let slip the tale about the underage drinking and crap shoplifting, just to pile on the bad impression. Bloody hell!

As George waited for the call to connect, Em ducked away before she could see Charlotte's completely gorgeous, luscious face on the screen – not least because she was wearing her denim cut-offs and an ancient striped FatFace T-shirt that had gone comfortably soft and baggy. *My mummy is prettier than you,* she remembered Seren saying. Yeah, all right. No need to rub it in.

But – 'She's not answering, poppet,' George said after a few moments. 'She must be in a meeting or something.'

Seren sighed, her face still wet with tears. Seeing her so dispirited, clutching her bedraggled fox figure, Em felt a pang of sympathy for her. It couldn't be easy, being on holiday with much older children. Of course Seren wanted her dad to herself. Of course she missed her mum.

'Come on, lovey,' she said kindly, putting the sandwiches onto a plate. 'You'll be all right. We can give your fox a blast with the hairdryer later, dry him out. Or you could find a nice warm sunny spot for him. Do you want to help me with the lunch things now?'

Seren merely prodded at a rather grey, unlovely tuna-fish sandwich. 'Yuck. This is squidgy,' she said, at which point Em felt her patience and sympathy start to evaporate again.

'Can you wash your hands, please, before you start poking around in the lunch,' she said, unable to help her voice tightening with irritation. She thought wretchedly of Izzie, fuming upstairs no doubt, and vowed to take her up a cup of tea in a minute. Maybe suggest that the two of them have a Netflix binge that afternoon or something. Christ! Being a parent was hard at the best of times, but ever since they'd arrived in Cornwall she felt as if she'd been getting it all wrong. She was trying to play two different roles – mum vs girlfriend – and it didn't seem possible to combine them with any success. By avoiding conflict with George, she had let her daughter down. Did everyone find this sort of situation so hard?

Glancing round, she saw that Seren was still investigating the sandwiches, peeling the tops off to check the contents, and Em had to bite back a sharp telling-off. *Not now. Don't make things worse.* 'Hey, I've got a job for you,' she managed to say with forced brightness instead. 'Could you wash these strawberries for me?' She dumped the punnet into the colander and pushed it along the table towards Seren. 'Then we can whip up some cream and have them with the scones. Yum!'

Thudding footsteps were heard overhead – hopefully

Izzie coming down again, lured by the prospect of lunch, Em thought – but before she could go and check, Seren had dropped the colander of plump scarlet strawberries all over the floor. 'Whoops,' she said and Em had to bite her tongue as she crawled around retrieving them.

It was just an accident, she told herself, grabbing a cloth to wipe up the juicy red smears that now adorned the flagstones. Accidents happened. 'Don't worry,' she said. 'I'll do this – how about you go and shout to Izzie and Jack that lunch is ready instead?'

She and George exchanged a look as Seren left the room. 'This is going well,' he remarked, then came towards her and took her in his arms. 'Kids, eh? Shall we just turf them out in the nearest forest, leave them to it?'

She laughed, grateful for the reassurance of having him hold her, his warm solid body telling her, *We're still a team, you and me.* 'Don't tempt me,' she said. 'Not least because I'd quite like to get you all to myself for a while.' He slid his hands round to her bottom and they kissed one another for a delicious few minutes, Em pressed against the worktop with the colander of strawberries digging against her back.

But then –

'Izzie's not there,' said Seren, sounding agitated as she burst back into the room. 'She's gone.'

Em pulled away from George. 'What do you mean, she's gone? She must be in the bathroom.' Nevertheless a queasy feeling rippled through her and she ran past them both. 'Izzie? Izzie, where are you?'

No reply came. Jack tramped down the stairs, lifting his headphones off one ear to say, 'Did you shout for me?'

'No, I . . . Where's your sister?' Em thought about the clumping footsteps she'd heard minutes earlier, how Izzie had never actually appeared. She remembered how upset her daughter had been, the hurt look on her face after George had snapped at her on their way in.

Jack shrugged. 'I dunno. Why are you freaking out?'

Em didn't answer, just ran to the downstairs loo, flung the door open – nope – then had a thought and rushed to the hallway where they'd been keeping their bikes. 'She's taken her bike. She's gone off somewhere,' she said. Her heart was going into overdrive. Oh, help. Poor, upset Izzie, feeling as if no one was on her side. Where was she? Where had she gone? She grabbed her phone and dialled Izzie's number, only to hear it ringing upstairs in the house. 'She hasn't even taken her phone with her,' she said, anxiety rising.

'I'm sure she hasn't gone far,' George said calmly, but Em was in no mood for calm.

'I'm going out to look for her,' she said, voice trembling. For a split-second she found herself wishing that Dom was there; Dom who would take charge and tell her not to worry, who was always able to talk Izzie out of a snit.

'Wait, shall I—' George started saying behind her, but Em was too panicked to let him finish the sentence.

'You stay here in case she comes back,' she said. 'I need to find her.' If she hadn't been canoodling in the kitchen with George just now, if she'd gone up to Izzie to comfort her the moment it had occurred to her, this wouldn't be happening. Priorities, Em! Where are your priorities? Her heart still pounding, she snatched up the car keys and whirled out of the house, slamming the door behind her.

Chapter Fourteen

Earlier that morning Olivia had surfaced into wakefulness like a diver swimming up from the depths, a traveller returning from distant shores. She had *slept*, she marvelled, lying flat on her back in the gorgeously comfortable bed and staring up at the old beamed ceiling above. She had actually slept, for the whole night without a single disturbance. It felt . . . weird. Good, but wrong, as if it had been at someone else's expense.

Yeah, your husband's expense, and your kids', a sarcastic voice in her head pointed out. Do you think they slept well without you last night? Well, do you?

She blinked and rubbed her eyes, jangled fragments of her dream slipping from her mind. Something about giving birth, the shocking sensation of a small warm baby between her legs. How he'd cried out when he was taken away. She shook her head, not wanting to think about any of that, revelling instead in the strangeness of not having to throw the covers off and immediately run to attend to someone's yelled demands. She didn't have to make anyone's breakfast or attempt to squeeze squirming, sausagey boy limbs into items of clothing or sort the never-ending laundry or . . .

She shushed her mind, stopping the thoughts before they could whirl into an exhausting list. Before she could press the bruise of being here and not there. Misplaced. Dispossessed. She wouldn't think about Mack and the boys, or what might be happening at home. They could recede into the distance for a while until she was ready to conjure them back up, she decided. For the time being she would lie here, her head sinking into the soft pillows, the duvet protecting her from the rest of the world. It was all she could manage right now.

Some time later, after a blissful shower, she put on clean clothes and dried her hair. Even through her numbness, she could recognize that doing these things in peace and quiet felt pretty amazing. A holiday from reality. At this rate, she would never go back. *Don't think about that*, she reminded herself.

Toast, hot and buttery, came next, along with a cup of coffee that she would actually get to drink all the way to the bottom for once. Plus the simple pleasure of merely sitting still at the kitchen table, just breathing in and out, whilst doing absolutely nothing. Watching idly as a family in another cottage trooped out laden with a windbreak and picnic bag, the littlest girl holding buckets and spades. Listening calmly as two seagulls duked it out in aerial combat, their harsh battle-cries carrying to her through the open window. She felt like a character in an arcade game, gradually being powered back up to full strength. Perhaps because of this, she took a deep breath and switched on her phone, braced for the bombardment of messages she knew she was in for.

Ping ping ping ping ping. The noise of so many notifications tumbling forward onto the screen was an accusation in itself. All from Mack, all saying pretty much the same thing. *What the hell? Where are you? Ring me!*

Olivia closed her eyes briefly as the words started to crowd in around her head like angry faces. Then she typed a reply, only marginally longer than the first one she'd sent: *I'm fine. Sorry.* She pressed Send, then switched the phone off again fast before Mack could ring her, before she had to think about the boys asking, 'Where's Mummy?' in puzzlement. Her heart pounded and she felt the toast churn greasily in her stomach as their confused little faces swam up anyway. Oh God, what had she gone and done? What was *wrong* with her?

Her head in her hands, she found herself breathing raggedly as if she'd been running or in a fight. Now she was imagining the mums at the Stay and Play sessions she sometimes took the boys to; the judgement in their expressions as they discussed her disappearance. 'She did *what*? Just left them and drove off? What kind of mother does *that*?'

Mouths would be pursed, eyebrows lowered. 'Always thought there was something a bit odd about her. Didn't you? Something not right.'

Stop. Stop it! She put her arms around herself for a moment, as if she might break into pieces. Was this how her mother had felt? Had she sat alone tormenting herself with similar guilt and recriminations? Olivia wished she could somehow speak to her, woman-to-woman, and say, *Okay, I get it now. I'm in that place too.* It was not a good place, though. She felt terrible about everything.

She made another coffee and tried to push away her thoughts again, turn the white noise back up in order to block out the world. Deep breaths. The boys were safe with Mack. She had told him she was okay, which might stop him worrying so much and sending out the search parties. And, she reminded herself, this was the first real time she'd had to herself in three and a half years. Surely she was allowed a day or two to take a breather?

Face forward, her dad had been fond of saying when times were tough. Face forward and find the light. She had the whole day at her disposal. The sun was shining. So what should she do first?

A short while later Olivia was on the road, with the uncanny feeling that she had slipped down a wormhole and gone back twenty years in the blink of an eye. It was all so familiar, yet changed. She knew these streets so well that their maps were imprinted on her mind. She still dreamed about being here sometimes. And now she was back in person again for the first time in years.

After Aidan had died, life in Falmouth had become unbearable. How could she have stayed? Heartache had sent her away as soon as possible, and she'd gone to Bristol to take a business degree (eventually) and build a new life. She had returned to Cornwall for occasional weekends and at Christmas to see her dad and Gail, but steadfastly avoided the old haunts from her teenage years as too painful to revisit.

It had come as a surprise, then, to return to Marco's Café with Lorna and Roy yesterday and not feel the maelstrom of anguish she'd expected. Sure, it had been an emotional occasion and they'd all been thinking about Aidan, but the physical space, the actual being there, hadn't bothered Olivia at all. In fact there had been something surprisingly nice about going back. So many good memories of the place had flashed through her head, like a slideshow: the rainy afternoons she'd spent with Aidan and their friends, leaning against him in one of her black mohair jumpers with the sleeves pulled up over her hands on winter days, leafing through the music papers and talking about all the important topics of the hour – the new bands on the scene, the play someone was acting in, hair dye, politics, becoming vegetarian . . . And there had been the laughter too. The feeling that she belonged in a gang. She had forgotten all of those nice things, she realized.

As a child, her favourite toy had been a wooden marble run that once belonged to her dad: blocks that you built into towers, with chutes and runways attached with hooks to form a course for the racing marbles to whizz down. Sometimes you'd set your marbles rolling – her favourite was one with a pistachio-green twist in the middle, like an unblinking cat's eye – only for them to come to a premature halt, clicking together like a string of beads at a badly positioned link. You'd have to go back and reset the piece, pushing it more firmly into its hook so that the path was smooth.

It had occurred to her last night, moments before she slipped into blissful deep slumber, that maybe you could do this with life too – go back and sort out the obstacle. Reset the course. Maybe while she was here she could revisit some of her other special teenage places. Turn the trip into . . . not a pilgrimage, as such, but certainly something respectful and meaningful. A small, private tour that said, *I remember you. I remember us, I remember life here, for better or worse.* There might be some comfort to be had from walking in her own steps once more, twenty years on, and seeing things anew through adult eyes. Perhaps she could even lay a few ghosts to rest as well.

First stop: the yellow-painted house on Bar Terrace where her friend Nina had lived. It had been something of a party house, due to the cellar where their friends' band had practised and the fact that Nina's parents were fantastically laidback about all the cider-drinking and smoking that had gone on down there. It was also where she and Aidan had had their first kiss at a New Year's party when they were sixteen, out in the garden near the shed, with fireworks exploding above their heads. The smell of cordite and alcohol, stars spangling the velvety dark like fairy lights. The start of something magical.

Sitting on the wall now, Olivia allowed herself the pleasure of some happy memories. She'd been shy and giggly back then, laughing with embarrassment when he told her she was beautiful, because she didn't know how to take a compliment. 'I mean it,' he said, just as people started shouting the countdown to midnight. TEN! NINE! EIGHT! 'Let's kiss on "one",' he'd suggested boldly, and suddenly she wasn't shy any more; excited instead as the numbers decreased. THREE! TWO! ONE! Her first kiss! And then . . . HAPPY NEW YEAR! Fireworks were zooming and bursting, tearing up the dark sky with crackles and bangs. Their friends were all hugging each other and snogging, and someone was trying and failing to remember the words to 'Auld Lang Syne'.

'Happy New Year,' Aidan said to her with a grin before they kissed again.

'Two kisses in two years,' she'd joked, feeling fizzy and

dizzy, as if rockets and bangers were shooting all over her body as well as up in the sky. Aidan Brearley had kissed her!

Good times, she thought now, remembering the cold dark night, frost on the car windscreens as he walked her home later, hand-in-hand, both of them wondering what the new year would bring. Optimistic times. 'You were a bloody good kisser,' she said quietly now into the warm summer air. 'I haven't forgotten, you know.'

Next on her little tour was their old sixth-form college, out towards Kergilliack; really the first place where she had felt it was okay to be herself, after years of doubt. Secondary school had been an anxious period for her; she'd felt weighted down with the confusion and self-prescribed guilt of her mum having vanished, and had not felt able to care about making friends or studying or trying to get into any school teams. But at college it was as if her time had finally come – she had clicked with a few people in her classes: Nina, Beth and Spencer; she enjoyed the subjects she had chosen to study, and had discovered the excellent trinity of loud music, black eyeliner and crimped hair, assembling a whole new identity for herself. The world began to open up beyond the estate where she lived, to reveal bright and exciting horizons. All of a sudden she had started feeling upbeat about what the future might hold.

She walked around the buildings now, trying to orient herself, almost able to smell the chips from the cafeteria, the patchouli oil she and her friends had sprinkled on their hair, feeling the ghostly memory of a rucksack of library books on Tsarist and Communist Russia thumping weightily against her back. If her home life had left her feeling lost, it was here that she had found herself again.

Aidan had enjoyed sixth form too; maths and physics were his favourite subjects and he dreamed of being an engineer, leaving a legacy of beautiful constructions around the world. He could talk at length and with great enthusiasm about hydraulics and suspension, the beauty of geodesic domes, the science of pendulums, his hands flying around as he described and explained. Picturing his animated face made her smile now, but she was wistful too, because it had been from a time when they were so mad about each other, so completely entwined. Before she had been the one to oscillate like a pendulum herself, in fact, swinging uncertainly between Aidan and Pete Westgate, the guy in her history class with the brownest eyes she had ever seen.

One thing at a time, she begged her memory as it began peeling open the part of the story she most would have liked to remain closed. Don't start getting ahead of yourself.

She gave the college one last appreciative look, her hand on the gate. 'We were happy here, weren't we?' she murmured. 'Before it all went wrong.'

And then she went back to her car and drove away. *Keep it together*, she said under her breath.

Olivia had been meaning to head into town next, to the bar where she and Pete had met up that fateful day, but her subconscious must have had other ideas, because she realized after a few moments that she had missed the turn and was in fact heading in the opposite direction, towards the stretch of road where Aidan had died. The steering wheel wobbled under her hands as this occurred to her. Oh gosh. Was she ready for that? Could she really bear to go back?

In the days leading up to the accident, a prickly sort of mood had settled on her. Since the afternoon in the pub with Pete, it was as if a filter had dropped down before her eyes and she was suddenly seeing things in a new light. Aidan was irritating her in ways that she had never previously considered, for starters. He was so sensible. So reliable! Would it kill him to be spontaneous once in a while? Rebel against his nicey-nice parents and the world?

Driving along now, thinking about this made her want to turn right round and scuttle back for the safety of Lorna's cottage, where she could hide under the duvet until the memories receded again. Because this was the terrible twist in the tail, the horrible guilty secret she had never ever told anyone – not even Mack, not even her brother. She had buried it in her mind for so long that she was scared of what might happen if she began excavating.

She was getting close to the spot.

'Aidan, I've been thinking . . .' she had blurted out that night in the car as he drove her home. They had been to see a band in Truro and he was driving them back, because – being sensible and thoughtful – he had been drinking orange juice all night and – being hard-working and practical – he had saved up enough money from his Saturday job, plus birthday and Christmas, to have bought a car a couple of months earlier. A deeply uncool white Renault 5, which still smelled of an old lady's handbag, but it was his pride and joy.

Oh, Aidan. If she had just kept her mouth shut. If she had just kept her head!

The coroner had recorded a verdict of accidental death. The local newspaper had described it as a tragedy, with the chief reporter at the time calling for safety barriers to be put up at the side of the road. *We must never allow a senseless accident like this to happen in our town again*, he had written at the start of a passionate think-piece, alongside a picture of himself, stern-faced, standing at the edge of the road where it had happened.

No notice had been taken of his words, by the look of things, because she was approaching the bend now, for the first time in twenty years, and it all looked exactly the same. No barriers. No warning signs. Tears smarted in Olivia's eyes as memories bombarded her. 'Is he okay? Is he okay?' she had screamed at the paramedics when they finally came to cut them out of the mangled vehicle. Even though she knew the answer. Even though she'd been lying there beside Aidan in the wreckage and his face had already become quite waxy. Quite cold.

The thing was, only she knew the truth: that he wouldn't have died if she hadn't been sitting there next to him. It was all her fault.

She pulled over in the next lay-by and lost herself in a storm of weeping.

Some time later Olivia wiped her puffy red eyes, blew her nose and swigged from an ancient bottle of water that she found in the passenger footwell. Okay. Enough crying. What right did she have to cry when it came to Aidan, anyway?

Planning to head back to the cottage, she started the engine and drove away, but once she was on the other side of town, she realized she was approaching Swanpool, her and Aidan's favourite beach, a place they had both loved. Perhaps she had the energy for one last stop after all.

The beach was always heaving with tourists in summer, but she and Aidan had gone there loads of times in winter too with their friends, lighting big fires on the sand at night-time and playing music, or breaking into derelict beach huts and telling ghost stories by torchlight. She smiled to herself briefly, recalling how spooky it had been, with the boys surreptitiously making scratching sounds against the wooden boards to unnerve the girls, and how jumpy they had become as a result. A gust of wind had banged the door suddenly, right at the tensest moment of one story, and they'd practically screamed the place down, clutching at each other in hysterical fright.

She would go there again, she decided, slowing so that she wouldn't miss the turn-off. Remember the summer that Spencer had worked at the ice-cream stand, and had dished out so many freebies to his mates that he'd been sacked within ten days. Remember the warm September night that she and Aidan had come here, just the two of them, for some starlight skinny-dipping, the first and last time she'd ever done such a bold and thrilling thing. Remember—

Shit!

Olivia slammed her foot on the brake as she rounded the bend, punching the horn in alarm. What the hell . . . ? There was a girl on a bike right in the middle of the road, so close Olivia could see the whites of her eyes, the sudden panic on her face. Time seemed to slow down, but the car wasn't slowing fast enough. Could she swerve away? She was going to hit her. *She was going to hit her!*

Chapter Fifteen

All okay? Ring me if you want a chat, any time. I'll keep my
phone next to me in bed just in case.
Morning! Hope you slept well. Thinking about you. Hope
you're having fun!
How's it going? Let me know if you want me to pick you up
earlier. Miss you. xx

Maggie's unanswered texts were piling up in her phone like litter on a beach. Every time she glanced over and saw that there was still no message of reply, it felt like a rebuff. What did it mean? Was Amelia having such a wonderful time with Will that she didn't have a spare minute to glance at her in-box? Or was she desperately miserable, but too proud to say anything?

More than once her finger had hovered above the Call key, only for her to wrench it away again. Amelia seemed to resent her mother full stop these days and would almost certainly resent any intrusion into her Newton Abbot stay, however desperate Maggie was to hear from her. Oh God, how she wished this wasn't happening. Why had she allowed herself to be bulldozed into the situation, without more of a fight?

After leaving Amelia there in Devon yesterday, Maggie had driven away, feeling untethered, unhinged, as if she no longer knew the rules. She felt like weeping with the stress of what had just happened, especially when she passed a trampoline park and imagined the children inside bouncing wild and free, their hair spraying out around them, the shrieks, the laughter. Amelia used to love trampolining, she remembered with a pang. So did she herself, for that matter. They'd had a trampoline in their garden until a few years ago, and they'd ended up bouncing on there together many times. 'It's hard for the only ones, when they don't have brothers or sisters, isn't it?' her neighbour Tina had once said sorrowfully, peering over the fence at them. Maggie had felt so winded by this not-so-subtle jibe that she had bounced to a sudden halt and almost broken her knees.

The holiday just felt all wrong without Amelia. Waking up in the too-quiet cottage this morning had seemed so strange. Maggie had gone into the second bedroom and her throat had tightened as she saw the bed there, unslept in. She'd actually sat down on it for a moment and put her hand on Amelia's pillow because she felt so bereft. Then, in the kitchen, she'd automatically pushed two slices of bread down in the toaster for her, as she did every day. It was only as she was buttering the toast and opened her mouth to bawl Amelia's name that she had realized what she'd done. She'd ended up eating them herself, on top of the bowl of porridge she'd already put away.

'I miss you,' she said into the dead air of the room. 'I wish you were here.'

Surprise surprise, she imagined her sister-in-law Helena saying sarcastically, if she could see Maggie now. Helena had never bothered hiding the condescension she felt towards her, and Maggie still bristled whenever she thought about Helena and Ross's New Year's Eve dinner last year, when things had really come to a head. Helena was one of those people who intensely disliked not getting their own way and, having tried but failed to talk Maggie into staying over for the night, she then began jokingly calling her boring and a party-pooper – or Maggie had assumed she was joking anyway. But then a mean sort of light began shining from Helena's piggy eyes and the mood changed abruptly. 'I knew you wouldn't stay. You never do. You always use Amelia as an excuse – your cover story, stopping you doing anything interesting with your life. Ross thinks so too. What are you so scared of?'

Maggie had been so shocked and humiliated by the accusation that she had jerked Amelia away from her cousins and they'd left pretty much there and then, but the moment came back to her now. Helena's plump, scornful face looming at her, a small shred of bruschetta wedged between her two front teeth, the stale waft of alcohol drifting from her open mouth. *What are you so scared of?*

I'm not scared of anything, she had told herself indignantly that night as she drove home, the roads empty as the rest of the country poured another drink and danced the old year out. *Of course I'm not*, she had repeated once back at the house, alone on her sofa as she watched the London fireworks crack and pop above the celebrating crowds. She'd always prided herself on her competence, how she'd kept her little family going by pure strength of will – as opposed to the strength of Will, you could say. But today her sister-in-law's unkind words jabbed at her like thorns. They weren't true . . . were they?

Look at what she'd done so far that day, though: gone to the supermarket, filled in the newspaper crossword, eaten a boiled egg for lunch while listening to a dreary Radio 4 phone-in about pensions. On her *holiday* as well. The devil makes work for idle hands, her mum had been fond of warning, and Maggie was starting to think she might be better off – at least better entertained – considering the devil's options instead.

Just then, though, she almost jumped out of her skin when she heard a ferocious banging at the front door. 'Is anyone there? Hello?' came an urgent voice.

Well, it didn't sound like the devil, was her first ridiculous thought, before she snapped out of her strange mood and rushed to answer it, wiping her hands on her trousers. Wait – what if it was Amelia, tearful and heartbroken, having hitched all the way back to Falmouth? Maggie's mind was instantly teeming with panicky possibilities. If Will had upset her, after all this, if Will had *dared* make Amelia feel small or insignificant or stupid, she would wring his rotten neck with her own hands. She would *kill* him!

She yanked the door open, only to see the woman from the cottage next door standing outside, looking agitated. 'You haven't seen Izzie, have you? My daughter. She's not off with your girl somewhere, is she?'

The words burst forward in such a torrent, Maggie found herself blinking. 'No,' she replied, her heart rate decelerating. 'Amelia's in Devon. I   Is everything all right? I did see Izzie, about ten minutes ago,' she added, remembering how she'd been dully washing up her lunch things and happened to glance out of the window. She had seen the whole family coming back a short while before that, and noticed distractedly how cross they all seemed to be with one another. Then out had come the older girl on her own, hooking a leg over a bicycle and pedalling furiously away, shoulders hunched low for speed. No helmet, Maggie had thought in disapproval. 'She went off on her bike,' she said.

The woman – Em, was it? Emma? – sagged on the door-step. 'Okay, thanks. Did you see which way she went? Anything else at all?'

'Sorry, no,' Maggie said, trying and failing to dredge up further details. 'Can I help?' she asked in the next moment. 'Is everything all right?'

'I don't suppose you—' Then Em broke off, her mouth buckling as if she were about to burst into tears. 'No, don't worry about it. Thank you.'

'Honestly, ask me,' Maggie urged. At heart she was still a Girl Guide, wanting to do good whenever possible, wanting to please others. 'Amelia's not here, I've got no plans whatsoever – if there's anything I can do, just say it. You'll save me from cleaning the cooker.'

The woman's eyes were watery, but she managed a tiny smile. Perhaps she thought Maggie was joking about the cooker. What kind of saddo cleaned the cooker when they were on holiday, anyway? 'In that case . . . I don't suppose you could come with me, could you?' she asked. 'I'm going out to look for her and I just—'

'Of course I will,' said Maggie as the woman's voice got smaller and smaller. 'Absolutely. Let me just grab my key and I'll be right with you.'

So this was an unexpected road trip, she thought, clamber-ing into the passenger seat of Em's car moments later.

Inside, there were stickers all over the dashboard and crisp packets in the footwell, and it smelled like a cheese-and-onion pasty. Maggie wondered if it would be very rude of her to wind the window down. 'I've brought my map of the area; where do you think she might have gone?' she asked, unfolding it on her knee as Em started the engine. 'Gosh, it's warm, isn't it?' she murmured as stale air poured out of the vents. She spotted a button for the window and rested a hopeful finger there. 'Mind if I . . . ?'

'I don't know – into Falmouth, maybe?' Em said, answering Maggie's first question before she could finish asking the second. 'She just took off. She was upset. There was a . . . a small saga, and she was unfairly blamed. She must have felt disbelieved – I didn't back her up as roundly as I might have done.' Her mouth trembled again as she executed a clumsy three-point turn in the car park and stalled. 'Oh, bloody hell. Sorry. Excuse my atrocious driving.'

'Let's head for Falmouth then,' Maggie said. She knew how it was to feel like a rubbish mother, after all – she understood how you could beat yourself up over a badly handled argument. She also knew that teenagers could explode a small grievance into a whole furnace of drama. 'If she's on her bike, we might even catch her up. No speeding round the corners now,' she added, trying to sound as if she were joking, but meaning it too; Em had certainly set off at a far faster lick than Maggie was used to travelling. She pressed the button to open the window and gulped in the delicious cool air that streamed through.

'Good point,' Em said, slowing as they approached a bend. 'Talk about adding insult to injury, if I went and knocked her down now, on top of everything else. Injury to injury, more like.' She shuddered. 'Thank you, by the way. This is incredibly nice of you.' She sniffed loudly. 'I'm sure Izzie's fine, she'll just be blowing off some steam, but all the same . . .' Her voice wobbled on the words. 'All the same, thank you.'

'It's fine, honestly. I know what it's like. I can't do anything right with Amelia at the moment. She doesn't even want to spend our holiday with me any more,' Maggie found herself blurting out. What was it about being in a car next to someone that made the space feel like a confession booth? 'If it's any consolation, I'm not sure I'm handling the teenage years at all well. Quite badly, in fact.'

The two of them exchanged a small smile of understanding before Maggie, now shy at having revealed her vulnerable side, turned back to the map on her knee. She didn't really need it – she'd been this way already when she and Amelia went to Pendennis and was a good, instinctive navigator, but felt as if she was more useful with a physical prop to consult. Also, any excuse to have a map on the knee. It was like a comfort blanket. 'We're coming up to a bridge over the river,' she said, tracing a finger along the lines. 'And then you need to take a sharp left out of the village.'

Em slowed as they crossed the charming stone hump-back bridge, then took a left. 'They probably went along here on their bikes the other day, come to think of it,' she said. 'The teens, on their naughty trip into town,' she added, when Maggie looked blank.

For some reason Em flashed Maggie an expression that she couldn't quite interpret. A grimace of disapproval? What did she mean by 'their naughty trip' anyway? What had been naughty about it? Em was already speaking again, though, before Maggie could ask.

'That's why I assumed she would head into Falmouth,' she said, suddenly fretful. 'But what if she went completely the other way, just pedalled off, without a clue where she was going?' She bit her lip, staring anxiously ahead. 'She's a really sensible girl, but maybe it's been too much, George coming with us on holiday – that's my boyfriend, by the way. Man-friend? I don't actually know what to call him. We haven't been together for long and it's the first time I've dated anyone since my divorce, so . . .' She rolled her eyes. 'Sorry, too much information. Shut up, Em.' The road widened and she picked up speed. 'Oh, where *is* she? I'd have thought we'd have caught up with her by now.'

They turned a corner to see a small beach on their right and Em slowed once more, both of them scanning the car park and beyond for signs of a teenage girl on her bike. Nothing. 'This is probably pointless,' Em said. 'Maybe I should have waited for her to come home again, rather than dashing out in pursuit. But I just felt I had to do *something*. If I can find her, at least she'll know I care.'

'I know what you mean,' Maggie said. 'I would be the same. You just want to make things okay for them, don't you? To have their worlds turn a little more smoothly.' She gulped, unable to prevent her next words pouring out. 'It's when they won't let you do that – when they push you away – that it's really hurtful. In my experience.' She stopped and awkwardness took hold of her. Why did she keep saying such personal things? Maybe it was Em's own openness, or the fact that this was the first conversation she'd had all day. Either way, she should really get a grip on herself.

Sure enough, Em shot her a quizzical look. 'Tell me about your daughter, distract me,' she said as they continued on towards the town centre. 'Jack mentioned she'd gone away – I forgot in all the panic. She's in Devon, did you say?'

'Yes.' Maggie swallowed. 'She's gone to stay with her dad, who's practically never met her. It's all been a bit of a drama in our house as well, to be honest—' She broke off, spotting a cyclist ahead. 'That's not her, is it?'

'Nope,' said Em with a sigh.

These girls of theirs, thought Maggie as they overtook the cyclist and carried on. These girls who kept squirming away from their mothers. Had they any idea how much heartache they caused? She glanced down at her handbag, at the silent phone that she could see poking out of the top. Still no reply to her messages then. *Oh, Amelia,* she thought with a pang. *What's happening? Are you all right? Tell me he's being nice to you!*

Her feelings got the better of her again, and she found herself blurting out a potted version of events to Em – so much for getting a grip on herself. Her fears, her hurt, out they tumbled into the confined space of the car. *For God's sake, Mum, have some self-respect,* she imagined Amelia saying, with one of her withering glares.

Em let out a whistle as Maggie drew to a close. They had reached Falmouth by now, still without any glimpse of Izzie, and she was circling around, trying to find somewhere to park. 'Jesus,' she said. 'I thought my ex-husband was a cock, but I've got to say, yours sounds— Then she broke off and put a hand over her mouth. 'Sorry. No offence.'

'No, you can say it. Whatever it is, I'll agree. I hate him, you know. I really do. He's a . . . a *tosser*. A grade-A tosser. He started trying to apologize on the doorstep to me, can you believe. Too late, mate. Too bloody late!' Her voice was shaking. *Calm down, Maggie. Stop!*

Em had spotted an empty space and began making an absolute pig's ear of reversing into it. 'Yeah, well, I hear you, loud and clear,' she said, going forward and back a few times, trying to straighten up. She heaved the handbrake on with a sigh. 'My ex has gone for your archetypal bimbo – we're talking fake everything, and a brain the size of a pea, as far as I can tell. I mean, what does that say about me? That's his type, is it? I don't want to fall into the trap of competing with other women, but it's so bloody insulting.' She turned off the engine with a dramatic flourish. 'Especially when I'm clearly a thousand times better!'

Maggie spluttered with laughter at Em's indignation. 'I don't doubt it for a second,' she said.

They headed into the town and Maggie couldn't help thinking that they might as well have been looking for the proverbial needle amidst a haystack. For one thing, she'd only glimpsed Izzie a couple of times from her kitchen window and would struggle to recognize her in a police line-up. For another, Falmouth was absolutely heaving with shoppers and day-trippers, the streets thronged with slow-moving people, the shops and cafés all busy with customers. Nevertheless, she realized that she was glad to be here, doing something useful, rather than being stuck in the quiet, empty house wondering what to do with herself. She felt better, too, for getting the whole Will episode off her chest, and for having Em's support and solidarity in response. Em thought Celeste sounded priggish and up herself, that Will was a cock, and that Thistle and Rain would be changing their names to Dave and Tracey just as soon as they were old enough. Somehow this all helped enormously in taking the sting out of yesterday's pain.

'Well, I don't think she'll have gone into *this* shop at least,' Em was saying now, grimacing theatrically as they passed a chichi little gallery on their left. 'Not after what happened the other—Oh.' Now she seemed wary all of a sudden, her eyes narrowing. 'She didn't tell you, did she? Amelia.'

'Tell me what?' Maggie asked in surprise, glancing back from the gallery's shop front to Em.

'Um . . .' Em looked as if she wished she'd never opened her mouth. 'Their naughty little Truth or Dare game?'

Naughty – that word again. What was Em on about?

'Amelia didn't say anything,' Maggie replied. 'She seemed a bit subdued once she came home, but didn't really go into any details. In fact, between you and me, I wondered if she'd been . . . Well, you know. Being with older children, I think she was maybe rather . . . overawed?'

Em made a strange sort of choking noise. '*Seriously?* I'm not sure about that. Er . . .'

'Oh!' said Maggie as her phone beeped. She glanced down at it to see that Amelia had at last replied.

All okay, was the message. That was it.

Maggie stared at the two words, which told her so little, and sighed. Did that mean she was having such a great time that she didn't have a minute to spare for a longer text? Or such a terrible time that she was in denial and didn't want to talk about it? She passed a hand over her eyes, feeling despairing, then remembered Em still standing beside her. 'Sorry. You were saying something about the gallery?'

'It's nothing,' Em said quickly, resuming walking again. 'Oh God, this is hopeless,' she added after a moment, as they wove their way around a large family and then what might have been a canoeing club: a crocodile of children in fluorescent life-jackets, walking in a chain of twos. 'We've got no chance. Maybe we should—'

From her expression she looked to be on the verge of saying 'give up', but just then her phone started ringing. She pounced on it at once, scrabbling to press the right button. 'Hello?' she asked, standing still as the crowds swirled around her. 'What's happening? Any news?' Then her whole face changed. 'She *what*?'

What an absolute shit-show of a day Izzie was having. Could this holiday get any worse? She hadn't even *wanted* to go and look for shells with stupid Seren in the first place; she had been having a laugh playing Frisbee with Jack and George, having actually forgotten about trying to score any points for the Summer of Yes leaderboard for once. And yet, surprise surprise, as soon as they walked away together, there was Princess Whinge kicking off again. George was *her* daddy. Em was mean and Seren didn't like her. Mummy was better. Blah-blah frigging blah. Was it any wonder that Izzie lost her temper and gave the uber-brat a bit of a nudge? It hadn't been a *push* exactly, but yeah, there was kind of an elbow going in there. And yeah, Seren had fallen pretty hard into that rock pool. Served her right, though, frankly.

After that . . . Jesus. You'd think she'd broken her leg, or had several toes hacked off, the fuss and the faff. And it had been horrible for Izzie, coming back to the cottage and feeling as if nobody was on her side. George had looked at her so angrily, spoken to her so coldly, as if he was a cross Victorian father whom she'd thoroughly let down. Almost as bad had been the visible doubt on her mum's face too, as if she was torn between siding with Izzie or with her new boyfriend – only for him to win! She'd actually chosen *George* over her. And then of course Seren's stupid misheard comments about her kissing 'a man's boyfriend' had only humiliated her further. Jack would never let her hear the end of it. God! Talk about the worst holiday ever – and it was still only Tuesday.

Even her own dad hadn't been interested, when she rang up to pour her heart out to him, up in the privacy of her bedroom with the door firmly shut. 'Come on, love, it'll blow over,' he'd said, sounding like he couldn't care less.

She found herself remembering how, when she was little, he'd always call her 'my girl'. *Where's my girl?* he'd yell when he got back from work, like she was important, she mattered. *That's my girl,* he'd grin, ruffling her hair when she scored a goal for the school team or got picked for the netball trials. It seemed so long ago now.

Worst of all, Izzie had been able to hear Michelle in the background of the phone call, saying things like 'Who is it? Are you going to have lunch with me or what?' and could imagine her tapping a polished fingernail on the table of whichever bar or restaurant they were in this time. Just picturing that cat's-bum mouth of hers, frosted lipstick crinkling as Michelle's pouty mood soaked up all her dad's attention, was enough to make Izzie boil with rage and self-pity. *Nobody* gave a shit! *Nobody* was on her side. *Nobody* saw her as their girl any more.

And so minutes later she was erupting from the house, throwing a leg over her bike and heading off. Who cared where, just as long as it was away from everyone. Sometimes Izzie liked to imagine herself in a reality-TV show where she was the star and found herself glowering at the invisible camera. 'I'm out of here,' she muttered.

The rage stayed with her, volcanic enough to see her flip the finger at one driver who cut her up at a crossroads, then shout, 'In your dreams' at a group of lads who wolf-whistled her as she flew through the village. Everyone could do one. Everyone could just sod right off! She'd had enough of the whole world – every single person, George and Seren especially. Why had Mum thought it was okay to invite them along on their holiday like that? Why did Seren have to be such a pain in the arse?

Well, they'd all be sorry, she thought, cycling grimly on. Because she was totally going to—

But then she realized three alarming things, one after another.

Suddenly there was a car coming round the corner.

She hadn't been concentrating and had somehow drifted into the middle of the road.

The car was coming right at her, horn blaring, and the woman driving it had opened her mouth in a big shocked NO!

There was a screech of brakes – car and bike – and a million fragmented thoughts hurtled through Izzie's head like instant camera flashes. How angry Mum would be if she died like this, stupidly, for not looking where she was going. How she'd never find out her GCSE results now (maybe that was a good thing). Should she fling herself off the bike? What would it feel like to have your bones broken? She was going to die and she'd never even kissed anyone!

But then the fourth thing happened, which was that the car stopped literally an inch from the front wheel of her bike. And she and the woman just sat there, staring at each other and panting. She could smell diesel and burnt rubber; she could feel the heat radiating from the car against her bare legs. It was as if the whole world had frozen still around them, or shrunk right down so that only they existed in that moment.

In the next second the woman leapt from her car, like someone in an action film, and ran over. 'Are you all right? You were on the wrong side of the road!'

Izzie blinked a couple of times. She could taste blood in her mouth where she'd bitten down on her lip, and her body was awash with adrenalin, her heart galloping like a racehorse. Okay. She was alive. She was unhurt. Stand down, everyone. No dramas. 'Sorry,' she mumbled. 'I wasn't looking.'

The woman let out a long breath. Her face had turned very pink beneath her blonde ponytail. She was small and rather plump, with a turquoise T-shirt that strained across her chest and a denim skirt. 'It's okay,' she said. 'No harm done.'

But something weird was happening to Izzie in the next second, as if contradicting those words. No harm done? Actually she was trembling all over, because her mind kept producing these awful images of her smacking to the tarmac with a horrible crunch, of her flattened beneath the car wheels, and then her mum, dressed in black, doing proper ugly-crying at her funeral. Shit. That had been *close.* All the hairs on her skin were standing on end. That had been so close!

She tried to pull herself together, but it wasn't happening.

Her arms and legs had gone to jelly, her head was swoony as if she was about to fall over. 'I . . .' she stuttered and then it was suddenly really hard to breathe, however valiantly she gasped for air. 'I . . .'

The woman gave her a sharp look. 'Okay, don't worry,' she said, and put an arm around her. 'You're just a bit shocked. You'll be all right in a minute. Take shallow breaths, get some air to your brain, that's it. We're fine, thank you,' she yelled to somebody else in a voice that Izzie's mum used sometimes, the sort of voice that said, *Sod off, none of your business.*

Izzie's lungs were burning. Her throat seemed to be closing up. Her vision was pixelating, the woman's lilac baseball boots turning grainy and weird as she looked down at them. Was this a heart attack? Was Fate having the last ironic laugh at her? *You thought you had avoided being hit by a car – and then you died anyway. Ha!*

But then, at last, with a gulp – a huge shuddering gulp – her body seemed to remember what to do again. Breath entered her lungs. She swallowed and unclenched her fists. 'Sorry,' she said again dazedly. 'I feel really . . .'

'You're a bit wobbly, aren't you? Listen, there's a café right there – how about sitting down for a few minutes and having a drink, just until you feel better again?'

Izzie gazed in the direction of the blonde woman's pointing finger to see a small cheerful-looking café, with benches and picnic umbrellas outside. People were eating pasties and drinking coffee from cardboard cups. Small children licked ice-cream cones while beady-eyed seagulls watched, heads cocked, hoping for a dropped cornet. Okay, yes, she could manage that. Except . . .

'Um. I . . . I don't actually have any money,' she said in a low voice, feeling embarrassed. She didn't have *anything*, she realized in the next moment: no phone, no money, no key to the holiday cottage; she had leapt on her bike and out of there as if she were some kind of crusading Tour de France contestant. Imagine if she had been knocked unconscious by the car and there was nothing to identify her. Mum would just have kittens, wondering what had happened.

The thought was enough to make Izzie's lungs tighten again, and then that horrible clammy feeling began to return, descending on her like a fog – until the woman said firmly, 'I've got some money. You wheel your bike over there and sit down; keep taking those shallow breaths. I'll park the car and meet you in a minute, okay?'

The woman – Olivia, she was called – was really kind. She bought Izzie a cold Diet Coke and then they walked right down to the end of the row of beach huts and just sat there together until Izzie began to feel more normal again. *How many points for a near-death experience?* she imagined herself putting on the group chat later, only – cringe-klaxon – she must actually have said the words out loud, because then

Olivia was frowning and saying, 'How many points for what?'

'Nothing,' Izzie mumbled, cheeks burning.

'Do you want to talk about it?' Olivia asked. 'What happened, I mean. You seemed miles away when you were cycling along. Is everything okay?'

Izzie sipped the drink. Its cold sweetness seemed to spread some calm through her and she let out a long exhalation. 'Just . . . family holiday stuff,' she said. Then her earlier feelings of rage caught up with her and bubbled out. 'I thought holidays were meant to be fun! Mine's rubbish so far. I just felt like getting away from everyone.'

Olivia didn't reply for a moment. 'I know what you mean,' she said eventually.

Izzie pressed her lips together. Adults – Mum, generally – were always saying that, but half the time they had no idea. They *didn't* know what she meant. Here was Olivia, for instance, nice and everything, but she had her own car with kiddie seats in the back: a grown-up life with responsibilities and money. What would she know about wanting to run away on a moment of impulse?

'At least holidays come to an end, though, right?' Olivia went on. A weird expression crossed her face. 'Well – most of the time. You'll be back in your real life again soon.'

'I suppose,' said Izzie. 'Although I'm not looking forward to that, either. Exam results and stuff with friends . . .' she added by way of explanation when Olivia gave her a quiz-zical look. Then she felt herself turning red. Look at her, pouring out her heart to this random middle-aged woman, having nearly been run over. Her friends would laugh their heads off if they could see her. *Er . . . Summer of Yes, remember? they'd jeer. Wild recklessness and bad behaviour! What the hell, Izzie?*

'Oh God, I remember those days. In fact I've spent all today remembering,' Olivia said, which was a bit odd, but then before Izzie could respond, she went on. 'But, you know, here's me, mid-thirties, living a life of domestic bore-dom' – her face became rather pained-looking as she said this – 'and I'd give anything to go back and have those teen-age years again, when everything was possible. I'd do half of it differently, mind, but . . . Well, that's life, isn't it?'

Izzie didn't know what to say. She was rubbish at talking to grown-ups. She felt embarrassed whenever she was round at her friends' houses and their mums would pop their heads around the bedroom door and ask friendly ques-tions. *Just smile if you don't know what to say, smile and be polite,* her mum – the least shy person in the world – was always badgering her. So she gave her best and politest smile. 'I guess so,' she replied vaguely.

Olivia tipped back her head to finish her drink. 'And there's plenty of the summer left to turn everything around, at least. In the meantime . . .' She turned to Izzie and raised an eyebrow. 'Sometimes you just have to fake it till you can make it, as they say.'

Izzie was about to do her polite smile again and agree, but found herself nodding thoughtfully instead as the words resonated through her head. *Sometimes you just have to fake it till you can make it.* Yes, maybe that was the answer. In fact maybe that had been the answer all along and she'd been too honest – or thick – to realize it. None of her friends knew what was going on here, after all. She could make up any crazy wild thing for the Summer of Yes group chat, and they wouldn't have a clue if she was telling the truth or not.

Words began appearing in her mind as if she was typing them there and then. *Oh my God! Have met the hottest boy. Summer fling here we come!*

Whoa! Got chatting to some eighteen-year-olds on the beach earlier – they invited me to a house party tonight. Obviously I said YES!

Went skinny-dipping with my new friends – so much fun. But COLD!!!

Why not? she thought, giddy with her own parallel universes. Why shouldn't she fake it? At least her friends might shut up, for a change. Then she hurriedly blinked her giddy thoughts away, realizing that Olivia was talking again.

'Now, are you okay to cycle to wherever you were going?' she was asking, getting to her feet and smoothing down her denim skirt. 'Legs not too wobbly any more? Otherwise I could give you a lift, if we can wedge your bike in my car. I'm staying in this tiny place called Parr's Head, if that means anything to—'

Izzie started. 'Parr's Head? The holiday cottages with the swimming pool? That's where *we're* staying too.'

'No way!' They both laughed and stared at each other with zero recognition. 'Well, then it was obviously destined that we nearly crashed into one another.' Olivia pulled a funny face. 'Although next time, feel free not to scare the living daylights out of me. So are you heading on into town or do you want a lift back?'

Chapter Sixteen

'Her car's back,' Lorna said to Roy, looking out of the kitchen window as he walked into the room. The farmhouse where they lived was up a short track from the cottages and she tried to keep her distance from her guests, in order to afford them some privacy, but she had been baking today and it was hard to miss the comings and goings. If she was honest with herself, she was curious about their new arrival too. Olivia had looked so wretched the day before, Lorna had been quite concerned about her. It had been a relief to see her striding purposefully out that morning, and then, an hour or so ago, Lorna had noticed that her car was back in the car park again and had found herself sighing a little in relief. Good. She was okay. And maybe, just maybe, she might want to talk with Lorna about Aidan a bit more. Would it be wrong of her to go over there on the pretence of checking in on her?

'Why don't you pop in and say hello, if you're worried?' Roy asked. He'd always been able to tell what she was thinking. His hands were filthy from the vegetable patch and he went over to the sink and began scrubbing up with the Palmolive. 'Rather than spying out the window like some nosy old biddy.' He tilted his head towards the cake cooling on the tray, its top sticky with deliciously gritty sugar. 'You could take her some of that lemon drizzle, before I ruin my diet with it. Save me from myself.'

'Who are you calling a nosy old biddy?' Lorna asked, before giving a snort at his diet comment. Roy was always going on about the diet that their GP had prescribed him – low-fat, low-sugar, low-joy, basically – but they both knew he'd chucked it in the recycling box with a sniff of mistrust the minute he'd come back from the appointment. 'Cake's not a bad idea, though.'

'You don't have to give her all of it, mind,' said Roy, watching as she plunged the knife in. He hesitated. 'And don't badger her, will you now? She looked a bit fragile to me.'

'I'm not going to badger her, you great lummox,' Lorna scoffed. 'I just . . .' She felt embarrassed to put into words how desperate she was to talk to Olivia about Aidan again. But oh, how wonderful it had been when Olivia had brought him alive with her stories and memories! Lorna had written up every single one on pieces of paper and stuck them into her scrapbook, and felt a warm glow inside, like a lit tea-light, whenever she replayed their conversation. It was amazing how even a small flame could brighten a dark corner. *Cherish the good days,* she'd read in magazine agony-columns before. *Recognize the happy moments when they arrive* – and she did, or she tried to anyway, pinning down every lovely memory like a butterfly, telling herself whenever she remembered that today was going to be a good day, even when that didn't always feel possible.

'I just want to say hello,' she said.

'That won't take long then, will it?' He met her gaze with his, steady and kind. *Don't get all worked up now,* that look said. *Don't you go upsetting yourself.*

'No,' she replied, getting a cake tin down from the cupboard. 'Probably not.'

'Lorna, hello! This is a nice surprise. Come in,' said Olivia when Lorna knocked a few minutes later.

'Are you sure? I'm not disturbing you? I've brought some cake,' Lorna said, holding the tin up rather self consciously. 'Lemon drizzle; it's still warm.'

'Thank you! That's so kind.'

They went through to the kitchen, where Olivia had been peeling vegetables. A small chicken joint sat pinkly in a tray on the worktop with a head of garlic and some olive oil standing in attendance nearby. 'Having someone round?' Lorna asked in surprise. It was always so strange to see her cottages with other people's belongings in them. Barring emergencies, when she had to pop over and replace a light bulb or inspect something that wasn't working, she only ever saw them empty, having been stripped of guests and their possessions once more.

'No, only me.' Olivia moved the chopping board and peelings off the table and onto the worktop, then put the kettle on. With her deft movements, she already seemed different from the broken woman she had been at Aidan's grave. 'I just fancied making something really delicious,' she went on. 'Treating myself. Roast chicken's the best comfort food I could think of.' There was a turquoise swimming costume on the table too, still with its price tag attached and somewhat incongruous amidst the potatoes, carrots and broccoli. 'I treated myself to that as well,' she explained rather bashfully, noticing Lorna looking at it. 'How could I not, when that beautiful pool is out there? I'm getting all the food prep done first, then I'll put the chicken in and take myself off for a swim while it's roasting.'

'Good idea!' Lorna said. Then, because she couldn't help herself, she added, 'Roast chicken was always Aidan's favourite too.' There he was in the room again, her beautiful son, still eighteen and piling roast potatoes onto his plate. *Is that you? It's me.* They'd had a running joke about how many roasties he could eat. Sixteen, on one memorable Christmas Day, could you believe? Growing boys and their appetites!

Olivia stiffened for a moment before turning to find two

mugs. 'I've been thinking about him a lot today,' she said. 'Revisiting some of our old haunts.'

Lorna leaned forward greedily, as bad as Roy with his eye on a cream bun. This was what she'd come for. Tell me everything, she wanted to say. Every detail you can remember. Bring him back for me. 'Where did you go?' she asked instead.

Olivia started listing the stops she'd made – their old college, a friend's house, a favourite beach – but there was something sort of closed about her face, Lorna noticed. Something she was holding back.

'And how did they make you feel?' Lorna prompted when Olivia's words dried up. 'Was it . . . Are you okay?'

Olivia was busy making tea, but Lorna saw her mouth twist at the questions. Oh dear. Had she gone in too personal too soon?

'I was worried it would be overwhelming,' Olivia confessed after a moment, in such a quiet voice that Lorna had to lean further towards her. 'I've hardly been back at all to any of these places in twenty years, I just cut myself off because . . .' She set a steaming mug down in front of Lorna and sat opposite her. 'Because I couldn't bear to revisit them, knowing he was gone,' she finished.

They exchanged a small sad smile of understanding. *Say no more, my darling,* thought Lorna.

'But today . . . I was surprised. I found myself thinking

about happy times. All the best moments. It was . . . It was cathartic. And at times really lovely.'

'Tell me,' Lorna urged. *Give me more. Please. Humour me.* She wanted to continue building the jigsaw of her son, patched together with everyone's nicest stories about him, to commemorate who he had been. Colour him in with bright memories so that he would never truly fade.

And so Olivia started recounting old tales, tiny snippets, moments of kindness. She talked about how she'd always felt Aidan had rescued her, brought out the best in her. Lorna drank in every word, every detail. Hadn't she just told herself that today was going to be a good day? And she was right!

'I just wish . . .' Olivia said after a while, her eyes glassy. 'I just wish I could have always been as nice to him as he was to me.'

'You *were* nice to him!' Lorna said in surprise. 'He thought you were the bee's knees, Olivia.'

'Yes, but sometimes I . . . Sometimes I wasn't.' And now there was a fearful edge in her voice, an anxious glance at Lorna before her gaze dropped away.

Lorna knew that face of regret, because she had worn the same one herself, she had felt those exact feelings. All the things she could have done for him and hadn't, it tortured her even now. She'd been meaning to paint Aidan's bedroom for weeks when he died, but had put it off and put if off for one reason or another – until it was too late and he was gone. She'd always promised she'd take him to Wimbledon one summer – they were both big tennis fans – but again, she'd never quite managed to sort out tickets, and he'd died without ever seeing a match. She could go on.

'Oh gosh, but nobody *is* nice around the clock, darling,' she told Olivia now. 'When I think about the times I told him off for coming in late, or nagged him about tidying his room, or was impatient with him . . . I could cut my tongue out for them. I wish I had been more patient and understanding, of course I do. I would give anything to have him back, and I'd never complain about a single thing he did, ever again! But . . .' She spread her hands. 'It's called being human, isn't it? That's just how we all are. We get frustrated and snappy with other people. Poor Roy, the things he has to put up with – the man's a saint for sticking with me sometimes. But it doesn't mean I don't love him any less. Like you always loved Aidan! He knew that.'

Olivia nodded but didn't say anything, just clutched the mug of tea with both hands and took a sip. Lorna found herself looking at those ringless fingers and felt sorry for her. 'It's a shame you never met anyone else,' she blurted out. 'I guess he was a hard act to follow, though.' Gratitude swelled inside her at Olivia's loyalty. Her devotion! If Aidan could only see how much he had meant to this girl.

But Olivia was frowning. 'What do you mean?'

'I mean . . .' Lorna felt bad for jumping to conclusions,

Roy was always telling her off for it, but she couldn't help another glance at the other woman's bare hands. 'I take it you aren't married. Is there a boyfriend, though, or anyone special?'

'Oh,' said Olivia. She put her mug down and her hands vanished under the table. 'I . . . Actually, I *am* married. I'm married with two little boys.' Her voice was getting lower with every word. 'But I've kind of messed everything up.'

Lorna swallowed hard because the first feeling she had was one of upset. Indignation, too. Olivia had married someone *else*, who wasn't Aidan? She'd had *children* with this man? Lorna couldn't believe how disconcerted this made her feel. Which – yes, okay – which she knew, rationally, was wrong of her. Wrong and unfair. Of course the poor thing was entitled to marry someone else, rather than live the rest of her life miserably alone, mourning her teenage boyfriend. But oh – Aidan. Poor Aidan! She hoped, if he *was* in the room with them, that he wasn't too devastated by this bombshell. *Don't listen, my love. Hands over your ears, just like when you were tiny and the fireworks scared you.*

'I see,' she managed to say. Oh dear, and now she sounded all stiff and formal, as if she disapproved. Probably because she did, just a little bit, even though she knew she shouldn't. 'I noticed you weren't wearing a ring and assumed . . .' She tailed off weakly, wishing she hadn't said anything now. To think two minutes ago she had actually felt *grateful* to Olivia, for not marrying anyone! What an idiot she was. Wait till she told Roy. 'No fool like an old fool,' he would say mildly, before giving her a consoling hug.

Olivia's head was bowed. 'I took the ring off,' she said. 'We're going through a bit of a bad patch. I just needed to get away.'

Thoughts were jumbling around in Lorna's head and she found that she didn't know how to articulate any of them. Olivia was a wife and a mother, but had walked out on the family? This didn't sound good. In fact it sounded very much like history repeating itself, she thought, remembering the stories about Olivia's own bad apple of a mum. Wild Sylvia Asbury of the kohl-rimmed eyes and tangled hennaed hair, that gap between her front teeth when she gave you one of her lazy smiles. The men had flocked around her like dazed bees to her honey. According to the gossip, she'd been having a very public fling with a man from St Mawes (the latest in a long line) and, word had it, they'd vanished to the States together when he was accused of a burglary and had promptly gone underground. It had all been hushed up to protect the children of course. 'Oh dear,' she said now. 'And do you ever . . . Sorry, I don't want to pry, but did you ever hear from your mum again? I know she went away, but is she around to help at all?'

Olivia's face closed up. 'She died.'

'Oh darling, I'm sorry,' said Lorna. 'It must be so hard,

not having her there to turn to. I remember when I first became a mum and—'

She was interrupted by a knock at the door and Olivia jumped up, as if grateful for a chance to get away from the conversation. Lorna finished the last of her now lukewarm tea, still reeling. What must be going on in Olivia's mind to have walked out of the family home like that, to have slept in her own car rather than in the marital bed? She must have been desperate to get away. What kind of man had she married? More to the point, what might she be doing with herself now, if Lorna and Roy hadn't come along in the nick of time?

Her fingers trembled on the mug, trying to make sense of it all as her feelings whirled. Roy had warned her, hadn't he; he had said that Olivia seemed fragile and not to go interfering – and he'd been right. But had Lorna listened? No. She'd gone blundering in with her lemon cake and interfering questions, like she always did, driven by her own selfish longing. She didn't *know* Olivia any more; it was none of her business to go poking around in her life, none at all.

Guilt jabbing her like pinpricks, she got to her feet and took the mug over to the kitchen sink, unable to avoid over-hearing the conversation at the front door.

'Oh, there was no need, honestly,' Olivia was saying. 'It wasn't as if I had to go out of my way or anything. That's very kind of you.'

'Yes, but it was so kind of *you* to bring her back, really

decent,' another woman was saying in a fast, rather breathless sort of voice. 'I was out there driving around like a maniac, trying to find her – I don't know if Izzie told you, but we'd had a bit of a bust-up earlier.'

'No, she didn't say anything, but . . . Sorry, do you want to come in?' Olivia asked. 'You don't have to stand on the doorstep.'

Feeling self-conscious about loitering there within earshot, Lorna rinsed the mug, splashing it noisily, even though there was a perfectly good dishwasher that Roy had plumbed in himself not two years ago. She was tired, she thought, noticing the ache in her knees as she stood there. She could do with a holiday herself really – get away from the area, take a break from running this place. Roy pestered her now and then with adverts for cruises, winter getaways, special package deals he had found on the Internet. *Mmm, maybe*, she said each time, but they never actually went anywhere. She hadn't done so for years, in fact. How could she, though, when Aidan was still here? How could she possibly leave him, cold in the ground and all alone?

She blinked away a tear. 'Well, I really appreciate it,' the woman at the door was saying. 'And obviously if there's anything I can do for you or your family, in return, I'm just over there, Briar Cottage.'

Ah, okay. It must be Emma, thought Lorna, the woman who had booked on Christmas Day. You always got a few people booking then – drunk, bored or a cheering-up exercise? she'd often wondered, fascinated. She put the mug upside down on the draining rack, then sat back down again, curious to know if Olivia was going to correct Emma on the mention of her family. No, it appeared not.

'Thank you' was all she said.

'I'll bump into you around the pool, no doubt,' the woman said. 'I'm Em, by the way.'

'Olivia,' replied Olivia. 'Nice to meet you. And thanks for this!'

She returned, rather pink in the cheeks, bearing a bottle of red wine, and Lorna got to her feet once more, feeling as if she had overstayed her welcome. 'I won't keep you,' she said. 'Thank you for the tea. Do knock, won't you, if you need anything? I'm always on hand if you want a chat.' Then, worried it might sound as if she were prying, she tried to adopt a brighter note. 'Especially if you've got anything else to tell me about Aidan!'

Was it Lorna's imagination or did a strange, almost fearful look pass over Olivia's face? The poor thing obviously still carried a torch for him, she thought, letting herself out and hurrying back home. But, let's face it – who wouldn't?

Chapter Seventeen

Em was starting to feel as if a curse had been put upon the holiday. If it wasn't one thing going tits-up this week, it was another. When George had rung her in Falmouth to say that Izzie was back home and seemed okay, she had actually burst into tears in front of kind Maggie, because she just couldn't cope with the drama any more. She'd got home, hugged Izzie and apologized, and then she'd had to apologize to George too, for tearing out of the house like a lunatic. God! If they made it to the end of this fortnight still together, it would be a miracle. She was longing for one single day when nothing catastrophic happened. One measly little day. Was it so much to ask?

Still, the main thing was that Izzie was all right, even though Em still hadn't got to the bottom of how it had come about that her daughter had been brought back by a fellow holidaymaker, no less, staying right there on the other side of the swimming pool. How on earth had the two of them recognized each other, for starters? She didn't even know there *was* another family in the third cottage, and she was not a woman to miss that sort of detail.

Anyway. Whatever. Em had plundered her booze stash and taken over a bottle of Merlot for Maggie, to thank her for her company and sanity on the Falmouth hunt, and then another for the mysterious Olivia, as thanks for her part in the story. (Yes, okay, also to have a little bit of a nosy at her.) *Jesus, Em, you've managed to get the whole bloody gang involved in your chaos,* her sister Jenny would have said, had she been here to witness the spectacle. Thank heavens she was not.

One day, Em was most definitely going to turn into the elegant, composed sort of woman she longed to be, whose life passed serenely without anyone yelling or fighting or running away. A woman like Charlotte, presumably. In the meantime, was she a person to let life knock her down? No, she was not. Which was why she'd suggested they spend the afternoon at the pool, in the hope of some happy bonding time. Izzie was kind of lukewarm about joining them and said she was going to catch up with her friends online, but everyone else gamely put on their swimming things and jumped right in. And soon they were having a good time, playing silly games together and laughing a lot, just like a proper family. The sun was out, the water was warm, Daddy Fox was drying out on his very own sun lounger and, oh goodness, George did look fantastically *hot* in a pair of swimming trunks. Seeing his bare sculpted chest and back, it was difficult to restrain herself from twining her legs around him under the water.

And yet . . . Did he still even want that from her? she wondered anxiously, retreating to a corner of the pool and propping her elbows on the wet concrete lip. Was he not tiring, just a little, of the real Em, now that he had seen her at her most shrill and stressed that afternoon? She had tried so hard to keep up appearances, to be the perfect holiday girlfriend for him, but she knew the mask had slipped earlier, revealing the mess of her true self beneath. Spending so much time in close proximity made you vulnerable, she had realized. With hindsight, it might have been better to keep the relationship on a more detached setting: dates where she only had to be charming and witty for a few hours, nights where she could throw her energies into being seductive and seduced, safe in the knowledge that he'd leave in the morning and she could slob about enjoyably in her old dressing gown in privacy afterwards. If only she had considered this earlier, before she went and blurted out her invitation to him!

As if sensing her doubts, George swam over to her and leaned on the edge of the pool beside her. 'You okay?' he asked. His bronzed wet arms gleamed in the sunlight, and she had to resist the urge to lay her head on them.

'Yeah,' she said. I'm just a girl in a slightly too-tight bikini standing in front of a boy with a sexy wet body, asking him to love her, she thought. Thankfully she didn't say that out loud, though. Not least because she hadn't qualified as being a 'girl' for more than twenty-five years. 'Sorry about earlier. Me flying off the handle in a panic.'

He seemed unperturbed. 'That's okay. It all got a bit hectic, didn't it?'

'It did a bit.' They smiled at each other rather apprehensively, then both spoke at once. 'I'm finding it—' she confessed just as he said, 'I guess that's the downside of—'

Then they stopped. 'You first,' she said, losing her nerve.

'I was just going to say, that's the downside of going on holiday with kids – your attention's divided all the time, there are so many people to please.'

'Yes,' she replied gratefully. Exactly. And for a people-pleaser like Em, she had felt pulled in all directions. 'It's not easy, trying to navigate our own thing when we're both having to be mum and dad as well. I hope this wasn't . . .' She swallowed, not sure if she dared say the words in case he went and agreed with them. 'I hope this wasn't too much too soon,' she managed after a moment, gazing up at him worriedly through her eyelashes.

He put his hand on her arm and her stomach gave a slow, delicious flip. Actual goosebumps pimpled up like soldiers standing to attention. 'At least we still get to be together,' he said.

She nodded, lost in his eyes, the world suddenly contracting around them to this small private moment. His skin on hers. The water gently rippling against their bodies. A universe where only the two of them existed and they understood one another perfectly. Maybe later on tonight they could sneak out for more of an X-rated dip together beneath the cover of darkness. She shivered with pleasure as all sorts of erotic images tumbled into her mind. Now *that* would improve the holiday no end.

Then she squealed in shock as a small person dive-bombed into the water beside her, spraying Em full in the face.

'Daddy!' cried the small person – Seren, unsurprisingly. 'Play with *me* now. My leg is still hurting a bit you know.'

George gave Em a rueful smile. *Here we go again.* 'Hold that thought,' he told her, winking as if he'd read her mind a moment earlier. Then he scooped up Seren and hoisted her high in the air, which made her shriek with excitement. 'Right, you little munchkin, where shall I throw you?'

Em tanked up and down a few times – the pool was too small to swim lengths really, but at least you could clock up five or six very easily, and then Jack suggested a lilo race, just the two of them, and soon she could feel her equilibrium returning. This was good. This was great, actually – the four of them, having fun, nobody arguing or being jealous or having a strop. Relax, Em. Capture it in your mind's eye like a perfect family photograph: proof that some parts of the holiday were a success. Click!

'Your turn, George,' Jack said, when it became clear that he was beating his mother with far too much ease. He turned a splashy somersault in the water and grinned. 'Front-crawl sprint. Although I hope you're not going to be a bad loser about this, when I win.'

George laughed. 'Tell you what,' he said. 'I'll swim with Seren on my back and I'll still beat you. Are we on?'

'In your dreams!' Jack retaliated. 'Me against you, so you don't have any excuses when I annihilate you. Prepare to weep man-tears of shame, George. Mum, you're the judge. Seren, give us a Ready, Steady, Go.'

The two of them lined up in racing positions on the far side of the pool, arms bent back behind them, feet against the wall, ready to push off.

'READY STEADY GO!' yelled Seren at the top of her voice.

SPLASH! Forward they plunged, water foaming around their shoulders as they surged across the pool. 'Go on, Jack!' Em cheered, recognizing the determination on her son's face. She dodged out of the way as they drew near, neck-and-neck, both finding an extra burst of speed for the final metre. Down slapped their hands on the pool's edge. 'Jack wins by a finger!' she decreed, which made him whoop and leap in the air.

'I'll get you next time,' George said, holding out a hand to shake. 'Oh hey, Izzie,' he said just then.

Em turned to see her daughter strutting towards them, wearing only a pair of mirrored aviator shades plus a tiny – and Em really did mean *tiny* – black bikini. Where had *that* come from? She must have picked it up in town with her mates, because Em certainly would not have willingly purchased it for her.

'My eyes, my eyes,' Jack groaned, clapping a hand over his face as he saw his sister. 'Jesus, Iz, you're scaring the horses.'

'What horses?' Seren asked.

Em felt flustered. There was something a bit seedy about seeing your own beautiful teenage daughter looking like a sex object. Looking *womanly*, with far shapelier thighs than her own mother and an enviably toned stomach. In the blink of an eye, Izzie had blossomed from a sporty, ponytailed girl in school uniform into this . . . well, this beautiful young woman, frankly, all hips and boobs. What with Jack suddenly becoming interested in girls and now Izzie turning into this goddess, Em felt as if someone had pressed a fast-forward button on her children's lives. Or was it that she hadn't paid enough attention to them lately?

'Jump in! The water's lovely,' she urged Izzie, with just a fraction of desperation in her voice. *Cover yourself up! Too much bare flesh on display here.*

Izzie didn't jump in, though. She sat at the edge of the pool, her legs dangling in the water, with a strange look on her face. It was hard to read her expression while those mirrored sunglasses were down. 'You had a phone call, George,' she said in this artless sort of way. She tossed her head so that her long tawny hair fell swishily down her back, then turned her gaze back towards him. 'It was a woman.'

It was weird, the way she said it, carefully enunciated, loaded almost. Oh God, thought Em immediately. What woman? What had happened?

George seemed to be taking great care not to look directly at Izzie. 'Ah,' he said. 'Any woman in particular, or did you not get that far?'

'Your ex-wife,' Izzie said, which was rude, seeing as Charlotte did have a name, and Em was fairly sure her daughter knew it. She raised an eyebrow. 'I told her you were semi-naked and a bit tied up with Mum, so . . .'

Oh Lord. Charlotte calling from Berlin, presumably to find out what the drama had been about earlier when George had tried to get through. And Izzie had felt it necessary to say *that*?

'Right,' said George. Despite being pretty much the most easy-going, amiable person Em had ever met, even he appeared kind of irritated at this. 'Another time just give me a shout, I could easily have come in to talk to her. Does she want me to call back?'

Izzie lifted a single shoulder in a couldn't-care-less shrug. She must still be smarting with George over the Seren business earlier, Em realized wretchedly.

'Right,' said George again, with a certain amount of weariness. 'I'd better go in and talk to her.' He hauled himself out of the pool, water running down his back and arms. 'Won't be long.'

'Me too,' Seren cried at once. 'I want to talk to Mummy as well!' A whining note had entered her voice as she clambered up the pool steps, still wearing the flamingo rubber ring. 'To tell her about being hurt. Being *pushed*!'

Izzie scowled and Em's smile became fixed like a mask as they went inside. Moments later, it was Jack's turn to heave himself onto the side. 'I'm starving,' he said, ambling towards the house.

'Okay, well, don't drip everywhere,' Em called after him. 'Dry your feet before you go in!'

He showed no sign of responding or even having heard her, and Em sighed, feeling her holiday-fun mood leaking away, like the stale air from a punctured lilo. 'Fancy a swim, Iz?' she asked weakly, but Izzie merely snorted and tossed her hair before padding back inside.

Right. And then there was one, Em thought, swishing her legs gently underwater as she leaned against the pool's smooth concrete lip. Maybe she would just stay here a while, leave George to deal with everything. Ignore any shouts of argument. Duck her head underwater so that she didn't have to hear the next fight.

But just then there came the slap of approaching flip-flop

footsteps, light and quick, and Olivia was walking towards the pool, wearing a bright turquoise one-piece with a towel around her waist. 'Hi,' she said shyly, as Em turned. 'You don't mind if I join you, do you?'

'Of course not,' cried Em, the erstwhile hostess.

Olivia put her towel down on one of the loungers and approached the pool, twizzling her long blonde hair up with a scrunchie. 'Oof,' she said, as she began descending the steps into the water. 'Not as warm as I was hoping.' She had a sweet high voice, a round face beneath her blonde hair. Late thirties, Em guessed.

'It's fine once you've done a few lengths,' Em promised as the other woman hesitated, two steps down. 'Just throw yourself in and swim fast for a minute and you'll be okay.' She glanced over to Briar Cottage, its windows reflecting blankly back at her. What was happening in there? she wondered distractedly.

There was a small muffled scream as Olivia plunged in and executed a splashy breaststroke across the pool and back, the blonde topknot wobbling frantically on top of her head. 'Okay, I'm warming up,' she said, bicycling her legs underwater and rubbing her plump pale shoulders. 'I'm all right. If I keep telling myself that, it might come true anyway.'

'I've been doing that a lot this holiday,' Em said, deadpan. She began swimming again herself, a lazy crawl that meant she could still talk. 'So are you here with your family? I didn't even know anyone was staying in your cottage. You must have been very quiet!'

'Oh,' said Olivia and, to Em's intrigue, two spots of colour appeared on her cheeks. 'Well, I'm sort of taking a breather from family life actually, so . . .'

Em reached the edge of the pool and turned, waiting for Olivia to finish the sentence, but the other woman didn't say anything else. Taking a breather from family life? What the hell did that mean? 'Ah,' she said, feeling awkward. 'Sorry. None of my business. Um . . . Are you staying here long?'

'Just a few days,' Olivia said vaguely. 'Surprise holiday, you could say.'

'Oh, right,' said Em. 'What, you mean . . . ?' Suddenly a whole new story was forming in her head. A really good, enviable sort of story. 'Don't tell me. Your husband sorted out a mini-break for you in Cornwall as a treat to get you through the summer holidays?'

'Something like that,' Olivia said, cheeks still pink. Perhaps a little embarrassed at how lucky she was.

'Oh my God,' sighed Em, unable to imagine such a scenario. 'How utterly blissful. What an amazing husband you've got! And it was a surprise, did you say?'

Olivia hesitated for a moment. 'I had no idea I was coming here till the day I set off,' she replied and Em let out a whistle.

'Nice,' she said, astonished that any woman could be so

fortunate. 'Jesus, I picked the wrong guy to marry. My first husband, I mean,' she clarified quickly, seeing Olivia's puzzled face. 'George is . . . a second try,' she said, lowering her voice. 'New boyfriend. First time holidaying together. Possibly the last too, if my children keep sabotaging things as they have been so far.'

Olivia laughed, probably thinking Em was joking.

If only, she thought, with another wary glance back at the cottage.

Chapter Eighteen

Right! Maggie was going out of the house. It was mid-afternoon, but she still had time to do something and act like a normal person on holiday, so there. So there, Will! He wasn't about to stop her enjoying herself.

It had been talking to Em earlier, on the way back from their abortive Falmouth trip, that had changed Maggie's perspective on this new aloneness. When she'd said, rather miserably, that Amelia was at her dad's and she was on her own as a result, her fellow holidaymaker's reaction had shone a whole different light on the situation. 'What, so you've got two days of holiday all to yourself? Mate!' Em had cried, slapping the steering wheel. 'Seriously? I am wildly jealous of you right now, Maggie. Wildly jealous! What are you going to *do*?'

'Well . . .' Maggie had started but then stopped again, not knowing where to take the rest of the sentence. Especially seeing as she'd been sweeping the floor and listening to Radio 4 earlier when Em had knocked on the door.

'I would totally book myself in for a spa,' Em said before the silence could develop. 'Just lie there for the day getting massaged and facialled, and emerge all sleek and pampered, having not lifted a bloody finger all day.' She sighed noisily, accelerating too fast around a corner at the sheer wistful thrill of such an occasion. 'Or – alternative plan – lounge indulgently by the pool, reading a massive fat blockbuster from start to finish. Only pausing to mix another cocktail.' She grimaced, self-consciously. 'Hmm, my day-off fantasies seem to involve a lot of lying down. How lazy. How about you? Are you going to shame me by doing loads of active, exciting things?'

Maggie had been on the verge of laughing and admitting that she was not a very exciting sort of person, but something had stopped her at the last minute. Em's positivity was surprisingly infectious. 'I might go for a long hike,' she said tentatively, the idea springing into her head at that moment. Yes! Why not? 'Somewhere really remote, just me and the elements.'

'Good one,' Em enthused. 'The great outdoors, with no teenagers whingeing about the poor phone reception or lack of Wi-Fi . . . yes, I would like that too. Oh – here we are,' she added, swinging into the car park at the cottages with a rattle of gravel.

It marked the end of the encounter – Em was, of course, desperate to see her daughter again, and after an appreciative thank-you, and a slightly rueful apology for having been a drama queen, they were saying goodbye and going their separate ways. By then, though, Maggie's imagination had been set ticking. Maybe Em was right: a couple of days to herself could be a pleasant thing after all. Spas and manicure weren't exactly her cup of tea, but there were loads of places she wanted to visit that Amelia had shown herself to be less keen on. This was her chance to really indulge in her hobbies, be completely selfish about what she fancied doing. Good!

And so she had turned to the guidebooks that her colleague Paul had lent her, flipping through the pages until she found a piece on Zennor, whereupon she remembered the promise she'd made to her mum. Perfect! According to her phone, it would take just under an hour to get there, where she would visit the church with its mermaid chair and take some photos for her mum, before returning home, possibly via the chippy for a proper fish supper with lashings of vinegar. There – see? Who said Maggie Laine couldn't enjoy herself on holiday?

Heading off moments later, she felt purposeful and focused, glad that she had something to do. According to the guidebook, the mermaid chair was a carved medieval bench end, thought to have been made in the fifteenth century or thereabouts, and featured an image of a mermaid holding a comb and mirror. *The most romantic legend of Cornwall,* the guidebook proclaimed although, in truth, Maggie was less interested in the romance angle. (That was her all over, she supposed: destined to be alone and peering at ancient relics rather than misty-eyed and waltzing off into the sunset with anyone.)

She *had* tried dating again, by the way. It wasn't as if Will had scraped every last romantic thought from her soul when he'd left her, but all subsequent attempts had resulted in bruising disaster. The first time she'd tried relaunching herself on the singles market had been via a dating agency, joined in a very un-Maggie-like moment of New Year rashness. 'Hold your nose and jump in,' a friend had advised her, and she'd taken the plunge, filled in the forms and been allotted a date. Arrangements had been made, a babysitter booked and a new haircut and dress purchased for the occasion, but once at the restaurant, she'd had a panicked call from the babysitter to say that Amelia, aged five at the time, had come down with a stomach bug. Maggie had to leave the date, having barely finished her starter. Arriving home to find her daughter flushed in the face and clammy, retching over the washing-up bowl with glazed eyes, the guilt had been acute.

'I wanted you, Mummy, but you weren't here,' Amelia had wheezed, words that had kept Maggie awake all night, bathed in reproach. The smell of Dettol had retained a particular whiff of blame ever since. (Oh, and the man in question? She couldn't even remember his name, let alone his face. She had cancelled her account with the dating agency the very next day; lesson learned.)

A few years later she had dipped a toe in the pool once again. Andrew, a supply teacher at school for most of the autumn term, had caught her eye. He was charming and attractive, ten years older than her and shamelessly flirty whenever they were paired together for playground duty. When he asked her for a drink, she'd almost choked on the staffroom coffee in her surprise and delight. 'Seriously?' she asked idiotically, feeling herself light up inside like a Christmas lantern. 'Absolutely,' he'd replied with a smile that sent her stomach into washing-machine spin cycle.

Oh, Andrew. It had started so well, too. She went out with him three times – twice for drinks and once for dinner – and had felt her old resistance actually starting to crumble in his garrulous, attentive presence. Her heart felt pleasantly fluttery whenever she saw him across the staffroom. Her tummy felt deliciously swoopy as they kissed goodnight at the end of the date. She was even starting to think this might be serious, wondering when she should sleep with him, fantasizing about how it would be. When should she introduce him to Amelia? What might the future hold for the three of them? Horizons were expanding before her, with new possibilities and dreams. They could be a family! Maybe 'second time lucky' was really a thing!

Not for her though, it wasn't. Because shortly afterwards she'd heard him in conversation in the staffroom just before the end of term and everything had changed. The two of them hadn't gone public about dating – that sort of thing was very much frowned upon by the head teacher – and she'd rather enjoyed the secrecy of their relationship, the subterfuge involved, all those knowing looks and smiles. But then she'd happened to hear Sandra Brewer, one of the French teachers, chatting with Andrew over by the coffee machine. 'I met your wife the other day – turns out your kids and mine are in the same drama club,' she'd said, and that was all it took for Maggie's blood to run cold, for the walls of the staffroom to start pulsing nightmarishly in and out, for her hopes and dreams to crash down to the ground in a shower of brick dust and rubble.

He had a wife and kids. He was a married man. Why hadn't he told her? Why had he let her believe that anything might come of their relationship? How could people be so deceitful, so cruel? She had sat there, cheeks burning, as she heard him prattle on about the drama group and their Christmas show and blah-blah-blah, like a normal parent, a good old family man. He knew that she was a mum, she'd told him about Amelia – he'd had every chance to reply with details of his own kids in return. And yet he'd hidden them away from her sight, along with his wife, and let her think that he was hers for the taking.

'You didn't tell me you had children,' she had said furiously the next time they were alone together. It was the end of the school day and she'd gone to find Andrew in the history block, where he was sat with a pile of marking. She had burst in there with such rage that her fists had actually been clenched, she remembered.

He had blinked at her, unperturbed. (Un-bloody-perturbed! She felt like perturbing him to death there and then for his irritatingly mild expression.) 'You didn't ask,' he'd replied. 'To be honest, I thought you knew. It's not like I've kept it a secret.'

'And a wife too,' she'd gone on, her nails digging into her own palms. Later on, she would examine those livid crescent-shaped indentations and almost wish they had scarred her forever: a reminder never to fall for a smooth-talker again.

'Would it have made any difference to you?' he'd asked with that same bland demeanour.

He'd genuinely said that. Would it have made any difference to her, like she was some kind of marriage-wrecker, like she *wanted* to go out with a man whose life had already been wrapped up in a neat parcel with another woman. Who had kids, a family life, drama-club appointments in the diary. 'Of *course* it would,' she had cried, scandalized. 'God, Andrew. You clearly don't know me at all, if you think otherwise!'

He'd just shrugged, though, as if he didn't care anyway. 'It was only a couple of drinks, Maggie. Friendly drinks. You didn't think there was anything more serious going on, did you?'

The question was like a dagger plunged into her heart. Friendly drinks? But we *kissed!* she wanted to yell. You pressed your leg against mine under the table! You looked into my eyes and said nice things to me! And now he was dismissing it as nothing, as friendly bloody drinks? Was she the deluded one or was he?

It had taken every bit of dignity she possessed to leave that room without crying. And from that moment on, she had walled up her heart like a tomb. No entry. Access denied. It was too dangerous, too hurtful even to *try*, she had decided. Forget it!

She gripped the steering wheel now, driving west, thinking about the boundaries she'd erected around herself, mighty and impenetrable. Her own fortress, in which she had kept herself safe, protected from idiots like Andrew or Will. The strategy had worked, at least – nobody had been able to break in and hurt her again, but sometimes it had felt like a lonely hill on which to stake your principles. Even Paul . . .

Well. She felt kind of bad about Paul, if she was honest with herself. A colleague of hers at the school, he had been a real rock over the years: not only with the advice and encouragement he'd given her as a novice teacher, but also with numerous helpful deeds, coming to her rescue when her car wouldn't start one snowy afternoon after school, popping round with a toolbox and new lock the horrible day she'd been broken into, and generally being on the end of the phone if she needed a pal. He was lovely, in short. Handsome too. As their friendship had developed, she had occasionally felt a funny sensation inside, a giddy, floaty sort of feeling, as if she might be falling for him, but she had stamped on it hard. Very hard. She had made a pact with herself always to put Amelia first, and that meant never getting involved with a man and becoming vulnerable to hurt again. So that had to be the end of it.

That said, there had been a couple of times when she had got the impression that Paul might be having similar feelings about her too, though, as if he would also like more to come of their friendship – an earnest look in his eye, a throat-clearing hesitancy as if he were building up to broach a tricky subject – but she had firmly pre-empted any such advances each time, making it clear that she only had room for Amelia in her life, before he could put her on the spot with an awkward question. Afterwards she had found herself cringing, feeling bad for the way his face had fallen, but she knew that refusing him was the right thing to do. Because how could she possibly get involved with anyone else?

She frowned, still unsure now whether or not she had done the right thing, then spotted the sign to the village and tried to concentrate on where she was going. It was only self-preservation, she told herself. Nothing wrong with that, was there?

Zennor was small and rather beautiful with its weathered stone buildings, narrow lanes and the backdrop of lush green fields. Maggie tucked her car in behind a Ford Focus with dog stickers all over the back window a short walk from St Senara's Church where, according to her mum and Paul's guidebook, the mermaid chair was located. *Uggggh,* she imagined Amelia complaining. *This looks so-o-o boring. Do I have to come in? Can't I stay in the car?*

'Oh God, tell me about it,' Em had groaned earlier when Maggie had mentioned Amelia's lack of enthusiasm for any of her suggestions. 'All my two want to do is go to those extreme sport places: zip-slides and death-plunges and the like. Zorbing, Jack keeps suggesting. I don't even know what that means, but I'm pretty sure my battered pelvic floor won't enjoy the challenge, whatever it is.'

Locking the car now, Maggie glanced back down the road, imagining her parents, young and athletic, cycling along there together. Her dad, the most competitive man alive, no doubt pedalling away in the lead, with her mum's ponytail streaming behind her as she did her best to keep up. Alec and Jan, love's young dream, pink in the cheeks after the fresh air and exercise. All of a sudden she had a lump in her throat. She was not too old and dried-up to remember how it felt to be young and caught up in a whirl of romantic love herself. When she and Will had first got together, it had been wonderful. She had felt so happy!

She walked towards the church, picturing her twenty-something parents alongside her, hooking their legs over their bikes as they dismounted, smiling at one another. The warm, still air almost seemed to shimmer with their ghostly figures as she went up the lichen-splattered stone steps into the grassy churchyard. Did people you'd loved ever really leave? she thought, following the path to the church ahead. She had tried talking to her dad a few times after he died, but always felt self-conscious and melodramatic. Besides, at first she had felt so angry with him for dying from his own stupid recklessness that she'd only been able to say accusatory things in his direction anyway. Today, though, it felt as if he was here with her, however implausible that seemed, and she was glad for his presence.

Inside, the church was calm and hushed, with colourful cushions in the pews and beautiful arched stonework. The mermaid chair was chunkily built from dark-brown wood with the carving still in incredibly good nick, Maggie marvelled, crouching to photograph it from the best angle for her mum. Had her parents held hands as they stood here, exchanging glances as they read about the legend? Had it really been this that prompted her dad to make his proposal outside? She wished he was still around to ask.

A wistfulness stole over her as she gazed around and noticed other couples together, wandering about in their twosomes and pausing to read the mermaid's love-story. How come everyone else seemed to manage their relationships so easily? she wondered. And what was wrong with her that she'd never been able to relinquish herself to love and romance again?

I'm not scared of anything, she had told herself when Helena challenged her, but in truth she *was* scared, she realized now. She was so weak and frightened in fact that she had said no to every opportunity, every man who had come her way for years. It had taken her this long to recognize the reality: that she *had* hidden behind Amelia, that she *had* used her as an excuse. The strategy had seemed the best option at the time, but look at her now, all alone, while the rest of the world moved in their cosy little pairs around her. How would that ever change, unless she did?

She felt numb with the unhappy self-realization, frozen to the church floor, no longer sure what to do with herself. A couple walked by just then, so wrapped up in themselves they didn't notice her there and the woman bumped against her. 'Sorry,' said Maggie automatically, but it seemed as if neither the woman nor her partner saw her even then. She was invisible. A total nobody. And suddenly she was sick of it always being this way.

'I am *here*, you know,' she said after their retreating

backs. Either they didn't hear her or they didn't care, because neither of them turned back to respond.

Maggie was not a confrontational sort of person. Usually she would have absorbed the snub and moved on. But today something had got under her skin, because rather than scuttling away as she ordinarily would have done, she raised her voice and said the words again. 'I *am* here, you know! I do exist!'

Now she had other people's attention, but not in a good way. Heads turned and she was met with wary glances. Uh-oh. Crazy-lady alert, their expressions said. Quick, drop eye contact and let's hope she goes away again. Nobody encourage her.

Cheeks flaming, hands curling defensively into fists, Maggie walked quickly towards the door and out of the church. Her own words kept ringing through her head like the breaking of an enchantment, though. *I am here! I do exist!*

Maybe, just maybe, it was time to smash down some of those self-built high walls and reintroduce herself to the rest of the world, she thought, as she got back into her car. Her blood was racing like a warrior's. Her heart was thudding. Then she pulled down the sunshade and flipped open the little mirror there, staring at herself as if seeing herself for the first time. The question was: who did she want to be? And what was she going to do about it?

Chapter Nineteen

Izzie flopped onto her bed, smarting as she heard George's voice through the wall. He was talking to his ex-wife, Charlotte, she could tell, because Seren was clamouring to speak too, like the annoying little brat she was. George sounded a bit irritable, she thought, and then, leaning closer to the wall, Izzie heard him ushering the little girl out of there so that he could talk to his ex in private. Oh, great. No doubt they were giving her a good old slagging. Just what she needed!

Okay, so she probably shouldn't have spoken to the woman *quite* so rudely earlier, but when she'd answered George's phone she'd been feeling so damn angry about everything that this sharp burst of nastiness had just spiked up through her. *Your girlfriend's daughter sounds a right charmer,* she imagined Charlotte bitching to George. *What the hell's wrong with her?*

Good question, Charlotte. *The* question, in fact.

Rolling over, Izzie put her face in the pillow, feeling

confused and tired, wishing she could start the day all over again. But how did you spool backwards from a bust-up like that when your own feelings were balanced so precariously? George was probably waiting for her to say sorry, but why should she, when she hadn't even done anything wrong? He should be the one apologizing to her, thank you very much – he and his crummy daughter. He had really pissed her off!

She reached for her phone and clicked on the Summer of Yes group chat to see what her friends were up to. Maybe they would distract her. Lily was swooning about her boyfriend as usual, Ruby was wanging on about some party or other at the weekend – great, another thing Izzie was going to miss – and all of a sudden she was utterly fed up of being the only one with nothing interesting to say for herself. Being the boring one of the group totally sucked.

'Take it till you can make it,' she remembered Olivia saying and then, in the next moment, her fingers began to fly unprompted over the keyboard. *Forget your party, how many points do I get for some hot naked action with an older man then??* she typed. *While my mum was in the next room!*

Her finger hovered above the Send button. For years afterwards, even when she was a grown woman with a job and a flat and a boyfriend of her own, Izzie would remember with a choking nausea that moment of hesitation when the future held its breath and waited for her choice. But a weird sort of momentum had taken hold of her and she felt powerless to stop it. *Send*, she decided, pressing the screen.

There followed a few seconds' silence, as if her friends were collectively gasping and reading the message again to check they weren't hallucinating – and then in poured the responses like an avalanche:

Ruby – NOOOOOO. WHAT?????
Tej – are you serious?
Izzie – hell, yeah
Lily – OMG
Alice – WHOA
Ruby – you broke the frickin leaderboard!!!
Miko – what was it like?? This is George the sexy older
man, right?
Izzie – yep. Fucking amazing!
Tej – tell us everything. EVERYTHING!!!!!!!!

Izzie let go of her phone and fell back on her bed, her heart pounding as if she'd been running hard and fast. How do you like me now, girls? Is that wild enough for you?

Sweat popped out on her forehead, both from the stuffiness of the room and the acid guilt curdling her stomach. She felt as if she was either about to throw up or collapse in hysterical laughter. Lying so outrageously felt exhilarating and kind of crazy too. She loved thinking of their shocked faces, trying to comprehend what she'd done. What she hadn't done, more like, but they didn't need to know that. If her friends called her bluff, she'd just laugh and express incredulity that they'd believed her at all. You really fell for it? You really thought I would? Thanks a lot, guys. Unbelievable!

She heard the door close in the room next to hers and then George's footsteps on the landing. 'Seren?' he yelled. 'Seren, where are you?'

Izzie's phone was still chiming and buzzing with new messages and questions, but she typed *Got to go* and then muted her notifications, not wanting to get entangled with elaborations. She'd tell them later that it was all a joke. Probably anyway. For now, though, the lie felt like a small, private strike back. A tiny victory that George didn't even know about. 'I win,' she said under her breath.

'What, so she *lied*? An out-and-out lie? Are you serious?' Em couldn't believe what she was hearing. She had eventually come in from the pool with vague thoughts about being hungry, only to see that it was almost five o'clock and she was shrivelled up like a prune. Then, as she towelled herself dry in the bedroom after a quick shower, George had come in to find her, stormy-faced.

'Everything all right?' she'd asked, her stomach turning in dread. Oh no. *Don't tell me*, she thought. Charlotte was so incensed with the way her daughter was being treated, she had insisted that George remove her from the house immediately and return Seren to the safety of Cheltenham. George had agreed that yes, Em and her family were a dangerous influence on his precious girl, and he was about to dump her *and* the holiday in one fell swoop. He hated her and never wanted to see her again!

His eyes were dark and severe, with none of their usual sparkle; she had never seen him look so forbidding. Back as a little girl, her childhood dog, Brandy, had always let out a nervous whimper whenever he felt he might be in line for a scolding, and Em could feel the same animal instinct inside her too, to make a similarly pitiful noise. *Don't be cross with me. I'm sorry. Whatever it is, I'm sorry!* But in the next moment George sank onto the bed with a sigh and she realized that his bad mood might not be directly connected to her after all.

'Well, I had an interesting chat with Charlotte,' he said heavily. 'Turns out Seren didn't tell the truth this morning about Izzie pushing her. She made the whole thing up.'

'What, so she *lied*? An out-and-out lie? Are you serious?' Okay, she had not been expecting *that*.

'Yeah.' He scratched his chin, a rueful look on his face. 'Charlotte got it out of her, with a few stern questions. Apparently it's happened before too. Getting other girls in her class told off, pretending they hurt her or scribbled on her artwork, when it turned out not to be true. Eventually there was this huge backlash at the end of term, when several parents complained to the teacher about Seren's behaviour.'

'God,' said Em, trying to take all of this in. 'So at the beach today . . .'

'Fake news. Well, presumably she did actually fall in the pool, but Izzie didn't push her.' His voice was becoming grimmer by the second, his face sagging as he spoke. 'I feel bad for instantly believing her now, thinking the worst of Izzie . . .'

Her daughter's newly proven innocence made Em instantly generous. 'Of course you believed her,' she soothed. 'Look, we're always going to be biased towards our own kids, that's just part of the deal here, isn't it?'

'I'll apologize to Izzie, obviously. And Seren will too.' He ran a hand through his hair. 'I'm a bit stunned by all of this, I have to say.'

He looked so downbeat, so disheartened by his daughter's mendacity, that Em felt sorry for him. Thank God her kids had always been straight with her. She hated the thought of them lying about anything. No wonder George seemed so stricken. Wrapped in her towel, she went over to hug him. 'Kids, eh?' she said, her voice muffled by his shoulder. Then she snorted. 'That seems to have become the catchphrase of this holiday.'

'Charlotte said to apologize too,' he said as they drew

apart. 'Seren's just finding it hard, she thinks, us being apart. It's the first summer she's had where she's been shuttled back and forth like this; she's probably thinking about other holidays where we were still a family and . . .'

'Charlotte doesn't have to apologize for anything,' Em said quickly, seeing George becoming more miserable by the second. 'And neither do you. If Seren says sorry to Izzie, we can clear the air, start again. Right?'

He nodded. 'Right. I'll bring about the truce, get the peace treaty signed and sealed and then how about I take us all out for pizza tonight?'

Em began combing her wet hair and smiled at him in the mirror. 'Sounds like a plan,' she said. He left the room and she heard him knocking gently on Izzie's door.

There. Over. Sorted. Even better, her own child wasn't in the wrong for once. She picked up the hairdryer, feeling as if they might just have turned a corner. Smooth roads and happy holidays ahead, she thought.

Chapter Twenty

'Are you sure this is safe?' Maggie asked with a nervous laugh. 'I'm not about to plunge to an early death or anything?'

The man tugging on the straps of her harness to check they were secure paused to consider her question. He was in his mid-twenties, she guessed, burly to the point of almost bursting out of his green 'forest ranger' uniform, and had a dimple in his cheek when he smiled. 'Let's see, it's Wednesday today, isn't it?' he said in reply. 'Nope. No early deaths booked in for today, you're all safe.'

'Ha-ha,' said Maggie apprehensively. 'That was a joke, right?'

'Let's hope so!' he replied. 'Okay, you're all set. Last question is: do you want a push or are you going to jump?'

Maggie stared down at the forest canopy below. TAKE THE PLUNGE! read the sign in front of her. Strapped into a harness, holding tight to a cable, she was standing at the top of a zip-slide, having impetuously picked this as the bravest and most un-Maggie-ish thing she could do today.

But now her stomach was saying, *Don't do this* and her head was saying, *You could die* and . . . Actually this was a ridiculous idea. What had she been *thinking*? She didn't need to throw herself off a tiny timber platform 150 feet high to prove anything to anyone, she—

'You're not scared, are you?' said the man, who looked a lot like Helena, now that she peered at him more closely. Wait, that was weird. What was *she* doing here? 'Okay, I'm taking your silence to mean you want a push,' said Helena. 'Ready . . .'

'No!' yelped Maggie, because she hated the thought of being pushed.

'Steady . . . GO!'

'WAAAARRRGGHHHHH!' Maggie screamed as she was shoved off the platform.

Then she sat bolt upright in bed, panting. Sweat broke out on her forehead. It was just a dream, she told herself shakily. Just a dream.

She blinked a few times and the morning swung into focus. Oh yeah. Now she remembered. Today was the first day of the rest of her life. So what was she going to do?

A few miles away, Olivia was clambering down a wooded slope. She was making her way tentatively, legs trembling with the exertion, when she skidded on some loose stones and had to clutch at a sapling to stop herself plunging all the way down. As she clung to the tree, her heart pounded, but she kept her balance and let out a shaky breath. This was not how she usually spent her Wednesday mornings. Then again, this was not a usual kind of day.

She had woken up following the luxury of another full night's sleep. Her fourth day in Cornwall and already she felt like a different person from the frazzled, crying woman who'd driven, shouting aloud, down the motorway. The white noise had quietened to a faint hiss of static in her head, but family life in Bristol still felt distant, as if it belonged to somebody else.

How are you? When will you be home? We all love and miss you so much, Mack kept texting, with accompanying photos and little videos of the boys. Any time she dared turn her phone on there would be another flood of new messages. But looking at them and the pictures was like gazing at another person's life. What did it mean, the complete lack of compulsion she felt about returning – her blank feelings of nothingness? Was she a monster? Or just malfunctioning?

Her relationship with Mack been so easy before the boys were born. They'd each had their separate jobs and friends and hobbies, but always clicked back like jigsaw pieces whenever they were together. She'd find her gaze drawn to his across a party and feel a throb of joy that she'd be going home with him later, that he was her other half. But then, with the arrival of their sons, it was as if they'd been cast into different corners with new labels slapped upon them. He was now the Big Provider, still with his own job, friends and hobbies, while she'd been given the role of Loving Homemaker, who had time for nothing and no one outside the home, least of all herself. They had been winched further and further apart until he seemed far out of reach. It was hard to remember now how they'd been as newly-weds; even harder to remember how it had felt to be her own self, Olivia, before she'd become Mrs Jim Mackintosh and Mum.

Until yesterday, that was. Yesterday, when she had been forced right out of her numbness, by almost colliding with Em's daughter Izzie on her bike down at Swanpool. And even though it had been a shocking experience – she could almost hear the brakes of her car still screeching in her ears – Olivia hadn't panicked or gone to pieces. She hadn't dwelt on the what-ifs and what-might-have-beens at all, despite the fact that car accidents had always been a terror of hers, still there in the back of her mind even after the many thousands of miles she must have driven by now. She'd actually coped pretty brilliantly, if she said so herself. She'd kept a cool head and looked after the girl when she dissolved into a panic attack, and got her home safely afterwards. It had felt really good, actually. Like she was a proper, responsible adult with some agency – a person who did things. Maybe not as worthless as she had been thinking.

Then there had been the time spent at the pool as well.

Having the chance to swim a few lengths alone, enjoy the relaxed feeling of floating in water, chatting to a friendly woman. Nobody needed their armbands fixing or saving from a potential drowning incident. When was the last time she'd been able to swim like that? Certainly before the boys were born. She hadn't done any form of exercise since then, unless you counted walking to the local shops and back, hauling along a double-buggy.

Afterwards she had eaten her roast dinner (delicious), drunk a massive glass of Sauvignon Blanc (ditto) and then lain on the sofa all evening, watching cookery shows and soap operas, deliberately not switching on her phone. She would return Mack's calls soon, she vowed. Just . . . not yet.

Olivia carried on down the wooded slope now, placing her feet with care. Here she was, just her and her bad memories, in the very place they had happened. Because today she was going to rip off the scab and feel the pain of the truth, for the first time in two decades. It was the least she could do.

Hesitating between the trees, she stared around her. Was this the spot? Right here? It was hard to tell. The night had been dark and the car had rolled over a few times before smashing into the tree with one final terrible crunch; remembering those fractured jumbled moments now and trying to relate them to her surroundings was impossible. Her legs were shaking, she realized, and she sat down suddenly in front of an oak tree. The ground was soft and springy beneath her and she leaned against the thick gnarled trunk to catch her breath. There. This would do. It was as good a place as any.

'Hello again,' she said. There was the faint hum now and then from the road above as a vehicle droned by, and sporadic birdsong from the trees, but otherwise it was quiet. Peaceful. The light was green and dappled through the leafy branches and her gaze was caught by an ant nearby, carrying a seed on its back. Tiny flies circled mesmerizingly in the air a short distance away. This miniature world was going about its creeping, murmuring business, wholly uninterested in her. She stretched out her legs in front of her, hands in her lap, and shut her eyes. Remembering.

It had been an ordinary day when she'd bumped into Pete in town. The exams were over and she was trying to get a holiday job for the summer. Aidan, of course, had already found a bar job at the golf club, but Olivia had left it to the last minute and was now dropping her details in at some of the hotels and B&Bs, in the hope that someone needed a waitress or chambermaid. She was getting nowhere and feeling increasingly fed up, so when she'd heard Pete calling, 'All right, Liv?' across the street she'd been glad of the distraction.

If college rumours were to be believed, Pete lived on his own, his dad having died, and his mum having gone off with a new bloke in Penryn. Whether this was true or not, there was something a bit damaged about him anyway, a bit broken. You could see it in his eyes. *Takes one to know one,* Olivia's wise old Devonshire gran would have said and, indeed, she did feel a connection between them, an understanding that she could never feel with Aidan, who had his comfortable home and such kind, loving parents. One thing had led to another that day anyway, and she and Pete had ended up drinking beer and setting the world to rights in the sunny little courtyard of a pub full of tourists. Several hours later, the sun and alcohol having gone completely to her head, Olivia hugged him as they said goodbye, just in the way that she would have hugged Nina or Spencer or any of her friends. The difference this time was that suddenly she and Pete were kissing and it was so passionate, so sexy, she felt her stomach turn over like a flipped pancake.

Stop! she wanted to protest.

Don't stop! she wanted to beg.

'Listen, a few of us are off inter-railing in August,' he murmured, his arms still slotted around her waist as they eventually drew apart. 'Why don't you come with us?' His hip ground against hers. 'With me.'

'Oh!' she had said, taken aback. Didn't he know? 'I'm going out with Aidan. I mean . . .'

He'd raised an eyebrow as her words trailed away. He had very expressive eyebrows, she remembered, and this one seemed to hint at disbelief and all sorts of badness with a single lift. 'Still?' He'd laughed. 'Didn't feel like that to me just now.'

There was a wildness about Pete that made her shiver even now, years later, to recall him. He reminded her of a hunting animal, bold and impulsive, eyeing her with a predatory air. Somehow the effect was seductive, though. Magnetic. By contrast, Aidan seemed more like a domestic pet: a soppy Labrador or Golden Retriever, who would lick your face and sit when told. Pets were overrated, in Olivia's opinion.

'It didn't feel like that to me, either,' she found herself replying huskily.

He'd laughed approvingly, the night air full of danger and temptations, and she'd just about had the wherewithal to get herself home then, before anything else happened. All the same, the encounter had left her whirling. Excited.

In hindsight, she should have glossed over that day as a mistake – a lesson not to go drinking in the afternoon with a handsome bad boy – and moved on, but it had turned into this doomed romantic melodrama in her head. It wasn't as if she'd ever particularly fancied Pete until that moment, but suddenly he was forbidden fruit; he had made a play for her, and she was flattered by the attention, giddy with the turmoil this had provoked in her heart. Imagine what would happen if they were inter-railing together, all the passion promised by that one single kiss! She would be ripping his clothes off in every European town and city they travelled through, collecting decadent new experiences like stamps in her passport.

And then, in the car with Aidan on the way back from the gig, it had all come to a head. 'I'm not sure if we're really right together any more,' she had said, carelessly and – yes – cruelly. He had been getting on her nerves all evening. First, the way he'd tucked his shirt into his jeans like some kind of mummy's boy. Also, the careful way he'd locked up the car and double-checked it in Truro – like anyone would want to nick that Gran-mobile! Even his natural chivalry wound her up, opening the door for her, buying her a drink – tiny acts of love that damaged, dirty Pete wouldn't think to bother with. God, it was so annoying! Why did he have to be so nice? Nice was boring.

Poor Aidan. Poor nice, kind, doomed Aidan, who only had moments left to live at this point. He had turned towards her, his astonished face yellow under the street lights. 'What are you saying?' he'd asked, and the fear made his voice tremble like a vibrato. (Pathetic! Pete would never have acted so wimpishly.)

'I mean . . .' she began – and it had been like a delicious game for a moment: this tragic love-triangle, with her right at the centre, loving the torment of her dilemma. But she'd never finished her sentence because all of a sudden, a sharp bend was coming up and Aidan was still staring at her, distraught. 'Watch the road. AIDAN, WATCH THE ROAD!'

Afterwards, everyone had wanted to establish how it had happened. The police, the doctors, Lorna, her dad, friends . . . they'd all asked so many questions.

Had he been drinking? Not a drop.

Was he speeding? She was pretty sure he wasn't.

He was such a careful driver, though! Did anything startle him or distract him? Well . . .

She'd never been able to tell the truth in answer to that last question. How could she have done? She was only just eighteen herself and was hazy about the liability of heartlessly trying to dump your boyfriend moments before he crashed his car. Did that make her responsible for his death? Would she be arrested if she confessed to the real story? The whole town would hate her and judge her for it. Lorna would probably have taken a swing at her. Her dad might have disowned her with the shame.

Instead they had all been so kind to her. So concerned and tender, as if she warranted any of their sympathy. In a horrific moment of irony, Lorna had even *apologized* on behalf of Aidan that Olivia had ended up in hospital with whiplash and concussion! How Olivia had managed to keep a poker face while she deflected the apology she would never know, but somehow or other, her secrets had remained intact. And here she was back in Falmouth, staying in Lorna and Roy's beautiful cottage, when there was so much they didn't know. What a hypocrite she was.

Maybe she should just tell them and allow them to get their hatred and anger out on her in return. Let them hurt her as much as she had hurt them. Maybe Lorna needed to know the kind of person Olivia really was. For Olivia to end up despised by the one woman who had looked after her would at least feel like a proper punishment.

'What do I do?' she murmured aloud. 'What do I do, Aidan?'

She waited for some kind of sign – anything at all. A bird alighting on her hand perhaps, its black beady eyes full of compassion and understanding. A white butterfly flitting past her that might represent absolution. Even, you know, a massive judgemental thunderclap above, then a bolt of lightning that stabbed through her head, killing her immediately, with Aidan's voice rumbling 'JUSTICE' amidst the thunder. At least that way she'd know where she stood.

'Ready when you are,' she said shakily, but nothing came. Nothing changed. No bird or butterfly, no crack of thunder above her head. Of course it didn't. She was being fanciful.

Leaning back against the tree trunk, she took a long deep breath. The ground was solid beneath her, the air smelled of baked earth with just a hint of ozone on the breeze, and there were dog roses flowering nearby in a brambly cluster, she noticed. The birds were still singing. Such summery woodland beauty only made her feel worse than ever.

'I'M SORRY!' she yelled at the top of her voice. 'I'M SORRY, OKAY?'

A bird flapped away, startled at the sudden noise and she put her head in her hands. Idiot.

Although there was still that one thing she could do, by way of penance to Lorna and Roy, mind, but . . .

She looked up in the next moment, turning it over in her head. No. It was unthinkable, after all this time. Think of how it would shake up all of their lives – not just Lorna's and Roy's, but hers and Mack's too. Stanley's. Harry's. And . . .

No, she thought again, before her thoughts could take her any further. Some things were best left undisturbed. She should leave well alone, keep the past behind her.

Shouldn't she?

Chapter Twenty-One

'So what are we doing for you today?'

Maggie met the eyes of the woman in the mirror. After her dream that morning, she had sat in bed and googled 'How to change your life' and one of the first pieces of advice that had come up was that sometimes, if you changed yourself from the outside, you then felt more able to change from the inside. *Try a new hairstyle,* the writer had enthused. *A great new cut is the perfect way to start reinventing yourself: you'll feel younger and more confident – it'll put a spring in your step!*

Maggie was in her forties and no longer believed in fairy stories, but what the hell – it was worth a go. Being on holiday meant you were removed from your usual boundaries and routines, she figured: you could branch out a little, try new things. Besides, she couldn't actually remember the last time a professional had been let loose on her hair – at least six months ago, she estimated, and as a result her thick brown hair currently fell like drab, heavy curtains around her face. Not for much longer, though, because here she was at Salon

Suzanne, just off the main street in Falmouth, and the hairdresser – Suzanne herself – was waiting for her to reply.

'I'm not exactly sure,' Maggie began apologetically. This was one of the many reasons why she was generally so reluctant to go to the hairdresser's – because she didn't know the terminology, she never quite knew what to ask for. She didn't even know what suited her. *Just a trim,* was what she usually said, and you could always see the disappointment in the hairdresser's face – yawn!

Today, here in Cornwall, she didn't feel like trotting out the same old, lame old phrase, though. Today she wanted to change her life. 'What do you think would suit me?' she asked instead.

Suzanne's eyes lit up at once. 'Ooh, let's see – well, we could take some of the weight out of your hair, perhaps bring it up to your shoulders, and add texture with a few layers.' She a ran a hand expertly through the strands, lifting up the hair so that it reached Maggie's shoulders to demonstrate. 'What do you think?'

Maggie turned her head from side to side. She had a neck! Who knew? 'Yes, please. That sounds good,' she said. And then, because Suzanne had such kind brown eyes and seemed to really care about Maggie's hair, she found herself adding, 'I just want to feel more confident, to be honest. I've felt a bit . . . invisible lately. An invisible middle-aged woman. You know?'

Suzanne probably *didn't* know, because even though she looked as if she might be a similar age to Maggie, she had beautiful dark-auburn hair that tumbled halfway down her back, thick and strong, and a really sharp fringe that fell just above her eyebrows. You could have used it as a ruler, it was so straight and angular. Not for Suzanne the humbling cloak of invisibility – and yet she was nodding sympathetically. 'It's a shock, isn't it, when you realize you're getting older,' she said. 'It happens to us all. But let's see what I can do to help. Now, did you want any colour today, with the cut? We're fairly quiet this morning, so I could do that for you as well, if you wanted.'

Colour! Maggie hadn't dyed her hair since she was a student, and that had been with cheap packet dyes that left her hair unnatural shades of tomato soup and aubergine. 'Um . . .' she said apprehensively.

'We have some lovely warm tones that might just soften things up a bit, that's all,' Suzanne went on. 'A nice shiny chestnut, perhaps, or more of a cocoa brown . . . Shall I show you the range so you can have a think?'

Maggie glanced in the mirror at the sprinkling of grey hairs that speckled her parting. Remembered how some of the Year 9s she taught had commented on them at the end of term and started calling her 'Granny Laine'. She was not a vain person by any means, but even so, she didn't want anyone thinking of her in grandmotherly terms just yet.

Take the plunge! the banner from her dream encouraged her and she found herself nodding. 'Yes, please,' she replied, suddenly emboldened. 'Why not?'

This was *nice*, she thought a few minutes later as a younger woman washed her hair and gave her a head massage so blissful it sent shivers down her body. When had anyone last touched her like this? It felt so good, so luxurious. She was not a naturally touchy-feely person herself, wasn't the type to go around hugging or kissing others willy-nilly, but her whole body was reacting to this woman's fingers as if it had been starved of attention for the longest time. As if she was ravenous for the human touch.

A lump the size of an egg seemed to be in her throat. 'Thank you,' she croaked at the end, as a towel was gently wrapped around her hair and wound into a neat turban. Her nerve-endings were still tingling. 'That was wonderful.'

Time passed pleasantly by as Suzanne pasted the dye onto sections of Maggie's hair, then wrapped them in foil, while they chatted about this and that. Before long, Maggie resembled a silvery hedgehog, a strange creature with shimmering scales around her face. 'Don't look so worried,' Suzanne laughed, seeing her apprehensive expression. 'You'll be feeling a million dollars when you walk out of my door, I promise.'

Once the dye was on, Maggie was given a selection of magazines and a fresh cup of tea as she waited for the colour to take. She glanced at her reflection, feeling excited at her own boldness. Amelia wouldn't believe it if she knew her boring old mum was here, getting a makeover. Should she take a photo – get her guessing? Or would that be kind of naff while Amelia was with her dad, as if Maggie was tugging at her daughter's sleeve: *Look at me, look at me, give ME some attention now?*

She sent a text without mentioning her whereabouts. It could be a surprise, her new image, when they saw each other again. (A good surprise, she hoped, rather than a moment of hilarity.) *How are you today, my love?* she wrote. *Hope you're having fun. Ring me if you get the chance, won't you? I tried a few times last night, but kept getting your voicemail. Love you. xx*

It was the not-knowing that was so hard to deal with, she thought, pressing Send. Of course she and Amelia had spent time away from one another in the past, what with school trips and sleepovers and Amelia's gradually increasing independence, but this was different. For the first time ever, she felt as if her daughter might be vulnerable and unprotected without her. Could Maggie rely on Will to look after and love her? No, not even slightly. Anything could be happening there.

After a while the foil squares were removed, the dye was rinsed off and Suzanne began deftly snipping. Maggie felt pliant and rather absent as locks of hair pattered softly to the floor around her. It was surprisingly relaxing, handing yourself over to another woman, an expert, and saying, *Please sort me out. Improve me.* And then, once Suzanne was satisfied with the cut, out came the blow-dryer, roaring heat around her head, and she watched, fascinated, as the new Maggie Laine took shape in the mirror.

Goodness. It was a transformation.

There in front of her was a woman with shiny conker-brown hair that looked light and swingy as it curled under at the neck. Suzanne had given her a side-parting, rather than her usual centre one, and Maggie turned her head slowly, marvelling at the way her hair framed her face so differently, how her cheekbones seemed more prominent all of a sudden. Goodbye, Granny Laine, she thought, noticing how the salon lights bounced pleasingly off the warm tones of her hair. Farewell, invisible woman. Here I am, world. What do you think?

'Lean forward just a fraction for me,' Suzanne said, snipping carefully against her neck. 'There. All done!' She held another mirror behind Maggie's head, and Maggie blinked a few times, startled to discover that her eyes were damp at the corners as she took in her lovely new style from all angles. She was almost embarrassed by how much hot, devout love she suddenly had for Suzanne, wrangler of miracles.

'It's gorgeous,' she said thickly, but the phrase didn't even touch how good she felt. 'I feel . . . amazing,' she went on. 'Like a new person.'

'You look like one too!' Suzanne replied. 'You look as if you're ready for anything now – and you're definitely not invisible. You're ready to take on the world!'

Maggie couldn't stop staring at herself. Then she smiled. 'I think I am,' she replied.

With pizza and apologies having restored some holiday harmony the night before and Izzie even deigning to spend time with Seren and her Sylvanian Families collection, once back at the cottage, Em was confident that they had all moved on a step. And the next day started pretty well too, with Jack and George having a bit of a kick-around with a football outside. They both seemed to enjoy that kind of argy-bargy and tussling, with George temporarily becoming a rather adorable teenage boy again in the process, while Jack couldn't get enough. He'd missed having a dad around since Em and Dom had separated, by the sound of things, Michelle never gave them much time alone to just hang out and be daft together.

She smiled, hearing their whoops float through the open kitchen window. This was good, she told herself, packing up a picnic for later on – but just as she was thinking those words, she heard a loud splash and a yell, and hurried to the window to see George flailing about in the pool fully dressed where he had fallen in. It was hard not to laugh as he emerged up the steps, absolutely drenched, with water pouring from his clothes – Jack was certainly roaring his head off in true unsympathetic style – until George clapped a hand to his back pocket and groaned. 'My phone,' he said in dismay, at which point even Jack managed to stop laughing. Oh dear. 'Shit. It's completely dead,' he said, examining it.

So that was the first setback of the day and then, minutes later, Izzie announced she wasn't coming out with them and wanted to stay at home, which had Em wheedling and cajoling, to no effect. 'I'm sixteen and I'm an introvert,' Izzie said, not budging an inch. 'And I'll be fine on my own. Don't worry, I won't drown or anything. Or let any burglars in while you're out.'

Sometimes you just couldn't force a person to have fun. Never mind. The remaining four of them could still have a good day out. George had suggested a boat trip out to Truro, stopping on the way at Trelissick, a beautiful old country house with gardens and woodland to explore. Lovely! That would do. 'We might not have mobile reception the whole time because we'll be out on the river,' Em told Izzie before they left, 'but if you have any problems, just go and knock at the big farmhouse up there. Remember Lorna, the lady who gave us the keys? She may be able to help if you need her.'

A picnic packed, sun cream applied, and with George's phone stuffed in a bag of rice to dry out, they finally set off in George's car. It was weird – and not completely to Em's liking – the way they had settled into holiday roles this week, she thought, opening the map on her phone so that she could give him directions. Before now, they had been just Em and George in their relationship: two adults who liked each other's company and found each other attractive. Simple. But ever since they'd been in Cornwall, they had become more like Mum and Dad, whose main preoccupations were their various children. Em seemed to be doing all the cooking and organizing, just like she'd done in her marriage to Dom. George seemed to be doing all the driving and the larking about with kids – again, just like Dom had done when they'd been together.

Em wasn't sure she relished being slotted back into that old pigeonhole. She'd preferred it when they had their own separate spaces and lives. It wasn't that she didn't like George any less than before, it was more that she didn't want to be Mum-Em when she was with him. How did anyone get the balance right? Was it even possible? She . . .

'What am I doing here?' George asked just then as they approached a T-junction and Em snapped out of her thoughts, prodding hurriedly at her screen, which had gone unhelpfully blank.

'Um . . . left, I think,' she guessed. 'No – right. Sorry! Right!'

Oh God, and wasn't this exactly how it had been with Dom too – stressful navigating, as he ended up becoming crosser and crosser at her flakiness and lapses of concentration? Did she *want* a man at the steering wheel groaning at her incompetence all over again, and making her feel useless? No. She bloody well did not. 'I'll drive on the way back, by the way,' she said lightly, feeling the need to assert her own ability. Pigeonholes were for pigeons.

'Say no, if you value your life, George,' Jack said immediately from the back seat.

'I want *Daddy* to drive!' Seren chipped in piously.

Em opened her mouth to protest – after all the effing football matches she'd driven Jack to and from as well – but George was too quick for her. 'I'd love you to drive back,' he said, with a sideways wink. 'That is *very* kind. What am I doing at this roundabout by the way?'

Once again Em had to stab frantically at her phone. 'Whoops. Sorry. Er – straight ahead! Is that the second exit? Yes – second exit,' she babbled. 'I hope that's not a smirk at me, mate,' she added, seeing Jack's grinning face in her sunshade mirror.

'As if!' he cried, the innocent.

'He's texting his girlfriend actually,' Seren replied smugly on his behalf. 'I *saw*.'

'What? Who?' cried Em, while Jack swung away in irritation, saying, 'No, you didn't. You don't know what you're talking about.'

'Yes, I *do*. And you put kisses. He put kisses on his message, I saw!'

'All right, that's enough,' said Em, wondering if the girl

in question was Maggie's daughter. She'd put the thumbscrews on him later, try to find out. In the meantime Seren really needed to learn that nobody liked a grass. 'Look, we're nearly there, let's just—'

'Am I following signs to the docks here or . . . ?' asked George, somewhat impatiently.

'Er.' How had this happened again? 'I'm not sure, sorry. Let's guess at . . . yes?'

'You do know the boats only go every two hours, don't you? I mean – if we miss this one . . .'

'We're not going to miss this one. I'm on it, don't worry. See that parking sign? We're turning off there. No – the one on the left. That one!'

To think that she would look back later on at this car journey with something bordering on nostalgia: a time when all she had to worry about was kids bickering, and the prospect of missing a boat trip, because of her crap navigation skills. Because what she didn't realize was that the day was about to get so much worse. Her entire holiday was about to collapse like a house of cards around her, and there was absolutely nothing she could do to prevent it falling.

Olivia was sitting cross-legged up on the headland, just her and the big sky, with the sea below, all shades from indigo to teal. Funny, she hadn't spent much time in Cornwall for twenty years and yet she could still name every seabird – the guillemots and cormorants and razorbills – without a second thought. She'd recognized the sea-pinks and vetch too, their names springing instantly to her mind as she noticed them. Cornwall ran through her veins, like it or not. Every place carried a memory for her. Being here, for instance, reminded her of the time she and Aidan had once made their way to this spot together, bunking off sixth form to smoke a badly rolled joint and lie in the warm tussocky grass hand-in-hand for a whole afternoon. It seemed a fitting place to write a letter of confession; she could practically feel his presence there with her, directing her hand.

Dear Lorna and Roy, she began. *I should have told you this a long time ago, but . . .*

Then she stopped, already swamped with shame and doubt. This was going to be the hardest letter to write. How on earth would she be able to find the words? How could she do this?

Because you owe them, a voice in her head told her. It sounded a lot like her conscience. *Don't you think you owe them that much?*

Her hand shook. She hadn't smoked for over fifteen years, but she suddenly felt desperate for a cigarette. A brandy, even, to stop her nerves.

She put the pen down and thought of Mack far away at home with the boys. Somewhere, beyond all the hills and fields and rivers, all those villages and towns and streets, the three of them were carrying on life without her. Eating breakfast, getting dressed, going to the park, digging in the sandpit, swinging on swings. They walked through her head like cutout paper dolls and she felt a small, dull ache inside for them. She missed them. She had failed them. Why had she ever thought she could be a good mother this time around?

Still searching for the right words with which to begin the letter, she switched on her phone and the familiar flurry of beeps and notifications chorused at her moments later. All from Mack at a guess – oh. No, actually. He must have been ringing around trying to find her, because there were some others too.

Dad: Everything all right, love? Where are you? Ring me if you want to talk. Mack's really worried about you.

Her brother Danny had texted too: *You okay? Is this about Mum? You're not her, remember. Don't do this, Liv. Call me?*

And – oh God, this was embarrassing. Some of the mums she knew had texted her as well: Mel and Ashleigh and Sara, all asking after her. *You all right? Can I help? Ring me if you need a friend,* they said and she bit her lip, slightly overwhelmed that everyone was being so concerned. So nice. She also felt kind of embarrassed. Just how many people had Mack told? Were they all gossiping about her now?

The phone vibrated in her hand as a new message appeared in the next moment: her brother again. *Hey – are you in Falmouth? Had a message on Facebook from Nick Barton, saying he thought he saw you in town. Want me to meet you somewhere? Can get out of work if you want to talk. x*

Tears misted Olivia's eyes. Now that Danny lived in London and was busy with work and dating, while she was so tied up with the boys, they hadn't seen much of each other recently, but he knew her, he understood. In some ways he knew her a lot better than her own husband. An image came to her of the two of them huddled on the back doorstep the night their mum had left, their small bodies shivering, their small tummies empty. For a short alarming time, it had felt as if it was just the two of them against the world, but they'd had each other at least.

Thanks, she replied to him. *Just figuring some stuff out. Will call in a few days, promise. x*

Mack next. Guilt pierced her as she read his messages and saw the latest photos of the boys he'd sent: a day-trip to Bristol Zoo, by the look of it, then the two of them in the bath later on with soap bubbles on their heads. A little video of them both waving at her and Stanley saying, 'We love Mummy!' while Harry loyally added, 'And Daddy!'

For so long she had felt weighed down by numbness, but she could feel it starting to lift off her at last, wisp by wisp peeling gradually away. The world seemed to be shifting back into focus again, as if she could see more clearly. She loved the three of them, so much. She always had done.

Feeling choked up, she typed a message to Mack: *Sorry*

about this. I miss you all too. I'm starting to feel a bit more human. There's just one thing I have left to do here. x

She sent the message, then switched off her phone again before anyone could ring her. Then she turned back to her letter. If she could somehow put things right here in Falmouth, she might just be able to face her real life in Bristol again, she thought. It was worth a try, wasn't it?

Chapter Twenty-Two

Outside the hair salon, crowds of cheerful holidaymakers were making their way through the bunting-laced streets, while seagulls cruised above, tracing wide arcs against the blue. Dogs sniffed out dropped pasty crumbs in the gutters, babies dozed in prams, small children in colourful T-shirts and sunglasses rode high up on their dads' necks. Maggie breathed in the seaside scents of vinegary chips, coconut sun cream and frying onions, then joined the melee, enjoying the sensation of her hair bouncing lightly with each step.

What next for the bold new Maggie? It was a warm day, the sun already high in the sky, and she decided to head down to the beach, past all of the pretty little shops and galleries – one of which had a sign up in the door saying: NO TEENAGERS. Then she stopped, remembering that this was the place Em had pointed out to her a few days earlier – something to do with their kids, but the full story had never come out. She must get to the bottom of that, she thought to herself with a frown. Moving on again, she kept catching sight of her own reflection in shop windows and being startled by how nice she looked, how much happier and younger she seemed without all that heavy hair weighing her down.

Once on the beach, she kicked off her sandals, the sand warm and gritty underfoot as she walked along. It was busy already there, with families laying out towels and beach mats, toddlers squatting in the shallows making mud pies in colourful buckets. A strong breeze whisked the newly bared back of her neck, and she smiled as she spotted a little girl gleefully licking an enormous chocolate ice-cream that was going all over her chin – 'Oh, Romy, you're *wearing* that ice-cream, my darling,' her mother said, half-exasperated, half-affectionate.

An elderly couple were sitting in a pair of deckchairs nearby and Maggie noticed they were holding hands across the sandy divide, their silvery heads turned to one another as they talked. Nearby there was a small wicker picnic basket and a Thermos flask, plus two paperbacks piled on a folded towel: a tableau that signalled companionship, a nice easy afternoon with the person you loved. It gave Maggie a similar feeling to the one she'd had in the church at Zennor, a pang of something she couldn't quite put her finger on: envy? Regret? Wistfulness?

'It's lonely sometimes being on your own, isn't it?' her mum had sighed in the years following her dad's death, but Maggie always refused to entertain the idea.

'Lonely? Ha! Chance would be a fine thing. I'm far too busy to be lonely,' she'd always replied, steadfastly turning away from the direction of self-pity. Turning down all the invitations she'd received, too, in dogged pursuit of being the best parent ever, running around after Amelia's wants and needs. Yet if she was honest with herself, she could see how gratifying it must be to have a decades-long loving relationship; to still be holding hands on a crowded beach, glad of each other.

Yes, well. Sometimes it wasn't as easy as all that.

Meanwhile, what might Amelia be doing with Will right now? Maggie checked her phone out of habit, but there was still no message. Maybe Will had taken her off to Exmoor with a load of camera equipment for a photography lesson, she thought, picturing him giving directions as he leaned over Amelia's shoulder, the two of them concentrating deeply on the moment. Perhaps they were walking along the river together, swapping stories and getting to know each other. Or maybe all five of them had gone out, one big new patchwork family, and Amelia was enjoying her role as older sister to the little ones. Maggie remembered how, aged five or six, Amelia had liked nothing more than lining up dolls and teddies and bossing them around with gusto. She would be a good big sister, she thought. Better late than never.

Further along the beach, a bohemian-looking woman caught her eye. There was something Pre-Raphaelite about her long red flowing dress and the headdress of flowers on her blonde hair, and she had set up some kind of stall near the kayak-hire place just along from the café. HAPPINESS ART PROJECT, Maggie read on a rippling banner.

'Hello, would you like to take part in my project?' the woman called out, seeing her looking. She was young – early twenties, at a guess – with a sweet round face.

Maggie smiled politely but kept walking. She never took part in avant-garde things if she could help it; they made her feel self-conscious. Plus she had a strong feeling that this young woman's project was going to be 'out there', as Amelia would say. *No, thank you,* she thought to herself.

'It's completely free and practically guarantees happiness,' the woman added winningly. 'Come on, it'll only take a few minutes. Have a go!'

For some reason, Maggie found herself hesitating. Stopping. Maybe it was her new haircut and Suzanne having told her she could take on the world that made her think twice. Maybe there was something in the sea air that day, opening her mind to new possibilities. Or maybe she was just plain old tired of saying, *No, thank you* all the time – to friends, to colleagues, to Paul, to strange random women on the beach.

'Go on then,' she said, approaching the stand with an unexpected prickle of curiosity. Whatever this was all about, it surely couldn't be any more embarrassing than her meltdown in Zennor yesterday, she decided.

A pile of large grey and white pebbles had been set out on a table, along with a box of colourful chalks, plus a selection of marker pens. 'Fabulous!' said the blonde woman. 'So this project is about releasing bad thoughts and thinking up new hopeful ones to replace them, as a means of making us all a little bit happier. I'm asking people to choose a pebble each and then to write on them with chalk any negative thoughts or messages that have been holding them back. Anything that's a worry.'

Maggie was starting to regret getting involved in this. 'Right,' she said suspiciously. Because achieving happiness was that simple, clearly. What a load of rubbish!

'I'll photograph the chalked pebble in your hand – it's all anonymous, by the way – and then the idea is that you walk down to the sea and throw the pebble out as far as you can. Really let it go! The tide will take it away – along with your worry.' She smiled a rather goofy smile. 'I know it sounds kooky, but the symbolism is really nice. And we all love chucking stones in the sea, right?'

'Well . . .' said Maggie, who was already worrying about hitting someone with hers. Followed by an arrest for grievous bodily harm shortly afterwards, knowing her luck.

'THEN – and this is the good bit – you take *another* pebble and with one of the permanent markers you write something hopeful and positive. Whatever you want. I'll photograph that too, then you get to take it away with you. Then we're done!'

'Right,' said Maggie, still dubious. She knew from her geologist days how the Coast Protection Act stated that taking stones from beaches was illegal but she could see a garden-centre bag of sandstone and shale pebbles behind the woman, so presumably these had already been bought, rather than collected from the surroundings. More importantly though, why did this person think anyone would want to pour out their secrets so publicly? On a *pebble*?

'You're looking unsure – let me show you some of the pictures so far,' the woman said, pulling out a folder from a bag. 'Here – see? I'm putting on an exhibition at the end of the season. You're welcome to come along if you'll still be in town.'

Maggie stared as the woman flicked through the pages of the folder. The photographs were beautifully shot: a hand holding the pebble each time, with their words springing out in coloured chalks. *Grandad dying,* was written in pink chalk on one. *Being alone,* read another in pale-blue capitals. *Exam results,* said a third.

Opposite them was a second photograph, the same hand with a different pebble. These ones carried much more upbeat pronouncements. *LOVE,* said one. *HOPE,* said another. *KEEP GOING,* said the third.

They were just *words* written on lumps of rock, but there

was something so simplistic about them, so poignant, that Maggie felt quite moved. 'Gosh,' she said. 'They're lovely.'

'The aim is that people take their pebbles away with them and just hold them now and then – because pebbles are *so* lovely to hold, aren't they? – and remember being here: a sunny beach, on a summer's day, feeling hopeful and positive. Like I said, almost a guarantee of happiness!'

'Okay,' said Maggie, even though she was more used to studying rocks rather than writing on them. The girl had charmed her with these photographs and her earnest goofy smile. It was impossible to refuse now.

'Great! Well . . . choose your pebble and chalk, and go for it!'

Maggie picked up a large grey pebble that had a thin white stripe running around its middle like a belt. It was cold and heavy, beautifully smooth. The girl was right, it did feel lovely to hold. Then she chose a yellow piece of chalk and considered a few options.

Anything bad happening to Amelia. No. She'd never fit all of those words on the pebble, for starters.

Will left me. Another no. That was an old wound, she wouldn't reopen it for the sake of an art project.

Dying alone surrounded by feral cats. Now she was just being silly. Come on, Maggie, for heaven's sake, get a grip.

'Sorry, I'm taking ages here,' she felt obliged to say, still hovering with her chalk in hand. 'I can't decide what to write.'

'It's fine, take your time,' the woman replied, removing the lens cap from a fancy-looking camera. 'Sometimes just letting the first and simplest thought pop into your head is best, but there's no rush.'

Maggie thought again of her dream, how she'd been paralysed at the top of the zip-slide, not wanting to jump. *What are you so scared of?* Helena had taunted her.

Maybe that summed it up: how bogged down she had become with all her no-thank-yous. How her own fear was perhaps holding her back. *Being too scared to try,* she chalked carefully onto the pebble, then grimaced a little as she held it out to the woman in the red dress. 'I know this is a bit pathetic,' she said, wanting to pre-empt any criticism.

But no criticism came. 'Not at all,' the woman said earnestly instead. 'It's perfect. Thank you so much. Now if you could just turn a little, so we can get the best light . . .' She angled the camera, leaning it over Maggie's hand, then began clicking off shots. 'And perhaps if you could hold it up against this piece of driftwood,' she went on, heaving a chunk of wood up from beside her table. 'Lovely. Yes. Super!' She beamed at Maggie and put the camera down. 'Okay. Now you can go ahead and hurl your worry into the sea. Throw with all your might.'

'I'll try not to hit anyone,' Maggie promised. Feeling

rather self-conscious, she walked down to the water's edge, found a stretch of shoreline where there were no swimmers or frolicking children within throwing distance and bowled the pebble underarm. It landed with a satisfying splosh, ten feet or so away, and vanished beneath the surface.

She knew it was symbolic rather than anything real, but all the same, the act of throwing the pebble away felt good. Surprisingly good. She imagined it sinking through the water before settling into the muddy depths, down below the waves, and the letters she had chalked gradually washing away. *Being too scared to try:* gone.

All the way back up to the art-project table, she could hear that splosh resounding in her ears and she smiled as she caught the woman's eye on returning. 'Nice,' she said. 'Thank you. Do you know, I feel oddly better for that.'

'Good! That's the whole point,' came the reply. 'Consider that worry lifted off your shoulders.' She grinned. 'Okay, now for the more upbeat part.'

This woman was *infectious,* she really was. Because not only was Maggie then absorbed in choosing the nicest pebble to keep and the marker with the prettiest colour (the sage-green was quite lovely, she eventually decided), but she then found herself deliberating for some time about what she wanted to write on it. On a pebble! She must be going soft in the head, she really must. And yet . . .

And yet it mattered, weirdly. She wanted to pick exactly

the right word. HOPE, she pondered. STRENGTH? LOVE? TOGETHERNESS?

In the end, she wrote COURAGE in her neatest lettering and awarded herself a small approving nod. Yes. That was what she was looking for.

'Wonderful! Perfect,' came the enthusiastic response from the artist. 'Great – nobody's done that yet, and it's such a good strong word. Right, last photograph and then I won't take up any more of your time. So, let me position your hand here . . . Lovely!'

Some clicking followed, a few rearrangements of angle and placing, and then it was all over. 'Thank you for taking part,' said the woman, passing her a small business card. 'Here are the details of the show, if you're in the area – otherwise, I'll be putting the prints online for you to look at.' Her flowered headdress had slipped sideways on her head, and there was lipstick on one of her front teeth, but she reminded Maggie of a sea nymph or even a good fairy, standing there amidst her pebbles and hopefulness. Her nose wrinkled as she smiled. 'You are now free to take your courage and leave. Have a lovely day.'

'You too,' said Maggie, smiling back. The pebble was weighty in her palm and she curled her fingers around it carefully, not wanting to smudge the ink. A handful of courage, she thought to herself, continuing along the sand. It was just what she needed.

Chapter Twenty-Three

Izzie was swimming in the pool. Length after length after length, feeling strong and energetic, enjoying being on her own for once. All the things that had stressed her out this summer didn't seem so important while she was here in the water, the sun warm on her shoulders, her muscles singing with the exertion of movement. The exams she'd taken – whatever. The pressure of trying to keep up with her friends – whatever. The thought of moving on to sixth form and a whole new chapter of her life beginning – pah. She'd deal with all that when the time came.

She did a splashy tumble-turn just for the sheer fun of it, surfacing halfway across the small pool. I am a dolphin, she thought. A mermaid. I am . . . being stared at by a man in a motorbike helmet. What? Where had he come from?

'Hi there,' said the man, pulling off his helmet and tucking it under one arm. Oh, okay, less of a 'man' actually, because he wasn't that much older than her, at a guess. Eighteen? Nineteen? He was quite sexy, with his flop of dark-brown hair and wide smile. 'Mrs Lorna Brearley?' he asked, peering at the address label of a parcel he was holding.

Izzie sniggered and swam to the side of the pool. 'Do I *look* like a Mrs Lorna Brearley?' she asked, then pointed up at the farmhouse. 'She lives there.'

'I know,' he said. 'She's my nan's friend, actually.' He grinned and a dimple poked a small attractive crater in his left cheek. He was wearing faded jeans with biker boots and she could see a white T-shirt under his leather jacket. The more she looked at him, the hotter her face seemed to get. He was *fit*. 'So what *is* your name?' he asked.

She laughed. Was he flirting with her? It felt as if there was a warm current crackling between the two of them. 'Izzie,' she replied, gazing up at him. 'What's yours?'

'Fraser,' he said, scooping a hand through his hair. He looked bashful suddenly. Maybe he was seventeen even, she thought. 'You on holiday here?' He rolled his eyes at himself. 'Stupid question.'

'Yeah,' she said. 'Here for another week.' They looked at one another and smiled again. 'You're local, are you?' she added, even though she was already pretty sure of the answer. She just wanted to keep him talking, have him there in her eyeline a while longer.

'Yeah, born and bred,' he said. Then he hesitated. 'So, um . . . What are you up to later?'

Her skin felt prickly even though the air was warm. Oh my God. Was he about to ask her out or something? Was this going to be a holiday romance? Her first kiss? Her mind was racing, but she did her best to play it cool. 'Not a lot,' she said. She was about to shrug, but the straps of her swimming costume felt too precariously balanced to risk it. Yikes! Do not flash the handsome biker dude, whatever you do. 'Why?' she added boldly. 'Got any bright ideas?'

'A few,' he said, one eyebrow quirked.

Her stomach seemed to turn inside out. He was gorgeous! Way better-looking than any of the boys back home.

'I'll probably be finished by two. We could . . . hang out?' he went on. 'Down at the beach – do you know Swanpool?'

'Nope,' she said. 'But I could find it.' Her heart was pounding so hard she was surprised the water wasn't pulsing around her. Just like that, her day had changed into something wildly exciting.

They both smiled at each other for a long hot second. The air quivered with possibilities. Then he waggled the parcel in the air, somewhat self-consciously. 'Right. Well, I should drop this off. Two o'clock, remember. See you by the café?'

'Yep,' she said dazedly. 'See you later. Bye, Fraser,' she added, just because she wanted to say his name out loud. *Fraser.* This handsome boy who wanted to meet her later. YES!

He strode away and she turned a fast splashy somersault, wanting to squeal with excitement. All of a sudden this holiday had got *so* much better. Miles better! As soon as he was round the corner and out of sight she got out of the pool and rushed back into the cottage. Thank God Mum and the others weren't here to make stupid comments and ask annoying questions. Thank goodness something *fun* had happened at last. She'd finally be able to go back on the group chat later with good news: Only joking about the older man, she would type with some laughing emojis. But guess what *did* happen today . . . !

She'd try and get a selfie of them together, she decided, thundering up the stairs, just to show her friends how hot he was. Ooh! Would he be wearing trunks at the beach? Would he try to kiss her? Help, and what was *she* going to wear?

Running into the bathroom, Izzie felt more cheerful than she had done in weeks. Now then: shower, blow-dry, make-up . . . she had a lot to do. There was no time to waste!

The temperature rose as the hours passed. The wind dropped away and the humidity stealthily increased, so that customers in outdoor cafés fanned themselves with paper menus and dogs lay panting in the shade. The air felt treacly; it became an effort to move. In cars and buildings, fans and air-conditioning were turned up higher. Men pulled at their shirt collars. Women dabbed their perspiring foreheads. Clouds massed threateningly in the sky, like an army gathering. In gardens around the town, laundry was unpegged and brought inside. There's a storm coming, people said knowingly to each other.

Em wasn't too fussed about the weather. At least while they were on the boat, it felt as if some air was still moving around, and she always quite enjoyed the drama of a thunderstorm. In fact despite the heat and general sweatiness of the atmosphere, she would go so far as to say that this was turning out to be the best day of the week so far. Trelissick was gorgeous. Jack had seemingly forgotten the argument in the car and was actually being really sweet with Seren, playing hide-and-seek with her in the woodland. She and George got to hold hands and feel romantic as they gazed out over the views together, as if they were a couple again, and not merely parents on manoeuvres. Without wanting to jinx anything, Em couldn't help wondering if they might just have cracked this holiday business at last.

Hope all okay with you, she tried texting Izzie, but there was no signal and the message kept failing to send. It was a shame Izzie hadn't come with them, but then she *was* sixteen and very hard to dislodge, when digging her heels in. Em hoped she wouldn't be too bored, all alone there today. Tomorrow she would get Izzie to suggest something she'd like to do with them all, she decided.

Truro was the next stop on their boat trip and proved

delightful with its cathedral and pretty streets. They stopped for a cold drink and Em saw that at some point her message had finally been delivered and that Izzie had replied – *Great, thanks!* – and felt reassured. Then they were back on the boat, the sea grey beneath the still-heavy clouds, and she was congratulating herself on everything turning out nicely, George's leg warm against hers as they bounced over the waves. 'I hope we can make it back to the car before the storm breaks,' he said, eyeing the flinty sky.

It turned out that there was more than one kind of storm. Because the boat was just puttering back into Falmouth harbour once more when Em's phone bleeped, back in range, and she saw that there were three missed calls from her friend Louise, as well as a text: *Ring me when you get this. V important – re Izzie.*

What the hell . . . ? Louise's daughter Ruby was friends with Izzie, and Em immediately began piecing together alarming scenarios of what might have happened while she'd been out on the boat, without a signal. She'd had that message in Truro, though, that Izzie was okay, so what could have gone wrong in the meantime? With her head in a whirl, and trying to help shepherd the children back onto the harbourside, her phone started ringing before she had the chance to return Louise's call. *Dom*, it said on the screen, and Em clambered onto the dock and fumbled to press Answer. 'Hello?' she said.

'What the hell is going on?' he said. He sounded really wound-up. Angry, even.

'What do you mean?' she asked. 'Is this about Louise? I've had really patchy phone service all day, I've only just—'

'Louise rang me because she couldn't get hold of you,' he said. God, yes, he was definitely angry. He was practically spitting out the words as if he was about to boil right over, so loud that both George and Jack could hear too, judging by their faces.

'Right – something about Izzie,' Em garbled, feeling defensive. Oh no, was he cross that he'd left Izzie on her own for the day? That was a bit rich, when he was always telling her that she didn't give the kids enough freedom. And she *was* sixteen! 'She was fine, last I heard. What did Louise say?'

'She said – and I can hardly believe I'm saying this – that Ruby's sister saw something on Ruby's phone.' He sounded as if he was about to explode. What on earth was this about? 'Saying that Izzie . . . that she's been naked and copping off with that man.'

'WHAT? What are you talking about? What man?' Em practically fell over. George shot her a worried look as he took Seren's hand and began leading her away, shooing Jack along too.

'Your *boyfriend*,' he yelled. 'I've a good mind to drive down there myself and—'

'WHAT?' said Em again, so shrill it was practically a

shriek. She turned away, her heart thumping. Had Dom gone mad? 'No,' she told him. 'No, no, no. That hasn't happened. That has *not* happened.'

Too late. He had gone full volcano. 'I trusted you to look after our child!' he was raging. 'She's sixteen years old, for crying out loud! What in God's name were you thinking? Is he some kind of weirdo or . . . ?'

People were staring at her. George was staring at her too, a frown creasing his forehead. Was that exasperation she could see in his eyes or something else? He must be getting sick of the constant soap opera of Em-and-her-kids, she thought with a lurch. 'This is ridiculous,' she said coldly, cutting Dom off mid-rant. 'Stop shouting at me and listen: whatever Louise has said, she's wrong. Nothing has happened, all right? Now I'm going to talk to Izzie and find out what this is all about, then I'll call you back, okay?' She hung up before he could say anything else and gulped in a breath. Her brain was whirring, unable to make sense of the conversation. Izzie had said *what*? She couldn't have done. It must be a misunderstanding, a joke – mustn't it?

'What was all that about?' George said, even though she was pretty sure he must have heard at least some of her ex-husband's accusations. Bloody hell. How was she supposed to explain *that*?

'I . . .' She couldn't even look at him. This was all too crazy. George wouldn't have done anything with Izzie. He just wouldn't. She was a child, and he was in his forties! But even so, her mind was already throwing up accusations, digging up old conversations.

How well do you actually know this man? Jenny had asked.

I wish George wasn't here on holiday with us, Izzie had sighed.

Had something happened? Em wondered now in sudden horror. Was that why Izzie had been so weird this week? She thought about the moment when Izzie had walked out in her bikini, so womanly, so . . . well, so *sexy*. George had averted his gaze from her as if he felt uncomfortable about Izzie's near-nudity. But that didn't mean . . . Em shut her eyes for a moment, her thoughts racing. What did it mean?

'Let's talk about it later,' she said, after a long awful moment, aware that Jack was eavesdropping like crazy. No doubt supergrass Seren was listening in too. She swallowed hard, trying to get a grip on the awful worries and fears that were already spinning wildly out of control. 'He's got the wrong end of the stick somehow – don't worry, we'll sort this out.' Her own words sounded hollow, though, and her heart was galloping so hard it was making her feel queasy.

Then the clouds above them broke and the rain started to pour.

Izzie cycled up the hill, thighs burning from the effort, as the rain hammered down. She could hear her phone ringing somewhere in her bag behind her and hoped it would be Fraser. Telling her he missed her! Telling her he couldn't wait to see her again! They had swapped numbers and arranged to meet up that very evening. 'I can borrow my brother's car and pick you up tonight,' he'd said. 'If you like.'

She *did* like. She really liked. In fact she felt positively giddy at the prospect of being in the small, enclosed space of a car with him later on. None of her friends had boyfriends with cars! It felt so grown-up and exciting. Plus it totally counted as a date, right?

They'd had such a nice time that afternoon. He'd bought her a Coke and they'd sat on a big rock together, talking and making each other laugh. Funnily enough, Swanpool turned out to be the same beach where she'd nearly been run over by that woman Olivia the other day, but Izzie felt like a different girl from the angry, stressed-out person she'd been back then, seething about the bust-up with Seren. Sitting next to Fraser in her nicest top and shorts, with her hair all bouncy and still smelling of shampoo, she felt as if her heart might combust with how good this felt, how happy she was. He was seventeen and working for his uncle's courier business over the summer; he liked the same music as her and wanted to study veterinary science at uni. Good-looking *and* clever *and* funny . . . Fraser was perfect. *Everything* was perfect!

'I bet you've got loads of boyfriends back home, haven't you?' he'd asked and she'd blushed at how wrong he was.

'No,' she laughed, feeling awkward. Hardly. 'How about you?' For all she knew, he did this every week with another holidaying girl. Surely he had them queuing round the block!

'What, have *I* got loads of boyfriends?' he teased. 'Nah.' He grinned at her. 'Or girlfriends, for that matter. I haven't met the right girl.'

'That's a shame,' she said, raising an eyebrow.

He put his hand up to his eyes and pretended to peer out at the horizon. 'Yeah. Hope she turns up soon,' he sighed.

She whacked him and he held onto her arm and then they were play-fighting and laughing, until all of a sudden he was looking at her with soft eyes, and the fighting ground to a heart-bursting halt. 'Ah, here she is,' he said to her and she held her breath, both of them just gazing at each other for a long, charged second.

Her blood raced around her. Was he going to . . .? Should she . . . ?

Then he leaned over and kissed her, really gently, on the mouth before she could answer any of her own questions. 'Here she is,' he said again, all soft and murmury.

The beach seemed to vanish as his lips met hers a second time. She closed her eyes, feeling the most delicious shivery thrill run through her. He tasted of Coke, he smelled of soap, he kissed like . . . Well, she didn't have a lot of experi-ence, in all honesty, but even she could judge that he kissed like a god. Her eyes felt swimmy as they eventually pulled apart, as if the world had drifted into soft-focus. As if she'd travelled through a portal into a whole new place.

They smiled at each other again. 'Your phone's been ringing,' he said. 'Did you not hear?'

'I didn't even notice,' she replied honestly, then blushed because it sounded like she was spinning him a cheesy line.

'Ah, I bet you say that to all the boys,' he teased and she elbowed him, feeling all goosebumpy as their skin touched again.

'Let me get a photo of us,' she said, changing the subject and rummaging in her bag for her phone. Missed calls and a text from Ruby – RING ME! RED ALERT! it said, but she doubted it was anywhere near as important as kissing hand-some Fraser and getting a selfie to prove it. Knowing Ruby, it would be some sixth-former liking one of her Instagram posts and her needing to analyse everything this might mean. 'Smile!'

She took three photos and they studied them. 'We look good together,' he said. 'Especially me.'

'You are such a—' She laughed, unsure what to say. In private, she agreed with him anyway – he looked so-o-o good – but it wouldn't be very cool to admit as much.

Fraser had to leave shortly afterwards, and it seemed as if

the crowds on the beach had the same idea, as a cool breeze began whipping across the sand. 'Reckon it's going to rain,' he said, casting an eye up at the sky. 'Will you be all right getting back?'

'I think I'll survive,' she told him, as the first few drops of rain pattered around them. In the next minute her phone started ringing – *Mum*, she read onscreen – and she sent the call to voicemail. *Bye, Mum. Not now. Busy falling in love here.* She stuffed the phone in her bag and picked up her bike, which she'd left leaning against the rocks. 'See you later on then. Text me when you're coming over, yeah?'

'Yeah.' They walked back up to the road together and he kissed her again, a slow lingering kiss that made her legs feel like jelly. 'Bye, Izzie.'

'Bye, Fraser,' she said, her voice practically a croak.

Almost back at the cottage now, her hair was plastered to her head and her top was drenched and practically transparent, but she felt as if she was glowing, radiant with happiness. Her lips still tingled where Fraser had kissed her, she felt swoony and liquid and weak. Oh my God. She had kissed a boy. She *liked* this boy! And he was going to pick her up later on – he could *drive!* – and they were going out together and she was almost certainly going to kiss him again and . . .

Just as she was approaching the driveway to the cottage, a car beeped and flashed its lights at her as it overtook, snapping her out of her dreamy thoughts. Was that George's car? Her mum's face whizzed past, pale and anxious, and Izzie stared after it with a frown, remembering the missed call. She had been so caught up in Fraser and the headiness of their encounter that the rest of the family had seemed remote the whole time. What had her mum been calling about? she wondered now.

Cycling quickly back to the house, she got off her bike and fumbled for the key in her pocket just as Mum, Jack, George and Seren walked round from the car park, hurrying through the rain. 'Hi,' she said, opening the front door and lifting her bike in. 'How was the boat trip?'

There was this weird sort of – well, it was like an *angry* silence, if that was even possible, Izzie thought in alarm, staring at them all as they followed her inside. 'Mum?' she prompted. What was going *on*? 'Are you okay?'

'You're soaked through,' her mum said, sounding simultaneously irritable and as if she was going to cry. 'Go and get those wet things off. I'll be up in a minute.'

'Okay,' Izzie said, puzzled. Jack pulled a face at her as he stomped through to the kitchen, while George didn't even meet her eye. Unsure what to think of all this, she went upstairs and began towelling her hair. Then she remembered the missed calls and message from Ruby and pulled out her phone.

Another text had arrived since the RING ME! RED ALERT! one, and her eyes widened as she read the words.

Major major shit, Ruby's new message declared. *Mum got hold of my phone – long story – and read our group chat. Am grounded for fortnight.* She is currently ringing everyone's mums and telling them what we've been up to. She was shocked about you and older man. SORRY. Apparently she rang your dad too. SORRY SORRY SORRY.

All the breath seemed to have left Izzie's lungs. All the blood had drained from her head. 'Shit,' she breathed as panic took hold of her. 'Shit shit SHIT.' *Seriously?* she typed, fingers clammy. *You're not winding me up??*

Ruby's mum Louise was such a gossip, she'd have been straight on to Mum with a full report. *Izzie says she's been getting off with your boyfriend – did you know about this, Emma?* And she'd told *Dad*, too? Oh my God. This was a disaster. She was never going to live this down.

Her mum came into the room just then, her face utterly grim, and shut the door behind her. 'Have you any idea what I'm about to say?' she asked tightly.

Izzie burst into horrified tears. 'Yes,' she sobbed.

Chapter Twenty-Four

'What on *earth*,' said Em, 'has been going on? I don't understand. Why is your dad ringing me up saying these terrible
things about George? Why have I got missed calls and texts
from Louise, saying I need to ring her back urgently, she's
worried about you?'

Izzie had gone completely white and was gulping with
such huge sobs she could hardly speak. 'It was a . . . a joke,'
she said, not looking at Em. 'I didn't mean . . . It was a private chat.'

Em still couldn't understand what had actually happened. 'Your dad is under the impression that . . .' It was
hard to get the words out. 'That you and George have . . .'
She stalled again. 'Well, that you two have – I don't know
how to say it. Got naked and copped off.' She stared at her
weeping daughter, incredulous. 'Why would he think that?
Did you *tell* someone that?'

Izzie put her head in her hands. 'Go away,' she sobbed.
'Please go away, Mum.'

There was no way Em was going anywhere. 'I don't think so,' she said, sitting down next to her on the bed. It went against all her maternal instincts not to soothe her, when Izzie was in such a state, but she felt too jangled by Dom's phone call, by this weird, unpleasant conversation. She took a deep breath, remembering the black bikini and Izzie's peachy young body. She *had* to ask. 'For my own peace of mind,' she said, 'I need to know the answer to this. Has something happened between you and George? Anything?'

Izzie shook her head, tears dripping from her chin. 'No,' she said in a tiny voice.

Thank Christ for that. 'Are you sure? Nothing? He hasn't made you feel . . . uncomfortable in any way, or . . . or . . . touched you?'

'No!' Izzie was shuddering, still in her soaking wet top. Em picked up her dressing gown from where it had been flung on the floor and draped it around Izzie's shoulders. Okay, well, that was something, she supposed shakily. Not that she had doubted George for more than a single freakish second, but all the same. Good to have it confirmed.

'So . . . Look, talk to me,' she said, wanting to establish the facts before she had to speak to Dom again. Louise too, for that matter. 'What's this all about? I don't understand.'

'I just . . .' Izzie was still hiding her face. 'I don't want to say,' she wailed.

338

'You have to say,' Em replied sternly. 'Your dad's making all kinds of accusations. I don't know where they're coming from.'

Izzie scrubbed her face with the dressing-gown sleeve, streaking make-up everywhere. 'They came from me,' she said in a low voice. She hiccuped. 'It was just a stupid game. I didn't think anyone would believe me. It was like . . .' She remembered Olivia's words from the beach that day. 'Fake it till you make it. You know?'

'So you *said* those things? About George? You said you'd got off with him?'

Izzie looked utterly mortified, as well she might. 'I want to go home,' she sobbed. 'I can't stay here. I've ruined the holiday. Can I go home?'

Em stared at her, unable to get her head around this. Her own daughter telling such vile, awful lies. Izzie had always been a good girl. Such a nice person! Whatever had possessed her? 'You could have got George into so much trouble,' she said. 'Your dad was all set to kill him, for one thing. Louise will have passed it on to everyone in town by now . . . they're all going to think the worst of him. When he's done nothing wrong!' This was just *horrible*, she thought in despair. So completely awful for George, if anyone were to believe Izzie's lies. The best and loveliest man, ruined by her daughter – for what? What was going on in her head?

'I'm . . . I'm sorry,' Izzie said, just as there was a knock at the front door downstairs. Then she jerked up in alarm and ran to the mirror. 'Oh, shit!' she said.

'I'll get it,' came George's muffled shout.

'If that's for me, I'll have to – oh God, look at my face,' groaned Izzie, staring at her reflection.

'What do you mean, if that's for you?' Em asked, feeling more bamboozled by the minute. 'Who's going to be knocking for you?' She could hear a female voice from downstairs – probably Lorna, she guessed, checking that everything was okay. Ha! What a time to be asking such a question. 'Look, you're going to have to put this right,' she said fiercely, turning back to the matter in hand. 'You've got to tell everyone – including Dad, including Louise – that you lied. You have to do that, do you understand? You need to apologize to George.'

'No! Please!' cried Izzie crumpling all over again. She looked petrified. 'Does he know, then? What I said? Please don't make me say anything to him. I'd rather die.'

Em didn't know what to say any more. She could see Izzie was limp and squirming with embarrassment – had she had a crush on him? she wondered. Was that what this was all about?

'Please, Mum, can't we just go home? Finish the holiday early?' Then something seemed to cross her mind, because in the next moment she blurted out, 'Oh, but then Fraser—' before snapping her mouth shut again.

Em felt very, very tired all of a sudden. Very tired and confused. Right now the prospect of going home early wasn't even such a bad idea. It had been a mistake asking George on holiday with them, she thought dully. They didn't know each other well enough. Their kids hadn't particularly gelled. And now here was Izzie, prostrate with guilt and wretchedness over some terrible crush she'd developed, some joking around that had gone horribly wrong. Izzie hadn't wanted to share the family holiday from the start – it had been Em who'd pushed everyone into it. What a disaster. Maybe it was time to pull the plug. Enact a mercy killing.

'Look,' she said weakly, 'how about if I ask George to go home early? Seren's due to go back tomorrow anyway, maybe I should just—'

But at that moment there came a gentle knock on Izzie's bedroom door and then George himself put his head around it. He looked strained and apologetic, and Em's lungs seized with terror that he might have been listening to their conversation.

It turned out that something even worse had happened, though. 'Er . . . Charlotte's here,' he said.

Chapter Twenty-Five

As the rain tipped down, Maggie sought shelter in the café, queuing up for a cup of tea and flapjack, then managing to bag the last free table. She had come to Trebah, a beautiful botanical garden, as recommended by Paul in the guide-book he'd lent her. After the encounter with the pebble artist on the beach, she had returned to the car and flicked through the pages, trying to decide what to do next. It was only then that she really took note of all the messages Paul had left for her amidst the entries.

This is lovely – highly recommended, he'd written on one page. *Watch out – expensive car park*, he'd warned elsewhere. *Fabulous at the end of the day when the crowds have all gone*, read another pencilled addition. In his own quiet way, Paul had been telling her for years that he cared about her, she real-ized. Just look how he'd annotated his own book for her. *You'll love this place. This is right up your street! Bit overrated*, she read on other pages. Even the act of studying his handwritten notes made her feel warm inside.

Paul was such a good person, with his shy smile and brown eyes, his habit of taking off his glasses and rumpling his thick sandy hair with the palm of his hand whenever he was thinking deeply. Seeing his handsome, smiling face across the staffroom always made her feel better: thank goodness, there he is, that person who understands me. And yet each time he had ever dared approach her about pushing their relationship to a different level, she had slammed down the shutters and backed away.

What are you so scared of, Maggie? It was a good question.

An image came to her of the pebble she'd thrown into the sea that morning, a slow-motion film running through her head of it tracing an arc across the forget-me-not-blue sky. The splash as it vanished beneath the surface. Would her chalked letters still be visible on the pebble or would the sea already have taken them away, washed the stone clean?

She reached down to find the other pebble at the bottom of her handbag and pulled it out. COURAGE, it said to her as she put it in the middle of the table. She bit the corner off her flapjack and chewed thoughtfully, then rummaged in her bag a second time and pulled out her phone.

Hi! Having a great time at Trebah today – thanks for the tip! She typed in a new message to Paul. *The guidebooks are coming in v handy – much appreciated. Hope you're having a lovely summer. Maggie.*

She scrolled through the photos she'd taken that day,

eventually settling on her favourite, which had been taken at the top of a downward path towards the water garden. From there you could see umpteen palms and cordylines, which looked fabulous silhouetted against the sky. Even by her own cack-handed photography standards, it was a good shot.

Attaching it to the text, she pressed Send. There. Okay, to a normal person, it wasn't particularly courageous or daring, but Maggie had never been the one to start a conversation with Paul, she realized now. Never initiated anything with him, preferring to wait and let him call all the shots. It was a tiny thing, but she didn't want to be the one who always reacted any longer.

Outside it was still raining. There was still no further word from Amelia, despite all of Maggie's many texts and attempts to call, and the nagging worry at the back of her mind was starting to build to an anxious crescendo. Will had seemed pretty shambolic in terms of health and safety; what was to stop Amelia falling off a cliff or into the river under his so-called supervision? Maybe she'd come down with a bout of salmonella – Maggie had seen that kitchen, after all. So full of angry pride at the time, she hadn't thought to ask for Will's number and now was unable to check that everything was all right and her daughter was still alive. Although she could have a quick look at Amelia's social media, she supposed.

Maggie dithered for a moment. She knew that some

parents were constantly snooping on their children's online activities, but her conscience was always faintly ill at ease with this idea. It wasn't *spying*, it was parental concern, she had to tell herself, opening the app. In fairness, she hardly ever looked at Amelia's Instagram account – and Amelia had no idea she even *knew* her account name there, let alone followed her – but needs must today, frankly. Was that so terrible?

Okay, so she *was* alive, Maggie saw as soon as she opened the app and clicked onto Amelia's account to see lots of new photos.

Having an amazing time with my famous dad!!! That was a selfie of them in a wood somewhere. Amelia looked happy enough, she decided, with her arm around Will, beaming into the camera.

First photography lesson with Dad – lucky me! Will on his own this time, setting up a tripod, looking earnest in a dark green T-shirt and knackered old jeans.

Some shots from the top of a hill – Maggie zoomed in, but couldn't tell where the pictures were taken, although Amelia had written *I love Devon* as her caption.

There were photos of the younger children too: the little boy pressing a cutter into some red rolled-out Play-Doh on the kitchen table at home. Amelia had caught him from the side and you could see his gorgeous long eyelashes and a frown of concentration; he looked lost in the moment.

There were pictures of the little girl as well: running after the chickens in the garden, barefoot, with a purple dress floating out at the sides as she charged about. A blurry smile, her curly hair springing around her face – good action shots, thoughtfully taken. Nice domestic scenes.

Then there was a selfie of Amelia alone, collapsed in the middle of the grass, her limbs arranged artistically like a model, with bright flowers spangling the green. She looked beatific, blissed-out, as if Celeste had slipped her something trippy in the green tea. (She better bloody not have done, Maggie thought immediately.) *So happy!* ran the accompanying caption.

Maggie sipped her tea and tried to swallow back the dark swirl of feelings inside her. Of *course* she was glad that Amelia was having such a good time, she told herself, although this reaction was battling quite strongly with a response that felt a lot like insecurity. She doubted Amelia usually posted anything quite so positive about days out with Maggie, for instance. In fact, now that Maggie checked, there had been a stony silence about their entire trip to Pendennis, although the day before *that* . . . wait. What? Why was there a picture of Amelia holding a tequila bottle down by Falmouth docks?

Startled, she flicked through the other photos from that day. The tequila bottle seemed to feature prominently, she thought, eyes wide. In fact . . . hold on. She zoomed in to take a closer look. If she wasn't mistaken, that was the exact same tequila bottle that Maggie had won at the tombola stall at the school summer fair in June. The tequila bottle that Linda Barber from the PTA had handed over to her with a wink, saying, 'Someone's in for a good night tonight!' Maggie had smiled politely and then, once home, had added the bottle to her meagre drinks collection, imagining it would be there for several years untouched, until she remembered to give it away for another school summer fair.

It was the same bottle, she was sure of it. And then Em's cryptic comments about that day came back to her in the next moment – what was it she'd said? *Those naughty teens*, or something. Was this what she'd been referring to? Oh my goodness. And there Maggie had been, assuming that the other two had been a bad influence on her angelic daughter. Had it actually been the other way round? She wouldn't have believed it herself, had the evidence not been right there, in front of her, captured for posterity on her daughter's camera roll.

Okay then. So that showed what she knew about her own flesh and blood: a lot less than she'd assumed. Did that make her a bad parent or Amelia a bad daughter? She picked up the pebble and stared at it. *Help me*, she thought. *Any ideas how I'm meant to tackle this one?*

*

After numerous attempts and several changes of mind, Olivia had finally finished her letter to Lorna and Roy, and now she was in Falmouth saying her goodbyes.

She probably wouldn't come back again, she had decided. After Lorna read what she had to say, she might not be welcome any more, for one thing, but also this was a place with so many memories of the past that she wanted to leave it behind now. So this would be her last day here and she was going to act like a holidaymaker: enjoy the town's loveliness before she went on to spend the evening indulgently alone, doing all the things that motherhood had taken away from her. Eating late, drinking a lot, another long bath, a silent luxurious night. And then tomorrow . . .

Her thoughts kept snagging on that word. It was Thursday tomorrow and by then she would have spent four nights away from home, by far the longest time she'd ever been separated from the twins. Lorna and Roy had made it clear that the cottage would be empty until Friday and she could stay that long if need be, but Olivia didn't want to overstay her welcome. Like it or not, she would have to make some decisions.

Not right now, though. Right now, she was going to revisit some old haunts around the town – her farewell tour, if you like, and then head out on her favourite walk, along the coastal path to Maenporth. Before she'd left them, her mum had loved this stretch of coastline and they'd gone there many times, rain or shine, in Olivia's childhood. She could still remember her mum crouching beside her, pointing into the sea where a seal's sleek fat head had popped up. 'Look! Can you see it?'

Her thoughts turned to her own boys then – how she had crouched similarly between them, pointing out a horse on the downs, a huge tipper truck, a cat on a shed roof. Their little faces lighting up with wonder, their eyes shining as they all watched together. It hadn't all been bad, she told herself. They'd shared some good moments, hadn't they?

She was on Church Street, the bunting flapping in cheery zigzags above her head, following the crowds past a surf shop and a café, the streets full now that the rain shower had blown over. Overtaking her just then was a mother who seemed to be in charge of five children, including a baby in a papoose and a dozing toddler in a pushchair. 'Okay, because you've all been *so* good this morning, you can each choose a book from the bookshop,' she told them, at which the older three whooped and ran into the shop ahead of her.

Olivia sighed, watching the woman steer the pushchair through the doorway and follow them in. A wave of self-doubt washed over her. Women like that made Olivia feel completely inadequate. Women like that made it look easy. Five children! They couldn't all be hers, could they? And even if they weren't, how was she managing to cope with them all single-handedly? If that was Olivia, she'd be in a hot sweat, utterly frazzled, frantically counting heads every thirty seconds, terrified of losing someone in the crowd. If that was Olivia, she probably wouldn't have left the house at all, let alone manoeuvred the whole group around the busy streets, let's face it.

She trudged miserably on, feeling worse by the minute. Then again, who would entrust her with five children to mind, after what she'd done? She didn't deserve her boys. She didn't deserve to have anyone at all.

The Summer of Yes group chat

Izzie – Guys, it was a lie, okay? Nothing happened with me and Mum's boyfriend. OBVIOUSLY. Because I am sixteen and he is, like, old. Also because he is MY MUM'S BOY-FRIEND. I just felt embarrassed because nothing fun was happening to me so I made it up. Sorry. If you have told anyone about it, please pass on the truth. Mum is about to kill me and hates me. I feel such a dick.

Izzie turned off her notifications before she could see or hear any of her friends' messages, which would no doubt pour in thick and fast. They would probably chuck her out of the friendship group for this, or someone would start a new group without her and they'd all bitch about what a weirdo she was and what a liar. She cringed, imagining how it would go round everyone from school like a flash. How she'd start at sixth form and be faced with loads of people she'd never met giving her the side-eye because they all knew about her.

Don't make friends with her, she's a liar.

Yeah, she makes stuff up about sleeping with old people. That's a bit creepy, don't you think?

Ew, gross! I'm steering well clear.

She flopped down onto the bed with a groan. Next she had to phone up her dad and confess to him as well, which was going to be equally horrendous. Meanwhile downstairs it was ominously quiet. Mum had looked as if she was about to puke when George put his head round the door and said that Charlotte had turned up. 'What?' she squawked, aghast. 'Here? Now?'

He'd nodded, looking glum. 'She flew back a day early to pick up Seren,' he said. 'She's been trying to ring me, but because of my phone going in the pool . . .'

Mum's face – it was as if something had cracked inside her, thought Izzie. It wasn't as if Em was particularly vain, but Izzie had switched on the family PC more than once to find that Mum had been googling this Charlotte woman, so she obviously felt pretty competitive about her. The fuss she always made about her appearance whenever Dad had brought Michelle round, you'd have thought the Queen was coming for tea. Clearly she would have liked a bit more notice to prepare for the Other Woman this time too.

'Right,' she'd said weakly. 'I'll come down. Actually, can we just have a word in private first?'

Izzie had hung her head. George hadn't looked at her once, she realized as Mum went out of the room, closing the door behind her. How embarrassing this was. How excruciating!

She dialled her dad's number, wishing that an enormous sinkhole would appear under the cottage and destroy it all in an instant. Make this nightmare end. 'Hi, it's me,' she said miserably when he answered.

'Izzie! About time! I've been going out of my mind here. Are you all right? I couldn't believe my ears when Louise—'

'Dad – stop. Let me speak,' she begged before he went off on one. 'Dad, it wasn't true,' she said in the next breath. 'What Louise told you – it didn't happen. Nothing happened.'

That took the wind out of his sails. '*What?*' She could tell he was frowning. He had such bushy eyebrows, her dad; she and Jack were always taking the mick out of him for them. Now she could practically hear them crashing together. 'What do you mean? Look, you don't have to cover up for him, love. If he has laid a *finger* on you . . .'

'He hasn't. He really hasn't,' Izzie said. She could hear footsteps on the stairs and Seren singing a Disney song at the top of her voice. At least someone was happy. 'Dad – please, take no notice of what Louise said. It was just a stupid joke to my friends. I swear. Nobody else was meant to see it.'

He didn't like being in the wrong, ever. If he was answering a football quiz show on the radio and said the wrong answer, he'd immediately go all defensive and make excuses. *They phrased the question misleadingly! How was anyone meant to know that?* Sometimes even: *Where do they get these facts from? Out of the presenter's backside?*

He was silent now, pondering. 'Dad?' she prompted. 'There's nothing to worry about.' From where he was sitting, anyway. Izzie had *plenty* to worry about, thanks to her own stupid attempts to impress. 'So you can call off the troops, okay? Stand down. George has done nothing wrong.'

'Right,' he said gruffly. 'Well, if he *does* . . .'

'He won't,' she assured him. Not least because George was probably going to dump Mum over this, just as fast as he could. You would, wouldn't you, if the teenage kid of the person you were dating started spreading lurid rumours about the two of you. You'd be backing right off, hands up, saying, 'Whoa, no, I did *not* sign up for any of this.'

They ended the call and she lay there feeling utterly flat. All the sparkle of seeing Fraser earlier had left her. Now she just felt like a stupid kid who had wrecked everything.

Chapter Twenty-Six

And then there were three, thought Em as she retreated wearily inside the cottage a short while later. Just like that, the magic was over, the bubble had popped and she was back to normality: one single mum and her kids. So that was that.

How humiliating that this had all happened in front of Charlotte too – beautiful, professional Charlotte, who had appeared looking miraculously uncreased and glamorous despite the flight from Berlin, followed by a hire-car drive down to Cornwall from the airport. Meanwhile Em was in the rattiest old cut-off jean shorts she possessed, along with a pink vest top that had a deodorant mark under one arm. Plus her hair was like a tangled fright-wig, thanks to the boat trip, and she had no make-up on and . . . Oh God. It was impossible trying to be competitive because she had already lost so badly; she had lost *everything*.

She'd had to drag George into their bedroom because she couldn't face having such a torturous conversation in front of his ex. 'Listen, I know everything's gone a bit mad today,' she said, 'and I'm so sorry. If I could explain properly, I would, but . . .' She bit her lip unhappily, thinking of Izzie in the next room, squirming with embarrassment. 'I can't really tell you what's happened. I know that sounds nuts, but I swear I'm going to make sure everything's put right and . . .'

George was already glancing past her towards the door, as if he wanted to get out of there as soon as possible. As if he couldn't bear being trapped in here with her for a minute longer. 'Look, don't worry about it,' he said, interrupting her rambling plea. 'This didn't really work, did it? It's probably best if I go back with Charlotte and Seren now; I think that's the most straightforward thing. Charlotte's going to drop her hire car in Truro, then I'll drive the three of us back.'

Em blinked, wounded, as the words hit her hard. *This didn't really work, did it?* Oh God, he had actually said that, kindly but with weariness. He wanted shot of her, and fast. Who could blame him, after what had just happened? 'You mean . . .' she began pathetically, then stopped herself because she knew what he meant and didn't need him to spell it out. 'Right,' she croaked, her heart breaking. *No, George, no. Please, no!* Her knees swayed as if they could no longer support her. Her eyes filled with tears and she had to dash them away quickly. Do not cry. Do not fall apart.

George gave her a half-smile, but his heart wasn't in it, she could tell. 'I should chivvy Seren along, get her to pack her stuff,' he said after a moment.

'Yes,' she said robotically as he left the room, trying not to torture herself with visions of the three of them on their unexpected road trip together. Seren would doze off contentedly in the back while George and Charlotte discussed the terrible holiday in low voices. *Oh God, what a nightmare*, she imagined Charlotte saying, appalled. *The ex-husband said WHAT? Because the daughter . . . ? Christ, thank goodness I could rescue you a day early!* Give it till the first service station and they'd be bonding over Em's ineptitude, and then they'd be looking into one another's eyes once more and re-evaluating their marriage in a new light. *We were good together, weren't we?* one of them would say. *We were so good. You know it's not too late to try again, right?*

Em hurled herself onto the bed and punched the pillow, allowing herself a silent scream of anguish. *This didn't really work, did it?* she heard him say again and it was like a pain in her chest, a huge rock crushing her. Goodbye, relationship. Goodbye, happiness. Goodbye, George. It had been so bloody lovely while it lasted. It was only the knowledge that Charlotte was downstairs that prevented her from bursting into full-blown howls. *Keep it together. Just keep it together.*

Then she scuttled through to the en-suite to splash cold water on her face and try to comb her hair into something less insane. She gave her lashes a lick of mascara and threw on a clean striped top before she hurried down, heart in mouth, to greet their surprise guest.

'Hi,' she said, finding Charlotte in the living room, helping Seren to pack up the books and toys she'd left there. Em found herself seeking out the big flashy diamond engagement ring on Charlotte's left hand as if that was any kind of reassurance, but it didn't make her feel better. *Okay, you win,* she thought, as the other woman straightened up and smiled at her. *He's all yours now.* Not that it was a competition – she was trying so hard for this not to be a competition – but Charlotte was indisputably beautiful and elegant in a crisp navy trouser suit and spindly heels. She had long dark hair and wide brown eyes, plus a full luscious mouth with perfect lipstick. Damn it, Em totally should have changed out of those jean shorts as well as her manky top, she thought with a stab of regret.

'Hi! Emma! I'm Charlotte,' the other woman said unnecessarily. 'I'm so sorry about turning up early like this – George is so rubbish at replying to texts normally that when he didn't this time, I just assumed he would have received them, but . . .' She rolled her eyes. 'Clearly not. Sorry if I've caused chaos.'

'No, not at all,' Em said brightly. *God no, I'm delighted that you turned up a day early before I could clean the house and make myself a tiny bit more attractive. I'm THRILLED you made it in time to see the fallout from my daughter's social-media lying frenzy, and to be here just as George realized he couldn't stand me any more. Cool!* 'Um . . . Can I get you anything? A drink, something to eat?'

'I'm fine, thanks. We'll be out of your hair as soon as we can,' Charlotte said.

It felt like a criticism, as if Em was pushing them out of the door. 'There's no hurry,' she felt obliged to say, then realized she'd run out of conversation. 'Um . . . so how was your conference?' she asked after an agonizingly blank few moments.

'Busy,' Charlotte replied, stuffing some picture books into a bag. Then she looked up at Em and wrinkled her nose. 'Kind of boring, actually. Loads of stiffs. I was quite glad when they changed the running order and I could leave, between you and me.'

Damn it, now she had to go and be nice, on top of everything else. Nice and not up-herself. Why couldn't she be an unpleasant airhead like Michelle? That made life a lot easier, in Em's experience. 'Conferences can be like another planet sometimes,' she said, hoping she sounded sage and savvy, a woman of the world herself. In truth she'd only ever been to one conference and it had been in a budget hotel just outside Swindon, and Em had got so pissed with the other delegates that she'd fallen over on the dance floor. Charlotte didn't need to know that, though. 'Anyway,' she said weakly, 'nice to meet you.'

George was in the kitchen, bagging up his hiking boots

with a nearly-dry towel draped over one shoulder. 'Listen, I'm sorry about this,' he said as she came in. It didn't seem possible for a conversation to take place without someone apologizing, all of a sudden.

'No, I'm sorry,' she replied. Make that two people apologizing. They were all just utterly sorry. She hesitated, feeling wretched, not wanting the connection between them to be severed quite so suddenly. Until this holiday, they'd been getting on so well! Was there no chance they could return to that place? She hadn't even really been able to explain what had happened with Izzie. 'Um . . .' she began tentatively, but her confidence deserted her. She was too scared that George might be more brutal about the split if she pushed things.

He didn't seem to notice her hesitation. In fact he was already striding past her. 'I'll just get my stuff from the bedroom,' he said over his shoulder.

In a matter of minutes it had become 'the bedroom', rather than 'our bedroom', she realized glumly. Shortly to be 'your bedroom'. 'Mum's bedroom'. And thus the dream was over, as was her chance to have a last private moment with him. With a bustle of packing and checking, the three of them were out of the house and driving away before she could muster the courage to try again.

An hour or so later, Em sank into one of the pool loungers with a very large and very cold glass of white wine. It was a beautiful tranquil evening, the sun casting streaks of bronze and pink across the sky and backlighting a cluster of small puffy clouds; she could hear the raspy clicking of crickets somewhere behind her, while a late-working bee nudged against the smudgy purple lavender heads. A gorgeous scene, in other words. Idyllic. The sort of moment that an artistic type might photograph and put on their social media (no filters!). Shame she felt like screaming her head off instead, frankly.

Aaaargh, though. Seriously: *aarrrrggghhhh!* So much for her perfect holiday. So much for her and George's families mingling in joyous harmony. Her dreamily scripted happy-ever-after had become a horror story, with one disaster after another, and now there had come one final terminal crash into the buffers as he'd packed up and gone. Gone for good? Who knew, although she wouldn't blame him if, after this week, he had decided to run for the hills, or at least to the nearest monastery.

'Why didn't you tell me any of this earlier?' she had all but howled to Izzie after George, Seren and Charlotte had left and the house had taken on the sombre feel of a recent bereavement. 'You could have told me stuff was going on with your friends – you can *always* talk to me about how you feel, however embarrassing it might be.'

Izzie had given her a *Get real* sort of look, though. 'Yeah, but when? *When* was I supposed to talk to you? I can never get you alone,' she'd pointed out. 'Apart from now, obviously – but I'm guessing it's a bit late for talking now.'

She'd guessed right. It was a bit late for everything now, unfortunately. Certainly too late for Em to have paid more attention to her own kid when she'd needed it. So that was another point to chalk up for bad parenting.

Staring glumly down at the ground, she noticed that Seren had left her little Sylvanian Families fox behind. It must have been blown off the sun lounger in a gust of wind at some point, because it was now lying face-down in the grass. You and me both, mate, she thought, reaching over to pick it up and wiping the dirt from its velvety nose.

Dinner had been cooked on autopilot: some white fish with lemony new potatoes and salad for dinner, but nobody seemed very hungry. 'So George and Seren have just . . . gone?' asked Jack in surprise, seeing the table only set for three. He had never been the most observant child when it came to joining dots; he sailed through life oblivious of his surroundings half the time. 'How come?'

Em gave him a weak imitation of a smile ('Your divorce smile,' Izzie had once called it, and the naming was apt). 'They just decided to go back early,' she said. 'Seren was always going to leave with her mum at the end of the week, remember, but . . . yeah. He went earlier too.' She had run out of steam and knew she must sound unconvincing, but Jack nodded, accepting it as fact.

'Oh, right,' was all he said. 'Hey, Amelia's back soon at least,' he added in the next moment, completely unrelatedly. As if that made up for anything. He slopped mayonnaise onto his potatoes in a shuddering dollop. 'You know, the girl from next door?'

'Um . . . That reminds me,' said Izzie just then. 'Is it okay if I go out tonight? With a friend?'

Em stared at her. Izzie had put on a lot of make-up, she noticed, but despite that, you could see that her cheeks had turned pink beneath it. 'What friend?' she asked, and then waved a fork impatiently. 'Forget I asked that, actually, because whoever it is, the answer's no. Not after today. I think we all need a quiet—'

'But, Mum, come on!'

'*No,*' she said, and all her frustration and misery gave the word extra weight, so that Izzie jerked in her seat as if she'd been kicked. 'You're not going anywhere. You can stay in and think about . . . about what you've done.'

Jack immediately looked interested. 'What *has* she done, anyway? What was that weird phone call from Dad about?'

'Oh, shut up!' yelled Izzie, tears springing from her eyes, and then she wrenched herself from the table and was running upstairs.

So that had been a nice mealtime. Call her a terrible parent (again), but Em just did not have the stamina to go up after her, to try and patch things up. She'd had her fill of drama for one day, without getting into an argument about why Izzie couldn't go out tonight, on top of it all. Even her wise friend Kathy wouldn't have been able to dredge up a single positive affirmation about this whole disaster.

'Bloody *hell*,' she muttered to herself now, taking a massive, medicinal swig of wine, and then jumped, because a voice quite nearby asked tentatively 'Are you all right?'

Em looked round, embarrassed to see that Maggie from the middle-sized cottage had appeared, seemingly out of nowhere, beside her. 'Oh,' she gulped in surprise. 'Hi.'

'Sorry,' said Maggie, looking awkward. 'I didn't mean to bother you.' She was clutching a wine glass and bottle of her own and held them up rather self-consciously. 'I just wondered if you wanted any company?'

Em managed a small smile. Not particularly, she felt like replying. Thanks and everything, Maggie, but right now I'd like to get very pissed on my own and feel sorry for myself. Perhaps even ruin the picture-postcard holiday scene with some ugly gulpy sobbing, once I've put this bottle away. But she was too polite for such honesty of course, so what she really said was, 'That would be lovely. Please do.' And then she realized something was different about her neighbour. 'Your hair,' she blurted out. 'Have you had it cut? It looks fabulous!'

Maggie blushed and looked delighted. 'Thank you,' she said, patting it self-consciously. 'It was a bit of an impulse decision, to be honest. I keep forgetting about it.' She hesitated, as if sensing Em wasn't exactly in a good place. 'Sure it's all right for me to join you?'

'Absolutely,' said Em, pulling herself out of her mood as best she could. 'So how are things with you?'

'Well . . . okay, actually,' Maggie said, as if surprised by her own words. She dragged the nearest pool lounger a little closer and sloshed wine into her glass. 'I had quite a nice day today – I'd been expecting to feel weird without Amelia being here, you know, but . . .'

Em was listening – she *was!* – but her attention was caught in the next moment by the sound of a car arriving at the property, at which point her heart leapt like a salmon and she promptly tuned out. From where they were sitting, it wasn't possible to see the driveway and the car park, but her imagination had already gone into overdrive and adrenalin throbbed through her. Oh my goodness. Had George come back? He couldn't live without her! He wanted to reassure her that they would be okay!

Maggie had broken off from whatever she was saying, sensing she was losing her audience. 'Is everything all right?'

Em blushed. How rude of her. 'Sorry,' she said. 'I was distracted by the car that's just come in. I'm wondering if it might be George, you see – long story, but he, er, had to leave early and . . .' Now it was her turn to break off, because she was tying herself in knots. There was the sound of a car door slamming and she prickled all over with nerves. 'He . . . I'm not sure . . . I don't really know what's happening,' she floundered, poised to leap up and rush over to him the second he appeared.

You came back, she would cry, weak with relief.

I love you, he would tell her as she ran into his arms.

In the next moment, though, around the corner came Olivia carrying a bag of shopping and the brief flare of hope Em had felt was extinguished like a snuffed candle. 'False alarm,' she mumbled, embarrassed. Of course it wasn't George. He was probably on the motorway, thanking his lucky stars he was rid of her by now. What an idiot she was.

Olivia gave a shy wave as she approached, and both Em and Maggie waved back. 'Come and join us, if you want,' Em called, feeling it would be churlish not to. 'We're just setting the world to rights here.' *Although one of us is likely to go into full nervous breakdown any minute now.*

Olivia looked pleased to be asked. 'Thank you,' she said, dimpling. 'That would be nice.' She patted her bag. 'I'll just put this lot away and I'll be right with you.'

She walked on towards her cottage and Em turned back to Maggie. 'You were telling me about Amelia,' she said, feeling bad for not listening properly earlier. 'I think she and Jack have been texting each other, actually – they seem to have hit it off. Is she getting on all right with your ex?'

'Um . . .' said Maggie. Her face had done something

peculiar when Em had mentioned Jack. Did that mean she disapproved of their friendship? 'Okay, I think,' Maggie replied, 'although it sounds as if Jack knows more than I do. She's not exactly been very forthcoming with me so far. In fact I've barely heard a word from her while she's been away.' She rubbed at a mark on the sun lounger for a moment before she spoke again. 'Er . . . Actually, I wanted to ask you something. About our kids going off to Falmouth that day. I think – well, I'm pretty sure – that Amelia behaved quite . . . badly.' She lowered her gaze as if she was ashamed. 'I think there may have been a bottle of tequila involved.'

Aha. 'That's what I heard too,' Em said. 'They're not our little babies any more, are they? More's the pity.'

Maggie looked very uncomfortable. 'I'm sorry,' she said. 'I had no idea Amelia had it – the tequila, I mean. Obviously I wouldn't have let her take it, had I known. I wouldn't have let her anywhere *near* it, frankly, but . . .'

Em shrugged. The whole episode didn't seem to matter so much any more. Not after today's saga. 'That's teenagers for you,' she said, then snorted. 'I take it you didn't know about the gallery incident, either?' Maggie's blank expression meant there was no need for a reply. 'Some drunken game of Truth or Dare apparently,' she went on. 'Where I got a phone call from an irate gallery owner, after Jack had been dared to nick something from the shop. The silly sod only went and did it.'

'What, he—'

'Yep. Lucky the police weren't called, to be honest. I had to buy a very expensive painting to talk the gallery owner round. Kids, eh?'

A strange expression came over Maggie's face. 'Oh my God. Wait, this is the place you pointed out to me the other day, wasn't it?' She pressed her lips together for a moment. 'I went past earlier today and noticed a sign on the door saying: NO TEENAGERS. I thought it was a bit harsh at the time, but I bet it's been put up there recently. Because of our kids!'

The two of them exchanged horrified looks, then burst out laughing. 'Oh dear. What great parents we are,' Em gurgled. She could feel herself verging on hysteria; the mood where you laugh so hard, you start crying and can't stop again. *Pull yourself together, Em.*

Maggie sipped her wine, looking rueful. 'I clearly don't know my own child as well as I thought I did,' she confessed.

'Tell me about it,' Em replied with feeling. 'Oh – here's Olivia,' she added, seeing the other woman approach with a beer bottle in hand. Thank goodness. Em did *not* want to get into how Izzie had surprised her so horribly earlier on.

She smiled at Olivia, trying to suppress an envious pang as she wondered how the other woman might have spent the day, in comparison with her own rather miserable recent hours. Perhaps this amazing husband of hers had shelled out for a day-spa somewhere really luxurious. Or Olivia had been for a mega shopping spree, or a gourmet dinner, or . . .

'Hello there,' Olivia said, drawing up a chair. She had let her blonde hair loose from its usually severe ponytail so that it fell in waves around her shoulders, and was wearing a floaty top and cropped wide trousers. Her feet were bare and her toenails glimmered with sparkly coral polish. She'd probably had a pedicure as well, Em guessed. Nice!

'I'm Olivia, by the way,' she was saying to Maggie. 'I don't think we've met.'

'Maggie,' said Maggie.

'And I'm Em, just in case you had forgotten and were too polite to ask,' Em said, trying not to look down at the chipped nail varnish on her own toes, with pale unpainted bands along the bottom where her nails had grown. There – she was slovenly at heart. Another reason for George to be whistling *The Great Escape* theme tune as he drove steadily eastwards. 'So here we are: impromptu girls' night out,' she said, trying to sound positive. 'Cheers, ladies. To good health – and happy holidays.'

Lord, what a hypocrite, she thought as she and Maggie clinked glasses with Olivia's beer bottle. Happy holidays indeed. I should be so lucky!

Just then there was a bleep from a phone. George? Em thought immediately, scrabbling to look at her screen. But it remained blank, unfortunately. Not George. It had been

Maggie's phone that had made the sound and she was already picking it up to check the message.

'Ooh!' she said, putting a hand up to her mouth and turning pink.

Despite her glum mood, Em was intrigued. 'Now that "Ooh" sounded to me like it might be related to an interesting man,' she guessed, arching an eyebrow. 'Am I right?'

'That's a good kind of "Ooh",' Olivia agreed, leaning in a little closer.

Maggie's blush deepened and her expression became distinctly bashful. *Definitely* a man, Em thought to herself with interest.

'Well,' Maggie said, glancing back at the message again, 'it's probably nothing. But there *is* this guy, Paul . . .'

'I knew it!' Em crowed.

'And . . . well, we've been friends for years and I really like him, but . . .' Her mouth gave an awkward sort of twist. 'Well, I couldn't face putting my heart on the line again, basically.' She hesitated, then added, 'I haven't exactly had much luck with men in the past.'

'But now?' Olivia prompted.

'I texted him earlier to thank him for lending me some guidebooks,' Maggie said. 'And he's replied . . . Hold on, let me read it. He's replied: *No problem, glad they were helpful. Hope you're having a good holiday. Let me know if you're around for a drink later in the summer – would be great to catch up.*' She put the phone in her lap and spread her hands, looking girlishly excited. 'What do I say? I think I want to be brave and go out with him, but I'm so rubbish at this sort of thing. Completely out of practice.'

'What's he like?' Em asked. 'If you've been friends for years, it sounds like he's trustworthy at least.'

'He is,' Maggie replied. 'He's . . . he's really great. He's been such a good friend to me and is actually quite . . . you know. *Hot*. But . . .' She was turning pinker by the second. 'The thing is, I don't know what the "but" *is* any more. I've been saying "no" and "but" and making excuses for years, even though I've felt the vibes from him and always felt a bit giddy about him in return.' She fiddled with her fingers, looking both fierce and shy at the same time. 'Maybe the time has come to just . . . take a leap.'

'Yes. Do!' cried Olivia. 'A date, how lovely. All that excitement and butterflies, getting dressed up, all the hope and anticipation.'

Em swallowed hard, remembering it well. All lost to her now, no doubt.

'Any words of wisdom, Em? How did you and George get together?' asked Maggie. Clunk. Presumably Em's face was saying *Catastrophe catastrophe*, because in the next moment Maggie began hastily backtracking. 'Um . . . If you want to tell us, that is. Oh dear. I haven't just put my foot in

it, have I? I did see him going out earlier and wondered—'
She broke off, grimacing. 'Sorry. Ignore me.'

'It's okay,' said Em, even though it really wasn't. She
stared at the inflatable flamingo that was drifting aimlessly
across the water in a breeze and did her best to dredge up
some semblance of composure. *Breathe.* 'Look, I'm not the
best person to ask about dating, sadly, seeing as George and
I might have . . .' She swallowed again, as if the words were
stuck inside her. 'Well, we might have ground to a halt,
actually. But don't let that put you off! Until this holiday, I
was blissfully happy.' Oh dear. Was that a sob? Had she just
ended that little speech with a sob?

Olivia and Maggie were both gazing at her with stricken
expressions. Damn it. She totally *had*.

Lorna was unstacking the dishwasher when she glanced out
of the window and saw the three women all sitting together
by the pool. She smiled with pleasure at the sight. So often
the women who came to stay here appeared stressed and
frazzled, exhausting themselves under the pressure of trying
to give their families the mythically perfect holiday experience. She'd much rather see her guests relax and have fun. It
was good that Olivia was out there too, joining in. Even from
this distance, Lorna could tell she'd picked up a bit of a tan
from the sunny weather, and her body language seemed less

tense. It made Lorna feel like a proud mother hen to see the difference in her.

'Look, Roy,' she said, gesturing towards the window as he came into the kitchen. 'Isn't that nice? I do like it when the families get to know each other.'

Roy came over, slotting his arms around her waist. He rested his head against her shoulder. 'Remember that holiday we went on when Aidan was – what, about fifteen? And we met that lovely family from Dundee.'

Until that moment, Lorna had forgotten all about the lovely family from Dundee, but then a memory flickered at the back of her mind like an old cine-film and she seized hold of it. 'Yes,' she said slowly, as the details coloured themselves in. 'Valencia, wasn't it? We rented that little white house.' And then she was remembering the warm evenings, sitting out in the communal courtyard with a bottle of Rioja, talking to the friendly couple they'd met, with the son around Aidan's age, the cicadas chirruping in the background. How she'd loved waking up in that quiet, plain bedroom every morning as the sun rose, orange and magnificent, sweeping its light across the whitewashed walls. 'That was a smashing holiday,' she sighed.

There was a silence as they both drifted through their own memories and she wondered if Roy was wishing they could go somewhere similar again. And actually . . . Well, it was the strangest thing, but for the first time since Aidan died, she thought she might be able to manage that. Find another whitewashed house and enjoy a calm, relaxing break away together; relax into the stillness and the warmth.

'Listen,' she said, turning around so that they were facing one another. 'We should look into going away in the autumn. Maybe the beginning of October, when the lettings have gone quiet. A little holiday, just the two of us, some-where warm.'

He looked surprised and happy to hear her say such a thing, then hugged her to him. 'I would really like that,' he said quietly into her hair.

Some hours later, Maggie, Em and Olivia were still out there by the pool, even though it was almost midnight. Up above, the stars were a handful of silver glitter against the inky black while the moon cast glimmering ripples of light into the water. The air smelled of wine and chlorine, with just a faint hint of ozone from the distant sea carried on the breeze.

There was quite a collection of empty bottles and glasses around them by now; that little drink and chat Maggie had envisaged when she'd first walked out towards Em had turned into a much longer session. At some point Olivia had pleaded starvation and gone inside to make herself dinner, returning with a plate of pasta and salad on a tray, as well as a whole garlic baguette for them to share. Some time after that, Em had popped indoors to make sure her children were okay and to tell them to start getting ready for bed. And once the sun had vanished and the temperature began to plummet, Maggie had suggested bringing their duvets out to keep themselves warm, because none of them quite wanted the evening to end just yet. Now they were comfortably rugged-up and cosy on their sun loungers, laughing and exchanging confidences like girls on a sleepover. And oh, what a lot of ground they had covered tonight.

Urged on by the others, Maggie had replied to Paul's text – and, believe it or not, *she'd* asked *him* out. Suggested a date and time and everything. He'd already replied saying Great, he'd love that, and she kept flipping from freaking out with panic to feeling excited and looking forward to it. *True passion awaits,* teased the memory of the fortune cookie. Well, she didn't know about that, but it definitely felt as if something lovely might be waiting on the horizon, hers for the taking.

They'd gone on to discuss Em's love life next, even though earlier she had told them she didn't want to talk about it. She was pretty circumspect about what had happened – something to do with her daughter, Maggie gleaned – and seemed pessimistic about the chances of getting back together with George. '*And* his ex is an absolute raving beauty,' she'd slurred, tossing another glass of wine down her throat.

Maggie couldn't help herself. 'So are you,' she had cried,

because truly Em was exactly the sort of woman she'd always envied: pretty, vivacious, sparklier than a whole string of Christmas lights. 'You're gorgeous,' she told her, 'and I've had more fun with you tonight than anyone else in years.'

Em looked quite choked up, squeezing Maggie's hand and thanking her. Then she deftly deflected the attention away from herself. 'Let's talk about more cheerful things,' she suggested, 'like someone who has, by the sound of it, cracked this whole relationship business.' She waggled an eyebrow at Olivia, then went on, 'Maggie, you'll never guess, Olivia's husband arranged for her to have a lovely break here on her own – how nice is that?'

'Wow! Lucky you,' said Maggie. 'That's so thoughtful. What a treat!'

But instead of smiling back at them, Olivia's face fell and she shook her head. 'It didn't really happen like that,' she confessed. She bit her lip. 'Sorry, Em, I didn't want to correct you the other day when you guessed that, because . . . Well, because the truth is a bit different. I'm not actually here because of any luxury treat. Far from it.'

She looked so distressed all of a sudden that Em and Maggie looked at one another in alarm. 'Is everything all right?' Maggie asked.

'Sorry, I shouldn't have been so nosy,' Em said. 'You don't have to tell us anything if you don't want to.'

Olivia pressed her lips together. 'It's okay. I need to start facing facts anyway,' she said, then sighed. 'I'm here because I ran away, because I'm a crap mum,' she went on, her voice trembling. 'And somehow I've got to put things right, but I still don't really know how.'

Em looked astonished. 'Oh, darling,' she cried in surprise. 'I'm sure you're not crap at all – it's the hardest thing in the world, being a mum. The steepest learning curve!'

'Nobody ever thinks they're doing a great job of it, trust me,' Maggie put in. 'Nobody.'

'We're all just bumbling along at the end of the day, aren't we?' said Em. 'Sometimes getting it right, sometimes getting it wrong. But you're doing your best, I'm sure.'

Olivia hung her head. 'I just . . . I mean, I do try, I really do, but it never seems to be good enough.' A tear rolled down her cheek and dropped to the ground. 'Thank you,' she said in a tiny voice as Maggie reached into her cardigan pocket and pulled out a small packet of tissues, passing them over. 'I'm not sure why I'm telling you all of this – sorry, I'm totally killing the ladies-night mood.'

'Don't be silly!' Em cried.

'Not at all,' Maggie agreed. Then she hesitated. 'So when you say you ran away . . .'

'That's what I did,' Olivia said dully. 'Just flipped out. Couldn't cope. Dropped the boys off with a neighbour – I have three-year-old twins – and got in the car. Total impulse decision. What kind of a mother does that?'

'We've all thought it, I bet,' Em said, reaching out and putting a hand on Olivia's. 'I know I've had those moments where I haven't been able to manage. Plenty of them. It's hard – and I didn't even have twins.'

Maggie felt sorry for Olivia too. There was something so young-seeming about her, so vulnerable. 'Do you have much help at home?' she asked. 'Family nearby or friends you can lean on?'

'Not really,' Olivia replied. 'My mum walked out when I was young – she's dead now – and my husband works stupidly long hours. My dad and brother are great, but they both live miles away, I hardly ever see them. As for my in-laws . . . they think my place is in the home with the boys, and that childcare for under-fives means you're a bad mother.'

'Harsh,' said Em indignantly.

'What century are they living in?' cried Maggie.

Olivia blew her nose. 'I really wanted to be good at it, you know? Because of . . .' She broke off, looking agonized. 'I really wanted to be this great mum. I tried so hard to do it all myself. But I just *can't*.'

Em got off her chair to put her arm around Olivia, and Maggie felt a pang for her too. 'Sorry to hear about your mum,' she said, remembering how much she'd always leaned on her own parents, especially in the early years. 'That must have been so hard.'

'I've always felt a bit . . . inadequate, with her leaving like that, out of the blue,' Olivia gulped. 'As if it was my fault, as if I somehow wasn't enough for her to stay.'

'Oh, love,' Em said. 'On a rational level, you must know yourself that isn't true, but . . .'

'It's always been like a hole in me. A hole I tried to fill up with boyfriends and work and friends.' Olivia wiped her eyes. 'And then I hoped my own children would stop up the gap. That I could somehow prove something by being this great mother myself. Except I've failed at that, too. I've failed at all of it.'

'It does get easier,' Em said. 'Those early years are gruelling, but I promise it gets easier. They sleep, for one thing. And dress themselves. And go to school for long periods of time . . .'

'Lack of sleep is the worst,' Maggie added with feeling. 'It's a form of torture. But you have to keep reminding yourself that it won't be like that forever – it's not a life sentence. None of it is.' She rolled her eyes. 'Now it's an effort to drag Amelia out of bed before midday at weekends and holidays. It's all just a phase.'

'Exactly,' Em agreed. 'And there are millions of women who understand what you're going through and sympathize. *We* do, for starters, and I bet everyone at toddler groups or wherever you go – they'll have felt the same way too, even if they've slapped on a brave face for the day. No one's going to judge you for finding it tough. It *is* tough.'

'Your GP can help,' Maggie put in. She looked at her hands for a moment, remembering the strain she had experienced being alone in the early years. 'I felt pretty low myself when Amelia was tiny. I'm not sure if it was full-blown Post-Natal Depression or what, but my doctor was amazing. Even telling her about it made me feel better. More able to cope.'

'Yes, and your husband should help, and all,' Em agreed. 'How come he's not pulling his weight?'

'He does – in his own way,' Olivia replied, then wrinkled her nose. 'But "his way", admittedly, is having an amazing career and bringing home the bacon. He doesn't really experience the day-to-day grind.' She gave a sudden snort. 'Mind you, he's been doing that this week, at least. I've had a *lot* of messages asking how to cook shepherd's pie so that the boys will actually eat it, and where the laundry powder is, and are the boys *really* allowed ice-cream every day . . . So I suppose he'll have a better idea of what it's been like for me, the last three years.'

'Good,' said Em. 'And once you're home again, hopefully he – and they – will appreciate you more for your absence too. For what it's worth, I don't think you sound like a rubbish mum at all, by the way. You cook your kids shepherd's pie and wash their clothes and lay down rules about ice-cream . . . That all seems pretty good to me. Not a failure at all.' She gave Olivia a last squeeze, then sat back down. 'I'm sorry you're going through this though. Really sorry. But there are people out there who can help you.'

Olivia dabbed at her eyes and gave them both a watery smile. 'Thank you,' she said. 'I know running away isn't the answer – your troubles just come with you, don't they? – but it's been good to have a break, even in these weird circumstances. Step out of my ordinary life and have some thinking space.'

'Yes,' said Maggie. 'Thinking space is always a bonus.'

'And hey,' said Em, 'a holiday *without* your family . . . I'm starting to think that might be the best kind of holiday of all. You might just be starting a trend here, Olivia.'

Olivia laughed, and the conversation took a much more upbeat tone. They moved on to funny parenting stories and most embarrassing moments and terrible teenage hairstyles. Somehow the hours just slipped by. Em made everyone a round of fried-egg sandwiches when they became peckish, and Maggie brought out mugs of hot chocolate sometime after that. Despite some of the more harrowing parts of the conversation, Maggie realized that she was enjoying herself enormously. She didn't really have girlfriends like this at home. It had been surprisingly lovely to talk so openly to the other two, to get things off her chest and to feel validated and supported in return. Chances were the three of them wouldn't see each other again, once they were back in their ordinary lives – Em was in Cheltenham and Olivia in

Bristol – but that just lent the evening an extra frisson of liberation; they could truly be honest, let off some real steam.

That said, it was getting very late now and Maggie was starting to think about her bed.

'This has been such a strange holiday,' she said, smothering a yawn. Strange but unexpectedly cheering in a lot of ways, she thought. She felt a different person, with her new haircut and attitude and, for the first time in years, the future felt . . . interesting. In two days she would pick up Amelia. In two weeks she would go on her date with Paul. She was going to be a better, bolder Maggie and there was plenty to look forward to.

'You're telling me,' said Em, with slightly less positivity. She had sunk lower beneath her duvet in the last half an hour, as if she was ready to sleep too.

Silence fell, except for the faint glugging of the water in the swimming-pool filter and the soft bumps of the inflatable flamingo against the metal steps as it cruised in slow, blind circles.

Maggie was just about to suggest they called it a night when Olivia spoke. 'I might regret this tomorrow,' she said hesitantly, 'but I was wondering . . . can I tell you guys a secret? Like – something really big?'

Chapter Twenty-Seven

It was the following morning and Olivia was packing up her belongings, feeling apprehensive. She had spent the last twenty years, pretty much, feeling weighed down by the past, dogged by the shadows. Maybe it went even further back to when her mum had disappeared and the colour had bleached out of her world. So what had changed today? On the face of it, nothing, apart from her hangover. She had woken up that morning the exact same person she had been the night before: the same combination of cells and nerves and muscles, the same history and memories and experience. Messy blonde hair that needed cutting, extra pounds lurking around the middle – yes, all still there. Nothing had changed, and yet everything had.

She sprayed perfume on her neck and breathed in the sweet scent. 'For the first few years after my kids were born, I did nothing for myself,' Em had said last night. 'I didn't wear make-up or perfume or jewellery, I didn't care about my clothes. Sometimes it felt an effort just to brush my hair.

But I've got to say, I always felt better whenever I did bother with any of those things, however small. If I put on some lipstick or a necklace, if I made it out to the hairdresser's or rang a friend to chat . . . You'd be surprised, you know, how much of an effect these tiny, tiny things can have. Don't underestimate them, because they make all the difference sometimes.'

Olivia put on some mascara and eyed her reflection. She was going to try Em's advice, she had decided. Make time for one little thing for herself every day – as well as some bigger things too, like catching up with her friends and her brother. Going swimming or out for a jog on her own, just to clear her head: positive actions that she knew would make her feel good, like Olivia again. She just had to make the effort, find the time, that was all. But she would. She was determined.

Last night, with Em and Maggie, had been lovely – such a relief to step out of the confines of her own worried head for a change. Talking to near-strangers had been like having a sounding board for her feelings. She had poured out her heart and neither of them had flinched or backed away, instead offering her support and kindness, just as Lorna had previously. *Women to the rescue,* Em had joked, but that was how it felt. Being listened to, being heard, had made her feel brave. Brave enough to spill out her secret at the end of the night. *He was called Leon,* she'd said, words she'd only ever spoken to Mack.

They had hugged her and assured her she was doing the right thing in telling Lorna and Roy. They had said, *You mustn't blame yourself* and *You were so young, give yourself a break.* She'd only been a few years older than their daughters, they'd reminded her. Would she be so hard on them, so judgemental?

She glanced down at the envelope that lay on the bed, the letter that had been so hard to write. Remembering Lorna's anguished face when they'd met at Aidan's grave, Olivia found herself wavering all over again. Handing over the letter was going to mean emotional upheaval for both of them. The landscape would shift and buckle, everything would change and it would not be easy. Once you threw a stone into water, you couldn't stop the ripples.

Rolling her new swimming costume into a ball, she tucked it into her bag, still considering. Lorna and Roy had been so kind, letting her stay here in her hour of need. Incredibly kind. The last thing she wanted to do was upset them. But didn't she owe it to them, too, to tell them the truth?

Having zipped the case shut, she heaved it downstairs and left it by the front door. Then she stripped the bedding, gathered it up with the towels she'd used and bundled the lot into the washing machine before setting it churning. She washed her breakfast things and stacked them neatly in the drying rack, bagged up her rubbish ready to go and then checked over the cottage one last time. Her heart was thumping suddenly at the prospect of what lay ahead, and she found herself sinking unsteadily into the armchair, struck by a queasy rush of nerves. Not only did she have to say her piece to Lorna, but after that she planned to drive somewhere quiet where she could phone Mack and talk to him, really talk, about where the two of them went from here. After that, she supposed she would have to go home and face the music. Hoping that it didn't completely deafen her.

Em's words came back to her – *Olivia, you're totally going to sort everything out and move on to happy times again* – and she found herself recalling how she'd lain in bed the night before, thinking, *Yes. Yes, it's time to sort everything out, once and for all.* Because she really did want to move out of the shadows at last and find those happy times.

She stood up, striding quickly towards the door before she could change her mind.

The wind was getting up, the trees rattling their branches threateningly as Olivia put her belongings in the car and then walked the short distance to Lorna and Roy's farmhouse. It was a lovely old stone building: double-fronted with a shingled roof. A cat snoozed on an upstairs windowsill, oblivious to the birds that whistled and cheeped in the hedgerow. It looked the sort of house where nothing bad could ever happen. How ironic, she thought, knocking on the door.

Lorna answered, wearing a faded blue apron with a dusting of flour on the front and her sleeves rolled up: the image of contented domesticity. At the sight of Olivia standing there, her face creased with a smile. 'Come in, love. Roy's just putting the kettle on, aren't you, Roy? Roy! Put the kettle on, Olivia's popped round.'

Something folded in Olivia's heart, but then she forced herself to toughen up. She had to do this. 'Um . . . thanks, but I won't stop,' she said. If she ventured into Lorna's sunny kitchen, no doubt with warm jam tarts from the oven cooling on a tray and a teapot with a brightly knitted cosy, she would never be able to steel herself and do what she intended. 'I'm actually leaving. Heading off to sort everything out and . . .' She shrugged self-consciously. 'You know, try and be a proper grown-up.'

'Good for you,' said Lorna. Her small gold earrings gleamed in the light as she nodded approvingly. 'I'm really glad. I hope everything works out.'

Olivia gave her a small smile – *so do I* – but could feel her hands trembling by her sides and knotted them together in a clammy tangle. *Here we go.* 'Before I leave, I just wanted to thank you and Roy, so much, for everything,' she went on. 'For taking me in like that when I was at rock-bottom. You are just the best, both of you. Aidan was really lucky to have you.'

Lorna's eyes glistened at the mention of his name. 'And I

want to thank *you*,' she replied warmly. 'For bringing him back to us with your stories. Honestly, it has been the best gift hearing your memories, I can't tell you. Any time you want to stay with us, you're more than welcome. Bring the family next time, I'd love to meet them.'

'Thank you,' said Olivia, her stomach twisting. She wasn't sure Lorna would be saying that any more once she'd read the letter. 'Um,' she said, still undecided even now. Then she pulled the envelope from her handbag and held it out. You could almost hear it ticking like a bomb. 'Here,' she said, her voice wavering. No going back now. 'This is for you. Please don't open it until I'm gone,' she added, hoping she wasn't making a terrible mistake. Lorna looked at her, eyes questioning, and Olivia shoved it into her hand. 'There was a baby,' she blurted out and then walked quickly away.

Olivia's body must have known what to do even if her mind was blanking on her, like a dying light bulb, because somehow or other it got her into the car and then she was driving off, gripping the wheel as nausea rose inside, too fearful to look back in case Lorna was already racing after her, shaking a fist, having been unable to wait to read the letter.

She would never tell Lorna and Roy what had happened just before Aidan had died; the cruel things she had said to him. No way. How could she do that to them and break their hearts all over again, knowing that his last thought, his last emotion, had been one of devastation at her betrayal? No, she would have to live with the guilt of her worst secret alone, and it would be only what she deserved.

As for her other secret . . . it had become impossible to keep back any longer. Having so much time to herself, seeing Lorna and Roy again, revisiting her teenage hangouts – it was no wonder that her first pregnancy and birth had come pushing to the surface. She'd even blurted the story out to Em and Maggie the night before – *Can I tell you guys a secret? Like – something really big?* – and then out it had come, albeit a pared-down version, with scant details around the event. *His dad was dead, I was all alone,* she had confessed, the words bursting out of her, and the other women had ended up soothing and comforting her as if she were a child herself.

And now Lorna and Roy knew too, presumably. *There was a baby*: all eight pounds and eight ounces of the secret that she had suppressed for nineteen years. *He was born in Dorset on April the fourth, 1999,* she had written:

He had blue eyes and dark hair like Aidan and roared like a lion as he met the world. But I couldn't keep him. I gave him away to be adopted. I'm sorry that I never told you before now. For a long, long time I put him out of my mind and tried to start a new chapter. But you and Roy deserve to know that you have a grandson out there. A little piece of Aidan. I hope you don't hate me too much.

The countryside was flashing by on either side of her as she sped along the road, putting mile upon mile between her and the letter. She imagined Lorna's cry of shock, a tear perhaps dropping onto that floury apron-front as she read Olivia's confession. She pictured Roy's sudden anger, their shared hurt and bewilderment – how could she have kept this from us? How could she have given our grandchild away?

'I'm sorry, I'm sorry,' she groaned aloud. The rushing noise she could hear wasn't the wind battering against the car, but Fate, she thought, hurrying to catch up with her. An old ghost breathing down her neck.

Meanwhile the ripples would already be spreading outwards. The secret, finally freed, would be covering ground like wildfire. Lorna and Roy would want to track him down, she was certain, and then it would only be a matter of time before her name was mentioned too. Would he want to see her, or would he loathe her for what she had done?

It was hard to concentrate on anything, let alone driving, with such huge thoughts crowding her head and, seeing a lay-by, Olivia indicated and pulled over, her breath coming in gulps as she hauled up the handbrake. Calm down. It's all right. You're okay, she reminded herself, but the past was filling her up like smoke all of a sudden, and she could no longer block it out.

It had come as the most enormous shock to her, two months into her university course, to discover that she was four months pregnant. As if Aidan was calling back from the grave, a hand reaching out to grab her by the ankle as she'd made her escape. *You can't get rid of me that easily.* He always did have to have the last word, and here it was: real and unavoidable. Literally a part of her now.

Life before then had been something of a Choose-Your-Own-Adventure game – this is what I want to study! This is where I want to live! This is where I'm going out tonight! – but all of a sudden, it was as if the choices had been taken away. She had dropped out, deferring her place on the course, telling none of her new friends the reason why. Then, having miserably confessed the situation to her dad, she went to stay with her aunt in Dorset for the duration of the pregnancy. It had felt as if she were a fallen woman from a cheap Victorian novel as she grew larger and larger, lonelier and lonelier, waddling unhappily through the streets of picturesque honey-coloured cottages for something to do while she saw out her confinement. No, she didn't want the baby, she told the midwives – she was too young; how could she manage on her own? – and opted instead to give it away to be adopted.

'It' – that was how she had seen the baby back then. Right up until the moment he was born and she was confronted by his curly black hair and his angry red face, when she realized, with a punch of emotions, that he was a he, not an it. *He* was a real small person. Her and Aidan's son.

She had never even held a baby before then. She had not expected to be quite so entranced by this tiny warm being that her body had miraculously known how to assemble. It had taken her by surprise just how miniature and perfect he was. The softness of his skin, the whorl of dark hair on his head and the way his wet pink mouth opened and closed like a fish. His shoulders had been so little! His tummy rounded like a peach. She had marvelled at his ears, so delicately curled.

Two days they'd had together, a bubble of time when the outside world had receded, when she held her baby and fed him and gazed at him. Her dad came to visit her, and Danny too, plus her aunt, but that was it. Nobody else seemed to exist. Then the brisk, matronly woman from social services had arrived with her clipboard and forms and plucked him away – 'Come on then, little one,' she had said kindly enough – and Olivia started to wonder if she was making a terrible mistake in letting him go.

'Wait,' she said, already missing the warm weight of him in her arms. It no longer seemed to matter that she was only nineteen and that she'd had to drop out of university for this. 'I think I've changed my mind.'

But the woman was presumably used to bewildered postpartum mothers calling these things when they too noticed the sudden emptiness in their arms, and she reminded Olivia of the new family that had been approved for the baby, how they lived in a lovely house with a big garden, how they'd already decorated a nursery for him and picked out his name – Leon. They were grown-ups with plenty of money and could give him, in other words, all the things that single, teenage, penniless Olivia couldn't.

And so she'd squashed down her feelings and let him go. Off to his new family and painted nursery and big garden, off to his life of plenty, without her. Because let's face it, she'd only muck things up anyway, she'd only let him down somewhere along the line, just like her own mother had in fact. Was it her imagination or had the baby yelled something out as the woman departed with him? A cry of protest, she'd thought – *Take me back to my mother!* – although maybe it had been an angry one, directed at her: *How could you do this to me?*

Afterwards the guilt had been terrible. It had swallowed her up whole for months. She still thought about him whenever April came around with its cherry blossom and tulips, still remembered the warm, milky solidity of his small body. Wondered if she had made a mistake. Told herself she probably had. It was why she had been so determined, so dogged that she would be the best mother ever, second time around with Stanley and Harry. But seeing them growing up milestone by milestone – first teeth and first words, crawling and then walking – only compounded her feelings of shame, reminding her of what she had missed by giving Leon away.

What was done was done, she reminded herself now, motionless in the driver's seat of her car as other vehicles zoomed by. She couldn't change what had happened even if she wanted to – and now that she'd told Lorna and Roy her secret, there would be no more denial or pretending. She'd given them Leon's birth date and the name of the hospital, details that would hopefully act as signposts if they went looking for him. It was up to them now.

Rain started pattering against the roof, leaving thin diagonal streaks across the windscreen. She felt very far away from the rest of the world all of a sudden, a small sad satellite spinning alone in the darkness. Mack had been kind when she had eventually told him about Leon, but she hadn't exactly picked the best moment. In truth, she hadn't ever intended to let him know the story at all, but then he'd come with her to her initial midwife booking-in appointment and when asked, 'Is this your first pregnancy?' she'd had to apologetically correct him when he'd enthusiastically answered 'Yes!' on her behalf. Which was something of a giveaway.

A moment passed and then Olivia switched on her phone and started scrolling through her photos. The boys in the bath, with flannels on their heads. A party tea, where they were wearing red and purple paper crowns, Stanley with both fists pumped excitedly in the air. Harry lying on his side on the living-room carpet, playing with his trains. She had never taken a picture of Leon, she thought in sorrow. Her dad had gently suggested it after the birth, but Olivia had said no because the thought was too weird and she'd naively hoped she would be able to forget all about him, although of course that had been impossible. On reflection, it had been the wrong decision. Yet another wrong decision!

She pressed the heels of her hands into her eye sockets wearily and sighed, feeling her emotions catch up with her. Then she looked at her phone again. At least she had Stanley and Harry, she reminded herself. And she missed them, she realized, feeling an ache inside. For all her doubts and self-blame, she missed her children and husband. *I've just got one thing left to do,* she had promised Mack when she'd last texted him – but now that she'd divulged her secret to Lorna and Roy, she wasn't sure what the next step might be. Where did she go from here?

A lorry thundered alongside her and the car rocked from side to side. Momentum had brought her this far, but now it was as if her clockwork had wound right down and she found herself paralysed with indecision, motionless with uncertainty. Before she could possibly go home again, she needed to come clean with Mack: open the door a little wider on how she had been feeling and try to articulate her sense of worthlessness, her difficulty in coping. He must know by now that she was not the perfect mother she had tried so hard to be, but talking to Em and Maggie had made Olivia see that perhaps nobody was. Maggie had even been to the doctor to talk about how hard she was finding everything when her daughter was little. Maybe Olivia's old habit of keeping her own anxieties disguised and pushed down wasn't working any more. Maybe it was time that she too plucked up the courage and asked for help.

And if she did . . . would Mack still be saying, *Come home, just come home,* once he knew the extent of her struggles? Or would there be judgement in his eyes? Disappointment at her shortcomings?

Well, there was only one way to find out. She took a deep breath and dialled his number. 'Hi,' she said when he answered, then swallowed hard. 'Have you got a minute? I need to say a few things.'

Chapter Twenty-Eight

Amelia lay on the hard, narrow camp bed and shut her eyes, feeling disgustingly homesick. Or Mum-sick, rather, if there was such a thing.

All around her she could hear the rest of the household moving about, getting on with the day. Thistle and Rain had been up for hours already, it seemed, watching cartoons in the living room and shouting out catchphrases. Then she'd heard Celeste running a bath and detected the faint herbal pong of whatever she was stewing herself in that particular day. Will . . . Dad – she still didn't quite know what to call him – had been in the kitchen, whistling cheerfully as he organized breakfast and then she'd heard him calling to Celeste that he was going for a run, and the front door banging.

Meanwhile here she was, warm and a bit ripe in her sleeping bag, feeling as if she didn't want to do anything at all any more. Thistle and Rain had pounded on her door at occasional intervals – 'Melia? Melia!' – but she'd ignored them, and Celeste had eventually gently chided them to leave her be. 'Teenagers need their sleep,' Amelia had heard her say and she'd rolled over unhappily. *She* didn't need any more sleep. She'd been going to bed really early at night just because it was all so overwhelming. What she needed was to feel like someone gave a shit. Like she belonged somewhere. Because she sure as hell didn't belong here.

She stared at her phone and at the glossy images she'd put up on social media over the last few days. *Having an amazing time with my famous dad!!! My gorgeous stepbrother and sis!!! First photography lesson with Dad – lucky me!* There were a few new likes since the last time she'd looked. A few new comments. It all felt hollow, though, when her own dad hadn't followed her back on Instagram yet. She'd dropped it into the conversation yesterday, trying not to sound too keen or desperate – 'Hey! How come you're not following me then?' – and he'd laughed, but made no comment. Was he embarrassed by her? Or just not that interested? She wasn't sure which was worse.

She flicked through to the last image, a photo of herself posed artfully in the back garden. There were some blurry blue cornflowers behind her and the sun was falling on her face as she smiled. *Happy,* she'd captioned the shot, but just seconds after it had been taken, a chicken had waddled up to her and she'd yelped in fright, and then Thistle had wandered out with a storybook, wanting Amelia to read to her, and then Rain had fallen over and started crying, and then Celeste had snapped at Amelia for not keeping an eye on the kids. Er . . . do I *look* like your nanny? Amelia had thought sarcastically, scowling and stomping back inside.

Happy indeed. A picture might paint a thousand words, but her pictures only told lies. A more representative image of her stay here would be a photo taken right now, of her huddled in a sleeping bag, with no inclination whatsoever to get up. Willing the time to pass so that she could go back to Cornwall with her mum. Then a thought struck her.

'Mum?' she said when Maggie answered the call. 'I don't suppose you could pick me up a bit early, could you? Like . . . today?'

Izzie had hardly slept all night, such were the depths of her turmoil and guilt. She had wrecked everything. To think that a few short weeks ago she'd written brave, carefree words in her diary about how this would be her rite-of-passage summer, how she was on the brink of becoming a woman . . . ha! Cue mocking laughter from the rest of the world, she thought, pulling the pillow over her head. Now George had left, apparently having dumped Mum, and it was all because of her: a stupid girl.

As if that wasn't bad enough, she had totally blown everything with Fraser too. Having been grounded the night before, she'd texted him saying that she couldn't go out that evening after all and could they hang out today instead?

He hadn't replied. Not a single word. He must have thought she had gone cold on him and couldn't be bothered to answer her. He was probably already chatting up some other girl in a swimming pool by now.

A sob burst out of her at how rubbish everything had become. Then another sob, because it was all her fault. She imagined pressing the pillow harder and harder against her nose and mouth so that she could no longer breathe. Was it possible to kill yourself that way, she wondered, or did the body's survival instinct kick in and somehow push the pillow away in its fight for air? She didn't have the energy to try it, though. That was how pathetic she was. She couldn't even be bothered to suffocate herself.

It was ten o'clock in the morning and they were having a lazy day at the cottage. Earlier on, Mum had made an effort and rustled up bacon sandwiches for breakfast, but she'd looked tired and red-eyed. For a horrible moment, Izzie had thought her mum might go into misery meltdown all over again when she realized she'd accidentally made two coffees, one for George, somehow forgetting that he had already left. She had stared at that mug as if it were possessed by the devil, and her lower lip had actually begun to tremble as the fact of his departure clicked back into place. *He's gone. You idiot.* You could see it on her face.

'I'll have it,' Izzie had said quickly, snatching the mug away, even though she'd never liked coffee. Anything to stop that wobbling lip. Anything to prevent her mum's face from sagging with renewed despair.

'What are we doing today?' Jack had asked just then, ambling into the room with his headphones on and completely misreading the mood. 'Hey, when are we gonna go zorbing by the way? You did say we could.'

'Let's just have a quiet one today,' Mum replied in this sad, dreary sort of voice, as if she had completely given up on the notion of holiday fun. Which in itself was so disturbingly un-Mum-ish that the words made Izzie want to throw herself on the floor and clutch at Em's dressing gown, pleading forgiveness for the hundredth time.

'Mum, I really am so sorry,' she mumbled, knotted up with guilt and shame, while Jack went over to the fridge and began gulping orange juice straight from the carton. There – another sign that Mum was still flattened by yesterday's events, because she didn't even start bollocking him about hygiene and *Just get a glass and pour it out, it's not difficult,* as she usually would have done. No, her gaze just slid right over him with supreme indifference. Bloody hell. This was *bad*.

'It doesn't matter,' Em replied dully – which was clearly a massive lie. Of *course* it mattered, Izzie thought, plunging slices of bread down in the toaster and silently fetching three plates. Mum had been nuts about George, and now

Izzie had inadvertently destroyed the relationship and sent him packing. She had to find a way to haul her mother back up again, and fast.

After breakfast, an uneasy silence settled upon the house. Mum trudged upstairs saying she thought she was getting a migraine and was going back to bed, and Jack was plugged glassy-eyed into some game or other and would almost certainly not move a muscle until lunchtime. Izzie didn't know what else to do other than slope back into bed herself. One family: broken, she thought. One holiday: ruined.

Over Christmas last year she'd worked in a gift shop in town, selling ornaments and vases and little wooden signs with cheesy slogans like *The Sun Might Not Be Shining But We've Always Got Gin!* to middle-class people who had nothing better to spend their money on. There had been notices up everywhere: *You break it, you pay for it* and clumsy Izzie had spent every shift dreading the moment when she was sure to elbow a cocktail glass off a shelf or trip over one of the tweedy Scottie-dog doorstops and go flying straight into the bone-china dinner-service display. The phrase kept coming back to her now as if it was a command: *You broke this, Izzie Hughes, you'd better damn well pay for it.* But how?

Scrolling through her phone – and deliberately not looking at any of her group-chat notifications – she saw George's name in her list of contacts from the time when he'd picked her up from babysitting, and her finger hesitated on the screen. Should she ring him? God, no, she thought with a shudder in the next moment. He probably wouldn't even answer anyway. Still, she could send him a message, she supposed. Tell him the whole thing was her fault, not Mum's, and ask him to give Mum another chance.

She grimaced, imagining her mum's face if she discovered Izzie had gone behind her back like that, trying to patch things up. And who was she, anyway, to go poking about in other people's relationships, when she'd never even managed to get as far as a second date herself? It was the equivalent of a child with a junior doctor's kit attempting to perform open-heart surgery. Broken-heart surgery, more like. Still, there was no harm in saying sorry, was there? Maybe that was a good place to start.

She rolled onto her front, propped herself up on her elbows and began to type. *Hello. Sorry things have gone wrong. If you want someone to blame, blame me, not Mum.*

Oh God, she was cringing already. Even she could see that this sounded so dramatically teenage, so pathetic. Would it be better if she sneaked Mum's phone from her room and pretended to be Em? *Hey, Em here. My daughter is insane, but don't let that put you off!*

Even worse. Just imagine Mum's livid expression when she rumbled what Izzie had done – the screeches that would rip through the house. *You did WHAT? For crying out loud!*

Haven't you caused enough trouble? What the hell were you THINKING?

Maybe not, on second thoughts. She valued her life too much to risk it.

Her eye fell upon her sketchbook just then and she remembered with a pang the conversations she'd enjoyed with George about drawing, about art. There would be no more of those now. No one in her corner saying yes, of course she should go for A-level Art, she should absolutely study the things that made her happy. She remembered how George had stood up to Mum on her behalf, arguing her case, and how validated he had made her feel, as if her view counted for something after all. Let's face it, her own dad wouldn't do the same. 'Art? How's that going to lead to a decent job?' Dom would snort, without even listening to how she felt on the matter.

Come on, Iz. She *had* to get George back onside, for Mum's sake as well as for her own conscience. For all her earlier misgivings, she didn't want him simply to vanish from the Hughes family's life, gone forever in a puff of cologne-tinged smoke. She opened her tin of pencils, ran a finger along them thoughtfully. Maybe there was some kind of artistic gesture she could make. A funny cartoon of her saying sorry? She probably wasn't a good enough artist to do the situation justice, though. In fact she could offend him by drawing him badly.

Then another idea came to her. What was the name of that painting they'd both been giggling over the other day? The girl with the guitar, or banjo, whatever it was. Caravaggio was the artist, yes, because she'd had to stop herself from making puerile jokes about his name.

She switched on her tablet and started searching – *The Lute Player*, there it was. The painting showed a pensive-looking girl in a white peasant-style blouse plucking the strings of a round-bellied lute, with several other instruments arranged in front of her. *Whoa – check out those eyebrows!* Izzie had snorted at the time, and then they'd had a bit of a laugh about the most inappropriate tune the girl could have been playing on that lute. 'He's got the whole world in his hands,' George had sung in full happy-clappy style, while Izzie argued that the girl was more of a rock fan instead. 'She's about to break into the chorus and go full headbanger,' she'd joked. 'WHOA-OH! Livin' on a prayer!' George had yelled, pretending to rock out, and then they'd both burst out laughing.

Izzie smiled wistfully now, remembering the conversation. *What on earth are you two cackling about?* Mum had asked, mystified, but you could tell she'd been pleased that they'd hit it off all the same.

Sitting up a little straighter, Izzie flexed her fingers, the idea taking shape in her mind. Okay, Lute-Playing Girl, forgive me for what I'm about to do to you, in terms of

Photoshopping and ridicule, she told the painting in her head. As for you, Caravaggio, do not choose this moment to turn your spectral eye on a holiday cottage in Cornwall, mate, or you'll be totally spinning in your grave.

Then she got to work.

Chapter Twenty-Nine

Olivia's parting words had rung in Lorna's head all morning like the reverberations from a struck gong. *There was a baby.*

As the front door closed, she had staggered a little with the shock. She clutched at the radiator for a moment, unable to fully comprehend the magnitude of what she had just heard. *There was a baby. A baby!* She blinked a few times, her mind racing with impossible questions. Did this mean . . . ? Could it be that . . . ?

'Roy!' she cried, turning the envelope between her fingers and gazing down at it as if it contained the mysteries of the universe. In a funny sort of way, it did. 'Roy, where are you?'

They had sat on the sofa together, the letter between them. Her hands were shaking so much, he ended up having to hold the closely written pages. 'It's a boy,' she said, a sob in her throat. She could hardly read the words any more because the tears in her eyes were making the world blur and shimmer. It was as if an enchantment had been revealed, changing everything. 'Our *grandson*, Roy. He's out there somewhere, Aidan's boy. Can you believe it?'

They held hands and stared at one another, neither of them able to quite find the words that adequately described their feelings. For twenty long painful years, she had thought their little family had come to the end of its journey; that it would terminate with them, in a dead-end of a disused siding, never to go any further. But now . . . But here . . . According to this letter, there was another stop on the family line, after all. Another person in the world with Aidan's genes. A grandchild, just as they'd always wanted. Longed for!

'What will we do?' Roy asked. His voice was hoarse as if he too had a lump in his throat.

'We'll find him, of course,' said Lorna. She wiped her eyes and read the letter all over again, just to make sure she hadn't imagined any of it. *A baby. Their grandson.* 'He'd be nineteen now,' she worked out. 'A young man. Older than Aidan ever lived to be . . .' Sadness pushed up through her, the usual sadness at the injustice of their having lost their only child, at imagining all the things he could have achieved: a career, a family, great happiness. And yet there was a strange elation mingled in there too; bubbles ascending. The story wasn't over yet, after all. If they could just find this boy – this young man, rather – it would be the closest thing to having Aidan back again. 'So he was born in

Dorchester . . . there must be records of the birth and adoption. We'll find a way to trace him.' She blew her nose. 'Our *grandson*, Roy!'

Roy's chin was wobbling. 'We might never even have known about him,' he said, eyes moist. All of a sudden, he sounded upset, his face twisting in such an ugly way she almost didn't recognize him. 'We could have gone to our graves not knowing!'

'I know, love, but . . .' Lorna bit her lip. She was too overcome with happiness right now to go near any recriminations. It was as if she didn't dare jinx this extraordinary news by allowing negative feelings to invade. 'Olivia was very young, though. It must have been such a hard decision for her, what with having lost Aidan and . . . Look, she's told us now anyway, hasn't she? And that can't have been easy.'

'Yes, well, bully for her. But she could have considered our feelings before, couldn't she? Just because *she* didn't want to deal with the consequences didn't mean . . .' He took his glasses off and rubbed his eyes. '*We* could have had him,' he said savagely. 'Rather than give him up to be adopted, *we* could have had him!'

'Roy, we can't think like that,' Lorna said helplessly, although now that he had said these words, it was hard to ignore them. She too was picturing them building train-sets with Aidan's little boy, finger-painting in the kitchen with him, playing football in the garden. The house mocked them with its emptiness. All the memories that could have been. How she would have *doted* on that child.

'Can't we?' Roy replied. 'Well, I do. Because she didn't think of us for a moment when she robbed us of the chance to know our grandchild, did she? That's nineteen years of his life gone, which we'll never get back.'

'I know, but . . .' She reminded herself of Olivia back then as a teenager: a quiet, polite girl, with a wariness about her that told Lorna she took nothing for granted. Olivia had not had an easy life, growing up; she didn't have the secure sort of background that could have coped with an unexpected pregnancy thrown into the mix. They had to take that into account, remember that she must have been devastated and despairing. They had all been! 'I'm not sure we'd have been up to the job of looking after a baby at the time,' she said slowly. 'We were in pieces ourselves, remember. I was, anyway.' She pictured herself unmoving in the bed, a silent mound of unhappiness. Maybe she'd have been able to drag herself up to look after a small motherless baby, but grief had numbed her for a long time. Realistically, it might well have been too much for her, she knew. Perhaps it was only right that the baby had grown up somewhere devoid of tragedy, at least in those early years. She patted her husband's hand. 'Come on,' she said. 'Let's be positive. We'll find him and we'll make up for lost time. Well, I'm going to anyway. If you want to sit and sulk, then that's your lookout.'

Give him credit, Roy did have the grace to look sheepish at that. 'I'm not sulking, I'm just . . .' he began, then sighed. 'I'm just sad. But you're right – this is good news.' He wiped his eyes again and put his glasses back on. 'So. Now we need to find him.'

Chapter Thirty

Maggie zoomed down the road, singing along to the radio, and felt joy swelling inside her chest as the miles between her and Amelia ticked down and down. Her voice wobbled with sudden emotion as the melody reached a higher pitch and she had to break off, rolling her eyes at herself. Goodness! What had *happened* to her on this holiday? She seemed to have shed a restrictive cocoon that had always kept her in check, emerging as a far more carefree butterfly. Someone with a swishy new haircut who sang loudly in the car and became choked up with unexpected sentiment at a deeply uncool soft-rock ballad in fact. Someone who, just the evening before, had dared to ask a man out on a date and became alarmingly fizzy and giddy about the pleased *Great idea!* text that had come in reply.

'Go, Maggie!' Em and Olivia had cheered her last night and she'd felt positively buoyant with good cheer, as if she might very well float on up into the warm night sky. It was funny how, at the start of the week, she'd felt so old and frumpy compared to fun, impulsive Em, and yet now, with her new hairdo and mindset, she felt younger again. Energized. Ready to take on the world, as Suzanne the hairdresser had said.

What a peculiar holiday this had been so far. In the first few days it seemed as if she had lost her daughter, but by dealing with that, she appeared to have regained her own self. Her past had caught her off-guard, yet had also pushed her into a bolder new future. Yes, she *would* try dating again. Yes, she *would* be more open to new invitations and experiences. She would allow her world to expand, make sure there was room for friends and hobbies and possibilities, rather than focusing her spotlight solely on Amelia, shrinking her life down to its small, safe bubble.

Talking of whom, Maggie had been thrilled to get Amelia's call that morning as she sat there in the kitchen, trying to get rid of her hangover with an enormous fry-up and approximately twenty gallons of tea. 'You want to come back early?' she'd echoed in surprise. 'How come? Is everything okay?' *Has he not treated you well? I will kill him, if so, I swear to God, I will.*

'Everything's fine,' Amelia said without a huge amount of conviction, then hesitated. 'I mean . . . they're all right. No one's been horrible to me or anything, but . . .' You could practically hear her pulling a face. 'But the kids are doing my head in,' she went on, lowering her voice. Then she gave a snort. 'I am *so glad* I don't have little brothers or sisters, you know. Man, they are a nightmare. And Celeste is . . . well, she's getting on my nerves too. She acts like she's this total earth mother, but do you know what I saw in her car when we went out earlier? Big Mac wrappers. I'm not kidding. Big Mac wrappers!'

'No!' cried Maggie, and then they were both laughing. 'Really?'

'Yep. Really. But even so, you've got to get me out of here. Please? She does all this drumming and shit, with bongos and whatever, it's driving me nuts. Oh yeah, and get this, she "doesn't believe" in washing-up liquid. She says it's unhygienic. I'm like . . . Right. Yeah. Whatever you say, love. But I'm kind of not wanting to eat off your plates any more.'

Well, she was her mother's daughter on that front at least, Maggie thought, remembering how she too had blanched at the filthy kitchen. 'You should get her to take you with her next time she goes to McDonald's,' she joked and then they both started giggling again.

'I might – you know, her cooking is absolutely rank. Dad's is even worse. They basically just serve up mush. I haven't actually *chewed* anything in, like, the whole time I've been here.' There was a loud groan down the phone. 'I'm like, hello, have these people never *heard* of pizza?'

'What about . . .' Maggie stumbled over the unfamiliar construction, 'your dad? How are you getting on with him?'

She thought about the photos she'd seen the day before, Amelia's breathless comments and enthusiasm. *Having an amazing time with my famous dad!!!*

The reply was somewhat less gushing. 'He's all right. But I don't think he's met many teenagers. You know? He either talks to me like I'm about five or like I'm twenty-five. I'm educating him, basically.'

Maggie couldn't resist smirking as she sipped her tea. Teenagers were so brutal. 'Well . . . It'll take you a while to get to know each other, I guess,' she said.

'Mmm,' said Amelia.

'It's good that you've met, though, isn't it? And you can build things up?' Maggie went on. Check out Lady Magnanimous, she thought, unused to feeling so gracious.

'Yeah,' said Amelia, although she didn't sound wholly enthusiastic. Certainly not the blissed-out joyful person of her social-media accounts. 'I'd kind of like to get to know him more slowly, without all the others here, though. Say, for an afternoon at a time. A day even, now and then. Maybe he could come round to ours sometimes, when we're back in Reading? You know, like you were saying about him coming over for Sunday dinner – that sort of thing. Just until we know each other better. What do you think?'

'That sounds very sensible to me,' said Maggie, scooping up the last forkful of baked beans. 'So do you still want me to pick you up later on, or would you rather stick things out until Friday?'

'Can you get me today? Like, as soon as possible?' Amelia asked, her voice small. 'Please? If it's not any trouble or anything . . .'

'Sure,' Maggie said. It was only then that she remembered the other photos she'd seen on her daughter's Instagram account: the antics with the tequila, the 'naughty trip into town' that Em had referenced. 'It's no trouble,' she went on, 'although I would like to have a proper chat with you later. About things that have been going on.'

There was a pause. No doubt Amelia was pulling one of her *Mu-u-u-u-m* grimaces at the prospect of a 'proper chat'. 'What sort of things?'

'We'll discuss all that later,' Maggie said. 'But right now I'd better get dressed and hit the road, hadn't I?'

'You're not *dressed*?' Amelia's shock was almost gleeful. 'Mum! I'm appalled. Standards are slipping without me.'

'You're not wrong,' said Maggie, thinking about all the wine she, Em and Olivia had put away last night. 'See you later then, love.'

The two of them would start again, she'd decided with a new optimism, finishing her breakfast and then hurrying up to the shower. They'd be honest with one another from now on. She'd have to admit to snooping on Amelia's social-media life, but in turn Amelia would have to come clean about the tequila incident. And then Maggie would lay down a few strict new rules and insist that this was not a bargaining matter. Oh, help. Amelia would be hot-footing it straight back to Will's at that rate, saying she'd changed her mind, you wait. But possibly not, she thought, remembering Amelia's lukewarm comments about staying there just now.

Her thoughts turned to the conversation she'd had with Em the night before, about how their children were growing up, finding their own ways, for better or worse. About how Em's kids had to be dragged places with her these days, how they'd rather be doing more adventurous, adrenalin-rushing activities better suited to their age. For the rest of the evening, Maggie's mind had kept returning to the subject, nudging at it with the uncomfortable feeling that she might have been going about this holiday all wrong. For whatever reason, Amelia had made it clear she no longer wanted to do the type of things they'd done when she was little. So maybe Maggie had to find an acceptable middle ground, be a bit more adventurous herself in suggesting other day-trips and activities they could try.

It was only as she was brushing her teeth that an idea struck her and she grinned at herself in the mirror. Of course. Perfect! Within a few minutes she was searching online and then entering her credit-card details, too quickly for her to go and bottle out. *There!* she thought with a mixture of triumph and trepidation, as the email confirmation beeped through on her phone moments later. Let it not be said that Maggie Laine couldn't surprise her own daughter now and then. Let it not be said that she couldn't surprise *herself*, for that matter.

Driving along now, she turned up the car radio and sang louder than ever. Even added a lung-busting harmony on the chorus for good measure. Maggie, you devil, she thought with a grin, indicating and moving into the fast lane.

'Hey!' Will opened the door with a cautious smile; the unconvincing sort of smile you might find yourself wearing when dipping a toe in the North Sea. 'Hello, Maggie, do you want to come in for a cup of tea?' Then he blinked. 'You look different. New haircut?'

'Ten out of ten for observation,' she replied, smiling. 'And yes please to the tea.' Here she was again at Will's house, but she was no longer the tense, uptight woman of her previous visit. Since then she had transformed, both inside and out.

'Hi,' she added joyfully as Amelia appeared in the hallway behind her father. As she saw her daughter's shy smile again, she felt the old connection twanging between them, the invisible umbilical that had always linked them so closely, so tightly. Surely Amelia hadn't grown taller in the scant few days she'd been here? No, she couldn't have. Yet the separation, however brief, meant that Maggie could appraise her through new eyes. Just look at her, so leggy and gorgeous, with that cloud of dark hair and those amazing cheekbones. Her girl. Her wonderful girl!

'Mum, why are you staring like that?' Amelia protested, squirming under her mother's gaze. 'Whoa, and what did you do to your hair? You look . . . actually quite nice.'

Maggie laughed. 'Damned with faint praise,' she said, stepping forward and hugging her. 'Ooh, that's better. That's what I needed. I've missed you.'

It was strange how, once the threat of something terrible had eased, you could look upon the world with a new benevolence, she thought, walking into the kitchen moments later. This room, for instance, no longer seemed the revolting health hazard it had done last time – now it was diminished to merely a scruffy, homely sort of place that could do with a few antibacterial wipes and a good mopping. It didn't bother her. She could even acknowledge that it held a certain sort of rustic charm. Hark at her, turning mellow in her old age!

Even more surprising was how normal this already seemed – her, Will and Amelia sitting down together in the same room and it being . . . well, okay, really. Conversation was a little strained, admittedly, as if they were all on their very best behaviour, but everyone was trying, she realized, because everyone wanted the situation to work out. This was how grown-ups were supposed to deal with such matters: on civil, practical terms, leaving emotions at the door. Not that all the emotions were turning out to be dark ones anyway in this case, she was discovering. Because every now and then Will would say something affectionate to Amelia or tease her, and Maggie found herself experiencing unexpected prickles of gladness rather than jealousy. *This is how things could have been if . . .* she began thinking at one point, but then silenced her own voice. Could-have-beens were never helpful. And anyway was he still the man of her dreams, sitting there with his thinning, dyed hair, with his hipster T-shirt and stubble? No. He wasn't a patch on Paul, let's face it.

Gosh. And that was interesting too, she realized, as truths slotted into place in her head, like cogs clicking together. She had spent all these years thinking miserably that she hadn't been good enough for Will, and that must be why he'd left – when in actual fact perhaps the real story was that he just hadn't been quite good enough for *her*.

She blinked at this astonishing possibility as if a light had been switched on in her face. There was definitely some pondering over that idea to be done later on.

After a while Celeste appeared with the little ones, having returned from the local shops, and the children both rushed over to Amelia to show her the treasures they'd found along the way: a pebble with a hole in the middle, a fallen fuchsia bloom that was as pink and fulsome as a pair of harem pants. There was something rather touching about their eager faces, so much so that Maggie didn't even feel irritated by

Celeste saying 'Maggie! Hello' in her low, dreamy voice and coming over to kiss her.

(Actually, she *did* feel a little bit irritated, but only because she was not a kissy sort of person. But never mind. It only lasted a moment. She would get over it.)

This is Amelia's family, she found herself thinking tentatively. These people are connected to her now and I can't change that. She had a slight pang as Amelia pulled the little boy (what was his name again? Nettle? Rain?) onto her knee – and yes, there it was, she acknowledged: the ache that a mother of one sometimes felt, when imagining your child with a sibling or two. The guilty stab that maybe they wished they weren't an only child. There was Amelia bending her face down to hear what the little boy was saying to her, as he related some tale or other about a ginger cat they had seen and, for a second, Maggie's heart cracked just a tiny bit that this was a scene in which she had no part, one where she could only be an onlooker. But it was sweet the way that Amelia and the boy – Thistle, that was it – could chat in this easy way. Nice that they had formed a new bond of their own. Perhaps as they both grew older they would choose to develop that bond, call each other brother and sister, ring up one another to grumble about Will or exchange funny stories about him. Perhaps this would be as close as they ever came, though, this moment about a ginger cat – and their paths would diverge from here and never really connect fully again and . . .

Okay, stop, Maggie. She was taking all this way too seriously. The details could all be worked out in the future.

Draining her mug of disappointingly weak tea, she caught Amelia's eye. 'We should head off soon,' she said. She wanted to reclaim her daughter now, to sit with her in the car and return to being on holiday together. They'd all survived this strange family shift more or less intact; perhaps it was time to get out while the going was good. 'Shall we?'

Amelia lifted Thistle from her knee and stood up. 'Thanks for having me,' she said to Will and Celeste, suddenly formal once more and a little shy, Maggie thought, as she pushed a lock of hair out of her eyes.

'Any time,' said Will, following them to the front door. He looked uncharacteristically vulnerable as Amelia heaved her bag up on her shoulder. Uncertain even. 'So . . .' he began awkwardly. 'So, it's been a pleasure getting to know you.'

'You too,' Amelia said. Oh gosh, now *everyone* was becoming formal and mannered. Perhaps this wasn't going to be as straightforward as Maggie had anticipated.

'Er . . . So where do we go from here?' Will asked.

And that was him all over, Maggie thought, trying to mask her exasperation. Still a man-child at the end of the day, still unable to be the adult in a situation. *Really, Will? It's*

up to Amelia *to broker another meeting? It's your move now, pal.*
You are the grown-up here, remember.

'Well,' she put in, so that Amelia didn't feel she had to
reply, 'where would you *like* things to go from here, Will?'
Come on, mate, she urged him in her head. Take the lead
for once. Make your firstborn feel wanted. Wasn't that what
this was all about?

He scratched his chin. Perhaps he was so used to other
people throwing themselves at him that he found it difficult
to be the one having to ask the big, scary *Do you like me?*
question. 'I would love to do this again,' he said eventually.
'I know I haven't been a great dad to you before now – or
any kind of dad to you – but I'd like to make up for that. For
us to get to know each other. If you want that too?'

There. Congratulations, Will – you did it. One heart on
a plate, handed out hopefully. And Amelia was nodding.
'Sure,' she said, hiding her pleasure with a casually offhand
shrug. 'Cool.'

Maggie felt a tiny bit sorry for Will, having finally made
his grand gesture only for it to be greeted by this typically
underwhelming response. 'That's teenagers for you,' she
said, winking at him. Then she slung an arm around Amelia.
'Come on, you,' she said. 'Let's hit the road.'

'Can I just have a quick word?' Will asked her abruptly.
'In private?'

'Sure,' said Maggie, handing Amelia the car keys. They both watched her slope away. 'What is it?'

He leaned against the doorway, his gaze sliding down to his tatty Converse momentarily before back up at her. 'Look, I . . .' he began. 'She's amazing,' he said quietly. 'And I regret being such a self-absorbed idiot that I thought I didn't care. That I cut myself off. It's not an excuse, but I think I had a sort of . . . breakdown. Like, an empathy break-down. I was so caught up in my career taking off that I . . . God, I got it all wrong. I'm sorry, Mag.'

She couldn't reply immediately because a wave of emotion was brimming inside her. All the angry things she'd wanted to say over the years had risen to the surface. Then they boiled over. 'You hurt me,' she blurted out because no, she couldn't just shrug this off and pretend it didn't matter. 'The things you said to me as you left . . . they've been torturing me for years.'

He had the grace to look ashamed and stared down at his feet again. 'I guess it was easier to direct the blame at you rather than myself,' he replied after a moment. 'Whatever I said – please, just put it out of your head. I was looking for a way out, that's all. You're a good person. You've always been a good person.'

Gosh, he looked so humble, so meek right now, just like in all those fantasy conversations she'd imagined where he prostrated himself at her feet and begged her forgiveness.

Of course it was pretty much at this point in her fantasy that she always kicked him with the toe of her boot, shouted 'Never!' and walked away, nose in the air. Except she didn't feel like doing that so much any more.

'Thanks,' she said instead. 'Well . . . Let's just see how it goes. I'm glad you're back in Amelia's life at least. And she is too. Thanks for having her.'

He smiled. 'It's been a pleasure. Bye, Maggie.'

'Bye, Will.'

She was whistling as she walked to the car and got inside. Then, clicking in her seatbelt, she asked, 'All okay?'

'Yep,' said Amelia, leaning back expansively and kicking off her sandals in the footwell. 'What was that all about?'

'Oh, he was just saying how great you were,' she replied, starting the engine.

There was a moment's silence as they both waved to Will, still there in the doorway, then Maggie pushed her foot down, feeling the sweet feeling of freedom as they accelerated away.

'Ahhh,' sighed Amelia, in exaggerated relief. 'No more having to pretend to be nice. Thanks, Mum.'

Maggie laughed. 'You *are* nice,' she said.

'Not when it comes to annoying little children, I'm not,' Amelia said, shifting around to get comfortable.

'What do you mean – didn't you like them?' Come on, let's hear it, she thought. All the bitching. There was only so much magnanimity and graciousness a person could dredge up in a single day, after all.

'I *like* them, but they're just in your face all the time. Totally full-on. Last night they were begging Celeste for a sleepover with me. Rain actually started having a tantrum – like, proper banging fists on the floor and everything. I was like: sorry, no way. That will not be happening for at *least* ten years. Twenty, if you keep this up. Jesus!'

'How about your dad?' asked Maggie, doing her best at nonchalance. 'Did you have to pretend with him too?'

'He's all right,' she replied. 'He's a bit . . . well, I like him, but I can see why you got rid of him. He's kind of flaky and woo-woo sometimes.'

'Wait – what? *I* got rid of him? He walked out!' Maggie spluttered. There was a charged moment of silence bristling with the shock of old presumptions having been challenged, and then they both spoke at once. 'You didn't think that—?'

'I just assumed that—'

'He left!' Maggie said. 'He went off to be a famous photographer. I was devastated!' They stared at one another before Maggie remembered to stare at the road. 'I thought you knew!'

'No! Because you never talked about him!' Amelia retaliated.

Maggie felt bamboozled, racking her brain to try and figure out how this misunderstanding could have come about. She had been so careful not to blame Will aloud in front of Amelia, or bad-mouth him too disparagingly, that perhaps she hadn't ever actually spelled out the events themselves. Had she? And so perhaps Amelia, in turn, had taken Maggie's silent disapproval of Will and interpreted their history as being one where *she'd* gone off *him*. As if! Over the years, Amelia must have accepted her own assumption of truth as gospel, with a drum beating louder and faster as the accompanying bitterness took root. *Mum sent him away. Mum robbed me of my father.*

'That must have been pretty shit,' Amelia said eventually.

Pretty shit. You don't say, Maggie thought, remembering all those desperate lonely nights when she had paced up and down with her wailing infant, feeling simultaneously alone and smothered. 'It wasn't shit, because I had you at least, and I loved you enough for two parents,' she managed to say. 'But it was hard for a while, yes.' A stunned few seconds passed. 'Sorry, we probably should have had this conversation a long time ago, you and I, but I guess I didn't want you to feel that he'd rejected *you*,' she went on. 'When it was me he was breaking up with.'

Another stretch of silence followed. 'Anyway,' she added, switching up into a brighter gear. With the three of them having just forged a tentative new alliance, perhaps this wasn't the right time to go raking up old hurts. At the end of the day, they had all survived to tell the tale. 'Are you hungry? Because I am.'

'I'm *starving*,' said Amelia.

'Good, you can make yourself useful then,' said Maggie. 'Find the nearest pizza place on your phone and let's make a pit stop for lunch. And then I'm going to tell you about the surprise I've got planned for this afternoon. This *is* our holiday after all,' she declared over the sound of her daughter's whoop.

Chapter Thirty-One

Olivia was sitting on a slightly creaky rattan chair admiring the view from the old stone terrace: long formal gardens stretching out in front of her, with rolling purple moorland in the distance. The lawns were verdant, the flowerbeds well tended; there was no sound other than birdsong from the trees and the faint hum of conversation from another couple at the end of the terrace. The occasional clink of a cup being returned to its saucer.

'Earl Grey tea?' said a waiter, appearing beside her just then with a tray balanced on his hand.

'Thank you, yes,' she said, and he deftly set down the crockery on the table, followed by a milk jug and sugar bowl, then the white china teapot with steam curling in wisps from its spout.

'Can I get you anything else?' he asked, holding the empty tray behind his back. He was in his early twenties, she guessed, and terribly earnest. The sort of nice young man whose parents were undoubtedly very proud of him.

She wondered, as she had done so many times over the years, about Leon and what he was doing now; whether he was working like the waiter here, or a student. What he looked like. If he was happy.

'No, thank you,' she said, worried suddenly that she was staring at the waiter too intently. He made a slight bow and walked away and then she was alone again. Alone again, that was, but not for much longer. Here she had come, to a rather nice hotel on the fringes of Dartmoor, waiting for the rest of her life to begin. She hoped it was going to be okay.

Sitting parked up in the lay-by earlier as lorries and coaches hurtled by, she and Mack had gone on to have one of the most honest and revealing conversations of their lives. She had confessed the recent state of her head: how inadequate she had been feeling as a mother, how hard she found the day-to-day routine, and how she had gone to some pretty dark places in her mind; dark places that perhaps her own mother had visited before her.

Out it had all come, her secret self-doubt and unhappiness. She laid it out for him like an unrolling carpet – the raw, real Olivia, there to be trampled over. It had felt both liberating and terrifying to peel away the mask, to say, *Here I am. This is what you married.*

He didn't trample over her, though. He didn't flinch from the real her, either. Instead he listened, really listened, without interrupting and when eventually she had finished, ending with an anxious 'I'm sorry', his reply contained sincere compassion. 'Oh, Liv. You don't need to say sorry,' he told her. 'You have nothing to be sorry for. *I'm* sorry for not having realized you were feeling like that. I'm really, really sorry. But we're going to make a few changes from now on. Right? We'll dig you out of this hole together.'

She'd shut her eyes for a moment, surprised that he was even saying the word 'together'. 'Are you sure?' she asked, her voice practically a whisper. 'Even though I . . .' The words were lodged in her throat; she had to force them out. 'Even though I ran away?'

'Yes! Of course I'm sure. I love you. *We're married*,' he cried.

We're married. Such a strange line of reasoning, she thought. Marriage hadn't stopped her mum from leaving the family forever, had it? It hadn't stopped her from emigrating to another country and eventually dying there without an explanation, without an apology.

But then she remembered Danny's words earlier: *You're not Mum*, and she forced herself to listen to them. Accept them. No. She wasn't Sylvia. She had made mistakes – mistakes all over the place – but she wanted to put them right now.

'We're married,' she echoed, as if it was that simple. Maybe on one level it *was* that simple. We're married. Together. So we'll see this through together. The thought was immensely comforting, as if she'd only just noticed the safety net beneath her. She'd been running for so long, she realized. Not just this week down to Cornwall, but ever since Aidan had died, and Leon had been born, she had been ducking and dodging: from the truth, from her own actions and the pain they had caused. Perhaps part of loving someone was stopping and facing those things. Holding hands and standing firm.

'Anyway, now that I've had the pleasure of solo childcare since you left, I get it,' Mack was saying in her ear. 'I hadn't really appreciated before just how—Talk of the devil.' He broke off, a new severity appearing in his voice. 'Oi! Stanley, get off him. *Stanley!* I'm going to count to three and if you don't stop that, there's going to be trouble. *One* . . . Okay, that's better.'

Had Olivia ever even heard him tell the boys off before? Usually it was her who had to be the killjoy enforcer, while Mack got to play the fun guy all the time. She pressed the phone closer to her ear, suddenly desperate to hear the familiar sounds of home, acutely able to visualize the boys grappling on the carpet, all squirming limbs and shouts until Mack's intervention.

'Sorry,' he was saying, 'but it kind of illustrates my point. It's bloody hard work being a stay-at-home parent, isn't it? Knackering. I have never been so tired in my life.'

She swallowed, unable to say anything for a moment.

Yes. *Yes.* Yes, to all of that. He had stepped into her shoes and realized just how thin the soles were, how tightly the toes pinched. But at least he had done that much, she thought. Some men she knew would have farmed their children off to the nearest amenable woman, rather than muck in and experience the coal-face for themselves. 'It's not easy,' she agreed.

'No wonder you wanted a break,' he said with feeling. 'Hold on, I'm just going somewhere a bit quieter,' he added, and she could hear a door closing and muffled bumping sounds, presumably as he went upstairs. 'Now then,' he said. 'Where do we go from here? Do you want to come home? Because if you do, I promise we'll do things differently. I'll help more with the boys. We could start them at pre-school – or get a childminder, if you wanted to go back to work. Or . . .'

Her head swam with so many questions and options; she felt overwhelmed with all the decisions that lay ahead. 'Um . . .'

'Otherwise, if you're not ready to come back right away, then that's fine too,' he said into the silence, perhaps sensing her apprehension. 'We could always meet you somewhere in the middle. Geographically, I mean, as well as in the abstract sense.'

A Peugeot estate had pulled in just in front of her and a man emerged from the driver's seat to let a child out from the back: a wriggling, hopping child who was escorted round behind the car, where a woman appeared with a yellow potty in hand. There was a sticker from a zoo on the back windscreen of the car and two other small heads visible inside. Every family journey had a few emergency stops along the way, she found herself thinking. That was just part of the deal.

'Yes,' she said, suddenly wanting the comfort of a child on her knee again, the smell of her boys' necks. Remembering how adorable they were when they woke up with their flushed faces and hair standing up in tufts. 'Yes, let's meet in the middle.'

'Okay, let me think,' he said, because he was never happier than when he had a puzzle to solve, a plan to bring about. 'So where are you now? Right, well, keep going east and head for the Dartmoor area. In the meantime I'll find us somewhere to stay and book us in. If you stop at the next services, I'll text you details of where we're going. Then I'll get the boys all ready, stuff them into the car and meet you there later on. How does that sound?'

How did it sound? It was kind of a relief to have him deciding for her, actually. So much of his work was about scooping up failing businesses and turning them around. As it turned out, he seemed to be pretty good at scooping up a struggling mother and suggesting practical solutions for her too, albeit belatedly.

'Somewhere nice,' he added, when she didn't immediately respond. 'Somewhere with a swimming pool and room service. You won't have to do anything, if you don't feel like it.'

A swimming pool and room service . . . this was becoming better by the minute. The back of Olivia's throat felt prickly. It felt as if she was being rescued, looked after. She wasn't sure she deserved it, after having run away and flaked out on him all week, but she was grateful he still cared. 'Thank you,' she said.

'We're a team, remember,' he told her. 'Standing shoulder-to-shoulder. I promise you that we're going to get through this together and make it work. Okay?'

And so, once they'd finished the call, she'd started the car and driven on to the next service station where, as promised, a text awaited. It felt like a grown-up sort of treasure hunt, following the link to find herself at the website of a hotel on the far edge of Dartmoor, which had a spa, a very nice restaurant and a babysitting service. *They could only fit us in for three nights – fully booked otherwise, but it can be a little holiday while we work everything out,* he'd written beneath the link. *Hopefully see you later. Text me what you want me to pack for you. I love you.*

She loved him too, she thought now, pouring her tea and stirring in the milk, appreciating the light breeze that ruffled the heads of the roses and sent a sweet scent drifting her way. It was gorgeous here: serene and classy, yet comfortable and relaxing. This felt like a place where she and Mack could reconnect and talk to one another with honesty about what they both wanted, their visions of a future life together. A family holiday, but different.

Maybe later tonight when the boys were asleep, they could talk some more. About Aidan and her part in his death. About her own mum vanishing and how it had been as if a piece of Olivia had gone with her too. Mack knew the basics about Leon, but now she'd have to tell him that her first son might be returning to her life in the future, and that she hoped he'd be okay about this. Having started talking honestly at last, she wanted to delve further into these subjects, expose them to daylight and another opinion, rather than burying them all again. Perhaps it would help to find a counsellor to work through them as well, she thought. Someone who could maybe give her a few coping strategies while she was there, to shore up her defences against spiralling right down again. She gazed out at the wide white sky and felt as if she might be open to possibilities again – or at least to accepting some help.

She remembered her brother's concerned texts just then and sent him a message. *Hi Danny,* she wrote. *All good here. Thought for a minute I had turned into Mum – couldn't cope. But I'm going to sort things out with Mack. We're meeting up later. Think we will be okay. x*

He replied moments later. *I get it. You can always talk to me, remember. Good luck and let's catch up properly soon. x*

Feeling a hundred times better than she had done a week earlier, Olivia sipped her tea and let out a long exhalation. Then her phone rang, jerking her out of her reverie and she fumbled to answer it, assuming it was Mack again or maybe Danny. But there was an unfamiliar number on the screen. 'Hello?' she said.

'It's Lorna,' came the reply and Olivia's heart clenched with immediate dread. Oh no. That hadn't taken long.

'Hello,' she said warily. Following her letter that morning, Lorna and Roy were certain to have a lot of questions, some of them potentially very angry ones. There was a strong possibility, in fact, that they would hate her by now. Her grip tightened on the teacup, so tightly that she had to set it down, fearful it might shatter between her fingers. She wasn't sure she could bear hearing Lorna's wounded rage right now.

'I'm ringing to thank you,' Lorna said, though, which came as such a surprise to Olivia that she had to blink several times before she could register the words. 'For telling us, I mean. We're going to find Leon, we want him to be in our lives. We are so delighted by the news, I . . . Well, I'm as giddy as a kipper, to be honest. I can't believe it!'

Olivia gazed into the middle distance, but was no longer aware of the calm surroundings. She hadn't been able to believe it, either, that shocking day almost twenty years earlier when she had discovered the pregnancy. She had *never* quite been able to believe it, even as she sat there in that noisy, overheated maternity ward, dazed after the shock of the birth, holding that small warm person with a plastic tag around his ankle. The same small warm person who, if all went to plan, would shortly be discovering that he had two new grandparents. Lorna was right: it seemed impossible to believe, even now. 'I'm glad,' Olivia said, uncertain of what else to say.

'I was just wondering, though: if we do track him down, should we tell you?' asked Lorna. She sounded all fired up, as if she were about to jump in a car and go knocking on doors for Leon as soon as she put the phone down. 'Do you want to know whatever we find out? See him?'

Here they were: the biggest questions of all, ones that Olivia had avoided looking at for so many years. While her secret was sealed away, hidden from sight, it had been easier to put him out of her mind, that little baby whisked away who-knew-where. And yet now that the secret was out, she wasn't sure there was any way back. Maybe she didn't want to go back anyway, though, she thought.

'Yes,' she said. 'If he wants to, of course. I owe him that much.'

'Okay,' said Lorna. 'I'll keep you posted.' There was a pause and then she added, 'We're really grateful for this.

Can we stay in touch, whatever happens? There's a proper connection between us now, isn't there?'

'Yes,' said Olivia with a lump in her throat. Lorna had helped her when she had been down on her knees, at her lowest point. Who *wouldn't* want a person like that to stay in their life? 'Of course we can keep in touch.'

'I know you've lost your mum, but you've got me now, don't forget,' Lorna went on. 'You know where I am, if you ever want to come back – with or without the rest of your family. And I'm just at the end of the phone if you need a chat, okay?'

She might have buried her only child, but Lorna was still such a good mum, Olivia thought with a pang. And as someone who'd been feeling as if she could really do with a compass and set of directions when it came to motherhood, this offer couldn't have come at a more welcome time. A huge tide of emotion rose over her. Gratitude that both Lorna and Mack were reaching out to her, offering their hands to haul her up from the depths. She'd even go as far as to say she felt the first glimmerings of hope. 'I would really like that,' she said.

'Good,' replied Lorna. 'Because I would really like that too.'

Chapter Thirty-Two

Izzie had muted the notifications from her group chat for this long, but now she took a deep breath and braved herself to take a look at how the others had responded to her confession. Just to get the recriminations and probable banishment over with. Opening up the chat, though, she quickly realized that she hadn't been the only one who had embellished details of their wild summer.

While it was true that Lily was going to the music festival, her boyfriend couldn't afford a ticket after all, so her mum had arranged for her to tag along with her older cousin's crowd instead, which was going to be way less fun.

Miko *had* noticed plenty of hot boys at the lido, but she hadn't dared chat any of them up and she definitely hadn't flashed anyone in the changing rooms.

Tej *had* crashed a party, but in truth had spent most of her time there vomiting in the upstairs loo after too much vodka. Then she'd fallen over in the garden, right in front of the girl she fancied, and some of the sixth-form boys had taken photos of her and laughed at her, so she'd gone home early.

Ruby *had* ended up kissing the gorgeous boy she had a crush on, but he'd made a horrible comment about her braces and she'd been so embarrassed she'd hit him, then he'd walked off without saying another word. She'd seen him in town the day before yesterday and he'd totally blanked her.

Out they all came, one confession after another, points knocked off each girl's totals until they were all rubbishly low. Somehow or other Ruby was even on minus figures. *This is exactly the sort of thing that Miss Crowley used to go on about in PSHE,* Miko had said, with several eye-rolling emojis. *Peer-pressure meltdown!!*

New hashtag: Summer of Fail, suggested Tej, deadpan.

Reading their confessions, Izzie didn't feel completely exonerated – it wasn't like anyone else's exaggerated claims had caused their mum's actual relationship to crash and burn in such an embarrassingly public way, but all the same, she felt slightly less of a boring freak. They understood why she had gone so overboard.

You're not going to believe this, I know, but I did actually meet a really nice boy yesterday, she posted mournfully, adding some of the photos she'd taken of the two of them on Swanpool beach. *We hung out and kissed (true!) and were meant to be meeting up last night, but I had to bail on him because I'm grounded. Will probably never see him again now. TYPICAL!!!!!*

So typical you could almost laugh. Or give up. No, she still hadn't heard anything back from Fraser, despite checking her messages every five seconds or so. Karma, she thought glumly each time she refreshed her in-box to find nothing new there. No reply had come from George, either, following the message she had eventually sent him earlier: a digitally tweaked picture of *The Lute Player*, now with a rock-star headband and skull patterns on her peasanty white shirt, plus a speech bubble coming from her mouth, which read, *I'M SORRY.*

Dear George, this is my fault, not Mum's, she had written. *She can't tell you the details of what happened because she knows it will embarrass me, but basically she really, really likes you and is sorry that you got dragged into my stupid mess. And me and Jack like you too, so please give her another chance. Sorry again, love Izzie.*

She'd even – and this was a measure of just how sorry she was – added a PS about Seren.

PS: I meant to say, Seren can have all my old Sylvanian Families if she wants them, there's a massive boxful in the loft.

But, like Fraser, George had gone quiet on her too. Perhaps she'd blown it with both of them. Being rational and philosophical about it, she could see there was a certain balance at work there, in terms of justice: she had lost Mum George, therefore she had to sacrifice Fraser and lose him too. When she *wasn't* being rational and philosophical, though, it just felt bloody rubbish.

In the room next door, Em was still in bed, drearily wondering if she had the energy to get up and make lunch for everyone, or whether the kids would have to forage for their own food today. The latter, she decided. Meanwhile she had never felt less like eating. It seemed just another worthless pursuit, like falling in love or trying to be a good person. What was the point?

From now on, she had decided, she would be single forever. Yes, she was resigned to it, absolutely. Relationships were for optimistic idiots, those who didn't know better. They never worked out, and it was too difficult when you had teenage children in tow anyway; her loyalties were always going to be divided. Maybe once the children were grown-up – say, thirty or so – she'd muster up the stamina to try again, but for now she would be better off slogging along on her own. In fact she'd go as far as to say that she'd sooner get a dog than another relationship. At least with a dog, you were guaranteed uncomplicated loyalty.

So that was cheering – not. Added to which, she had a raging hangover, whimperingly bad, thanks to the impromptu holiday women's piss-up last night. Still, she'd enjoyed herself at least, what with the three of them setting the world to rights, and they'd had a laugh too, in between their confessionals. Honestly, what was it about being on holiday that made a person throw caution to the wind? She had certainly poured her heart out – well, they all had, to be fair. They'd even ended up swapping numbers and promising to keep in touch. She wondered how Maggie and Olivia were both bearing up so far today, and if they were currently enduring the same drilling headache that she was. God, and Olivia had been planning to ring her husband as well, to broach some peace talks! She was clearly a tougher woman than Em, if she had managed such a thing.

Hope all going well, she texted her spontaneously. *Good to chat last night. Best of luck, whatever you decide.*

Best of luck to all of them, she thought rousingly, feeling a tiny bit better. Best of luck to every goddamn woman, in fact, who was struggling along this summer, trying to survive the holiday period as best as she goddamn could.

The rallying sentiment was enough to make her sit up, suddenly sick of lying around feeling sorry for herself. No, she would not flop about moping for a moment longer. She was in beautiful Cornwall, in a lovely cottage and she had worked bloody hard to pay for this fortnight away. There was still a week left here and she would damn well enjoy it too – George or no George. Onwards and upwards!

'Kids!' she called, fluffing up her hair in the mirror. She had been lying down for so long it had completely flattened against her head. 'Come and have some lunch, and let's make a plan for this afternoon. Something really fun! Jack, we could go zorbing, if you still want to do that?'

Just at that moment her phone rang. *George*, she read on the screen.

'Are you sure this is safe?' Maggie asked with a nervous laugh. 'I'm not about to plunge to an early death or anything?'

The man tugging on the straps of her harness to check they were secure considered her question for a moment. He was in his mid-thirties, she guessed, tall and rangy, with an infectious enthusiasm. 'Absolutely not. You're going to have the best and most exciting ten minutes of your life. Or at least this week,' he amended, with a wink.

Amelia seemed gleeful about her mother's shortcomings. 'Mum, you're such a wuss,' she said, loud enough for the queuing people behind them to hear.

Here they were, on a timber platform 150 feet high up in a forest, just like the dream Maggie had had the other night, only this time there was a dual zip-line and she and Amelia were about to take the plunge together, side-by-side. Elsewhere at the activity centre you could try water sports, a terrifying-looking giant swing and go-karting. None of these things sounded remotely sensible or unscary to Maggie, but Amelia had actually squealed in delight upon hearing where they would be spending the rest of the day. 'Oh my God, amazing! Thanks, Mum,' she had cried, apparently ecstatic at the prospect of throwing herself off cliffs in the name of fun.

Following their separation, today felt very much like a new start. They'd stopped at a small Devon pizzeria en route, to share thickly cheesed pizza and far too many side dishes – 'Whatever you want,' Maggie had said, feeling generous with happiness. There Amelia had given a lengthier account of her stay, with topics ranging from the disgustingness of Celeste's BO to Will's taste in music (as cheesy as the pizza, apparently), but also how the two of them planned to message each other a single photo encapsulating their week every Sunday night from here on in. A digital father–daughter exchange.

'I love that idea,' Maggie said in delight. 'What a great way to get to know each other.'

'I know! His challenge to me, he said,' Amelia replied through a mouthful of garlic bread. 'I think it'll be quite cool, trying to sum up my news in one image each time. I mean, we *are* going to chat as well,' she went on. 'We're not going to be, like, silent weirdos, communicating only by photos or anything. He said he would try and come to my parents' evening and everything this year. And when I said I was going to audition for the choir, he was like, "Right, I'm coming to see any concerts you're in then, try and stop me." ' She licked her fingers and Maggie noticed her small, proud smile.

'Which is kind of nice. Although the music probably won't be tragic enough for his taste, so . . .'

Maggie laughed. 'More education for him,' she said. 'But yes, that *will* be nice.' Her heart swelled a little that Will had come good like this, that he had suggested such things moreover, rather than feeling obliged to out of some grudging duty. Then she girded her loins for the next part of the conversation. 'Now then,' she said, rather more sternly. 'Moving on: I was wondering if there was anything you might need to confess to me. Regarding a tequila bottle?'

Amelia's face went dark pink and she froze, stricken, a triangle of pizza sagging midway up to her mouth. Any hopes Maggie had nursed about there somehow being a good reason for the bottle in the pictures resembling the one she'd won on the tombola immediately went up in smoke. Guilty as hell.

'Ah,' Amelia said carefully. You could practically hear the gears in her brain spinning as she tried to think of a plausible excuse. 'Right. This is what you meant on the phone, about needing to talk.'

'Exactly. So talk.'

The dark pink was spreading out from Amelia's cheeks and down into her neck. 'I'm sorry,' she mumbled, staring at her coleslaw as if it might somehow help her out here.

Maggie eyed her over a forkful of salad. 'I need more than that. Come on, Amelia, this isn't like you. Or is it? Is this what hanging around with Tara Webster and that crowd has turned you into?'

Amelia's gaze was still lowered. 'No.'

'That stuff is so strong,' Maggie went on. 'Really, really strong. Drinking spirits might seem wild and grown-up to you, but while your brain is still developing, it's a bad idea. Plus it's illegal, by the way. If a police officer had caught you, you'd have been in even bigger trouble.' She frowned. 'If you're going off on your own with friends, I need to be able to trust you.'

'You can!' Amelia said.

'Well, I can't, can I, if you're sneaking bottles of booze out and drinking them in broad daylight? Were you trying to impress that boy? Jack, is it? Is that why you did it?'

Amelia scowled and put her pizza down. 'Dunno,' she said darkly. *Yes*, in other words.

'You don't need tequila to impress anyone,' Maggie said, leaning forward. It felt as if she was imparting the biggest life lesson of all; she had to find the right words. 'Just be *you* – because being you is more than good enough. You are *wonderful*, Amelia: funny and clever and fantastic. And anyone who doesn't think so can . . . Well, they can fuck off, frankly.'

'MUM!' Amelia sounded utterly scandalized to hear her mother swear so fruitily. Scandalized and not a little delighted too, Maggie thought, seeing her mouth quirk at the corners.

'Look, you can talk to me, you know,' she said. 'About anything. Boys, growing up, friend dramas . . . any of it. I was young once too, remember.'

Judging from her daughter's face, Amelia was finding that hard to believe. 'And we'll make it a two-way thing, obviously,' she went on. 'For instance, you may or may not want to know about the hot date that *I've* got lined up once we're home, but . . .'

'WHAT?' Amelia had screeched so loudly that a couple three tables away turned to stare. And then the lecture was most definitely over, because they were straight into a whole other conversation about Paul, and where Maggie and he were going on their first date, and what she might wear, and how they both felt about the whole thing ('Quite excited actually,' Maggie confessed. 'Go, Mum!' Amelia cried) and they were laughing and confiding in each other, and yes, thought Maggie, they were going to be okay, she and her girl. She was certain of it.

Waiting now, rather wobbly-legged on the high timber platform amidst the trees, their final harness checks had been completed. 'You're all set,' the staff member assured them.

'Cool,' said Amelia, then eyed Maggie suspiciously. 'Are you sure you want to do this, Mum? You look like you're about to wet yourself.'

'I probably *am* about to wet myself,' Maggie admitted,

rolling her eyes, 'but I'm doing it anyway. I'm taking the plunge. Ready . . . Steady . . . WAAARRRGGHHHH!'

They leapt off together, Maggie holding on for dear life to the cable as she went whizzing at exhilarating speed down through the forest canopy and over a huge lake. 'Oh my Goooooooooodddd!' she shrieked, the air punching out of her lungs.

'Whoaaaaaaa!' yelled Amelia. 'Lean back, Mum, it's awesome! Woohoooooo!'

'We're flying!' cried Maggie joyfully.

It felt so good. *I took the plunge and it felt so good*, she thought in astonishment. *Look at me go, world. Just watch me fly!*

Walking through the exquisitely scented rose garden in the hotel grounds, Olivia heard Mack and the boys before she saw them. It was mid-afternoon and the sun was doing its best to break out through the gauzy clouds when she became aware of the sound of two high-pitched voices somewhere nearby. Her heart thumped immediately, an almost painful sensation, and she found herself turning wildly around to find them, breaking into a run when she saw their matching blonde heads leaning over an ornamental fountain. 'I'm here! I'm here!' she called.

'Mummy!'

'It's Mummy!' they yelped, charging towards her at once.

'Boys!' she cried, as they flung themselves at her, Stanley, then Harry. Their small hands gripped her skirt as if they were tethering her to the ground, preventing her from vanishing from them again. Would they remember the week when their mum had disappeared? Would it leave them with insecurities and doubts for evermore? She would make it up to them. She would put this right. If she could look after herself at the same time, she was sure they'd all be better off for it. 'Oh, I've missed you,' she said and bent her knees into a crouch so that she could hold them properly, her two squirming boys, both clamouring to tell her important things: first, that they'd spotted a penny in the fountain, as well as a gruesome dinosaur story they had listened to in the car on the way.

'It's in the water, Mummy, it's just there, but Daddy said we couldn't have it because . . .'

'And the Diplodderers was like BOOF! BAM! And the T-rex was like CHOMP! KILL!'

'We might fall in and get WET! Or bump our HEADS! So I said . . .'

'And then they had a fight, and guess who was the winner?'

'Hello, love,' said Mack, catching up with them just then, and Olivia gently set the boys down again so that she could stand up and hug him, and remember how good it was to have his arms around her. They stood there for a moment, just leaning against one another, and her eyes felt hot with love for them all, as well as the sheer relief of having made it safely back to them.

'Mummy, you're not listening!'

'Mummy! I *said*, guess who was the winner?'

Mack laughed at the barrage of protest and interruption currently assailing them from knee height, and they drew apart and smiled at each other. 'I'm the winner,' Olivia said to him. That was how it felt, anyway – forget the dinosaurs. 'Thank you for coming, and for sorting all of this out,' she added. Mack was so handsome, with his cropped hair and blue eyes, she thought, seeing him anew. So capable and strong. Thank God for him, she thought with a rush of feeling. 'It's gorgeous here.'

'It's good to see you,' he said, kissing her. 'And from now on, things will be different.' He was so keen to show her he understood, she realized. So earnest about proving his love. 'I've already been looking at my schedule, and I'm going to start delegating more so that I can get home earlier in the evening, help out more often. Whatever needs fixing, we'll make sure it happens, okay?'

She nodded and then looked down at the boys, both of whose faces were upturned, still talking, still desperate to get her attention. How close she had come to the edge, she thought, with a shudder. How distraught she had felt the last time she'd seen them. But they would fix things, like Mack said, together. They would reset the marble run, have everything running smoothly. Or at least functioning. 'Have you two been really good for Daddy?' she asked them.

'Yes! *I* have!'

'I've been *really* good. Haven't I, Daddy?'

She smiled at their earnestness, their vigorous assurance of model behaviour, times two. 'Oh, I *am* glad,' she said. 'Because do you know what I saw earlier? A really brilliant playground for good children. Would you like to see it?'

The whoops and shouts were reply enough, as was the bouncing about like blond pogo sticks. After a bit of tussling, because both Harry and Stanley wanted to hold her left hand and seemed prepared to fight to the death for the privilege, they set off towards the playground, all four of them in a line. Anyone glancing over at them would assume they were a normal family on holiday together, nothing more, nothing less. They'd be wrong, but nevertheless Olivia felt okay about hiding behind that interpretation for the time being. She and Mack could work everything else out later.

Chapter Thirty-Three

'Hi,' said Em, her hand clammy on the phone as she pressed it to her ear. She sank down onto the bed and pulled an anguished face at her reflection in the mirror, as a troupe of butterflies appeared for aerobatics practice in her stomach. She had gone through so many feelings since George's dismissal of her the night before – devastation, self-recrimination, the acceptance that she was destined to be single forever now, and finally a smouldering sort of anger. Because – hello! – it was kind of rude just to dump someone like that, to say things hadn't worked out, bye, as they were halfway out of the door with their ex. Not that she was particularly keen to explore in detail all her faults that had led him to this decision or anything – quite the opposite in fact – but you know. Manners cost nothing, right?

'Hi,' George said. Mind you, at least she got to hear that lovely low voice of his one last time, she thought with a pang. She was going to miss it afterwards, if this was the final time they ever spoke. 'How are you?'

Ugh, and now they were having to be all polite and weird, as if they barely knew each other. How was she? Oh, just marvellous, thanks, George. Bloody peachy! Her hangover was still banging away in her head like a carpenter on a mission and she had barely slept a wink, but she wasn't about to tell him that. 'Fine, thanks,' she said, rolling her eyes. 'How are you?'

'Good,' he said. 'Sorry I didn't text last night when we got back – my phone's only just dried out.'

'Right,' she replied, not sure what else to say. It wasn't as if she'd *expected* him to text her, after all. Who cared about his journey home when it had meant him leaving her?

Then the conversation took a decidedly unexpected turn. 'It felt weird waking up without you this morning,' he went on breezily. 'I miss you.'

It was lucky she was sitting down, because she forgot to breathe for a moment in her confusion. Why was he saying such a thing?

'Are you still there?' he asked, when she didn't reply.

'Yes,' she croaked suspiciously. 'Look, I . . . I don't understand.'

There was a pause. 'What do you mean?'

'After yesterday . . . what you said.' George didn't respond and Em gritted her teeth in frustration. Oh, for heaven's sake, did she have to spell it out? 'About us splitting up.'

'*What?*'

'What you said about us not working out – I don't understand why you're ringing me now to tell me—'

'Wait – I didn't say anything about *us* not working out. I said *the holiday* hadn't worked out, but I didn't mean *us*. Did you really think . . .'

He stopped mid-sentence and her head reeled. She stared at her reflection wide-eyed. 'You . . . oh. *Oh,*' she said, blinking. So he *hadn't* dumped her? This *wasn't* the end? She found herself rewinding that whole scene yesterday and seeing it from a different angle. George, recognizing that things were difficult with Izzie, and giving the two of them space to work it out. George, being a responsible dad and decent human being, not wanting to put his ex through another long car journey.

'Did you think I was breaking things off?' he went on. 'Because of one slightly eventful week in Cornwall?' He sounded incredulous, she realized, as if such a thing had never occurred to him. He even sounded a bit hurt.

'Well . . . *yes*! It hasn't been the easiest few days,' she said, thoughts still racing. 'I mean, it wasn't exactly the restful, fun time I promised you, was it, what with all the teen dramas and kids falling out and . . .' *And my daughter telling her friends she'd seduced you, and my ex-husband ringing up to bollock me loudly and proclaim you're some kind of nonce.* 'It's been a disaster! I just felt so mortified by everything that . . . well, I guess

I just assumed the worst.' She tailed off, feeling like an idiot. A catastrophizing idiot.

'God, that's not enough to put me off, Em! You'll have to try a lot harder than that, you know,' he said. 'Besides, we had some really good days too. I enjoyed the holiday! Believe me, I've had worse.'

She tried to laugh, but it sounded more like a bleat. 'I'm sorry,' she sighed. She still couldn't believe she had got everything so wrong. 'Again.'

'It's okay,' he said. 'You prat. Honestly.'

'I am a prat,' she admitted.

'Yeah and, just for the record, I'm not planning to ditch our relationship any time soon, but if I was, it wouldn't be that kind of casual, drive-by dumping,' he said. 'Give a man some credit.'

'Good to know,' she said drily.

He laughed and then she did too. The ground suddenly seemed more solid beneath her. 'Anyway. We're okay, aren't we?' he asked. 'We can move on from this and be all right?'

Her breath came back to her. Here was her second chance. 'Yes,' she said gratefully before he could change his mind. 'We totally can.'

'Good,' he said. 'I had a message from Izzie, by the way. Really sweet. She said the whole thing yesterday was her fault and nothing to do with you, and apologized for causing trouble.'

'Gosh. I didn't know anything about that,' Em said, blinking. 'That was nice of her.' She hesitated, wondering where they went from here. 'So . . .' she began, just as he said, 'Anyway . . .'

She smiled. 'You go first.'

'I was ringing to say – as well as hello and I miss you, and I most definitely did not dump you yesterday – that I won't come back for the rest of the holiday, because I made the mistake of looking at work emails last night and something's come up. But can we sort out dinner for when you get back? There's a new tapas place in Suffolk Parade – I thought we could maybe try it out?'

A lightness was filling Em, like air into a balloon. They were going to be okay, she realized. Despite all her angst and misery the night before, they were going to be okay. 'I'd love to try it out,' she said. 'Patatas bravas and Rioja in Suffolk Parade sounds much easier to handle than a fortnight away.'

He laughed. 'That's what I thought. Go back a few steps, keep it simple. Is that a yes, then?'

'Absolutely it's a yes. And let's promise never to go on holiday again.'

'Well, I wouldn't say that. I'm sure there's a way we could get away for a few days, just the two of us, if Charlotte has Seren and your ex has Izzie and Jack . . .'

Her eyes lit up at the prospect, her imagination already leaping ahead. A boutique bolthole somewhere gorgeous, wandering old streets together hand-in-hand, ordering exotic cocktails in romantic bars and snogging in a corner. An enormous hotel bed with crisp white sheets – and not an interrupting or arguing child in sight, either. 'Ooh, now you're talking,' she said. 'A proper holiday.' And why not? They had bloody well earned it, after the week that had just gone by. 'That's a great idea.'

'Good. I thought so too. Well, I'd better go,' he said. 'But let's make a plan once you're back.'

'Tapas and plans – I'm in,' she said, feeling a goofy smile spreading across her face. 'Good to talk to you, George.'

'You too,' he said.

Em felt starry-eyed as they said goodbye and hung up, then she flopped back onto her bed and danced her legs around with happiness. Yes! Yes! A second chance lay ahead, at a tapas bar in Suffolk Parade, and an as-yet-unbooked hotel room somewhere sexy. There was hope still to be had, and by the bucket-load. And a daughter to thank, too!

She knocked on Izzie's door and poked her head round to see Izzie lying on her bed, smiling as she typed into her phone. 'Hi,' said Em. 'I've just spoken to George – I gather you sent him a message earlier.'

Izzie's smile froze and then became something resembling anxiety. She rolled over and sat up, her phone abandoned. 'Is that okay?' she asked worriedly. 'I just wanted to make things right. Is he . . . cross?'

Em sat on the bed and put an arm around her. 'No, he's not cross. I think we're going to be all right, to be honest. Disaster averted.' She gave Izzie a squeeze. 'Thank you for whatever you said to him. It was really thoughtful of you. Really mature.'

'That's okay. I'm sorry I . . . you know. Mucked things up to start with.'

Em stroked her hair. 'Well, *I'm* sorry that I mucked up *your* holiday by inviting George and Seren along, without talking to you and Jack first. I won't do that again, okay? And we've got the second week all to ourselves, so from now on, your wish is my command. I know Jack is very keen to go rafting and zorbing and what have you, and if there's something special you want to do, then please do say the word. I'm all yours.'

Izzie's face became suffused with a blush. 'Um. Well. Actually . . .' Her eyes swung down to the phone beside her. 'So you know how last night I was asking if I could go out with a friend, and you said no?'

Aha. Somehow, in all the palaver of the night before, Em had forgotten about this mysterious new friend. 'Yes,' she replied, intrigued.

Izzie started twizzling her hair round one finger, her face practically aglow with her smile. 'Well, I met this boy yesterday . . .'

'Oh, you did, did you?'

'And I was wondering . . . Could I maybe meet him this afternoon? He's called Fraser and he just texted to see if I was around.'

'I see.' Oh goodness. *Fraser.* Was this Izzie's first holiday romance waiting to unfurl and blossom? It had to happen sooner or later, she supposed. 'And . . . do you think I would approve of this Fraser? Is he nice to you? How old is he?' She had to snap her mouth shut before she went full Spanish Inquisition.

'He's really nice,' said Izzie. 'He's seventeen and . . . Well, I approve, so . . .'

Em smiled. A very diplomatic answer. 'Then . . . yes. Sure. Do you want me to give you a lift somewhere?' She remembered then how they'd driven past Izzie just as they'd got back to the cottage yesterday, how sparkly-eyed and radiant she had looked, despite the drenching rain, despite the slog uphill on her bike. With the drama of Charlotte arriving and Dom's phone call, it hadn't even occurred to Em to wonder where her daughter had been all day. Getting to know this Fraser, apparently. Nice, seventeen-year-old, approval-worthy Fraser. It was all happening, this week, that was for sure.

'It's okay, I'll go on my bike,' Izzie replied.

'Okay, well . . .' Em felt she should be giving Izzie a lecture here, a list of dos and don'ts, but perhaps she wasn't the best-qualified person to give any kind of dating advice. So instead she gave her a hug and said, 'Have a lovely time. Keep me posted, won't you? He can join us for dinner if you want or . . .'

Em stopped again, because Izzie was giving her a look. 'I'm going,' she said, ducking out of the room again with a smile. Then she went along and knocked on Jack's door. 'Looks like it's just me and you this afternoon, kid,' she said to him. 'Any ideas?'

The earlier rain had blown right away and the sun shone over the south-west for the next few hours, gilding the corn fields, glittering off the rivers as they wound down to the sea, and prompting sunglasses and sun-cream applications everywhere.

Following their zip-slide adrenalin rush – and yes, they *did* buy the souvenir photos and fridge magnet – Maggie and Amelia tried a terrifying giant swing that had them both shrieking as they swung out from a cliff edge at dizzying height. After a restorative ice cream, they ventured to the go-karts where Maggie found herself laughing so hard, she could hardly breathe. *I've got my girl back*, she thought joyfully as Amelia took a selfie of them together afterwards. *Even better, I think I might have got myself back too.*

Em and Jack, meanwhile, had gone to an aqua park and, despite her initial qualms about squeezing into a wetsuit (Christ!), they ended up having a brilliant time. There was nothing like bouncing on giant inflatables, flinging yourself from an enormous catapult and skidding about on a huge trampoline in the middle of a lake to sweep away the last traces of a hangover. Not to mention the deeply rewarding glow that came from hearing your son say, 'This has been one of the best days ever in my *life.*'

Meanwhile, on the waterfront in Falmouth, Izzie and Fraser were practising the fine art of kissing. They were getting pretty good at it, even if they did have to pause for breath now and then. *I approve,* thought Izzie, swooning a little as she smiled into his gorgeous brown eyes. *I totally approve.* The group-chat leaderboard might have been abandoned now, but even so, she could still hear the points ringing in for her: win win win win WIN.

Further east, Olivia, Mack, Stanley and Harry had spent quite some time in the playground. The swings and slides had had a rigorous testing out and there had been much laughter. There was talk of driving out to find fish and chips for tea, and then the boys wanted Mummy *and* Daddy to bath them back at the hotel, all of which sounded good to Olivia. She was looking forward to the four of them snuggling on the huge double bed later on and quietly counting her blessings. According to Mack, you could get cocktails sent up via room service, which they were totally planning to try out, once the boys were asleep.

Lorna and Roy hadn't gone anywhere, but they still felt

as if they were on a journey. Had this been a normal day, they would have been cleaning Mawnan Cottage following Olivia's departure, ready for the new couple who were due to arrive tomorrow for a two-week stay. However, this was not a normal day and so instead they'd been sitting at the dining-room table, filling in an online form for the Adoption Agency together. It seemed as if they were on the brink of something truly momentous. 'Oh, I hope we can find him,' Lorna fretted every now and then, but Roy squeezed her hand each time, sure and steady. 'We will,' he said. 'However long it takes, we'll find him.'

Epilogue

'This is it,' said Roy, indicating to turn into the car park and then reversing into a space.

Lorna's heart felt as skittery as a newborn lamb. Without knowing it, she had waited years for this moment and yet, now that they were here and the moment was about to happen, she was no longer sure she was ready at all. What if he didn't like her? What if she had built her hopes up for nothing and he wasn't interested? Would he even turn up?

She was worried too that she would overreact and overwhelm him with the love she already felt for him. *You're not going to smother the lad now, are you?* Roy had asked her when they'd first made contact. *Of course I'm not!* she had tutted in response, but they both knew what she was like. Oh, she was desperate to love him, though! How she hoped he would let her.

She flipped down the passenger mirror for one last application of lipstick, fretting suddenly that she was wearing the wrong outfit, that she should have picked something dressier for the occasion. What were you supposed to wear anyway, the first time you met your long-lost grandson? She felt as if there should be trumpets playing a fanfare for his arrival. A master of ceremonies overseeing the whole situation. It seemed almost as life-changing as her own wedding.

'You look fine,' said Roy, as if reading her mind. Perhaps he noticed the pulse that seemed to be beating double-time at her throat. The plucking of her hands at a wrinkle in her skirt. 'Shall we go in then? We're five minutes early, so if you'd rather sit here and have a panic we could do that instead, though.'

She huffed at him for teasing her when this was such a huge day, such a big deal. That was Roy's coping mechanism, though, just as flapping and worrying were hers. They made a right pair, honestly. 'Let's go in,' she said, pressing her lips together, then blotting them on a tissue. She glanced again in the mirror and wrinkled her nose at herself. When had she got so *old*? Well, she'd just have to do.

Leon Andrew Waterford, that was his name: her nineteen-year-old grandson. He was studying physics at Glasgow University, but had spent the summer inter-railing around Europe, picking up bits of work here and there apparently, which was why it had taken them this long to be able to meet. He was now back home in Bournemouth, spending a few weeks with his adoptive parents before he returned to Scotland for his second year. The three of them were meeting today in a pub just outside Plymouth – neutral ground for everyone concerned.

It seemed to take forever to walk the short distance to the pub entrance. It was a smart whitewashed building, with baskets of trailing pink petunias hanging outside and blackboards propped up advertising their lunch menu and that night's fish specials. Lorna's hands felt clammy as she and Roy reached the door. She hoped Leon wouldn't be there yet, so that she could have a cup of tea and compose herself – but then changed her mind in the next moment. Of *course* she hoped he was already there! How would she be able to wait any longer?

It hadn't taken them long to track him down, once they had filled in the various forms and sent them off. Finding out his name had been like being handed the key to a treasure chest full of riches – thanks to the Internet, they had been able to track Leon's life through the years: from swimming galas he'd competed in, to pictures in the Bournemouth newspaper of his school play and GCSE celebrations . . . As for the photographs of him, Lorna had burst into tears the first time she saw one, because he had exactly the same dark shaggy hair and shy smile as Aidan. Two peas in a pod. It was a miracle.

Of course Lorna was biased, but he did sound a *remarkable* young man: handsome and talented, a prize-winning swimmer, a gifted student. He had made it to university, just as

Aidan should have done, and by all accounts was enjoying himself there. What an accomplished lad he seemed! She hadn't even met him yet, but could already burst with pride whenever she reflected on all his achievements. His adoptive parents had done a good job, clearly. Perhaps even a better job than two grieving grandparents might have done. Whichever, she felt nothing but gratitude towards them for loving him and looking after him while she'd been oblivious to his existence.

We've found him, she had texted Olivia, with links to the photos and other pieces of information. *This is him. Your boy. Our boy! Isn't he handsome?*

Olivia had phoned her, almost immediately. 'Oh my goodness,' she had said. 'Doesn't he look like Aidan? Isn't he gorgeous?' She'd sounded emotional, as if she was struggling to take the news in. 'He's a real person,' she'd added, her voice cracking. 'I know that sounds silly – of course he's a person, he's a nineteen-year-old young man! – but he's never quite seemed real in my head before. He's been frozen in time for me, a crying baby being taken away from my arms. Until now.'

'We're going to try and meet him soon,' Lorna had replied, unable to stop looking at the pictures in front of her. 'How about you? Will you want to get in touch too, do you think?'

There had been a pause, when Lorna could imagine

Olivia glancing around her home – the place she shared with her own small family – and weighing up the consequences. 'Yes,' she said eventually. 'If he wants to, that is.'

Lorna had promised to report back after their meeting today. She and Roy had been on tenterhooks for the last few weeks, able to think of nothing else but how it would go.

'You know, I've been wondering,' Roy had said yesterday, when they'd been cleaning Briar Cottage in readiness for a new set of guests. Now into mid-September, the holiday season was beginning to slow, with the children back at school and the weather just starting to turn. 'If Aidan hadn't died, would he and Olivia even have gone ahead and *had* Leon, do you think? Or would they have decided that they were far too young to settle down at that point? Because maybe . . . well, it's horrible to dwell on now, but they might have decided they didn't want a baby. Leon might not have made it this far. If you know what I mean.'

Lorna had winced, not sure she wanted to imagine that outcome. And yet Roy had a point. With a terrible irony, it was perhaps only through losing Aidan that Leon had come into the world at all. Realistically, Aidan probably wouldn't have wanted his own child at the age of eighteen, just as Olivia hadn't – the possibility of having both Aidan and Leon in the world might not even have existed. Gaining a grandson would never make up for losing a son, but it was definitely a consolation.

It had been a summer of revelations, all in all. She and Olivia had been in touch several times since July, and the younger woman sounded much happier and more settled these days. Lorna and Roy were going to travel to Bristol next month, actually, to visit Olivia and her family, and Lorna was very much looking forward to it. She'd had some lovely cards and messages from happy holidaymakers too – one lady whose boyfriend had proposed to her at the cottage, a couple who'd celebrated their Silver Wedding anniversary there, and a woman who wrote the loveliest note saying that she and her teenage daughter had really connected on their holiday for what felt like the first time all year. Oh yes, and there had been one very funny review left on the booking site, from a lady called Em: *My relationship might have wobbled, my kids had umpteen dramas, but the cottage was still so beautiful and homely we ended up having the most wonderful family holiday together. Perfect!*

Who could ask for more? When you had such nice messages and feedback, it did really make you feel good about what you did. And, of course, she and Roy would be off on their own holiday very soon: a two-week cruise around the Mediterranean. She had bought a new swimming costume and everything for the occasion. It was going to be heavenly!

But enough of all that. She was walking into the pub now, her heart in her mouth, scanning the people at the bar and wondering if her grandson was already waiting for her.

Roy nudged her. 'Do you think that's him?'

Lorna turned in the direction he was pointing, to see a young man with dark hair and broad shoulders rising from a seat in the corner. He looked as tall as his dad had been and had the same way of standing with a slightly tilted head, glancing at them through lashes every bit as thick and sooty as Aidan's. It was him all right. She would have known him anywhere. Every cell in her body reacted to the sight of him. *Is that you? It's me. It's me!*

And then they were moving towards each other across the pub and a laugh was spilling out of her, a laugh of joyful recognition. 'Hello, my love,' she said, feeling the most over-whelming rush of joy. 'I'm Lorna, your grandmother, and this is Roy. We're so happy to meet you.'

He smiled and it was like having her boy back again. Just for a moment. 'Same,' Leon said, then laughed and wrinkled his nose self-consciously. 'This is strange, isn't it? Not every day you meet someone you're related to. Sorry, I'm babbling. Bit nervous. Would you like a drink?'

But Roy was clapping him on the back and Lorna could see how thrilled he was, how proud he was to be meeting this handsome young man who was something of the past and something of the present – and a whole new future for them too. 'Hello there, Leon,' he said. 'If anyone's buying drinks, it'll be us two. We're made up, we really are. You don't half look like your dad, you know. You must have so many questions about him, I bet! We've brought some photos with us, just in case you wanted to look at them . . .'

And then they were walking together to a table in the corner, all smiling with delight at each other's presence. For once she didn't need to kid herself that this was going to be a good day, thought Lorna, marvelling at her grandson's easy-going confidence, his manners as he pulled out a chair for her, drinking in every last bit of this miracle. Because she knew already – she was sure of it – that this would be a really, *really* good day.

Something to Tell You

by Lucy Diamond

What's your biggest secret?

When Frankie stumbles upon an unopened letter from her late mother, she's delighted to have one last message from her . . . until she reads the contents and discovers the truth about her birth. Brimming with questions, she travels to York to seek further answers from the Mortimer family, but her appearance sends shockwaves through them all.

Meanwhile, Robyn Mortimer has problems of her own. Her husband has become distant, and she begins to wonder exactly what he's keeping hidden. Dare she find out more?

As for Bunny, she fell head over heels in love when she first arrived in town, but now it seems her past is catching up with her. She can't help wondering if her relationship will survive when everyone discovers who she really is – and what she did.

As secrets tumble out and loyalties are tested, the Mortimers have to face up to some difficult decisions. With love, betrayal and dramatic revelations in the mix, this is one summer they'll never forget.